James Lovegrove   ess
Allen Steele // A   ed
Norman Spinrad   on

EDITED BY

IAN WHATES

SOLARIS
RISING 2

THE NEW SOLARIS BOOK OF
SCIENCE FICTION

'One of the best SF anthologies published this year...
there's almost nothing here that isn't good or outstanding.'
Gardner Dozois, *Locus* on *Solaris Rising*

SOLARIS

US $8.99
CAN $10.99

ISBN 978-1-78108-088-7

50899

EAN

Praise for *Solaris Rising*

EDITED BY
IAN WHATES

SOLARIS
RISING 2

THE NEW SOLARIS BOOK OF
SCIENCE FICTION

SOLARIS RISING 2

THE NEW SOLARIS BOOK OF SCIENCE FICTION

EDITED BY
IAN WHATES

INCLUDING STORIES BY

Paul Cornell
Nancy Kress
James Lovegrove
Adrian Tchaikovsky
Eugie Foster
Neil Williamson
Nick Harkaway
Kristine Kathryn Rusch
Robert Reed
Allen Steele
Kim Lakin-Smith
Kay Kenyon
Mercurio D. Riviera
Martin Sketchley
Norman Spinrad
Liz Williams
Martin McGrath
Mike Allen
Vandana Singh

SOLARIS

First published 2013 by Solaris
an imprint of Rebellion Publishing Ltd,
Riverside House, Osney Mead,
Oxford, OX2 0ES, UK

www.solarisbooks.com

ISBN: 978 1 78108 088 7

Cover Art by Pye Parr

Printed in the US

CONTENTS

Extensions: An Introduction, Ian Whates   9

Tom, Paul Cornell   17

More, Nancy Kress   35

Shall Inherit, James Lovegrove   59

Feast and Famine, Adrian Tchaikovsky   79

Whatever Skin You Wear, Eugie Foster   101

Pearl in the Shell, Neil Williamson   123

The Time Gun, Nick Harkaway   139

When Thomas Jefferson Dined Alone,
    Kristine Kathryn Rusch   151

Bonds, Robert Reed   185

Ticking, Allen Steele   213

Before Hope, Kim Lakin-Smith   235

The Spires of Greme, Kay Kenyon   259

Manmade, Mercurio D. Rivera   285

The Circle of Least Confusion,
    Martin Sketchley   311

Far Distant Suns, Norman Spinrad   345

Lighthouse, Liz Williams   357

The First Dance, Martin McGrath   371

Still Life with Skull, Mike Allen   387

With Fate Conspire, Vandana Singh   409

EXTENSIONS: AN INTRODUCTION

IAN WHATES

SOLARIS' CONFIRMATION IN late December 2011 that they wanted me to compile a second volume of *Solaris Rising* provided the perfect end to a very good year. The original volume had been a joy to work on, the critical acclaim it subsequently received both humbling and gratifying. To me, *Solaris Rising 2* is not so much a sequel as an extension to that first book; an expansion, if you will. The whole idea of *Solaris Rising* is to demonstrate the diversity, vitality, and sheer strength of modern SF; here was my chance to take that concept a step further.

I would be happy to work again with any of the authors who feature in *SR1*, and the simplest way to proceed would have been to go back to those same talented wordsmiths and solicit submissions, but how would that demonstrate 'diversity'? Instead, I determined to do the opposite: to gather an entirely new cast of contributors. So I sat down and began to draw up an approach list…

The very first story I accepted for the book was from Paul Cornell. In a career that is still gathering momentum, Paul has already achieved success in writing for TV (not just for Doctor Who) and comics (both Marvel and DC) as well as literary SF. I've come close to publishing Paul a couple of times in the past but it never quite happened, so when he assured me that he would be submitting a story for *SR2* I was sceptical. Then he delivered "Tom", dispelling any doubts. I rate this as one of Paul's finest stories to date, and that says a lot bearing in mind that his work has been shortlisted no fewer than five times for Hugo Awards in various categories.

Liz Williams has more strings to her bow than the average elven archer. Liz holds degrees in philosophy and artificial intelligence and boasts a past that includes tarot reading on Brighton Pier and being caught up in civil unrest while teaching English in Kazakhstan. These days she seems content to teach creative writing, report on all things pagan for the Guardian newspaper, co-run a witchcraft supply and retail business in Glastonbury (check out the hugely entertaining *Diary of a Witchcraft Shop*) and write some of the most profound science fiction and fantasy around. Liz invariably brings a unique dimension to any project, as "Lighthouse" amply demonstrates.

I first met Nick Harkaway in 2009, shortly after his debut novel *The Gone-Away World* had been shortlisted for a BSFA Award. I was immediately impressed by his charismatic vitality – a quality that spills over into his writing. I approached Nick regarding a story for *SR2* during the launch party for his second novel, *Angelmaker*, thus catching him at a moment of ebullient weakness (and who wouldn't be happy when your new novel has just received glowing

endorsements from the likes of William Gibson?).
This, of course, gave him little opportunity to say no.
Nick's story, "The Time Gun", has a lot in common
with its author: quirky, clever, and fizzing with energy.

I've been a fan of Nancy Kress since the 1990s, when
I bought a signed limited edition of her wonderful
Beggars in Spain. Nancy is someone I've long hoped
to work with. Little did I realise when accepting Jack
Skillingstead's poignant "Steel Lake" for *Solaris Rising*
that Jack is married to Nancy (hey, bear with me –
there's a big ocean between here and the US). How
could I spurn such an opportunity? Nancy's story was
one of the first to be accepted for *SR2* and would, I'm
sure, be a highlight of any book.

A few years ago, Kim Lakin-Smith and I found
ourselves pitted as bitter rivals when we each had a
story shortlisted for the BSFA Award. It was a role
we spectacularly failed to master, even grabbing a
bite to eat together before the awards ceremony. In
the event, neither of us won, though I wasn't *too*
disappointed as the winning story (co-written by Ian
Watson and Roberto Quaglia) was one I'd published.
Subsequently, I was privileged to also publish Kim's
novel *Cyber Circus*, which has garnered considerable
critical acclaim and was itself shortlisted for a couple
of awards. I had no hesitation in inviting Kim to
submit for *SR2*, which proved a wise move; "Before
Hope" is one of her best stories to date.

Neil Williamson and I became friends before I'd
actually read any of his work. I cannot begin to describe
my relief on picking up his short story collection *The
Ephemera* and finding that I loved it. A musician as
well as a writer, Neil is part of a Glasgow-based cabal

of talented authors whose members have included the likes of Hal Duncan, Michael Cobley, Gary Gibson, and Andrew J. Wilson. I was delighted when Neil's story "Arrhythmia" made the shortlist for the BSFA Award in 2011. In my humble opinion, "Pearl in the Shell" is even better.

Martin Sketchley is another writer with an alternative identity as a musician. Rather bizarrely, we first met at an air show. As RAF jets roared past overhead, wowing the crowd, we discovered that we both wrote science fiction. Martin's stories invariably examine the complexity of relationships and cut to the very heart of what it means to be human, and his contribution here is no exception.

Robert Reed has mastered the tricky art of producing short fiction in prolific quantity at a standard that never drops below 'good' and frequently rises a great deal higher than that. I first encountered his work in the pages of *Asimov's* and *Fantasy & SF*; indeed, there seemed a period when every month a new Robert Reed story would appear in one or other of those prestigious magazines, or even in both. I read them avidly, waiting for the quality to fall, but it never did. "Bonds" provides further proof of just how fine a writer Robert is.

Some years ago, when my own NewCon Press first started, I exchanged emails with the then editor of TTA Press' review webzine *The Fix*. Her name? Eugie Foster. We've never met, but Eugie was always helpful and impressed me as a genuine, likeable individual. I took an interest in her writing career thereafter and was chuffed to see her novelette (and that's just a reference to the length of its title) "Sinner, Baker…"

make the shortlist for both the Hugo and BSFA Awards, even more so when the same piece went on to win the Nebula. Eugie's was one of the first names I pencilled in when drawing up an approach list for *SR2* and, needless to say, she hasn't disappointed.

I'm not sure that James Lovegrove has yet forgiven me for mislabelling several online photos of him with another author's name (for no reason I can explain). Actually, he has, because James isn't the sort to hold a grudge... I hope. I first discovered James' writing more than a decade ago via the novella "How the Other Half Lives" and his novel *The Foreigners*. Both demonstrate what a thoughtful yet entertaining writer he is; qualities that have seen his Pantheon series of novels breach the New York Times best seller lists in recent years, and which infuse "Shall Inherit".

Before I ever met Adrian Tchaikovsky I was aware of him as the 'new kid on the block' in the epic fantasy scene, making a significant impression with his *Shadows of the Apt* series. Subsequently, I discovered that his writing encompasses a great deal more than that. Having already commissioned and published a couple of pieces by Adrian – a modern ghost story as well as a slice of reality-hopping SF – I felt confident that he could write something a little more 'hard SF'. My faith was fully justified by "Feast and Famine", which delivers on all fronts.

My first experience of Mercurio D. Rivera's work came via "Longing for Langalana", a story that appeared in a 2006 issue of *Interzone*. I rated this the best thing I'd read in the magazine for quite a while, and evidently I wasn't alone: it went on to win the readers' poll for that year. Nor has Mr. Rivera sat on his haunches since, producing a growing number of original and well-crafted tales for *Interzone, Asimov's* and elsewhere. "Manmade", which he referred to as 'a reverse Pinocchio story' when submitting, is the latest in a long line of gems from this exciting, still-emerging author.

Kay Kenyon writes science fiction of sweeping scope in plausibly-depicted settings populated by vividly-drawn characters – as evidenced by her *Entire and the Rose* novels. But she doesn't write enough short fiction for my liking; a situation I determined to remedy to some small degree. Thankfully, Kay accepted the challenge, and duly delivered the intriguingly named "The Spires of Greme", which proved just as inventive as its title and should not, under any circumstances, be confused with Kristine Kathryn Rusch's 2009 novella "The Spires of Denon". Kristine is someone who has succeeded as author, editor, and publisher (no mean feat, trust me). In the process, she has covered almost every area of genre fiction. It was SF I was interested in for this project, though, and Kristine has come up with a clever story of time travelling academia that manages to avoid stepping on Connie Willis' toes (which is no mean feat either).

I initially crossed paths with Mike Allen when submitting for his first *Clockwork Phoenix* anthology. He declined my effort with an encouraging 'I really like this, but...' rejection message. Tempting though it was to respond in kind, his madcap and frenetic "Still Life with Skull" proved too good a piece to turn down. Damn!

Martin McGrath is someone I know as a dedicated and hard-working individual from our years of service together on the BSFA committee, but I hadn't appreciated how good a writer he is. Not until I ran a 'blind reading' competition (how's that for a paradox?) to choose a story for an anthology, *Subterfuge*. Although Martin's story didn't win, it came a close second and later featured in the anthology *Conflicts*. A very good piece, but one that ill-prepared me for just how effective "The First Dance" would be.

Allen Steele's *Coyote* novels comprise one of the most compelling and convincing accounts of humanity colonising a new world in recent memory. I came into contact with Allen when Ian Watson and I included his story "The War Memorial" in *The Mammoth Book of SF Wars* (2012), and didn't hesitate in approaching him regarding *SR2*.

I recall reading Norman Spinrad's novels with a combination of pleasure and awe. It never occurred to me that I would one day have the opportunity to communicate with Norman, let alone commission a story from him. Then, by coincidence, I discovered that we have a mutual friend in the form of author Michael Cobley. I contacted Mike and, kind fellow that he is, he instantly put Norman and I in touch. The rest, as they say, is history.

I haven't read enough Vandana Singh; though, in this particular instance, I suspect the only worthwhile definition of 'enough' is 'everything by'. What I *have* read has unfailingly impressed me, and Vandana is another author I determined to approach from the off. Unlike many of the contributors, I had no real link to Vandana – either direct or otherwise – and feared that my invitation would be given short shrift. Nothing could have been further from the truth. Vandana has been enthusiastic and gracious throughout. Her "With Fate Conspire" was one of the last submissions to arrive, but it proved well worth the wait.

There we have it: the component elements of *Solaris Rising 2*; a collection of stories that will take you from the furthest reaches of space to the deepest corners of the human psyche. Enjoy the ride.

Ian Whates
Cambridgeshire
August 2012

TOM

PAUL CORNELL

Paul Cornell has been Hugo Award-nominated for his work in prose, TV and comics. He's won the BSFA Award and the Eagle Award. His latest novel is the urban fantasy London Falling, *out from Tor.*

YOU EXPECT THE platform to be stable. But actually it sways like a boat, gently, even though its legs are sunk into rock under the reef. That means if you come out on the launch just about keeping your nausea under control, you should get underwater as quickly as possible, let your inner ear sort itself. Having been an instructor here for five years, I'd stopped noticing that sway. But now I appreciate it again, because Tom appreciates it.

That feeling, looking at Tom's face, takes me back to a moment when the platform was swaying more violently. When the big guy showed up. I never got a name. Swav would never tell me. I don't know who that was meant to protect. Or maybe the males don't bother with names. I can see him even now, leaping, all blue muscle, with bright yellow stripes down his flanks, all the other colours on his skin that were at the edge of what we're able to see, that made strange rainbows through the spray. He hurled himself against the platform, time after time, making the tourists and the other scuba guides scream and fall around. He was the size of two or three orca. I couldn't see any similarity between him and Swav. I couldn't see a face, even. If there were eyes they were hidden in the dark lines along what might have been his head. I couldn't imagine how they could ever be together. I was holding onto Swav, both of us getting soaked. All I was thinking was that, emotionally, I was fucked. I could hear him calling her name. He was booming it underwater, her name vibrating the platform as much as the waves did.

I looked into Swav's face, and there was an expression there I couldn't read at all. It was an arrangement of muscles on something very like a human face that wasn't akin to any expression I'd seen before. She broke from my arms, suddenly slippery, like I'd loved a mermaid. She ran for the rail. She leapt into the water as I was calling her name, my shout lost in his. She jumped into water that was suddenly full of him rising around her, an enormous mass that overwhelmed her. He twisted her round and slammed her against the side of the platform, so hard I was sure it had killed her. He held her there with slaps, battering her, left and right with his fins or wings or whatever they were. I'd run to the side, but there was nothing I could do but shout. She'd told me what she expected, but she'd never experienced it. Would she have dived in if she'd known what it would be like? She was pinned there, against the metal over the underwater dock, her fingers gripping the wire netting now, her knuckles, suddenly so human, white with the effort. I remember Annie, the biologist, came up behind me and grabbed me when I looked like I was going to jump in after her. I don't know if I really would have. We watched together as that huge white puppet snake of a penis rose out of the water, a flap like a flower jerking atop it, sucking air. Swav threw her head back and I could see something odd at her neck, kind of like a wound, and I screamed her name again because again I thought he'd killed her. And then the penis wrapped round her, impossibly fast, and the flap rose above her head like a snake about to strike. In that second, she turned and looked at me, and this time what I saw on her face I read as terror. Then the flap grabbed her around her head. He let himself fall from the platform and with an enormous splash took her with him into the depths.

I recall the water hitting us again. How we were swept aside. And then how we all found ourselves just sliding against the rails, the water draining off in seconds, as it was meant to, children screaming, guides yelling to grab onto the cables. But everyone was safe, it turned out. Except me. I felt as if I'd been beaten. I'd had something ripped out of me. Annie made me look her in the face, and I could see every detail of what she was feeling, such a contrast, like coming back to reality after a dream, just for a moment. "She'll come back to you," she said. "I'm pretty sure of it."

I WAS ONE of the first, I guess, to have that experience. My working on the Great Barrier Reef made it more likely. The Carviv always asked to visit reefs, and because they always asked to work, a lot of them in the first party ended up as tour guides, things like that. Their hosts tried to dissuade them, but the companies that took them on were delighted. Mate, we've got a guide who is herself a tourist attraction. The Carviv presence funded the regrowth initiative and the carbon sinks. It was so unthreatening, you know? They didn't want to see our armed forces, they wanted to be near our water. The females separated, integrated by not staying in groups at all, spreading out all round the Pacific Rim. The males, we saw on television, lay on the ocean surface, somewhere off Hawaii, sleeping most of the time. Aussie blokes identified with that. That was a good first year, with the whole planet kind of sighing in relief. We'd met the aliens, and they turned out to be quite like us, really. None of the predictions of outrage and uprising came true. After a little while, nobody had that much of a problem. Humanity looked at itself in comparison with these guys, and decided we weren't that bad or that good, and stopped worrying so much about the end of the world. There was, after all, another one just over there, seventy light years away, and those guys didn't seem to think we were so bad. Looking back, I guess we started tidying the place up, now that the neighbours had come visiting. So much ecological repair in such a short time. The Carviv refused, even when asked, to express any negative opinions about the world they were visiting. But I think their love for the water contributed to us turning a corner, ecologically.

And the years after have continued to be good. But I still occasionally feel... well, just sometimes I don't know how I feel. Until I look at Tom.

*   *   *

EVERYONE TURNED OUT to welcome Swav when she arrived at the platform. She travelled on one of their boats, those slim white shells, their hulls shaped reassuringly like our own yachts, but with some sort of power source that made no sound, the sail only for braking, billowing out to do so as it approached us.

"Hi, everyone," she said as she stepped off the ladder onto the platform. Her accent already sounded Aussie. "Thanks for having me." She was sparkling white, a rounded head like a bowling pin, a diagonal sash that was decorated with dense designs as her only clothing, slim shoulders, big, three-fingered hands like a cartoon character. She swept downwards to a tiny pair of feet, her whole body leaning to one side or the other with every step. There were no visible... well, it's weird to use a word like "genitalia" thinking back to that moment, but that's how biologists, how Annie, actually, would have been looking at her. Her chest was just... rounded, as if she was a clothed human. But it was her face that was the most extraordinary thing. Those enormous blue eyes; utterly like ours, but impossibly expressive. The ridges above them which danced like extraordinary eyebrows. The button nose with a single nostril. The wry squiggle of a mouth, never open enough so that you could see her teeth, but always in motion, saying so much even when she wasn't. She had a waterproof rucksack on her back that looked like she'd just bought it.

The others clustered around her, Helena, the boss, doing the air kissing which we'd been told delighted the Carviv. And it seemed, indeed, to do the business with Swav. That was when I heard that huge, honest, laugh for the first time. I was holding back for some reason, Annie, her arms folded, beside me. Swav glanced over and looked at me. And held my gaze, her laugh suddenly turning into what looked like quite a shy smile. I found myself smiling back.

UNDERWATER, SWAV WAS incredible. She swam in a blur of motion, her whole body vibrating, able to turn on a dime and talk to us in our scuba gear by directing individual yells right at our ears. Which must have been, as Annie put it, like shooting daisies from a rollercoaster. The fish, initially, hated her. Carl, our bump-headed parrot fish, who'd learned to come to the diving pit beside the platform twice a day for food and photo opportunities, actually left. Which made the crew feel kind of awkward: nobody knew how long swimming with Swav would be a tourist attraction, while Carl had served us well for a decade. There was one night at dinner when Swav became aware that there was something nobody was talking to her about. She made Helena tell her about Carl. And the sadness on her face when she heard, oh man! It was breaking my heart. She suddenly got up, and ran to the door, and stopped and made a gesture for nobody to follow her, that it would all be okay. And then she was gone and we heard a splash, and we all got to our feet, and went to see, but all there was in the moonlight was a trail of foam that already stretched out past the reef.

She was back for breakfast, hardly able to contain herself. "Guys, come and see!" she said. I jumped over the side with a couple of the others, and there was Carl, laid back as ever, but a notch hungrier, if his bumping against us was anything to go by. And behind him, as if intrigued by this food they'd heard about, was a shoal of clownfish, our other major attraction, or they had been, when they'd been more common around here. "I found out what they were smelling about me," whispered Swav in my ear as she rocketed past, going round and round the platform in excitement. "I reversed it."

That night, in her honour, we got the grog out. There'd been a few who were a little awkward around Swav. Mostly I think they felt it was like being around, you know, someone who's very religious or a tranny or something; you get tense because you want to make sure you do everything right and don't offend them. But I had to admit, when I caught her in the corner of my eye, or ran into her without expecting to, I did react to her like she was a ghost. In a nanosecond, your brain realises you're not looking at what you thought you were, only she's enough like us that it slips gears a bit, and you find yourself jumping a moment *after* the conscious part of you has thought 'oh, it's just Swav'. She noticed, the second time it happened, and stopped me from making some sort of awkward apology. "It's okay," she said, "it happens to me too. You guys are kind of... large, you know?"

I laughed. "Not as large as your blokes! Oh, sorry –"

"Stop saying sorry! They're their sort of thing, not the sort of thing I expect to run into in a corridor."

"Are we ever going to get a visit from one of them?"

She laughed, like she was embarrassed. "Well, let's see how things work out." It was like I'd said something a little racy. Then she realised I was looking awkward again. "No, come on, I love them, honestly, but I like to get away, and... you know. Do stuff." Those huge eyes had been moving quickly, her attention resting briefly on every part of my face, as if she was taking me in. And enjoying it. She was waiting to see what I did next.

You hear blokes saying they fancy a cartoon character: Wilma Flintstone; Daphne from *Scooby Doo*; Mrs Incredible. But Swav kind of brought that feeling front and centre. Confronted you with it. I'd seen some of the other guys look at her, and then look away, awkward. Your eyes got halfway with it, and stayed on a curve or a motion, then they were lured into applying that feeling to something completely outside the lexicon of love. It felt kind of like fancying Carl. The women had started to make jokes about it. "And she walks about starkers," said Mia, another of the guides. "It's shameless." Swav looked puzzled when people said things like that, but now I think that was an affectation, to let everyone stay comfortable. Or maybe it was kind of like someone laughing along with a racist joke about them, I don't know.

"Is this...?" I wanted to ask her if she was coming on to me, but the thought seemed vastly weird and conceited and hey, potential diplomatic incident, plus all the guys laughing at me, forever. So I shut up again.

But she cocked her head on one side. "I guess. Maybe." While I was processing that, she took my hand in what felt very like a normal hand. "We've got a couple of hours. Let's have a cuppa."

* * *

SHE LED ME into her cabin. I didn't close the door, she did. I went to the kettle, but she came up behind me and put her hand on my chest. I started to turn around, and she very gently kissed me.

People always used to ask what it was like, before enough of them experienced it for themselves. I've got a bit fed up with describing it, honestly. It was great. It didn't feel very weird. I kept feeling that I wanted to close my eyes and then stopping myself because that might be insulting. What I was seeing might have been more complicated than I was used to, but it was still good. She didn't have breasts, but a curve that felt like them from behind. Her skin became softer and softer as I touched her. She laughed as she showed me all the incredibly complicated folds and openings and protrusions of her, and put my fingers where it would give her most pleasure, and I felt a huge sense of pride that I was arousing her so much, that I was seeing all this extra detail in what was normally a smooth surface. That she could even want me. She wanted to see me then, so I showed her, and what to do. She took to that! She told me not to worry about her teeth. I enjoyed that for a while, and then told her not to worry about mine. Although, you know, that was like my first time had been; I had no idea if I was doing it right, or even what I was aiming for. She smelt great, not like anything I'd ever smelt before, so there were no associations with it. It didn't take me back to any other time; there was just this enormous great now, this tremendous focus on this being just her and me. And even now, the smell of Tom takes me back only to her. I thought it was all going to be like teenagers playing around. While that was kind of frustrating, emotionally, for me, I assumed there couldn't be anything more. But then she told me that there wasn't really any equivalent of orgasm for her without penetration, that actually it was only the feeling of her partner coming that could set her off. She leaned over the bed, and moved her gorgeous roundness a little. "So, erm... how would you feel about...? I mean, I know it's a bit scary –"

It was, but no way was that enough to stop me. It had been established pretty quickly that, having evolved in different biospheres, there wasn't any need to worry about humans and Carviv catching anything off... you know, I regret mentioning that now. "No possibility of biological interaction", that's what we thought back then. Well, I guess it's what a lot of people still think now. A lot of idiots. But that was nowhere in my head just then. I positioned myself behind her and let her reach for me and guide me into one of the many channels. "Push," she whispered, and I did. Something bigger than it needed to be suddenly contracted around me, until it was just the right size, so welcoming and tight that it felt like an invitation and a violation at the same time. Things were touching me that wouldn't normally be, let us say. Part of her slid urgently into place to cup me around my balls as I was inside her. She must have heard the noise I made and realised what that was about. She looked over my shoulder and grinned. "You all right there?"

I laughed. "God, you're beautiful. Is this the first time you've... you know, I mean with...?" I had visions in my head of one of those big guys lying in the ocean. I'd wondered about what she was used to, if you know what I mean.

"With anyone. My lot either."

"Oh –!" I suddenly felt like I should have acted a lot differently, somehow, but I wasn't sure exactly how.

She laughed again. "Mate, it's not such a big deal for us. There are plants that have evolved on my world to do basically what you're... and there's a lot of jokes about that amongst the shoal, you know, I'm just going to leave Mum and all the guys and go on to the land to have a walk among the pretty flowers. La la la! Your girl friends tell you about it and so then you kind of want a go, and your mum gets all emotional, and the guys all take turns saying surely you're not ready to go exploring on unsettled land yet, shit like that. Until Mum basically put me in the boat and said do what you like! That's how the plants pollinate, so you get these enormous forests of flowers on the islands. We look over to them every now and then and go, hey, we were pretty horny this year." Her voice became softer again, serious. "But I wanted to know what it was like with, you know, someone here. Someone cool. And you don't need to worry. I shrink. I clutch. You feel..." and she raised one of those things that looked a lot like eyebrows and now her voice dropped to a whisper, "pretty big, actually. So, you just go ahead and... let yourself go."

So I did.

WE LAY TOGETHER afterwards. I watched, fascinated, as her bits sorted themselves out, retracted and relaxed until she looked smooth again. I was feeling pretty emotional. I mean, not that I wouldn't normally be, but... I felt I'd just gone through something intense, and I wasn't quite sure how I was meant to feel about it. Had we done something wrong? She must have realised that I wasn't feeling right. "It's okay," she said.

"Was it... all right?"

"It was brilliant. Mate, you're much better than a flower."

"I've never been told that before."

She looked suddenly serious. "Now you have to fight one of our males."

I looked at her shocked, and she burst out laughing. "Sucked in! You should have seen your face!" She wrapped her arms around me and I lay against her chest. "You needn't worry. I know I'm going home eventually."

"I wasn't going to say –!"

"It was fun. Lovely fun." She kissed me again, and I felt a kind of ache at what she'd just said. But she was right, it couldn't be more than that. Or so I thought then.

OVER THE NEXT few weeks, the crew cottoned on to what we were getting up to. I got a lot of ribbing, but it was all good natured. The only person who seemed to have a problem was Annie, who looked away whenever I tried to make eye contact. I guess that was the start of the jealousy that would lead her to hurt me so much later on.

ONE NIGHT, SWAV came to my cabin and held me back when I tried to kiss her. "I've had a message," she said, indicating a patch on her sash, "one of our males is on his way here. Now, you mustn't freak out..."

And she told me that he was coming to the platform in order to mate with her, that something had changed in the water temperature that made it feel like mating season back home, and so the males were all about to swim in various directions, meet up with the females and, well –

"It's not like you and me," she said. "I've seen it, and... you might want to go ashore rather than wait for –"

"What, and think about you and him? Do you *have* to do this? I mean, are you and he –?"

"It's not like anything you guys have. You shouldn't be jealous."

I asked loads more questions, none of which mattered, and she answered all of them, and, you know, I like to think I'm a guy who accepts different cultures, but I was still left feeling pretty damn small.

I WATCHED FOR any sign of mockery from the others. I knew Helena had told them about the forthcoming visit. They didn't say a word until the evening, when Ben clapped me round the shoulder. "What can I say, mate? You're about to be publically cuckolded by a fucking enormous whale."

"It's like the porn version of *Moby Dick*," added Mia.

"We can only hope," finished off Helena, "that he's not bi-curious."

I started to laugh. "You bastards." And we had a few drinks. They'd waited until Swav wasn't around, and they hadn't let it stay silent and terrible and I was grateful for that.

* * *

EVERYONE WAS SHOCKED by how the male arrived. That he surged like a torpedo towards the platform, without any message to us, that it swiftly became clear that that day's tourists were going to be at the very least alarmed, and not, as expected, entertained by the spectacle of seeing one of the larger Carviv up close. Once we helped them to their feet, Helena elected to give them their money back and send them to dry land on the launch. The kids were already starting to ask awkward questions about the violence of what Swav had said would take place entirely underwater and out of sight. Maybe that had been the male's choice, and what she'd seen before had been different. Maybe the bastard had just been showing off.

I stayed by the rail, Annie beside me. "Why are you so sure she'll be back?" I asked.

She shook her head.

At that moment, Swav's head burst to the surface. We all helped her back on deck. She looked dazed, and she kept putting a hand to her neck. "It's sealed again," she said. "My... you know."

"I don't think I do," I said, and I couldn't keep the bitterness out of my voice.

She wrapped her arms around me and I let her, in front of everyone. The smell of her had changed. I realised I still liked it. Only that felt wrong now. Or for just a moment it did. "He's gone now," she said. "It's all going to be okay."

I helped her back to her cabin.

I HAD TO ask how it had been. I had to. I don't know what I was expecting to hear. It was always going to be bad. "Just this enormous... natural experience," she said.

"Good?"

She looked pained for me, like she didn't want to lie to me. After that, she wouldn't say any more about it. It took us a few nights to get back to our old routine, but we did. I might have been kind of rough with her the first time, I don't know.

Swav apologised hugely to the crew for what the male's arrival had been like, even offered Helena her resignation. She hadn't known he'd make such a show of it, most didn't. Helena said her leaving was out of the question. Was there going to be a... happy event? Swav looked shocked for a moment at Helena's directness, then touched her neck and said she didn't know.

But in the next few weeks, it became obvious. The side of her neck and her lower back swelled, and you could see something shifting inside the translucent skin. She'd been spending a lot more time in the water, going deep under for hours at a stretch, for a long time now, even before there had been visible signs of her pregnancy. "And I'm going to have to be down there," she told me, "when it bursts." I spent as much time as I could down there with her. I didn't know how I felt about what she was carrying, but I wanted to be there for her, to help.

* * *

OF COURSE, WHEN it finally happened, I was on the platform, making dinner. I heard a weird cry from outside the galley, and rushed out, leaving the others, who hadn't heard it. Swav, who'd been deep underwater for most of that day, was bobbing on the surface, and in her arms was... Tom.

I looked at him, the little fella, small and blue and sleek, and I could see something about him, an expression in those eyes that were almost hidden in the folds of his face, an expression which just hadn't been there on that big male.

Swav smiled up at me, such an enormous smile of joy, and she didn't have to tell me what had happened. *How* it happened... well, they're still debating that.

It was something chemical. The greatest rush of my life. I leapt into the water and took my boy into my arms.

IN THE NEXT few weeks we took turns looking after Tom. Swav was going out to the edge of the reef on a regular basis to consult with a whole pack of males, yeah, including that one. They were talking, she said, about heading home soon.

"Do I get to come with?" I said.

"There's no way you could live on my world."

"But –"

"You want to be around Tom. I get that. So that's something else we've been talking about. How about you look after him for a bit? Then he comes back home with the second party, back to visit you again with the third?"

I was pleased at that. Though of course I'd miss Swav too. This arrangement would make it all feel much more grown up, and less like I'd feared, an adolescent melodrama, spurred on by my out of control hormones. I'd asked if her lot's scientists had come up with any ideas about how the two of us could have conceived, and she'd looked awkward. "Tom's not the only one," she said. "It's happened a lot."

AND INDEED, IT was soon all over the news, proud fathers clutching human/Carviv kids. Though I've got to say, I didn't think any of them looked as much like them as Tom looked like me.

It was then that Annie made her feelings plain. I found her watching a clip of some nature show in the galley. She switched it off before I could see what it was, which made me ask if it was porn.

"Yeah," she said, "if you're a dunnock."

She didn't take much persuading to show it to me. It was a whole bunch of garden birds hopping about. "It's for this thesis I'm writing," she said. "The female dunnock mates with a number of males, each of which ends up thinking it's the father of her kids. So when the eggs are laid, all of them protect them."

"I thought you specialised in marine life?"

She paused, but I guess she couldn't help herself. "These days," she said, "I specialise in the Carviv."

It took me a moment to get what she meant. I think I was pretty harsh back to her. She deserved it. It was the last time we spoke.

EVEN AFTER ALL these years, looking after Tom is still a joy. He swims like a torpedo. He's still only got a few words of English, but I've learned a lot of Carviv off him. He gets that just by listening to the sea. It sometimes makes me a little jealous about the guys who had Carviv daughters, the oldest of which are in school now, and charming the world. But no, I couldn't ask for more. There's this incredible bond between me and him, it just takes a while for others to see it. Every now and then I think about what Annie said, I mean, it comes up in some debate, but no... no, and anyway, even if it was true, so what?

Swav's been back once, and we took Tom over to Hawaii together, where the Carviv, having helped us sort out our climate issues, have started building an underwater holiday destination for their people. There are all these little islands covered in... well, those flowers Swav told me about.

"Tempted?" I asked.

"'Course not," she said, "I've got you."

MORE

NANCY KRESS

Nancy Kress is the author of 30 books, most recently
After the Fall, Before the Fall, During the Fall, *a stand-
alone novella from Tachyon. Her work has earned
four Nebulas, two Hugos, a Sturgeon, and the John W.
Campbell. She writes often about genetic engineering
and is best known for her Sleepless trilogy, beginning
with* Beggars in Spain. *Kress lives in Seattle with her
husband, writer Jack Skillingstead, and Cosette, the
world's most spoiled toy poodle.*

MY PRISON NAME is FMA16549EW. 'F' for female, 'MA'
for maximum security, 'EW' for eastern Washington
state, 16549 for who-the-fuck-knows. This is stenciled
on my coverall, db-ed in my records, and tattooed
on my butt. I own this number – or it owns me – for
perhaps thirty more minutes. Today I am getting out.

I don't need to tell you my name. The whole world
already knows it.

The steel gate clangs as it slides open, triggered by
the guard in the booth. Clanging gate, silent electronic

trigger: old technology manipulated by new. But of course that scenario doesn't always end well. The whole world knows that now, too, due at least in part to me.

Two more clangs and I reach the lobby. A clerk hands me the personal effects I surrendered fifteen years ago: lipstick, pocket flashlight, cheap watch, massively outdated cell phone. I'm already wearing my own clothes. Jeans and sweatshirt don't date that much.

The clerk smiles. "Good luck, Ms –" he glances at his tablet "– Jaworski."

Incredibly, he does not recognize me. But, then, he appears to be about fifteen, although surely that can't be true. So perhaps the whole world doesn't recognize my name, after all.

The only man who matters will recognize it. He shares it.

Wayne is waiting at the prison gates, at the wheel of a sleek black car. He's grown a short beard, which oddly enough gives him the look of an Edwardian dandy. He's fifty now but still looks good; he's one of those men who only get better looking as they age. He leans over to kiss me, then answers my disapproval before I can even voice it. "Electric, not gas, and the juice comes from the Green River Dam. No carbon footprint, no resource depletion."

"And the rubber tires will never end up in a landfill? You'll paint them white and plant daisies in them on the front lawn?"

He grins at me. "Prison hasn't changed you, Caitlin."

The fuck it hasn't. But Wayne doesn't need to know that. He has another girlfriend now, and she's pregnant, and anyway he's too valuable an eco-fighter to risk. Despite the car.

"So who does it belong to?"

"Friend of a friend."

"Dangerous, Wayne."

"This one can be trusted."

"None of them can be trusted. You used to know that."

He doesn't answer. Fifteen years ago, it was someone we trusted who tipped off the CEO of HomeWalls, Inc.

I say, "Are we going to the compound?"

He glances over at me. "Would you rather I take you somewhere else?"

We both know I don't have anywhere else to go. I gaze out the window at the shimmer in the distance and yes, as we speed along the highway toward Spokane in traffic even lighter than when I went into prison, there is the first of them. The shimmer takes form, an upside-down translucent bowl. Wayne speeds up and I say sharply, "No. Pull over. I want to look at it."

"Caitlin –"

"Do it!"

He does, and I look my fill, letting the look sink deep into my mind, where it can become rich fertilizer to nourish equally rich hatred.

The dome, a singleton, covers perhaps thirty acres: Model C-2, then, the largest possible. Sunlight striking at just the right angle glints off it, as if it were solid. It is not. The HomeWalls dome is a force field, proprietary to the corporation. It keeps out objects, including projectiles, air, and selective wavelengths of electromagnetic radiation. Visible light can get through; X-rays, gamma rays, microwaves cannot. The bowl shape is open at the top, to allow air exchange and weather, and through the opening rises a single communication tower. I stare a long time at that curve up to the opening, which is as small as the engineers deemed feasible.

The dome entrance, with its heavily guarded double-door access chamber, must be on the other side, at the end of the road merging into the highway. Through the translucent wall, which is precisely 1.8 inches 'thick', I see the blurred outlines of houses, a few shops and restaurants, a small apartment building, trees and flowerbeds and a tennis court. Two people on bicycles ride on the bike path that circles fairly close to the wall. The translucence gives everything the wavery, magical look of an impressionist painting.

Outside the dome the squatters have erected ragged tents, shacks of tin and old lumber, piss pits beside which children play. Most of the squatters, I know, will be on the other side of the dome, hoping to someday rush the access chamber. It's a stupid and futile hope. If they do, they will be shot by the guards. The courts have upheld these shootings as "legal defense of one's home and person in the face of credible threat." But still the squatters try, wanting more than the miserable little they have.

What hurts me the most is the gardens. Some of these squatters have planted corn and vegetables. In the summer heat the plants are spindly and brownish. There must be a public well here somewhere, or the people couldn't be here, but water would have to be hand-carried to water these brave little attempts at self-sufficiency. In the closest plot, a woman hoes weeds by hand. She raises her head to stare at the car.

Wayne and I have only minutes. He steps on the gas as the first of the squatters rush the road ahead of us, waving clubs and shovels. They can't take out their rage on the people in the domes, but we will do, in our luxurious car. Wayne revs the engine and we easily outdistance them without hurting anyone.

Moments of silence, while the dry plains of Eastern Washington roll by. Finally Wayne says, "We can't do it the same way, Catie."

"I know that." And then, "Why haven't you been trying a different way? For fifteen fucking years you haven't tried anything real!"

"We've tried what we could. Broadcasts, rallies, education –"

"And look at all your great results!"

Wayne doesn't answer. Truth roils between us like deadly gas.

"THE COLORS OF the spectrum, Catie," my father said.

"Red, orange, yellow…" I froze. What came next? Then the right color popped into my six-year-old mind and I shouted, "Green! Blue, indigo, violet."

"Very good! Now the name of the glass triangle that breaks light into all those pretty colors."

"Prism!"

"And the instrument that lets us study those colors."

This was one of the hard words, but I was sure. I said it extra carefully. "Spec-trom-e-ter."

My father smiled at me. We sat in the back seat of his big car, while Desmond drove with Ray, the bodyguard, beside him. When Daddy took me to school in the car on his way to work, it was our special time. Mama was in heaven and Daddy was usually busy, so busy, inventing things to keep people safe. I hardly ever saw him. Mostly I just saw my nanny, who pinched me to make me be good.

"Daddy," I said, "today in school we're going to start learning Chinese!"

"Good," he said, still smiling at me. "Study hard. Make me proud of you."

"I will!" I liked school. All the kids there were smart, and most of them were nice, and the school was safe behind its high fences. Not every place was safe, I knew. We were driving right now through a part of the city that wasn't safe, but we had to go through it to get to my school and Daddy's work. This place was ugly, too, with litter on the streets and men – "the lazy out-of-work," Daddy called them – sitting on sagging porches and steps in their undershirts. I saw a house with broken windows, the glass lying all over and nobody even sweeping it up.

"Opaque the windows," I begged.

Daddy pressed a button. The car windows opaqued, and we were safe in our own cozy world, with its exciting smells of leather and aftershave, its quiet hum of the powerful car engine carrying us along.

THE COMPOUND HAS indeed changed in fifteen years. It's shrunk.

How many of us had there been when I was here last, just before my arrest? Nearly a thousand. We hadn't been like the naïve commune-founders of two generations before mine. We assigned roles, established a working government, used appropriate technology even if it wasn't green, until the time came when the eco-war would be over and we could dispense with our toxic cell phones and tablets. We even recognized that the war might never be over.

Now the compound holds fewer than a hundred die-hards. Many of the buildings are boarded-up. The radio station still works, and in prison I managed to hear a few of Wayne's careful, chicken-hearted broadcasts on Washington state's one public channel. The news channels, of course, are state-dominated ever since the Rescue that put the United States under military rule. What was supposed to be rescued was the economy, but of course it hadn't been, except for those who already had enough. They just ended up with more.

A woman comes toward us from the closest ramshackle building. She walks with the swaying waddle of the heavily pregnant, and she is very young. Her gaze on Wayne is soft and adoring. Her gaze on me holds no sexual jealousy – he must not have told her of our history together. Probably wise. It no longer matters, although once my passion for him flamed just as strong as both our passions for justice.

"This is Tara," Wayne says, putting an arm around her. "Tara, Catie Jaworski."

"Welcome," she says, and I hear the fear in her voice, and below fear, the hostility. So she is brighter than she looks. She knows that I could threaten her precarious security. And I will.

"Hi," I say. And to Wayne, "Let's get to work."

* * *

"DADDY, IT HURTS!"

"I know it does, Catie. I know. But the operation was a success and you're fine now. The pain is just the stitches."

He stands beside my hospital bed, holding my hand. I am furious at him. "It hurt worse before and you weren't even here!"

"I came as soon as I could. I had to come from the other side of the world, pumpkin."

"I don't care! I hate you!"

The nurse, a scrawny old woman in stupid clothes with teddy bears on them, smiles at Daddy. "They always want more parent than they can get, Dr. Jaworski."

"Shut up!" I say. I hate the nurse, too.

"Caitlin, apologize," Daddy says.

"I'm sorry," I say, but I don't mean it. I don't mean that I hate Daddy, either. I know he was on the other side of the world, doing important work in physics. Everybody knows who Daddy is, and everybody knows about the new thing he invented, the clear energy walls to keep bad people from hurting little girls. It's wonderful and important, but I wanted him here when my appendix broke. Before that, I didn't even know I had an appendix. He never told me.

Daddy says to the nurse, "Can't she have more pain killers?"

"Her chart says absolutely not," the nurse said. "Her atypical allergies –"

"Never mind," Daddy says, in his important voice. "You can go."

The nurse looks startled, then frowns, then goes. Daddy sits in a chair beside my bed, still holding my hand. "Pumpkin, I know something better than painkillers."

"What?"

"It's a game that makes everything stop hurting. Close your eyes. Now think of a place where you were really, really happy... Are you thinking of one?"

"Yes." I think about being in the car with him, back when he sometimes had time to take me to school. Talking with him, laughing with him, the smells of leather and aftershave... me so happy I thought something in me would burst. Not, though, my appendix.

"Picture that happy place in your mind, Catie. Are you doing it? Good. Now picture even more of it. More of all the good things."

More. I saw the car driving on and on for the whole day, not just the morning. With a picnic basket. More talking, more laughing. More Daddy.

And it worked. I forgot that I hurt, and Daddy sat there holding my hand until his cell phone rang and he had to go. He didn't visit me in the hospital again.

WAYNE AND I have it out that night. Tara has gone to bed, and the welcoming party held for me is over. I'd sized up the 'eco-terrorists' gathered in the compound: one-third free-loaders professing beliefs they wouldn't act on, one-third committed to the same soft 'education' of voters that had accomplished squat in the last fifteen years, and one-third fiery enough but incapable of planning, of detail, of an after-life spent underground. They wanted to blow things up, all right, but not to live with the consequences. Useless to me.

"The tunnels are the weak point," I say to Wayne. "I studied everything in the prison library."

"They let *you* have access to articles on dome construction?"

"No, of course not. But there were ways." In prison, there are always ways.

Wayne fiddles with his beer. We sit at a homemade wooden table, lovingly carved by someone who could better have used his or her time in subverting the domes, not creating tiny local beauty outside them. The TV is on, as it has been all evening, to the state-sponsored news channel. I need to keep up.

"Catie, I'm not going to engage in anything illegal. Not with the baby coming. I have family responsibilities now."

"You mean that you've caved to the system."

"I mean that your arrest and imprisonment should have taught you that your tactics won't work."

"'Your' tactics? They were yours, too, Wayne! We made that plan together!"

"I know." He raises his eyes to mine. "Do you blame me for not getting caught along with you? For staying outside these fifteen years?"

I am astonished. "No, of course not. What good would it have done for both of us to go to prison?"

He laughs, reluctantly. "You always had courage."

"So did you. But I was the one stuck with the Jaworski name."

"Yes." For just a second the old feeling sparks between us, but it's only an ember, a pathetic flicker of what once was. I don't bother to fan the ember. Wayne had courage, all right, but never vision. Not really. He could kindle small fires to attract attention to injustice, but he would never start a conflagration that would burn the old order to the ground. I would have to do that.

I had tried to do that. This time, I would succeed.

Wayne says, "The domes are impregnable."

"Nothing is impregnable."

"Okay, that's the wrong word. But I think that if the tunnels –"

"Wayne, don't you –"

"Catie, give it up. We can succeed best with the slow drip of water on stone. Law makers are starting to come around. The Goodman-DiBenetti Act –"

"Is a sop to environmentalists! A pathetic old dog with no teeth!"

"No, it –"

"You're a coward, Wayne. Admit it."

He slammed down his beer glass on the table. "I'm a realist!"

"You've been seduced by the same thing the people living under the domes have sold their lives to: *more*. More security, more comfort, more soft living. More more more, and the rest of the world be damned!"

"And you think you're any different? You want 'more' as well! No incremental victory is ever enough for you. They have to be bigger, gaudier, more spectacular, because what you really love isn't winning battles to help the poor, it's the excitement of the battles themselves!"

Silence. There isn't any more to say. Except maybe one thing.

"Wayne, was it you who made that call fifteen years ago?"

"No." He's telling the truth. But the way his gaze shifts to the left, the slight droop of his head –

I say, "You know who did."

"You weren't doing what everyone agreed on! You made that substitution of –"

But abruptly, shockingly, I'm no longer listening to him. For fifteen years I've wondered who betrayed me that night, and now I'm no longer listening. The TV screen suddenly shows my father, wearing his solemn-exalted look. The news guy beside him looks not just exalted but positively beatified. I turn up the sound.

"– such a major breakthrough! Now no family need choose between living near a job or living near loved ones! Can you tell us, Dr. Jaworski, any more about the science behind this development? Of course we all know that HomeWalls Incorporated possesses all its tech on a proprietary basis and –"

I watch the entire program, and then the next one. My father has discovered a way to extend the force fields of the domes. The new tech will allow them to cover not just a maximum of thirty acres but entire cities. The rich and middle-class will never have to see, hear, or even be aware of the domeless poor again.

All my plans will need to change. Attacking the tunnels will not work now. My father has ensured there will be no more tunnels.

Wayne has slipped off to join Tara. I don't see him again before I leave the compound in the morning.

THE FIRST HOMEWALLS went up when I was fourteen. They went up around our house.

The house sat on the shores of Lake Michigan, on Chicago's Gold Coast. Twenty thousand square feet, plus guest cottage and pool house and boathouse by the dock. The force field 'circle of protection' extended six feet below ground, into ditches dug for the purpose, and out onto the lake, where it had to stop at the surface of the water. Those early walls were opaque and, of course, open at the top; the tech to create domes came later. We had weather. We had seagulls and winter snow and seismic detectors to warn of tunneling beneath the walls and complete safety from kidnapping. The dome had to be turned off briefly to let yachts sail to and from docks, but this was considered a minor inconvenience.

The thieves swam in from the lake, at dusk, when they were least expected because my father had a house full of guests. I had had some teenage argument with my father, gone into sulks, and refused to attend the party. So I was loitering by the curved eastern wall, finishing off a bottle of wine I was not supposed to have, when the intruders in their wet suits reached the control room and shot the guard. One of them – inadvertently, it later came out at his trial – deactivated the walls. Not a good step if you plan on stealing valuables and then slipping silently away. Most thieves are stupid.

So was I. Until then I hadn't known anything, not anything at all. When the wall collapsed, dissolving like dark rain, I lurched into squatters that the police had not yet removed, huddled around a small fire.

"No!" I screamed, smashed the bottle on the ground, and held out the jagged neck as a weapon. Who the hell did I think I was, some video fighter?

"No!" screamed a ragged woman, clutching two kids to her.

No men. After a moment the older kid, a girl maybe nine years old, snatched up a rock and threw it at me. It hit me in the arm and, drunk, I started to cry.

"Annie, you stop that!" the woman said. "Don't you be throwing no rocks!"

She was protecting me.

I dropped the bottle. The stupid tears came faster. Alarms sounded from the house, police sirens from the street, shouts from all sides. The woman came up to me, her face creased with fear, with resentment, with hope. "Miss, Annie didn't mean nothing. Please don't tell the cops that she –"

"I won't," I had time to gasp, before I vomited up a bottle of wine on both of us.

Later, I looked for the woman and her kids. I didn't find them, of course. They'd vanished into the growing horde of the homeless and the desperate. As well look for a single pebble on the shores of Lake Michigan. No, not on the lake – under it. The country was sinking into economic collapse, into despair, into violence. The demand for my father's walls was immediate and enormous.

But I did look for the woman. And looking, I saw.

By sixteen, I had found Wayne's group. By seventeen, I was gone. I didn't see my father again for four years, at the Cook County jail, where we shouted accusations at each other and he did not even try to make my bail or find me a lawyer.

"SunnyJay," I say. "You haven't changed."

This is a blatant lie. Unlike Wayne, SunnyJay has decayed over fifteen years. Fat now, bald, food stains on the shirt that stretches across his vast belly. But the black eyes still shine with malicious humor. He is the smartest man I've ever known, and I include my father.

"How you find me, snowflake?"

"Oh, drop the lingo, SunnyJay. Please." He is about as down-home as a Jesuit scholar.

He laughs at me. "By what means did you manage to locate me so quickly after termination of your incarceration, Ms. Jaworski?"

"You aren't exactly a secret on the street." Nor does he intend to be. For twenty years SunnyJay has eluded legal conviction, in an age of sophisticated military surveillance, with two simple stratagems: First, hide in plain sight. Second, keep everything in your head, with no electronic footprint at all. Everybody, including several levels of law enforcement, know where he is and what he does. None of them can prove anything at all in court.

"Buy me a cup of coffee," I tell him.

He leads me about a mile from his house, then another mile, through the slums and ruins of Spokane. No one bothers us. By the time we reach a more-or-less middle-class coffee house, SunnyJay is puffing and sweating. He sinks appreciatively into a chair and looks around as if he's never been here before. I would bet he hasn't. The feds can't bug every place in the entire city, although certainly they try.

When we have our coffee, I say, "I need something."

"We all need love, Catie."

"Love, yeah. I need love. Can you find me the right man?" SunnyJay knows exactly what I mean.

"Depends on what kind of sex you like."

I tell him. Do those dark eyes widen a little? It isn't easy to shock SunnyJay, who's seen everything. The thought that I might have shocked him is exhilarating.

"Heavy price for that," he says.

"To you?" The trust my grandmother left me has been piling up for me for fifteen years.

"No. To you."

"I know."

"You still want love anyway?"

"Yes."

"You're that angry?"

"About injustice I am, yes – that angry!"

"Uh, huh. Sure you are. This is all about social injustice."

"It –"

"I'll do it."

I look down, into my coffee cup. There is risk here to SunnyJay, too, and he's going to take it. I say, "Who was it?"

He doesn't pretend to misunderstand me. "My mama."

"How?"

"Stroke. She died on the ground outside the private hospital."

"The hospital was behind a HomeWall?"

"You know it. I was eleven."

I don't ask what had happened to SunnyJay after that. I know. But, on impulse, I ask something else.

"You ever gone away in your mind? Just eased the pain by picturing someplace where you were really happy and then willing yourself there?"

SunnyJay's lip curls. "Transcendental shit. Buddhist meditation. Christian mysticism. Taoist fucking pathways. No, I never do that."

"Sorry I asked." In prison, going away in my mind had saved me. How dare he sneer at it?

SunnyJay says, "Go to the Hammet Hotel, on Sixth

at West Carrington. Live there a while. Maybe love will find you."

Two cops walk in, staring hard at SunnyJay. He beams at them as if they are his long-lost friends.

I AM THE reason that my father's company's walls became domes.

I gather that the physics to do this – to maintain a force field that curved at the top and then left a gap for air exchange – was very difficult. The air exchange is necessary. Sealed biodomes have never worked for long: without weather, atmosphere separates into layers, soil- and rock-fixed molecules break loose, trees become etiolated and weak-wooded. For four years my father's company produced energy walls that circled two, ten, twenty, or a maximum of thirty acres. The walls went up around mansions, gated communities, prisons, factories. Then they went up around empty swatches of land and new communities were built inside. Only certain people could buy their way in. You needed money, of course, but you also needed a clean criminal record, a thorough drug screen, a psychiatric evaluation. You needed to agree to rules of behavior. If you violated those rules, you and your family were out. But inside – ah, inside! Safety for you and your children! No ugly poor people pan-handling, no desperate homeless squatting in the flower beds, no need to think about those stuck outside. All across the United states HomeWall communities sprang up like mushrooms after rain.

The community leaders weren't stupid. They knew that twenty-feet-high walls, the most that the technology permitted, could be gotten over. The richest of them cleared a wide area around the outside of the circle and put it under continual electronic surveillance: visual, infrared, and metal detection.

The plan that Wayne's group – we never gave ourselves a name – came up with was ingenious in its simplicity. We joined a tent community just beyond a cleared area. Inside a ragged tent we built a medieval catapult of wood. We obtained a canister to be lobbed over the wall and break apart on contact, releasing tear gas into the gated community right at dinner time on a sweet summer night, when everyone was outside barbequing, playing tennis, drinking cocktails in designer lawn chairs whose cost would have fed the hungry people all around us for a week. Everything was in place.

Except that the week before, in the tent camp, I had met Aisha.

She was skinny and Muslim and starving and she reminded me of myself, who had never been any of those things. She was six years old, and she was dying. She coughed blood. I took her and her frantic mother to a hospital, but even though I paid for her care, she died. Too little, too late. I never even got to tell her to go to that happy place in her mind.

The doctor, not knowing I was with her mother, said to me, "Just as well. One less sewer rat in the world. Keeps the rest of us safer in the long run."

I heard my father's voice: "*The weak look pitiable, Catie, but they're actually dangerous. They will bring down the strong if they can – from envy.*"

Two days later Wayne sent me to buy the canister. I made an elaborate, blind-folded journey through

Chicago, arranged by SunnyJay, and followed by even more elaborate blind transfers of electronic funds. On the black market, you can buy anything, and it was my money, from grandmother's trust. I didn't get a break-apart canister of tear gas. I got one of sarin.

THE HAMMET HOTEL, named for a famous seaside resort in Tunisia, is seedy but not overly dangerous. I wait there, paying cash for everything and producing SunnyJay's fake ID as needed, for fully three weeks. Most of the time I watch TV, newscast after newscast about the breakthrough that will permit HomeWalls to "shield entire towns from terrorists and violent criminals." No one ever said how many would be evicted from those towns, or where the evicted would then go. Hour after hour I watch these state-run broadcasts. It's pretty much like again being in prison.

Then my 'lover' arrives, with my package. The next day I catch a greyhound to Chicago.

EVEN FIFTEEN YEARS ago, Wayne was a careful person. Inside our tent, beside the catapult, he meticulously examined the canister. "It doesn't look like tear gas."

"It is. Unless you think they pulled a bait-and-switch on us?"

"No, I don't think that." And then, "Catie?"

"It's tear gas."

And he nodded. We were sleeping together, we were passionately in love. The canister went into the catapult.

But someone else in our group must have checked, too. Because there was an anonymous call – not to the cops, who would eventually have ferreted out the caller. The call was to my father, on condition that he not reveal it to the cops. He agreed. The cold-feet traitor to our unnamed movement told him that people, inhabitants of a HomeWall his company had created, were about to die.

The quisling called Wayne, too. We had just enough time to scatter. When I was caught, I was charged with attempted assault. It would have been attempted murder had not Wayne already changed the canister that the feds found in the catapult. He'd known the original wasn't tear gas. He'd asked me about it not to obtain information, but to see if I would lie to him.

I might never have been caught, since even back then, SunnyJay had been that good. The cops might not have found me, except for Douglas Jaworski. They asked him if he knew of anyone, besides the organizations they were already watching, who might have planned such an attack.

"My daughter," he said. "Caitlin Maria Jaworski." And gave them DNA samples, retina scans from house security, and enough personal information to find any pebble on any beach, anywhere at all.

IF MY FATHER refused to see me, my plan would be at an end. His house, the same one I grew up in, stands under a HomeWall dome, Model D-2, the second generation of the original two-acre shield. D for Douglas. C for Caitlin.

But when I give my name to the guard at the access, he nods. Not without bristling – almost I can see the hairs on his neck raise. But he has his orders, and after I'm retina-scanned and DNA-sampled for a positive ID, he passes me on to house security.

They strip-search me. They run full-body metal and plastic scans. They analyze my breath and urine. When it's clear there is no way I can harbor a weapon, they give me a soft, expensive robe and slippers, and usher me to the library.

"Caitlin."

He stands by the fireplace, alone. A curt nod dismisses the bodyguard, who scowls ferociously but leaves. No way Douglas Jaworski wants the hired hand to hear his daughter's vitriol. And I had just been rendered perfectly safe.

He's aged in fifteen years, even more than was evident on TV, even more than SunnyJay. But unlike that jolly criminal, this criminal has gone scrawnier, thin as shadow, shadowy as dusk. The lights are low, as if he can't bear to see me too clearly. Some things never change.

Thousands of times I've rehearsed what I would say to him. Five thousand four hundred seventy-five times, in fact: every night in prison. But now that my father is in the same room, I don't feel like saying any of it. What would be the point?

But it turns out he has something to say to me. "I knew you would come for me. Eventually."

It sets off all the old, battered, primeval rage. "You did not! You don't know anything about me! You never took the time or effort to know!"

"You're wrong, Catie."

Not a quaver in his voice. He thinks he's safe, that because of his crack security team and his careful planning and his fucking dome, I'm walled away from him. I reach under my robe for my thigh. The only thing that will go through state-of-the-art surveillance devices is the human body. The pocket of skin on my thigh, its thin scar indistinguishable from all the other scars I acquired in prison, opens easily if painfully. From within I pull the slim knife made of bone, not unlike what might have been used on the savannah ten thousand years ago. But much sharper.

I have only seconds before my father, or my own motion, activates whatever defenses the room has: gas, electric shocks, something so new I haven't even thought of it. But my father doesn't move. Instead he says, "You're going to kill me. But first let me explain something to you."

It's a trick, of course. Keep me talking until help comes. But all at once I want to hear him, more than anything I've ever wanted in my entire life. An irrational desire, as strong as sex, or despair.

"You never had a child, Catie. But if you did, and you saw that child embrace beliefs you didn't share, immoral beliefs, you'd try to stop her. You'd lock her in her room, force her into therapy, even use mind-altering drugs, all the things I did and you resented me for. But what you were doing was immoral. I was trying to make the world safer and you were adding to its sum of violence."

"Safer by condemning a fifth of the population to misery!"

"They were already miserable, and I was making it possible for the other four-fifths to raise strong and happy children who might have found ways to rescue a world descending into darkness. Mine was the moral act because it aimed at the future."

He believes it. The self-serving son-of-a-bitch believes it.

"Imagine one step further, Catie. You have a child set to commit a terrible crime, in which people might die. Do you turn that child in?"

"It was tear gas!"

"But you didn't know that, did you? You weren't content with tear gas. You wanted more."

I lunge. But now I've waited too long, listening to his bullshit – *why*? Whatever defenses are built into this room will take me down before I can reach him.

Except that they don't.

I cross the room. My bone knife connects with his chest. He's not wearing body armor. No alarms sound. My knife slides in. He gasps and sags against me.

He never even calls for help.

His body is so light.

I sink to my knees, my father in my arms. Blood trickles from his mouth. Still no one comes. My rage threatens to blind me. But I can speak.

"*Why?*"

"My... punishment."

"For the domes?"

"For... wanting... more for you... than..."

Than what? He can't finish speaking. Yet he doesn't die. His eyes, full of pain, stare at me, and what I see in them is not anger but infinite regret.

I begin to babble crazily, hardly knowing what I'm saying. "Think of a good time! Think of when we were in the car going to school – back in the car! You're asking me about the colors, remember?

We're in the car, it smells of aftershave and leather, we're cozy and warm and safe... Daddy!" He's gone. I sit there, waiting. After all, I knew right along that I would not survive this meeting. Either immediately or in the aftermath, it would be my death, too. I knew it – and yet now I just want a few additional moments, a few more words from him, a few seconds –

– more.

SHALL INHERIT

JAMES LOVEGROVE

Prolific author James Lovegrove's most recent novels are Age of Aztec, *latest in his bestselling Pantheon series, and* Redlaw. *He has written extensively for teenagers and younger children, and his work has been translated into a dozen languages and shortlisted for numerous awards, including the Arthur C. Clarke Award, the John W. Campbell Memorial Award, the Bram Stoker Award, the British Fantasy Society Award, and the Manchester Book Award. His "Carry The Moon In My Pocket" won the 2011 Seiun Award in Japan for Best Translated Short Story. James is a regular reviewer of fiction for the* Financial Times *and contributes frequently to the magazine* Comic Heroes. *He lives in Eastbourne with his wife, two sons and cat.*

MORNING, CLOUD CROWD! *It's Johnny Nimbus, your AI network host, comin' atcha with a streamcast of all your views, all your news, all the time. And the big topic of discussion today is – what else? – the launches. In a few short hours the crew of the IS Pandora will*

*be getting hoicked up to near-Earth orbit to take
their places aboard the super space ark that's going
to fly them to a galaxy far, far away, never to return.
The forums are open, as ever, so get commenting
and communing, tweeting and browbeating, 'cause
without your thoughts there's no show and without
the show where will your thoughts go?*

THE LIMO ARRIVED punctually at eight. Serene and black
and unforgivably ostentatious. Everyone in the street
would know who it was for, why it had come. Furtive
curtains twitched. Brazen neighbours came out onto
their front doorsteps and stared, arms folded.

I went upstairs to chivvy Martin out of his room. He
was on his computer, piffling about on the internet.
Astronomy sites and the like, as usual. Just as though
it was any other morning, in no way a special or
different day.

Special or different meant nothing to Martin.

"Time to go," I said.

"Yeah." He didn't look round; didn't move.

"Now."

"Okay. Coming."

"Really now. Not 'soon' now."

"I said okay."

Ten minutes later he deigned to descend. The limo
driver had already put his suitcase in the boot. Martin
had met the 20kg luggage allowance exactly, down to
the gramme. He'd made an eclectic choice of belongings
to take with him. A few of his favourite books,
cherished physical copies. T-shirts with videogame
characters on. A penny jar that accounted for nearly

a fifth of the suitcase's laden weight. A nightlight that he probably wouldn't be able to plug in anywhere. A handful of Lego models and Warhammer figurines.

He had needed some persuading to include a framed photo of us, his family, and the Good Luck card his classmates at school had signed.

Outside, he started quizzing the limo driver about the car. Maximum speed. Fuel consumption. Brake horse power. Stopping distances. All the Top Trumps stats.

"How should I know, son?" the driver said, despairing. "I just drive the thing."

THEY'RE NOT EVEN *proper astronauts. What's up with that? NASA didn't send civilian nobodies on the* Apollo *missions. Armstrong and Aldrin and the others, they were test pilots, air force guys, elite. Best of the best. Trained within an inch of their lives. Now it's a bunch of randoms? That's what we're manning a trillion-dollar spaceship with? Don't make me laugh.*

A YEAR EARLIER, someone from the government had come round to interview us. We weren't sure why at the time. Claire and I thought maybe it was a benefit-fraud investigation. We'd done something wrong, claimed money we weren't entitled to, ticked an incorrect box on the disability living allowance form, something of that sort.

Why an infraction like that should have seemed important to anyone, given what else was going on in the world, I didn't know. But it was the government.

Rules were still rules, even as civilisation inched inexorably towards the precipice.

The woman conducting the interview, Maggie, tried to put us at our ease. "It's just a formality," she insisted, "an assessment, nothing more. You don't have anything to be anxious about."

"Don't have anything to –?" I exclaimed. I may have sounded a little hysterical. It wouldn't surprise me if I had. "Have you been reading the headlines?"

"I mean this," Maggie said patiently, giving the edge of her electronic clipboard a tap with the stylus. "I was talking about this. Not the Incident."

A true professional. Everyone else was calling it Armageddon. Apocalypse. The End Of Days. The Slow Extinction. The Terminal Fuck-up. Only a public sector employee could calmly refer to it by its official designation, the Incident, and not add an eye roll or an ironic grimace.

"Martin, you see," she went on, "is a very interesting young man. He has certain... qualities. I need to know as much as I can about him. Whatever you can tell me, anything at all, will be very helpful."

What was there to say? What, that she couldn't already have known? Asperger's syndrome. High-functioning autism. Near the upper end of the spectrum. Incredibly smart. Incredibly unemotional. Like a robot in many ways. His brain working at unimaginable speeds. His heart aloof, unknowable. Impenetrable.

That was Martin.

IN OTHER WORDS, *they've selected the geeks. The nerds. The boffins. Not the prime physical specimens.*

The trolls who live in their parents' basements. The screen jockeys with the spaghetti limbs and cathode tans. The boys who could never get the girls, the girls who repel the boys. Total space cadets. The future of the human race is in their baby-soft hands. Pardon me while I puke. Why not football players? Farmers? Construction workers? Carpenters? Cops? People with some experience of life. Tough, physical people who know what pain and hard work is. It wasn't accountants or – or – or shut-ins who colonised the American West, was it? It was pioneers, outdoorsmen, cattle ranchers, rugged frontier folk. This is a disaster in the making. This has EPIC FAIL written all over it. As if we haven't screwed up badly enough already, we've got to go for the double.

THE LIMO CRUISED towards Heathrow. It felt, weirdly, like going on holiday. Me, Claire, Martin and his sister Jenny, all in one car, heading for the airport. Incongruously normal. A trip to Spain, maybe, or Greece. Except there was no sense of urgency or expectation, no fear that we might arrive late and miss the plane.

The roads were more or less empty. People didn't travel much these days. Didn't go anywhere. Would rather stay at home. In the first few months after the Incident, everyone went everywhere. Governments poured money into subsidising aviation fuel, airlines dropped their seat prices to rock bottom, and we all become globetrotters and jetsetters. Crossing those must-see destinations off our bucket lists. The Taj Mahal. Ayers Rock. The Great Wall. The Pyramids.

But then, in time, the novelty wore off. That weird sense of exhilaration died. Dull mundanity set in again. We turned into hermits, favouring the familiar over the strange, the known over the unknown, friends over foreigners, people over places.

Conversation in the limo was stilted. Claire kept trying not to cry. She had vowed not to make a scene, for Martin's sake. Outpourings of sadness or affection made him uncomfortable. He would actively squirm.

Finally, to combat the awkward silence, Jenny switched on the in-car TV. A news channel came up. There it was, a satellite shot of the Incident site. Facts and figures scrolled along the bottom. Width of site: now standing at 798.7 miles in diameter. Expansion rate: constant at a mile a day. Estimated number of ecophages: almost uncountable – a sextillion and rising.

A jet black stain on the ocean, like an immense ink blot. Widening. Encroaching. Spreading outwards and downwards ravenously, insatiably. A tumour on the planet, metastasising like mad.

The story switched to the trial of the eco-terrorist group responsible. For weeks the hearings had dragged on, bogged down in legal technicalities and fine print. The International Court was deliberating whether to prosecute the ten men and women for crimes against humanity, genocide, mass murder, or simply for industrial sabotage and destruction of property. Since nobody had died yet as a direct consequence of the Incident, it was all a bit moot. Besides, what punishment was there that could possibly fit the crime? Meanwhile, outside the Peace Palace in the

Hague, thousands of protestors were baying for the culprits' heads. Placards read HANG THEM ALL and JUSTICE FOR HUMANITY.

Martin appeared oblivious. He sat with his head canted against the window, gazing out. Perhaps he was counting lampposts. Or establishing the limo's speed from the rate at which the road markings flickered by. Or logging the number of windows in every house we passed so as to be able to produce an average at the end of the journey. Any of those.

THAT LAST CONTRIBUTOR, what bullshit. Who better to go than some of the brightest among us? We don't need jocks up there, we need brainiacs. What they don't have in terms of survival skills, they'll pick up from Pandora's *tutorial programmes. They'll arrive at the other end ready and capable to colonise their new home. Plus – and this is true because I read it in the* New Scientist *– people with autistic tendencies are ideal for space flight, especially one that's going to last a decade and a half. They cope better with boredom. They can amuse themselves for long periods. They're less likely to suffer claustrophobia or mental breakdown. Think of it this way. They're* homo sapiens *to us* Neanderthals. *The way forward. The next step. Evolution has given them to us, and now we need them. So let's use them.*

I REMEMBER WHEN it first sank in – the news that the march of the von Neumann replicators could not be retarded or contained. They would just keep copying themselves, turning everything they touched into more of the same, for ever and ever.

It was supposed to be safe. The perfect way to clean up an oil spill. The BP supertanker *Tony Hayward* foundered in a mid-Atlantic storm, her hull was breached, her cargo began to leak out, and a plane was despatched to lob a canister of dedicated ecophages into the water. The nanotech machines were designed to eat crude oil, multiply, and then, when their work was done, disintegrate harmlessly, converting back into carbon and hydrogen. There would be no slick, no cordoned-off black beaches, no fish floating belly up, no seabirds tarred as well as feathered.

Only, someone had contaminated the replicators with a code virus that was triggered the moment they were activated. The automatic shutoff did not kick in. An oil-only diet would not suffice. The replicators had been transformed from short-lived, self-destructing monovores into relentlessly self-perpetuating omnivores.

Earth Abides, the extremist eco-activist group, proudly claimed responsibility on their website. Some guff about rampant fossil fuel usage. Pollution. Proving a point. Striking a blow.

More like scoring an own goal.

And we hoped, oh God we hoped, that the pundits' direst prophecies would not come true. That someone would be able to put an end to it. That what human ingenuity had set in motion, human ingenuity would halt.

But time went by, the nanomachine cluster kept expanding, and everyone's best efforts were in vain.

Even detonating a low-yield nuke at the site made

no difference. The von Neumann replicators sucked up that thermal energy and thrived, like manmade molecular-scale cockroaches.

Slowly it dawned on us. This was Twilight Time. The nanomachines would not give up. They would eat on, reproduce wildly, until there was no Earth left, only them. A planet-sized ball of twinkling blackness, floating in space, adrift, lifeless. Nothing but that.

Accepting fate – a *fait accompli* – the governments of the world got together, pooled resources, and commissioned the building of *Pandora*. The International Spaceship *Pandora*. Furnished with nuclear pulse propulsion engines. Able to achieve something akin to light speed. Pointed at Gliese 581g, an extrasolar planet just inside the Goldilocks zone of a red dwarf star. A new Earth, habitable, with landmasses, oceans, atmosphere.

Sophisticated onboard systems would control navigation, waste recycling and life support.

But who should be the passengers?

IT's ALL A front, a scam, this programme of recruiting the autistic. That's just what we're being told by the powers-that-be. Actually, all the places on board Pandora *have been bagged by politicians, billionaires and their families. They've all cronied together and they're going to bugger off and leave the rest of us poor sods behind to die. This is no conspiracy theory. It's how it is. I have proof. They get the lifeboat, we all go down with the ship.*

* * *

"Dad?"

"Yes, Martin?"

"You'll feed Tyke after I'm gone?"

The cat. Tyke, short for Tycho. Named after Tycho Brahe, the sixteenth-century Danish astronomer, a hero of Martin's.

"Of course," I said. "Don't worry."

"Oh, I'm not worried. I'm just confirming. He likes his wet food in the morning, no later than seven, and his dry food in the evening, no later than six."

"I know."

"Sometimes you forget."

"I'll try not to."

"Martin?" said Claire. I could tell she was about to say something she shouldn't. Something that wouldn't get her the answer she wanted. "Will you miss us? When you're up there? Off in space?"

"I wish you were there to do my laundry," Martin replied, having considered the question for barely a moment. "And to cook tuna bake for me. That'll be a shame, not to have your tuna bake any more."

I took Claire's hand. Felt it tremble.

"There are worse things," I said to her, trying for consolation. "Your tuna bake *is* very good."

WHO WOULD YOU *rather share a starship with? Kirk or Spock? That's what it comes down to. Kirk will either beat up or shag everything in sight. Spock will actually get you where you want to go. It's a no-brainer.*

*   *   *

Martin was our first kid, so we didn't know any differently. We didn't know that not all babies were as taciturn as he was, not all toddlers were so laser-focused on their play that they ignored the other children in the room, not all three-year-olds failed to respond to verbal or visual prompts and couldn't meet your eye, not all youngsters were born so old. It wasn't until Jenny came along that we realised how – for want of a better word – abnormal Martin was. Jenny did all the things the child-rearing manuals said were supposed to happen. She hit all her marks, a textbook baby, whereas Martin was an exception to every rule. He was formally diagnosed when he was five, statemented when he was eight. He could read like a demon but his handwriting was infantile. He could solve complex logic puzzles but found tying a shoelace a challenge. He could work a computer like a virtuoso pianist but not ride a bike. He was superior in so many ways, and in so many other ways inferior.

Sometimes he would look at me across the dinner table, or I would look at him, and I'd have no idea what was going on inside his head. There was no expression on his face, just a flat affect. His eyes seemed lost, deep in thought, but perhaps there was nothing going on behind them, just cogs whirring aimlessly, a humming blankness. Only Martin knew what he was thinking, but he rarely told us. Rarely let us in.

We got used to it, but I couldn't escape the feeling that we were cursed, our family blighted somehow. A chance permutation of our combined DNA, Claire's and mine, had let Martin down. We had created, between us, a hollow being, an emptiness that looked like a person, a living automaton. He could never interact with others on any meaningful level. He was destined to be eternally apart. He would not belong anywhere.

Little did we realise that we had, in fact, given birth to the future of the human race.

WHAT'LL THEY DO *when they get there? They'll need to get on with building shelters, sowing crops and mating – especially the last. But they'll be too busy playing* World Of Warcraft *to "get busy", tee hee hee.*

HEATHROW NEARED. THE shuttles were going up from major airports all across the world simultaneously, a co-ordinated programme of launches to send a message to the inhabitants of this doomed ecosphere: *see them go, watch them ascend as one, weep if you must, but also rejoice.*

The shuttles were riding atop modified Boeing 747s, a piggyback ride to take them close to the stratosphere. Safer and surer than booster rockets, and simpler too. They would detach in flight, break through the ionosphere, then converge on the geostationary drydock where *Pandora* was berthed. Four hundred autistic youths would file through umbilicuses and airlocks onto a ship that looked not unlike a snowflake, a glorious confection of solar panels and habitat arms that would spin as it flew, its whirl generating artificial gravity. Fifteen years later they would touch down on Gliese 581g, fully grown now, physically mature, in the prime of life and ready to face the rigours of starting from scratch on strange soil under strange skies.

* * *

HI! JOHNNY NIMBUS here. You know I don't like to butt in, but every so often people need reminding of the rules. Keep 'em clean, don't be mean. That's what it comes down to, Cloud Crowders.

JENNY DECIDED TO annoy Martin. Because she liked to and could. One last go, for old times' sake.

"Martin."

"Yes?"

"Will you be eating Wookie steaks when you're in space?"

"I'm sorry?"

"I said, will you be eating Wookie steaks when you're in space?"

"No. Wookies aren't real. And if they were, I wouldn't eat one because it might be Chewie."

"Chewy, you mean?" said Jenny, sniggering, triumphant. He had fallen into her trap.

"Chewie. As in Chewbacca. First mate of the *Millennium Falcon*."

"But you can't eat a steak if it's too chewy."

"No, you can't. Oh, I see. A pun."

"Duh."

"You're very juvenile, Jenny."

"Come on. Give us a smile. It's funny."

"No, it isn't. It's facile," said Martin irritably. "It relies on the inadvertent homophonic resemblance between the words Chewie and chewy. It's not that clever. Why did you bother?"

"Because I knew it would bug you."

"And what's the point of that?"

"I dunno. Why not?"

"Well, in future, don't."

"Yeah." And suddenly Jenny was sad. "Anyway, what future?" And morose. "We don't have a future. Unlike you."

"Jenny…" chided her mother.

"It isn't fair. It just isn't. How come Special Needs Martin gets a ticket to another planet and we don't? Why can't we go with him? We're his bloody family!"

"Jenny, that's enough," I said.

"We ought to be allowed to go too. What if he gets lonely?"

"I don't get lonely," Martin pointed out.

Jenny burst into tears. Claire slid across the plush leather bench seat to cradle her. It was hard to say which upset Jenny more: losing her brother or being obliged to stay behind. All said and done, she did love Martin. And she didn't want to die, any more than I did, or Claire, or anyone.

"There isn't room on *Pandora*," I said to Jenny as soothingly as I could. "They can't take everybody. Just be grateful that one of us is going. Martin met the criteria. Be glad for him."

"Why should I be glad," my daughter pouted, "when he isn't even glad himself?"

"He is," I said. "I'm sure he is."

Just not so as you would notice.

THERE'S THIS RUMOUR going round that some of them are faking it. These parents, they've schooled their kids to, like, pretend they've got Asperger's, or bribed *a doctor to give them a certificate. To get them on board, yeah? It's despicable. But then, if I had a kid, maybe I'd do the same. You never know.*

WE PULLED UP virtually on the runway. No need for customs, immigration, passports, check-in, baggage inspection, any of it. A smooth, first-class ride straight onto the tarmac, where a dozen similar limos were already parked. Families stood in knots. A throng of journalists jostled behind barriers, shouting out questions, begging for interviews, and not far from them stood a horde of onlookers, the public, some cheering, some jeering, held back by a line of police. The racket was tremendous. There was a podium with a microphone and a PA system. The prime minister was due to make a speech shortly, a tightly-scripted homily of hope and good wishes.

Martin got out of the car. It didn't seem to faze him, the enormity of this moment, the significance of it, the irrevocability. He could have been just paying a visit to the local Games Workshop branch in town, for all the excitement he demonstrated. Perhaps that was just as well.

"Will there be Seven Up on board?" was all he said. It was the one, the only carbonated beverage he could stomach. Other than milk, it was the only thing he drank.

"I'm not sure there will be, Martin," I said. "I think we were told it would be shakes, power smoothies, that sort of thing."

"Oh. Yes. Well, I don't like them much."

"You won't have a choice. It's interstellar travel, not popping out for a picnic."

"I know. I was only asking. I'll manage."

Claire fussed over him, finger-combing his hair. Jenny moped by the limo, disconsolate. A cold wind blew. The sky was overcast, the clouds low. The plane and its shuttle hitchhiker would be lost from view mere moments after takeoff.

I looked up at the clouds and shivered in the chill of an unseasonably cold June day. The Incident, making its presence felt. The black blot of nanotech-gone-mad was already affecting weather patterns. It had altered the course of the Gulf Stream and the mean temperature of the Atlantic, which meant mild winters and rainy summers for Europe and beyond. The climate was destined only to get crazier. It was predicted that there would be terrible atmospheric disruption, thunderstorms of biblical proportions, hurricanes, tsunamis, the whole *Revelation* gamut of acts of God. Within five years, if not sooner, crop yields would go into steep decline, there would be mass starvation, death on an epic scale, followed by epidemics of typhus and cholera, and then, to add to the general cheery forecast, the planet itself would begin to wobble on its axis, its balance skewed by the relative density of the von Neumann replicators. Eventually things would arrive at a literal tipping point, when fully half of the world's surface area was black, like a permanent eclipse, and the Earth would sheer from its orbital path, the whole delicate equilibrium of celestial mechanics utterly spannered. There was debate as to whether the planet would shoot off into outer space or be drawn in towards the sun, whether our mudball would freeze or burn. Either way, we, its inhabitants, were – what's the technical term? – oh yes. Fucked. Well and truly fucked.

*   *   *

LAST NIGHT, ANGELS came to me. It wasn't a dream, it was a vision. They told me everything is going to be fine. This is all part of God's plan. If we just have enough faith, pray hard enough, the Incident will reverse itself. It will heal itself. The angels were beautiful. I'm so happy. I'm not making any of this up. It's true. Don't be afraid. Believe.

"THE LUCKY FEW," the prime minister said. "Chosen. Chosen not by committee, nor by lottery, but by natural selection. The fittest under the circumstances. A representative cross-section of a certain stratum of the population – pragmatic, efficient, dogged, regimented – who will take the human narrative on to the next chapter, continue our story elsewhere, on a distant world. I congratulate you, I envy you, I salute you..."

Blah, blah, blah. I tuned him out. There was only so much high-flown flannel you could endure, especially on the day you and your son were parting company for good.

"Martin," I said. The time had come. "I love you. You know that."

"Yeah," he said.

"And you love me too, in your way. I'm sure of that."

"If you say so."

"I'm proud of you."

"Thanks."

"I couldn't be happier for you. And if there've been times when I've been impatient with you, angry with you, lost my temper, then I'm sorry. I never meant to. It's been difficult. We've tried our hardest, Mum and me. We've done everything we can to understand you and accept you."

"Okay, Dad."

"We'll live on in you."

"Genetically speaking, that's true."

"So remember us."

"I imagine I will."

I just want to say, I'm terrified. I don't want to die. Everybody out there, do you hear me? I'm so scared. Johnny Nimbus? Is there an afterlife? Are we all going to heaven? Does anyone know? Please, someone, tell me.

And then he was gone, strolling with his suitcase towards the mobile stairs that led to the shuttle entrance hatch. He was in a long line with all the other kids. Some were in their mid to late teens like him, the rest not much older than eleven or twelve. Yet all of them strangely adult, serious and sombre as they walked, here and there someone with an oddball gait, a peculiar hand twitch.

Clutching a sobbing Claire and Jenny, I waited for him to look back.

And waited.

All Martin had to do was turn, look at us, maybe raise a hand, possibly smile. That was all he had to do to prove he cared.

Not much.

He reached the stairs.

He climbed the stairs.

And I realised that the only option for me was to look away. So I did. I lowered my head. Turned my gaze aside. Concentrated on a spot on the tarmac to my left.

So that I would never have to know.

Because who wants posterity to deny them? Who can bear, not simply to be forgotten, but to be unacknowledged? Unrecognised? Dismissed as irrelevant by their most precious possession?

Seeing Martin go off to live was a kind of death.

KEEP 'EM COMING, Cloud Crowd! This is Johnny Nimbus, on the air, in the ether, wireless and tireless, your sentient social network, up all hours and hungry for chat. The shuttles are airborne, the pigeons are eagles, and the stars await, while down here we've got terminal cancer of the planet and the lights are going out one by one. So talk. Talk to each other. Talk to me. Tell my silicon soul your innermost secrets. I'm all heart and all ears. My hard drive is wide open to you, my memory stands at a petabyte and counting, and I'm not going anywhere. I'm staying right here to be your confidant and best friend to the end. To the very bitter end.

FEAST AND FAMINE

ADRIAN TCHAIKOVSKY

Adrian Tchaikovsky was born in Lincolnshire, studied and trained in Reading and now lives in Leeds. He is known for the Shadows of the Apt fantasy series starting with Empire in Black and Gold *and currently up to Book 8,* The Air War. *His hobbies include medieval combat, and tabletop, live and online role-playing. More information and short stories can be found at www.shadowsoftheapt.com*

"MOTHER, PRODIGAL, CONFIRM crew and cargo secured, ready to depart. Telemetry incoming. Initial course mapped, confirm check on our exit solution. Prodigal out."

(eleven minute pause)

"Prodigal, Mother. Telemetry confirmed flight path clear. Come on in. Mother out."

(eleven minute pause)

"Mother, Prodigal. Commencing countdown, separation from Oregon in one minute.

"Twenty seconds.

"Ten... nine..."

* * *

Counting down to oblivion, the final transmission of Doctor Astrid Veighl, as she patiently numbered the last seconds of her crew's lives down to zero. And then she died.

There was a general conspiracy, back at Mother, to pretend that there might just be a radio glitch. Even as we made our approach towards her last known location – a course plotted to more decimal places than even God normally bothers with – there was a vacuous suggestion that Veighl would have passed us in the night, would reach Mother *any moment now*, and our four day investigatory flight would turn out just to be a criminal waste of fuel and resources.

After the abrupt cessation of any transmission from Veighl a swift decision had been made to send us out after her. 'Swift' meant a seven-hour prep for departure: that a returning, radio-mute Veighl would have arrived at Mother long before we reached her take-off point was the sort of maths that needed no computer. It was a subject that neither we nor Mother touched on when we checked in, as though to point it out would be to look in the box and kill a cat that we all knew was stone dead already.

Syrenka, to whose song everything danced, was an ugly green-purple bruise to starboard as we came in: a gas giant with twenty-one variously barren moons and enough of a debris ring to suggest the demise of at least five more. And in that ring, a secret, like the oyster's pearl.

The computers back at Mother, our own Onboard, and Pelovska's Expert System, had all put their heads together at our launch to plot out the sort of four-dimensional map that no unaugmented human mind could conceive of, so that when we kicked off from Mother on our fact-finder (nobody had ever said 'rescue mission' in the briefing) our course would keep us clear of each piece of the great field of murdered moon clutter that was Syrenka's waist. Oregon, our destination, was one of the larger pieces of rock, too small for a moon, but making a large asteroid. Very loosely comparable in length and breadth to Oregon USA, in fact. Eventually some peeved astronomer would throw something from the classics at it, but for now it proudly carried the monicker of the Beaver State because someone back on Mother was homesick for Astoria.

"There's another beauty." Osman was designated pilot, which meant that, unless someone had dropped a decimal back at Mother, he was here to sightsee. He was referring to a rock tumbling past, less than half the size of Oregon and a hundred kilometres away: he had magnified the image to show the blue starburst flower of Anchorite. Or an Anchorite. Or some Anchorites. Veighl, the departed, had been working on the answer to that problem of nomenclature. Pelovska, our geologist and Expert System, had reviewed the raw data Veighl had sent before her decision to return home, and subsequent abrupt silence. The question had remained unanswered.

Gliese 876 had been the second extrasolar system reached by human technology. The supposed 'earth-like planet' present had been a bust, but the probe, programmed for pattern-recognition, had sent back one picture, just one, that sparked a furore back home. Passing through this very debris field within the shadow of Syrenka (then just Gliese 876f) – and minutes before becoming several billion dollars of metal pizza that must exist still on the side of some moonlet somewhere – it sent out an image very similar to what we were seeing now. There were plenty of them, in fact, throughout the debris ring and on some of the smaller moons – geometrically irregular crystal formations like sea-urchins clinging on in the vacuum of space. *Life!* had gone the cry, back home – the first indication that we might not be alone, and life within reach, just about, for a team that was willing to be severed from the planet of their genesis for decades. We liked to think that everyone back there hung on our every years-old word. Possibly nobody cared.

The Anchorite was a phenomenon that existed throughout the ring in quantities from the microscopic to the sunburst array that Osman had pointed out. Veighl reported the largest known such specimen at two metres ninety centimetres diameter, and one metre eighty-eight projection from its substrate. Veighl, who had qualifications in geology and biology, had failed to get off the fence and come to any premature conclusion – a scientist to the end.

Pelovska summarised: "Veighl's data shows that the Anchorite is a carbon-rich crystal lattice, the structure of which appears homogenous no matter how large or small the sample. Veighl's data further shows that the Anchorite is capable of breaking down the material upon which, or within which, it is embedded and converting it into more Anchorite. It replicates. Does that alone make it life? If we *are* looking at an ecology, we're looking at one with incredibly low levels of energy: whatever tidal heating you can squeeze from an elliptical orbit around Syrenka, plus the background radiation and what pittance of light you can get this far out." The system's star was a cold, pale lamp far off in the alien heavens. You'd get more of a tan on Mars. "Still, Veighl took samples and treated them to the same intensity of illumination, and her results suggest that a day of that was enough for molecular-level conversion of asteroidal material into Anchorite." Pelovska had come down heavily on the 'geology' side of the argument long before. Efficient geology, though, which took the faint light and heat of its surroundings and grew like lichen, converting its substrate into its substance so resourcefully that there was no waste, as close to thumbing its nose at the laws of thermodynamics as anything we had ever seen.

Our shuttle had been decelerating smoothly for some time and now Osman reported needlessly, "Oregon ahead."

Just as there was no current need for our pilot to actually fly the vessel, as captain there was no need for me to give orders. A conclave of computers had already worked out the best approach, and our vessel ran through its paces nimbly as the state-sized asteroid grew and grew before us, until it filled our universe, until the naked eye could make out the sparse blue pinpricks of Anchorite, each in its crater. That was another observation of Veighl's. The stuff seemed to grow best at impact sites, if 'grow' is the word. That was why she had set down on Oregon in the first place.

Pelovska's headset light was on, which told us she was communing with her Expert System implant, that was in turn taking advice from our Onboard. The light itself served no function beside the social

– letting Osman and I know that her attention was away with the electronic fairies. In this case she was supervising our sensor arrays, bouncing signals off Oregon's nearest neighbours to try for any sign of Veighl. By that time, our craft had matched velocity and rotation with the asteroid – so that we seemed, to our primate eyes, to be magically suspended above a stationary wasteland.

"Ping," she announced, deadpan. "Captain?"

There was a moment's silence before I was ready to catch that ball, because it was confirmation of what we had known all along, that Veighl had never left Oregon. I tried to form the words "rescue mission" in my head, but they wouldn't come. "Let's get them past the horizon and see what we've got. Generate a solution for coming down nearby if we want to – but not right on them." Human social instinct prompted me to ask all sorts of other questions, to seek confirmation from her of what my own instruments could tell me just as easily. Principally: no signals, no signs of life. No surprises, therefore.

Then Veighl's craft was hauled over the shallow horizon, and Osman swore, and we simply coasted in silence for some time while the Onboard, devoid of either wonder or horror, made the necessary adjustments to stabilise the motion of the rock beneath us.

Doctor Veighl had dodged the "is it life?" issue in her cursory report – and we would never hear the detailed one that she would have prepared back on Mother after processing her data. Veighl had talked about the life/not-life boundary, and whether we even had valid criteria to make the call – at what point self-replicating chemistry could be said to make the jump into something more akin to us than rocks. Her data showed her painstaking experimentation on the Anchorite, taking samples and watching its glacial growth.

My first thought, unprofessional and yet unavoidable, was that the Anchorite had got its revenge.

There was a crystal flower there, but it was a jagged crown of thorns nineteen metres across and at its heart was some of Veighl's shuttle, embedded, part-metabolised, like a fly in a sundew. Everything from midway back towards the thrusters was either buried or just gone. Only six metres of nose, canted at a slight angle, stood proud of the hungry mass.

We hung there above it, our stationary orbit re-established, and I numbly checked that our cameras were getting it all. Something terrible and sudden had happened here, that made a nonsense of all Veighl's data, and I would keep transmitting a visual record of our mission in case terrible, sudden events came in twos. Still, I could not shake off the feeling that it would not help. Veighl had been in *mid-transmission* when this happened, cut off with no time to give a warning or to cry for help.

"At least it was quick." Until the others looked at me, I hadn't realised that I had said this aloud.

"Depending on how long life support lasted, or if it's still active, there is a possibility that the crew may be alive, maybe in their suits," Pelovska stated. In the stunned silence that followed I guessed that this thought had been given her by her Expert System, following its best guidance for the furtherance of the mission. It would be my decision, but the computers had already cast their vote.

"There's no sign of anything: no signals, no emissions, no heat at all," Osman reported. Then, more quietly, "It killed them."

"No speculation," I stated.

"Wasn't aware that counted as speculation. So, am I putting us down?"

"Everyone suit up," I decided, which entailed nothing more than securing our helmets. They were uncomfortable, restricted our vision, made our breathing stale, and nobody argued with me. The space around us, the asteroid below, now thronged with invisible dangers.

I ran some checks of Oregon's surface, bouncing waves off it and cross-referencing with Veighl's data, particularly the signature of Anchorite. The echo from the great spiked star of crystal matched its smaller brethren, and the balance of the asteroid showed nothing more than rock and the expected dusting of microscopic Anchorite flecks.

The Onboard tallied the cost of a stationary orbit over Oregon, not only the fuel and the constant adjustments to stay clear of the rest of the debris field, but the disruption to the asteroid's course as Oregon, in turn, would be marginally influenced by our mass. The rock's tiny gravity was giving us very little help, and the projected adjustments we would have to make over the course of an hour were falling foul of fuel conservation. The entire mission was on a penurious fuel budget, and our little trip hadn't been catered for in the projections.

The alternative was setting down, which would conserve fuel and fool with Oregon less, making any danger from other debris that much more foreseeable.

"Anna's right," I said reluctantly. "We need to be sure." Meaning that we would be pilloried if we simply got the jitters and left. "Bring us down at least two hundred metres away and be ready for a quick exit if we need one."

Osman swore again, and he and Pelovska put their heads together with the Onboard to come up with a landing solution, ran the result through some quick simulations, and pronounced it good. Oregon gravity was something in the region of two per cent of earth standard, a great deal for an asteroid, barely enough for us to notice. It made me think of all those people back in the Beaver State, whether they felt that little extra patriotic pull as part of Earth's grounding.

We had already matched Oregon's speed and rotation, and now we were allowed to drift closer and closer into the weak, weak hands of Oregon's gravity, so much in tandem with the asteroid that human senses saw only a very gentle approach to a stationary surface, when in reality we and Oregon were gyring our manic way through the cluttered ring of broken moons that belted Syrenka. Decelerating with our thrusters would have spoiled that close harmony, bouncing us back from the pull of that feeble gravity, and so the computers allowed us to drift, dream-like, until our craft's extended feet were brushing the ancient, vacuum-corroded stone. All we felt, when the claws were deployed, was the faintest of grinding shudders. If we had been asleep, it would not have woken us. Except for Pelovska, of course. Her implant would update her moment to moment, so that she spent her life being immaculately well-informed and, I suspect, lonely.

There was a fraught pause, no more than a second, and I think all of us were waiting for the jaws of the trap – the sudden eruption beneath us as a hidden crystal monster lunged up to feed. Of course, nothing happened.

Now we had a stable platform from which to investigate, and we were no longer haemorrhaging fuel simply matching our motion to Oregon's. Our claws, and the meagre gravity, would suffice to keep us anchored, but I made sure that the Onboard would keep plotting escape vectors so that we were ready to fire all thrusters and take off into the debris field if things got bad. Correction: if things got bad and we had the chance to do anything about it.

"Drone out?" Osman asked, and I nodded. We did not have anything particularly fit for search and rescue, and the mission's drones had been designed for scientific exploration, sampling and testing. Right then I didn't care how poor an ambassador ours would make. Better the drone than me.

What we had was something like a metal springtail programmed to think it was a flying squirrel. Osman deployed the drone from a compartment on top of the ship and gave it directions. The drone did the sums, checked them with the Onboard and Pelovska, and leapt. Leapt being a relative term, of course. In order to arrive at Veighl's ravaged craft in a controlled manner, rather than just bouncing from it like a fly on a windscreen, the drone put a minimum of force into the jump, departing our hull in an absurdly leisurely fashion, correcting its spin with minute applications of its jets but letting the simple force of the initial push carry it on a minutes-long, agonisingly slow drift across the intervening vacuum, letting the microgravity counteract upward motion just enough to bring it into a shallow arc that would end on Veighl's shuttle's nose. It could have got over there a good deal quicker on jets alone, but had the same problem we did. Mechanical movement used up stored battery, that could be replenished eventually by drinking in even the weak and distant light of the system's star. Thrusters used fuel, stored solid and then flash-ignited into superheated gas, Newton's third law in action. But when the fuel was gone, when that mass was cast away, there was no more, not for the drone and not for us. Fuel was matter, and once we had used it up there would be no more. We lived by an economy as harsh and limiting as the Anchorite's own.

The drone landed awkwardly – sometimes nobody's sums are perfect – and Osman took over, extending its handful of legs until one magnetic pad got purchase. For a moment we saw the magnified view of the drone dangling out at an angle by one limb, but then it had jack-knifed down its own length and was crawling over Veighl's hull, its cameras serving as our eyes.

"Emergency hatch is clear of the... of the stuff," Osman said. "Want me to open it?"

Again there was an awkward pause before Pelovska put in, "They may be inside without suits." We didn't believe it, not that they were alive, but her Expert System kept trawling the known data for even the most remote possibility.

Osman deployed some of the drone's sensors. "No vibrations. No heat. No power at all. If they're in there without suits, they're frozen dead."

A beat. "Granted," said Pelovska, the Expert System giving up on even that faint hope.

"Get it open," I decided.

A search and rescue drone would have had stronger manipulators, and a cutting torch if all else failed. Our science model had neither, and for the best part of an hour we watched it scrabble and drift and flail at the hatch release, and utterly fail to open it. Eventually Osman's monotonous swearing got too much, and I told him to abandon the attempt.

"Prep the airlock. My command, my responsibility. I'll go over."

There was no argument, much as I might wish for some. I did not want to go over to that partially-consumed shuttle. I did not want to get close to the alien thing that had murdered it. I did not want to confirm the patently obvious certainty that all three of us held in common, that Veighl's crew was dead, impossibly dead, destroyed by the unexpected malice of the phenomenon they had come to study.

Ten minutes later I was in our cramped airlock, breathing loud in my own ears, as they pumped the air from around me. I had an open radio channel and a camera running, and my suit would be transmitting all the minutiae of my body's workings, ready to sound the alarm the moment anything happened to me. Nobody got this far into space without mastering their instincts and conquering some deep-imprinted fears, but when the airlock doors opened onto the grim surface of Oregon I felt my innards lurch. We had come out here because we thought that we were not alone. Now that seemed a good reason to be anywhere else.

I had my own little thruster-pack, because I could

not do calculations as well as our drone, and my first step was too energetic for Oregon's feeble gravity, my nerves bouncing me high so that I had to use some of my own precious fuel stock to prevent me departing the asteroid altogether. After that I took it easy, crawling over the surface like a crab across some vast drowned cliff, trying to keep a constant proximity to the cratered surface without either colliding with it or losing contact altogether.

There were Anchorite flowers between me and Veighl, just little ones, a hand-span across or less, nestled in craters as though they were lurking there. Of course they could not move. They could not have killed Veighl either, according to her data. I gave them a wide berth.

A warning word from Osman told me I was close – I was so intent on my painstaking progress I had lost track. I slowed and regarded the vast crystal explosion before me. The footage that I was relaying would become the most viewed recording on Earth, when it arrived there years later.

The tilted nose of Veighl's vessel was plain, and the Anchorite had not visibly expanded since we arrived. I told myself that this was not some alien fly trap, that its spray of spines would not close on me. I told myself again. It didn't help much.

"Good luck, Captain," came Osman's voice in my ear. I bent my knees and jumped, kicking off from the surface, and then burning a little fuel to cast me with painful slowness at Veighl's craft. I think I touched down more gently than the drone had.

My suit lamp made little headway through the small ports, but I thought I made out a shape. "Is that…?"

"That would be the pilot's seat. Veighl herself was piloting," came Pelovska. A moment's image-cleaning later and she added, "Ninety per cent certain that's Veighl you're seeing."

"I'm going to open the hatch." Even then I hesitated because, however certain we and our computers were that Veighl's crew was dead, I was about to open the interior of their shuttle onto vacuum.

Opening their tomb was not something that would appear in my report.

I fumbled with glove-clumsy hands at the release for the hatch, making sure that I was well out of the way of it. There was no pressure of air within, though, not at that end of the Kelvin scale. Instead the freed hatch just drifted from its mountings, falling in slow, slow motion towards the rigid starburst of the Anchorite below.

I froze. I should have kept hold of the hatch, but you can't plan for everything.

It came to rest amidst those jagged spines. Nothing happened. Osman's oath in my earpiece was pure relief.

Then I turned my camera and my attention to the interior and he had no words for it, and neither did I.

It was a snapshot of crystal hell, looking down into the inclined cabin of Veighl's craft. The Anchorite had eaten the vessel from the stern up, swallowed its engines and reactor entire, ravened out into the crew's living space from the back wall and just kept on going. The two back seats where Veighl's crewmembers had been strapped in for lift off were gone, but the unwelcome clarity of my lamps revealed a single boot still protruding from the razor-tipped wall. The

Anchorite was translucent enough that we could see there was no body within. Ship and crew both had been consumed and translated into more of the stuff that had done for them.

Veighl herself, sitting ahead of the others, had fared slightly better whilst being just as dead. The spines of the Anchorite had pierced through the back of her chair and into her body, where what looked like a small secondary growth had exploded in her chest cavity, flinging its jutting needles in every direction and shredding her from within.

Her face, like everything else, was covered with a rime of crystallized air, the frozen remnants of the cabin's atmosphere that had not been allowed to vent into space. Her expression was placidly accepting, as though she had just learned a great truth. Her last breath was bristling about her nose and mouth.

"None of this makes sense," Osman whispered in my ear. "Captain, we have no idea how this happened or whether it's going to happen again. We should get off this rock."

I looked into Veighl's open, crusted eyes. "The problem is that we need to make sense of it." My voice was admirably steady. "Because this is what we came to this system for." Then, and still so very steady, "Any change from the Anchorite?"

"Nothing measurable," Pelovska confirmed. "Don't touch it."

"No intention of doing so." Veighl's stare was giving me the shudders. "I'm coming back. Send to Mother for advice. No point wasting suit power and air while we twiddle our thumbs and decide what to do." It was sound reasoning that would look good in my report.

The drone stayed out there – we could use it to explore the interior of Veighl's vessel now that I had the hatch open. I made my desperately careful progress back towards our vessel, eyes down at the vacuum-ravaged ground. I missed the clue myself, but Osman saw it through my cameras.

"Hold, hold, Captain!" Just as I was about to clamber for the airlock. "Go back down. Go to the landing gear. Or I can get the drone back –"

"No, I'm going." I let Oregon's gravity draw me gently back down. "What have you seen?"

"Not sure, it's just…"

I had gone cold all over despite the close heat of the suit.

There was a delicate clutching fringe of Anchorite about the nearest landing claw. Had we landed on one of the flowers? If so then we had done so with all three claws at once. Magnification showed that each had that spiky rim of crystal about it.

"It's started," Osman breathed. "Get in here, Captain."

With shaking hands I scrambled for the airlock. Pelovska was saying something about bringing the drone back, but Osman and I were both telling her we had no time. The Anchorite, life or not, had crept up on us.

I got through the airlock in record time and half-kicked, half-drifted into my seat. "Tell me we're ready to go." I was picturing the clutching claws of the Anchorite already attacking our landing gear.

"We're ready," Osman confirmed.

"Pelovska?"

The light of her headset blinked. Her staring eyes were

all too much like Veighl's. She was in deep communion with her Expert System, lips moving silently.

"Captain, I have a trajectory," Osman insisted.

"Pelovska!" I snapped.

"Hold," she murmured. Her unseeing gaze flickered between imaginary objects, the representations of her calculations.

"Captain!" Osman insisted. We both felt the onrushing jaws of the Anchorite accelerating towards us impossibly from below. Millions of years of evolution were clamouring that we were *under threat*, and that we had to get away.

"Go!" I told Osman, and Pelovska hit her override. He swore and fought with the controls and the Onboard, but he was locked out. For a moment Pelovska and I wrestled for mastery over the shuttle's systems, a silent battle of keys and commands, because I *knew* as captain that I had seniority, and even her Expert System had to bow to my authority.

That was how I learned that the people back home who had designed our systems had not trusted me, or any mere human being, quite that much. When the chips were down, our Onboard sided with the Expert System, and I ended up staring at the gleaming visor of Pelovska's helmet, twisted around in my straps.

"I need to conduct an experiment," came her voice.

For a moment I could not speak. Then: "Do it when we're up."

"No, Captain." Meticulously polite. "When we get to Mother you may of course have me confined to quarters for... mutiny, possibly. For now I am going to conduct an experiment."

I could see that Osman had undone his straps in

order to go for her, but I stopped him with a gesture – at least *he* was still taking my orders. Pelovska's headset light was on, gleaming from her visor, her implant computer cycling its calculations. I thought, then, that she had gone mad.

"She's taken control of the drone," Osman reported hollowly.

"Mother, Errant," I called in, hoping that she was not blocking the radio as well. "I need you to countermand Pelovska's override." It was hopeless. There would be long minutes before Mother even heard me.

"I will be as quick as I can," Pelovska informed us impassively. Osman was back to his controls and I knew he would be trying to find a way past Pelovska's lockout while she was distracted, but of course the Expert System was never distracted.

I looked at the drone camera image. She had sent it off from Veighl's tomb to touch down, all sprawling limbs, on Oregon's surface.

"Has it got to you? The Anchorite?" These words, recorded and transmitted back to Mother, would not be the proudest moment noted on my permanent record.

Now the drone's eye view was of the dark space above us, with the orb of Syrenka just nudging into shot, but one of our shuttle's own cameras had acquired the drone, showing it on its back, legs drawn in like a dead beetle.

I was waiting for Mother's reply. They were watching everything, every moment of our mission. A quick response could lock Pelovska out and give me my ship back.

"Ignition," Pelovska announced, and the drone fired its thrusters.

It should have shot off into the void, a receding pinprick of metal in seconds. Instead...

Osman's bark of surprise was loud in my ear. Where the drone had been was a lunging hand of Anchorite, an exuberant spray of crystal, with some small scrap of the drone cupped in its heart.

"Do *not* fire our thrusters," Pelovska informed us.

"*Errant, Mother,*" came the distant voice of our surrogate home. "*That's a negative on overriding the Expert. You are instructed to follow its advice. Mother out.*"

"I have been assimilating Veighl's data," came Pelovska's calm voice. "There is a flaw with her experimental method. She only tested the Anchorite's capabilities in its native environment. It exists in vacuum, with a minimal energy input that it utilises very, very efficiently to replicate. This we knew. That does not account for the flowers."

"Account for them, then," challenged Osman, still sounding shaky.

"The Anchorite exists in microscopic quantities everywhere here, and under normal circumstances it would grow at a speed we would think of as geological, that much Veighl shows. Her mistake was to assume that, because it lives in a very low energy ecology, it is capable only of slow growth. When presented with a gift of energy, such as the heat of a debris impact, Anchorite uses that energy to grow. It uses that energy immediately to convert its surroundings, working with extreme speed and efficiency because otherwise that energy would be lost to the void. I can only conclude that it has adapted to do so, and that those fragments better able to make use of such windfalls have out-evolved their less fit siblings to give us what we now see. The Anchorite makes near-instantaneous use of whatever energy comes its way."

A pause.

"Life, then," I concluded, but Pelovska, like Veighl, would not commit.

"If you have a self-replicating system with an imperfect replicator and limited resources, what we think of as adaptive evolution *must* occur. It is a logical certainty. Where you place the label of 'life' is more subjective. However, I believe that we wanted to depart."

"The Anchorite under the landing gear," I put to her. "Are you saying that's just…?"

"The friction of our landing. It isn't going to increase measurably, if I'm right. The heat energy of the thrusters, though, would… well, you've seen what it would do. Although I think the sheer scale of Veighl's monument is more to do with when the Anchorite assimilated her reactor."

I thought of that secondary burst that had torn open Veighl's chest. I did not feel any better for realising that her own body heat had probably provided the fuel for it.

"Captain, I am submitting a departure solution. The Onboard is plotting an escape trajectory. This will of necessity be a little less exact than usual."

I looked over what she proposed. The hurdle was not great: Oregon's gravity, two per cent of earth's, would not be too jealous of our departure. Still, our shuttle had a great deal of mass, and we would be fighting our own inertia.

"Mother, Errant. Do you concur with Anna's calculations? Errant out." By this time I had given over any illusion that I, a poor human, was in command of the mission.

A tense wait, the minutes dragging silently by, until the voice came to us, "*Errant, Mother. Confirmed calculations and trajectory. Looks like your best chance. Mother out.*" A human telling a human that one set of computers agreed with another.

What Pelovska, her Expert and the Onboard had proposed, I acted upon, retracting the landing gear to ninety per cent whilst Osman used some of our precious air to fill the empty airlock.

"Deploying in one minute," I heard myself say, bitterly aware that all the necessary information was being shared freely between computers anyway. "Twenty seconds... ten, nine..." Counting down.

When we hit zero the shuttle retracted its claws and then extended its landing gear with considerably more force than the manual advised. For possibly the first time in human history a space vessel tried a standing jump.

It did very little. We cleared the surface of Oregon by inches, poised momentarily over our slightly enlarged Anchorite footprints, held between the weak gravity's pull and our own feeble push. Then the airlock opened and voided its precious cargo, and Newton's Third stepped in and shepherded us gently away, leaving Oregon to dance off, taking Veighl's crystal grave with it.

All sorts of alarms were going off, because we had come away on a variant trajectory that would have run us into something in an hour or so, but a little jockeying from Osman had us back on track, and we were headed home for Mother.

Around us, the wheeling shapes of Syrenka's debris field danced on, heedless. The scattered flowers of Anchorite glittered like eyes as they watched us go, the almost-life within our vessel taking us away from the almost-life without.

WHATEVER SKIN YOU WEAR

EUGIE FOSTER

Eugie Foster calls home a mildly haunted, fey-infested house in metro Atlanta that she shares with her husband, Matthew. Eugie received the 2009 Nebula Award for her novelette, "Sinner, Baker, Fabulist, Priest; Red Mask, Black Mask, Gentleman, Beast," the 2011 Drabblecast People's Choice Award for Best Story, and the 2002 Phobos Award. Her fiction has also been translated into eight languages and nominated for the Hugo and British Science Fiction Association awards. Her short story collection, Returning My Sister's Face and Other Far Eastern Tales of Whimsy and Malice, *has been used as a textbook at the University of Wisconsin-Milwaukee and the University of California-Davis. Visit her online at EugieFoster.com*

THE SIGNS INSCRIBED in paint and light at the perimeter read *green space*, although there is more magenta and turquoise foliage on display than green. In the not-green green space, a techno-fairy in a dress of chrome cobwebs dances beneath a fuchsia willow tree. She sways and pirouettes to a soundless melody among its candy floss tendrils. A cobalt-skinned demoness crowned by a fiery wreath admires herself in a mirror of air, flaring the skirt of her white lace pinafore around her thighs. The mirror obeys her like a well-trained dog, bounding to and fro to present whatever perspective she desires. An electric-eyed swan maiden with tribal tattoos coursing over her arms levels a Gatling blaster. A bright *UNDERAGE* display hovers over her head in oversized text.

Claie doesn't glance up from his handheld when the percussive burst smashes into him. A shield deflects the Gatling's discharge, erupting from the tactile contacts on his wrists and flaring to envelope his two companions – a mermaid with shimmering aquamarine scales and a fox woman with golden eyes. Neither of the women react either. But when the redirected blast strikes the cobalt-skinned demoness, bouncing her several meters back, Claie turns. He gestures, adjusting the gain slider on his audio setting.

"Sorry," he says. "Didn't realize the discharge had a ricochet animation."

The demoness floats to her feet unhurt. "No worries. Can't expect to spend any time in a sandbox without getting bounced a couple times." The white lace pinafore disappears, and, for a moment, she wears only a lavender bra and matching panties. The moment passes, and the demoness, now in a black leather jumpsuit with gold spikes at shoulders and knees, bends to examine a knee-spike.

Another detonation from the Gatling throws a swath of hot pink turf into the air. This time, Claie winces at the explosion. He hurries to tap the public mute toggle on his smartdev before resuming his discussion with his companions.

"So anyway, Buneh, did you have a chance to replicate my results and see how our prim loses its phantom indicator when another phantom overlaps it?"

The fox woman nods, an orange tongue flicking over her muzzle. "Not sure why it's doing that."

"Doesn't happen every time," the mermaid says. "Why's it going wonky on some phantoms but not others?"

Claie taps commands into his handheld. "Devi, I isolated the error sequence. Seems to have something to do with certain architectural structures used in older sims, mostly flying buttresses. I'm sending you my results now."

While Claie waits for the mermaid to review his findings, the green space blanches, tinting everything from the magenta trees to the cobalt demoness (now in a high-necked evening gown) in shades of gray. The achromatic palette is short-lived. A concentric ripple of color overwrites it, spreading subdued greens, tans, and browns – flora in gauche earth tones – in its wake.

Claie notes the change with a raised eyebrow. "Someone needs to tweak their hue overlay," he mutters.

Devi cocks her head, a waterfall of liquid-cyan curls spilling over her shoulders. "That's loco –"

Mid-syllable, Devi vanishes, as does Buneh. Simultaneously, Claie's vision blurs.

His head snaps up and he blinks several times, trying to recover crisp lines and hard shapes in a suddenly Monet-soft panorama. Half the people in the green space have disappeared: all the commuter avatars like Devi and Buneh. The remaining occupants mill, their surprise and confusion evident even to Claie's watering eyes, as is the cause of their subsequent distress. They have all diminished, become less vivid, less fanciful, and, on the whole, less attractive.

Claie inhales sharply, breath hissing through his teeth, as he takes in his own appearance. His periwinkle zoot suit is gone, leaving only the bland, beige-on-beige unisex with its embedded tactiles, the same garment – with minor variations in cut and fit – that everyone wears beneath their skins. His flesh has lightened from gold-touched bronze to pasty white, complete with annoying freckles.

He is naked, stripped of his avatar skin, and it makes him self-conscious, embarrassed. His dismay is only marginally defused by the surety that everyone in the vicinity shares his predicament.

What happened? Green space or not, this type of prank is deplorable, not to mention alarming. What sort of script could override so many privacy protocols – a labyrinth of passcode encryptions and DNA biometrics?

He raises his handheld, the customary source of answers. With a grimace, he raises it higher to accommodate his uncustomarily myopic eyes.

Whatever banished the commuters and skins has also crashed most of his apps. His smartdev's display is tidy, sans the clutter of icons and text that normally litter it. The zero bars indicator is conspicuously evident.

Claie gapes at the modest red icon. He's only seen it in documentation wikis before. No signal means no way to rebake his skin or reestablish his conference with Buneh and Devi. It also means no way to call home. Or for anyone to call him.

What if Shelby tries to reach him and she can't get through? What if she checks their You OK? app and his vitals don't register?

Swearing, he wills the little bars to illuminate. Just one. One would be enough.

They don't.

He wants to rush home, but without a connection to the network there's no GPS to tell him where he is, no map app to get him home, no clear sight app to let him see. Without a connection to the network, his smartdev is about as useful as a pretty rock.

Claie forces himself to take deep breaths, to calm himself. Shelby knows he's in a meeting, and she's considerate of his work. There's no reason for her to call. And also, he recalls, his smartdev is a pretty rock that can keep time and record data even disconnected from LivIT.

While the majority of his apps are remotely stored on LivIT's servers, he has a few that can run without the network – simple ones that can function locally. He launches a stopwatch app and begins a data capture session. Ingrained coder principles. It is always easier to debug a glitch with reliable error logs.

A smattering of echoing movements dot the region, blurry figures tapping or thumbing controls at temple or wrist. Other coders probably. There are always at least one or two at any given time in a green space.

Letting his smartdev drop to his side, Claie presses fingertips to temples. His head aches from the unaccustomed eye strain. Still, there is an unexpected benefit to his nearsightedness. He can't make out facial particulars beyond vague impressions of eyes, noses, and mouths. Admittedly, it feels a little head-in-sand, but not being privy to the raw details – and he knows they are raw – allows him to pretend that his own RL shortcomings and deficiencies aren't being ogled at either. The unsavory intimacies that he *can* make out, the fleshy bulges and sags, the disturbing homogeneity of flesh tones, and the unsettling absence of individual aesthetics, are more than enough for his abused sensibilities to cope with.

"What's going on?" The question is shaky, frightened.

Claie peers at the speaker, a skinny youth, almost certainly still in high school. Probably the *UNDERAGE* swan maiden with the Gatling blaster.

He smiles, trying to reassure. "Hey, don't worry. It's just a bad glitch. A gang of griefers most likely."

"Never heard of a glitch like this," the youth says, voice cracking. He edges closer until Claie can see how wide his eyes are.

"Used to happen all the time," Claie says in his best not-a-problem, everything's-fine voice. "The green space will re-rez as soon as the corrupted code gets cleaned out."

"It's sure taking a while. Did it use to take this long?"

"Don't know." Claie suppresses a prick of irritation. He's not *that* old. "I only read it in a wiki about when LivIT was transitioning from device-based service to global release and the server infrastructure hadn't fully propagated. Before my time."

"Not before mine." A dusky woman with gun-metal hair wanders over. Close up, Claie sees lines beneath her eyes and around her mouth, mahogany creases in hickory. It makes him uncomfortable, unsure where to look, not wanting to stare.

"They usually never lasted more than an hour," the woman continues. "Always felt longer, though. There was one when I was around your age —" she nods to the ex-swan maiden, "seemed like it was never going to end. Made me late for a date. When I could finally log in, he'd already left the sim. Turned out okay, though. That's where I met my wife." The woman winks, an organic chiaroscuro of creasing and uncreasing across her face. "That one lasted fifty-seven minutes."

"Fifty-seven minutes?" the youth gasps.

"I'm sure it won't be anywhere near that long," she says. "LivIT hasn't had a regionwide outage in ages."

"Regionwide?" Claie asks, startled. "You think it's more than this green space?"

The woman studies Claie. "Nearsighted?"

Claie shrugs. "Treading the verge of legally blind without my clear sight app."

"Ah. Sorry. Can you see Mu Shu's?" She points.

Claie strains, trying to make out the eatery that sits beyond the outskirts of the green space. After several moments of intense squinting, he realizes that the dragon bot that usually greets guests with bouts of fire at the entrance is gone.

"Not well," he admits. "Is the whole place down? Textures and all?"

"Yep. It's nothing but RL as far as I can see."

Claie resists the urge to rub his eyes. "Did I see you launching a local app after we lost the network?" he asks. "You wouldn't happen to be a coder too?"

"You're perceptive for a shortsighted fellow. It wasn't a local, though; I was triggering my lifeline status feed. I moderate Blip's Facelight community. 'Fraid I wouldn't know a line of code from a song."

Claie doesn't approve of lay people jiggering with their 911 utilities. It's possible to jam up a smartdev's auto hail if folks don't know what they're doing. But he understands why a mod would want to piggyback her comm feed to her lifeline, and it means this woman has a network connection, albeit a constricted one.

"Are your comm members saying the whole region is glitching?" he asks.

"You're a mod for Blip?" the youth chirps up, awed. "Do you know Kimiko Blaze?"

The woman laughs. "Not personally, but I've moderated a couple of her chatviews." She touches her wrist. "I'm not getting many incoming chirps. And I timed some major lag happening from outside the southeast region. I can't think of anything that would do that except if the whole region's borked."

Claie's heart skips. She's right. But a griefer script able to take out a whole region's AVs, skins, bots, and textures? That would mean GPS satellites as well as integral LivIT source code being affected.

His worrisome speculation is curtailed by the abrupt return of his visual acuity, his AV skin, and Devi and Buneh. The youth sprouts a good fifteen centimeters in height, a pair of white wings, and a buxom chest scrawled with tattoos. His – her now – Gatling blaster materializes in its thigh holster as the swan maiden skin completes its rebake.

Devi and Buneh wave their arms, gesturing at Claie's handheld. Puzzled, he looks down just in time to read Buneh's "Toggle yr mute!" IM before an acoustic holocaust of voices, music, and tones crashes through his in-ears, heralding a flurry of alerts, chirps, and updates.

Claie yelps and fumbles for the global mute, peripherally aware of the Blip mod and several others occupied in similarly frantic slaps and thumbings.

Scowling, ears ringing, Claie gingerly restores the conference audio.

"Gomen ne," Buneh says, fox ears twitching sympathetically. "Tried to warn you. It took a messy restart to clear the glitch, and lots of folks on Badger had all their app settings reset."

"What you get for being a Badgerbrain," Devi says.

Devi is as rabid a Lynx devotee as Claie is a Badger one. Claie smiles and gives her the finger before launching a script to restore his customized settings.

CLAIE'S STOPWATCH APP informs him that the glitch lasted for all of seven minutes 48 seconds and a decimal streak of milliseconds. The server tally is a little longer, accounting for the gap between the glitch's true start and when it occurred to Claie to time it.

Less than ten minutes, more than five. Yes, it felt much longer. And it was more widespread than even the Blip mod speculated, hitting Devi and Buneh too – in UTC-8 and UTC-6 time zones, respectively – with preliminary chirps suggesting it also affected UTC+ regions.

The official word from LivIT's network gurus attribute the glitch to an epic and unique confluence of misfortune: a malicious griefer script breaching a too hasty upgrade, dominoing GPS fail-safes clashing with network security protocols, extensive sunspot activity, and a spilled mug of tea. The restart – which by all accounts goes beyond Buneh's understated "messy" and into Frankensteinian mosh pit – is cascading west to east: why Devi and Buneh knew about the Badger issue before him. Buneh also runs Badger, and she'd been treated to the same audio barrage.

After all the excitement, none of them feels much like resuming their test session. Buneh confirms that their data is intact, and they exchange farewells. Devi promises to send out a timely reminder to reschedule as the mermaid and fox woman de-rez.

The Blip moderator has also absented herself. Claie isn't sure if she's the red-skinned geisha in the smoldering kimono or the vampire in the Catholic schoolgirl uniform. The swan maiden is gleefully blowing away chunks of scenery with her Gatling.

Claie verifies that his shield app is running and then hits the shortcut icon that will call Shelby's smartdev. When she doesn't pick up, he pings their home server. It answers promptly, and a quick query tells him that Shelby is indeed logged into the apartment. Frowning, Claie brings up their dedicated You OK? app, and it reassures him that all of Shelby's vitals are a-ok and she hasn't activated a 911 hail, auto or manual.

Claie relaxes. Shelby is often neglectful of her smartdev. (Claie is the detail-oriented one.) She has probably only forgotten to set the ringer to audible. He smiles, indulgent. She might even be asleep. It'd be typical of Shelby to have napped through the whole glitch.

Claie envisions Shelby curled up, sleepy and kittenish, in a nest of blankets. He imagines waking her and regaling her with his tale of the glitch and how her lilac eyes will round and her dove-wing hands flutter to her mouth, and also how she'll fly into his arms.

He sets out for home, his pace brisk.

Along the way, he witnesses more evidence of the ragged restart. Mu Shu's dragon is unwell, its normally kaleidoscopic scales a subdued peach. And it has rezed several feet from its normal post, lodging halfway in the eatery's entrance. It opens its mouth as he passes, and disembodied flames gout from a half meter away.

The local first responders are out in their opalescent skins, HUDs blinking emergency clearances in high contrast letters. At the corner, one is tending an auto hail 911: a man bleeding from a head wound, and Claie goes over to see if they need assistance.

"Can I help?" he asks.

Medic and injured glance up.

"No, but thanks," the responder says. "Just a minor laceration."

"What happened?"

"GPS wonked out," the bleeding man says ruefully. He's quite chipper despite his injury. "One second I'm scootering full speed down the sidewalk, the next I'm on a tundra, all permafrost, polar bears, and yeti. I probably would've been okay except the phantom-physicals screwed up."

"Ouch." Claie winces sympathetically.

"Tell me about it. Rolled into a snow curtain displaying as phantom and discovered it was a physical brick wall in RL. Bakayarou griefers."

Claie makes more sympathetic noises. He doesn't want to get in the way so takes his leave. But the conversation has made him apprehensive. He doesn't want to walk into any brick walls. Claie pauses to launch an app from his handheld. As it loads, he realizes that he has been a fool. He curses, furious that in the whole seven minutes, 48 seconds, and some decimal of milliseconds it never occurred to him to run this app.

Claie's job requires that he be able to drill down to raw code, reducing scripts, textures, bots, and animations to their basic syntax in order to mold LivIT's landscape: the prims which are his livelihood. Every structure developer and sim architect, anyone who wishes to manipulate the fundament of LivIT has a view source app. But Claie's isn't a run-of-the-mill third-party app. He coded it himself, personalized to accommodate and correct his optical deficiencies. And, like the Blip mod with her status feed, Claie has lifelined it.

Claie exhales. He is not in the habit of unduly beating himself up over his mistakes. The truth of the matter is that the glitch – being denuded of his skin, isolated among strangers, and unable to see – rattled him. Badly. Bad enough to affect his reason and to make him miss an obvious and elementary solution. He makes a mental note to do some brainstorming for an emergency scenarios app.

Up and running, his view source app transforms his surroundings into strata of densely packed text, coursing letters, symbols, and numbers stacked one atop another, onionskin fashion. Each layer represents some aspect of the world – its appearance, textures, sounds, even smells — all the myriad information broadcast through LivIT's network reduced to purest form.

It is much more congested than Claie is accustomed to. He doesn't develop his prims on public thoroughfares, and his office is much quieter.

He brushes aside layers of code until he reaches LivIT's bedrock. Now he knows for sure what is solid RL and what is phantom. But even after he locks onto the script he wants, a mishmash of overlays, animations, and other sensory snippets continue to rush in, defying his efforts to keep everything stacked into orderly piles. It is a bit like trying to stem a cascade of sand with his bare hands. Claie considers the problem, then wades in, sweeping aside only the code he needs to in order to take his next footstep. It's fun, exhilarating even, and he's breathless, a little dizzy too, by the time he gets home.

Claie shuts down his view source app as he unlocks his apartment's door. It was an enjoyable game, but he's glad to end it.

There is a longer interval between the switchover to the apartment's server than usual. He is through the door and in the foyer before his apartment recognizes his login.

Unlike most people's domiciles, his home is a self-contained sim, loaded and running from its own server box. It's another occupational necessity, like his view source app. But he also likes the added security against poorly wrought, malicious, or mischievous scripts.

His home finally acknowledges him. However, where there should be familiar furnishings and visions of domestic coziness, there is only darkness.

Claie isn't troubled. The illumination app just needs to be prompted. He calls for lights.

The darkness remains darkness.

Claie's heart quickens.

"Lights!" he says again. Louder.

"Claie? Is that you?"

A coil of tension releases in Claie's stomach. The voice is deeper than usual, husky instead of dulcet, but he recognizes Shelby's china doll lisp.

"Who else would it be?" His reply comes out sharper than he intended. He moderates his tone as he takes a tentative step, hands outstretched, in what he hopes is a Shelby-ward direction. "What happened to the lights?"

"Don't be mad, okay? I passworded them."

Claie trips over a shin-high object and lurches to a stop. He swears. "What possessed you to do that?" His groping hands identify the obstacle as their velvet ottoman.

"Can you come back later? Please? I'll call you, okay?"

"Oh for the love of –" Claie rubs his bruised shin. "Lights! Override login Shelby, password Yusuke Ono."

"Nooo –"

There is a tempestuous flurry and clatter. The override successful chime peals. "Yusuke Ono" is both Shelby's favorite anime character and default password. The lights come up at their daytime settings: overhead, half illumination; standup lamp, white.

Hands on hips, Claie storms over to the Shelby-shaped lump huddled on the chaise. Shelby is bundled and buried beneath a rose-pink afghan – hand crocheted by Claie's grandmother – and the downed burgundy curtain that normally separates Claie's office from the dining room, complete with unmoored curtain rod hardware.

"What the hell is going on?" he demands.

"G-go away." The reply is a muffled sob.

Claie has a weakness for tears, especially Shelby's. He sighs, gathers his frayed composure, and plops down on the chaise next to the Shelby-lump.

"Kitten, don't cry. I'm not mad. Come out and tell me what's wrong, okay?"

"No. You can't see me. Something h-happened. My skin went poof and I'm n-naked!" The last is a despairing wail.

Claie rolls his eyes, exasperated, and also relieved that it's only this. Shelby is a vain little thing.

"LivIT experienced a major glitch today, kitten," Claie explains. "It took out bots and overlays, all the commuters got knocked off, and everyone lost their skins. That's why your skin went poof. But a restart's restored everything. Have you tried rebaking?"

"Of c-course I have."

Claie recalls that Shelby also uses Badger. "The restart set a lot of apps to their defaults. One of them might be interfering with your rebake. Come out so I can help you restore your settings."

"I don't want you to see me naked."

Claie is about to force the issue with some ruthless tickling (Shelby is quite ticklish), but then he stops. His brow furrows.

Claie often works from home, and he frequently doesn't bother hibernating his view source app if he's only popping to the bathroom or getting a snack from the kitchen. Third-party view source apps don't reveal RL identities beneath privacy locked skins. But Claie's viewer isn't a third-party app. When Claie developed it, he set it to override all overlays at home. It is more convenient that way. But it means that every time he exchanged a quick kiss with Shelby in passing or a moment of chit-chat, Claie was kissing Shelby's RL lips, seeing Shelby's RL face, and feeling the RL shape of Shelby's body.

But Shelby doesn't know that.

Claie swallows against the sudden knot in his throat. He's not sure what he feels worse about, that in four years of living together, waking in each others' arms, sharing meals and jokes and laughter, having fights and making love, Shelby has never wanted Claie to see anything but an AV skin. Or that he has unintentionally violated Shelby's trust.

"Claie?" Shelby's voice is petulant. Beneath the layers of cloth, Shelby interprets Claie's silence as a rebuke.

Maybe he's wrong. Maybe it's something else altogether. "Is it nakedness that bothers you, kitten?" Claie ventures. "I'm sorry if I've been insensitive. I can go skinned all the time if you want."

"Dummy. Why would I want that? Besides, your usual skin's just you in RL with some highlights."

It's actually more than that, but Claie is flattered that Shelby thinks so. Claie can be vain too.

"Kitten –"

"Can't you just go away for a bit? I can ask Hammie to come over to help me rebake, and then you can come back."

"You don't mind Hammie seeing you naked but not me?" That stings a little.

"Well, duh. Why would I care if Hammie sees my RL?"

It stings more than a little. "I think I'm jealous."

The Shelby-lump shifts impatiently. "Are you being dense on purpose? You're special, of course."

"I am?" He's fishing and he knows it, but Claie's feelings are still hurt.

"You bakayarou, why would I care about being beautiful for anyone *but* you? I don't want *you* to see my ugly, stupid RL because you're the only one that matters. I can't bear the idea of you thinking my RL is me. It's not me. It's not!"

Claie wraps his arms around the Shelby-lump and gives it a squeeze. "Silly thing. Of course it's not. Your RL is only another skin, just a hardcoded one."

"I don't like it." The Shelby-lump crosses its arms.

Claie shakes his head, amused, tender, contemplative. Shelby can be unreasonable sometimes, but he's at fault too and needs to confess the truth. But he very much does not want to distress his lover.

"You know I had a conference meeting today, right?" he says. "I was in the green space with Buneh and Devi testing our new prim design when the glitch happened. One second we're evaluating structural integrity, the next they're gone and it's just RL folks in the green space, all of us completely naked."

The Shelby-lump shivers. "Was everyone completely hideous?"

"To tell you the truth, I couldn't see very well 'cause my clear sight app went poof same as the skins. But what I could see did shake me. All the chubbies and the scrawnies, the wrinklies and the shorties. Made me feel guilty, kind of pervy, like I was peeping at something private that I shouldn't.

"There was this woman, a Blip mod, actually, and her RL body was dumpy with age lines all over her face. She came over to talk about the glitch, and I could barely look at her. And there was also an underage there, scared, never even knew LivIT could glitch like that. But as soon as he heard who the woman was, he got excited about talking to a real, live Blip mod and forgot to be afraid. So you see, that kid really showed me up."

"He did?"

"Yep. The kid didn't care that the Blip mod wasn't beautiful and young, only that she was a Blip mod. Didn't even occur to him to flinch. He would've been the same if she were an eight-tentacled cyborg alien or a giant aardvark."

"Well, duh. Aardvarks are cute."

Claie pokes the Shelby-lump, and it squeals and bats at him. "I'm saying outsides don't matter, kitten, AV or RL. Whatever skin you wear, I will love *you*, the inside Shelby."

Shelby emerges from the folds of afghan and curtain, timid and blushing, unable to meet Claie's eyes. In RL, Shelby is a slight man with pale, thinning hair and close-set eyes, red from crying, in a long face with rough features – except for the nose, which is disproportionately delicate, a pixie-button of a nose.

Claie cups Shelby's cheek, tips it so his lover must look at him. "You're beautiful, kitten. How could you think you could be anything but beautiful to me?"

Shelby searches for subterfuge or artifice in Claie's eyes. She is terrified. A hint of either will devastate her, but she must look anyway.

Claie's eyes are suns alight with adoration and devotion, their brilliance proclaiming Shelby lovely and loved. Claie's eyes are the only mirror Shelby needs to feel precious and special, and yes, beautiful, and what she is most afraid of losing. But they burn for her the same as they always have, and her fear melts away. Shelby smiles shyly and lifts her mouth for Claie's kiss.

The kiss is soft, tender at first. But Claie, as he always does, finds Shelby's sweetness – the way she offers herself to him – adorable and charming, and very arousing. The kiss deepens, and Claie tugs away afghan and curtain, pressing Shelby deeper into the chaise.

Shelby's face is flushed, eyes unfocused, but she pushes at Claie's shoulders. "Hold on. Wait."

"Don't want to," Claie growls. "Want to fuck my kitten into the couch." He feels Shelby grow harder at his words, her breath quick and a little ragged.

Shelby laughs, throaty, shaky. "Fix my skin, first. I don't think any of my coupling apps are working either."

Claie nibbles Shelby's neck. "You're beautiful as you are. And it might be fun doing it without the apps. Just you and me, naked."

Shelby grabs Claie's face, pulling him away until they're eye-to-eye. "When you make love to me, I want to be who I am inside on the outside too, the true me, not the one random genetics stuck me with."

Claie shuts his eyes, conjuring forth images of icy showers and utterly unsexy progress reports and tax tables, and prays that whatever is wrong with Shelby's skin can be easily and swiftly remedied.

When Claie can trust himself not to devour Shelby whole, he opens his eyes. "Okay, kitten, let me see your display."

* * *

FORTUNATELY, THE FIX is relatively simple. In her panic, Shelby managed to trigger a shutdown sequence in her smartdev. Because of the glitch, instead of the apps resetting when the smartdev came back, the whole thing remained in standby mode, unresponsive.

They reboot her smartdev and as soon as they log Shelby back in, her skin rebakes – raven hair spilling to a slender waist, porcelain skin and cat-slitted lilac eyes restored, along with Shelby's dulcet voice and silver-gold cheongsam.

Claie wastes no time launching both their coupling apps and begins removing Shelby's cheongsam. He knows the keys to her body – feather touches to make her writhe, kisses to speed her pulse, and fierce caresses to arch her, gasping and eager, beneath him. He is impatient to unlock her, to glory in the feel, the taste of her, everything that she is, his Shelby.

"Claie, will you do something for me?" Shelby's whispered request is bashful, yet also daring.

"Anything."

"Can you have wings? Big feather ones, big enough to hold me with."

The symbolism is not lost on Claie, and he is touched. He thinks of the swan maiden's wings, and his body reshapes itself, reforming with feathery angel wings, just as Shelby requested. Although Claie's wings aren't white. They're a shimmering periwinkle like his (currently discarded) zoot suit.

They sweep open and enfold Shelby.

She purrs and rubs her cheek against periwinkle down. Her eyes are luminous, glowing with delight, declaring without words that this is the safest, best place in all the world, here in the softest of embraces.

Claie is enchanted, and emboldened. "Kitten, will you do something for me too?"

"Mmhmm. What?"

"Cat ears. Kitten ears."

Shelby giggles, and a pair of soft-furred triangles appear on her head, raven-black to match her hair, daintily tipped with pink. She pricks them forward and bats her lilac eyes, coy and inviting.

Claie's response is instant and urgent. He accepts.

MUCH LATER THEY lie entangled, languid and replete. Claie is relaxed, not quite awake but not yet asleep, when he remembers that there is something he must tell Shelby. It summons him back to wakefulness.

"Shelby, are you asleep?"

"Not yet," she mumbles against his shoulder, but her eyes stay shut.

"I need to tell you something. It's important."

She snuggles closer. "I'm listening."

"I think you should know that I've seen you in RL before today, kitten. My view source app, when we're at home, I didn't code it to comply with your skin's privacy lock. I'm so sorry."

Shelby opens cat-slitted eyes and yawns, revealing a strawberry tongue. "That's nice, dear." She rolls over, drawing Claie's wings over herself like a blanket, and falls asleep.

Claie laughs quietly, at himself mostly. He tightens his arms around his lover and nestles her snug against his chest. Then he too falls asleep.

PEARL IN
THE SHELL

NEIL WILLIAMSON

Many of Neil Williamson's award-nominated short stories are collected in The Ephemera *(Elastic Press, 2006 / Infinity Plus Books, 2011). Neil is a member of the notorious school of literary pugilism known as the Glasgow SF Writers Circle, and has the internal bruising to prove it. Neil is also a musician, of sorts.*

THE VICTAZ CREW bombs straight up the back of the bus but Paolo lingers at the top of the stairs, popping his pearls out, casting an ear around the other passengers, on the scope as always for a source of sounds. Over the road rumble and the motor's electric whine, the coughs and sniffs and murmured conversations, he zones in on the tapping of toes and tuneless sing-a-long; looking out for clues to what's cycling through their mixes, what might be hidden away in their shells. You can guess a lot from physical appearance, but a good sourcer uses their ears first and foremost. Paolo's crew haven't come across a shell they couldn't crack given enough time, but it helps to be certain it'll be worth the effort.

Best bet is usually students – wilfully obscure and ever resourceful – or old hipsters who've been around since the days of physical media. Anyone who might conceivably be hiding something a bit different in there. New popular music might have flatlined after ICoSP – the International Copyright Simplification Programme – but more people than the corporations would have you believe still value variety in their music.

Paolo is out of luck with this bunch of West End Wendies though. Exactly the sort that happily gobble down whatever the industry tarts up and slops out in the name of entertainment. Fools like that deserve what they get.

Moseying up to join the others, he passes a woman rattling her fingernails on her armrest with all the natural rhythm of a fibrillating pulse. He jostles her shoulder and is rewarded with a slow-focusing glower that chills right down when she checks him. The inked suit, the shirt with the stiletto-tip collar, the chessboard hair and the pearlescent array of shell-tech devices pierced around his face like a beachcomber's Christmas tree baubles. He grins. She snatches back into her shell and stays there. She's not the only one to notice the crew now. There are glances; distrustful, wary. Good. The crew expects that reaction, *covets* it. It's a proud tradition, rude kids sharing their music with the wider community whether the community likes it or not. Only difference nowadays is they don't know about it until a little present pops up in their mix with the tag: *Mashbombed by Victaz*.

Paolo topples into a seat, eases the pearls back into his ears. Nods approvingly. Swanny's got some beats rolling, ready in case Paolo turns up something of interest. Some mashers go about it full on, nailing a jumble of scraps and slices to a plank of Canto-dub and ending up with the musical equivalent of a horse chewing through a mains cable, but Swanny's subtler than that. His beats are aggressive but he's got a real feel for the dynamics of a good groove that spotlights each of those little snippets of song at the same time as binding them together. That's the secret of good mashing.

When Paolo lenses up a file list of recent finds in the crew's shell-share, Swanny lifts his head and grins.

"What's this?" He says it without moving his lips. Only the others can hear it, in the share. Older people look like bad ventriloquists when they do this, but it comes naturally to the crew. Cell phones were on their way out before they were born. They're the shell generation. Dinks laughs at Paolo when he says things like that. Usually follows it up with some tosh about making the most of every resource in a scarcity economy. *Bollocks*.

Swanny's used to Paolo's little finds but his eyes widen when he runs the first of the files. "Aw, come on, ya perv, that's no real."

"Classic 1970s porno. Lifted it off the lollipop man outside St Agnes's at lunchtime."

Swanny shakes his head. "Dirty old bastard."

"Who's a dirty old bastard?" Dinks drops her prized antique headphones around her neck, paying attention now. Girl's got a sixth sense for fanny. Even monster fanny like this. "Woah! What was it with the seventies man? They never heard of personal grooming?"

They share a round of lulz. Their toons roll around the share, giggling and clutching their sides.

"Sure, but check the music," Paolo says.

They both do. They both nod. "Ya perv," they both say.

This time their lulzing avatars hit Paolo's over the head with cartoon dildos.

"Aye, aye." Dinks is their cracker and, next to fanny and retro tech-chic, the one thing she's got an infallible instinct for is a poorly protected shell. A second or two later, a group of girls appears. Five of them, sixteen or seventeen, school blazers and full make-up, modest shell-tech jewellery: barnacle ear-studs and *chickering* winkle chain bangles. Absorbed in their shell-share, they don't even notice the crew and once Dinks gives Paolo the nod he makes quick work of skimming their files.

Strictly speaking at this time on a Wednesday morning, he and Dinks should be at college. There are exams coming up after all, but Paolo will ace them. Hell, he could write the questions.

Explain the effect that the International Copyright Simplification Programme had on the commercial music industry in the United Kingdom and the United States of America.

What that really boils down to is: *what's the magic number?* At the last count, the magic number was seventeen hundred and seventy eight. That's the exact number of individual and distinct songs recognised by the International Rights Authority. ICoSP came about because DRM didn't work and because the delivery platforms had moved to the automatic micropayment model and because corporate pop music had long been reduced to papping out variation after variation of the same old shit, eventually dispensing with the involvement of writers and performers entirely. So, now there are only so many unique "*combinations of melody, presentation and lyrical sense*". Everything else is designated a copy.

It shouldn't have been a surprise: ignoring the mostly ignored and easily ripped off fringe artists, the history of commercial music was always more about flogging a formula than it ever was about invention and art. ICoSP was merely the acknowledgement of that fact. It only got really silly with the Universal Pact amendment, proposed by the multinationals who, naturally, were terrified. Once the uber-algorithms had worked out which songs were classed as being essentially *the same*, the amendment determined that the rights would be awarded to the earliest variant still under copyright at the time the statute was adopted as law by the signatory territories.

So now whoever holds the rights for "I Will Always Love You" also gets the cash from a thousand other compositions whose words cover the same general subject matter and have a roughly similar arrangement (and the operative words in that sentence are *general* and *roughly*). It came as a shock to the writers of the huge Euro-pop hit, "Build You A Wall", that the bulk of their millions in royalties were suddenly diverted to the geniuses who came up with "Bob The Builder". It came as an even bigger shock to discover that the Sex Pistols owned the rights to much of the history of rock and roll. And with the duration limited to fifty years, irrespective of whether the creator was still alive or not, legal battles over the next inheritor of that particular golden chalice had been rumbling on for the best part of a decade.

There you go. Ignoring the looming monster next door represented by the Chinese industry who refused to touch ICoSP with the proverbial barge pole, that's the history of modern music. Sixty marks, please. If he has enough time at the end of the exam, Paolo might be tempted to add a caustic postscript to the effect that it completely sucks that music students actually spend the bulk of their education learning how not to get fined, sued or imprisoned. Hardly anyone writes new music. Some still try – *potentially*, if you managed to write a genuinely original song you'd have the rights brokers battering down your door – but if you attempt to release a composition that matches 51% or more of the 93 points of reference in an existing copyrighted song, the rights for your new effort are automatically awarded to the existing copyright holder and you have to pay them for the privilege of playing the song you thought you just wrote. You'd still get a performance royalty but, as the man said: *Fuck that*.

There is an exception, however. The preview clause. You're legally allowed to play up to two point seven seconds of any song before your app automatically identifies the rights holder and coughs up. And that's where mash comes in. Danceable patchworks stitched together by crews like Victaz – as in *Frankenstein*, yeah? – from slivers you don't have to pay for. It's a loophole they've been arguing about for years, even though mashes themselves are now also copyrightable. The whole thing is frowned upon of course, but the mash charts are one of the few growth areas in the industry.

The greyest area of the whole thing is that the only completely honest way of creating mash is from what you can preview on the net. There was a time when you could find almost anything online, but after ICoSP the former rights owners of tens of thousands of tracks removed them from sale rather than make someone else a little richer every time they were played.

That's why, if you're serious about the art of mashing, about conjuring some sort of originality from a rehash of existing work, you have to go that extra mile to make your source material different from everyone else's. Which means bending the rules a little to see what the world is hiding from you.

The girls are a surprise. One of them has a decent stash of obscure 50s soul, and another appears to have a fascination for the roaring twenties. Both are untapped areas for the crew so, invisibly, Paolo transfers a selection of files from their share to the crew's. Swanny drops them a mash bomb as a thank you. From the way he's smirking Paolo suspects that 1970s pornography will feature prominently.

In the Victaz's share, Dinks's avatar stomps a big boot and executes a shrill two fingered whistle. "Our stop, boyos."

Paolo's proud of the plan they're about to put into action. The problem with random public skimming is that the hit rate is low for the effort required, so they've been looking around for a higher yield potential scenario than the buses and the malls.

Then someone in the music business had conveniently died.

The crematorium is tucked away up on a hill on the city's eastern fringe, just green enough and distant enough from the traffic and general noise to give the illusion of peace. Trudging up the access road, all three find the silence unnerving, so Swanny pumps one of his latest mashes nice and loud and they kick into a swagger as they reach the rows of cars parked along the manicured verge.

Paolo pops open Heather Gilchrist's obituary for some last minute revision. The crew are posing as fans come to pay their respects so, should anyone ask, they have to know at least the names of the old band members, her grown up children, and a few of the songs that had made her famous.

The obit is more a sob story than a celebration. It spends too much time sentimentalising about how the rights crash ruined Heather's life; making the person secondary to the legal fight, the subsequent poverty and the final retreat into reclusiveness when the cancer was diagnosed. The bit that caught Paolo's interest though is tucked away at the bottom. A sentence of speculation about how it's believed that she kept writing, kept trying to make new music, just never released it to the public.

And that's bollocks. No one keeps their music to themselves. *Someone* among her nearest and dearest must have copies.

They join the queue of mourners filing towards the door of the crematorium. Dinks is busy with something. Her avatar has changed to her gal-at-work one: swinging pick axe, hard hat and butt cleavage complementing the boots. In the corner of the share is a scrolling shell connection list. By the time they near the door she's cracked over half of them. Paolo wastes no time.

It's amazing what goes on in people's shells. While the mourners shuffle forward, respectful and solemn faced, exchanging murmurs of condolence and regret, they're watching news feeds, playing games, trolling creationist blogs for lulz. One fella is watching a clip of the deceased naked and grinning shyly, her fingers circling an erection, presumably the viewer's own. Paolo wonders if this is a remembrance of a sweet, private moment or simply a spectacular display of lack of respect.

Paolo skims over all this activity without much real interest. What he wants to know is whether she shared those new songs with anyone here. He starts with the porn star: finds his music stash and starts shuffling through it. It's no bad selection, with a fair number of artists Paolo doesn't recognise. He instructs his shell to transfer the whole lot, and moves on to their next kind donor with relish.

Then, as he's about to delve into the shell of an older fella – neatly trimmed white beard and one of those old fringed suede country and western jackets that were all the rage a couple of years back – three things happen almost simultaneously. The queue shuffles forward, Dinks mutters, "*aw, baws!*" and a disconnection icon starts flashing above porno boy's transfer.

Paolo stares accusingly at the back of his neck but there's no sign that he's even aware of the crew's intrusion as he ducks under the lintel and nods seriously to someone inside.

"Bastard must have disconnected himself," Swanny says.

"Bit late for a show of respect," Paolo replies.

He's fervently hoping that this won't be a trend when the queue shuffles forward again and then Victaz are the ones under the lintel and their shell-share vanishes. Their faces are still stretched in cartoonish renderings of shock when the usher inside the door asks them: "Family, friends or fans?" The usher is a soft presence but his eyes are granite. They flick to the side and they all see the neatly printed sign on the wall. They all read the words.

"Fans are in the back three rows," the usher says. Meekly, they follow his indicating arm.

"This is no real. Bastards cannae dae that." Swanny thinks he's whispering, but that's not a skill any of them has ever had much practice at. Heads turn.

"Yes they can." Dinks is glowering. "They do it all the time during exams, don't they?" Swanny glowers back. Even at school he never had much reason to enter an exam hall.

As one the crew glare again at the usher, at the sign next to him.

Polite notice.

Out of respect for the deceased, the bereaved have requested that shell connectivity is suppressed in the chapel of rest.

Thank you.

"What are we going to do?" Swanny's not handling this well.

Paolo puts his hand on his arm, but the wee fella shakes it off. "We're going to see this through," he says. "Play our part here as we planned and then blag our way into the after party."

"Reception lunch," Dinks chips in.

"*Reception lunch*, whatever." Paolo takes an angry breath. "Plenty of time to do it then." But from the looks they're getting, the whispers exchanged, he's not at all sure they'll get that opportunity. "Let's just keep it together, eh? See what happens."

The other two nod, and they all sit down.

The assembly of mourners takes place to the accompaniment of sobs, sniffs and a piped acoustic guitar. It sounds familiar, maybe a diluted version of one of Heather's old hits. Then the big fella in the fringed coat steps around the coffin to get to the podium and makes a speech. Seems he was her friend and manager for thirty-five years, and now he's assumed the mantle of being angry and bitter on her behalf. He batters on about her talent, how she could've, would've, should've been a global star if she hadn't been screwed sidewise by the system.

"And no one cared." He grips the edges of the lectern, cheeks and neck pink beneath his white beard, and casts an accusation around the room.

"Except for us." His voice loses its bellow, as if he's been punctured in the heart. "Her family, her friends, her fans. When she went underground and had to resort to shell hacks to retain control over her own songs, we kept faith. So we broke a few laws, but I know there's not one soul here who would have not done at least that for her."

While the assembly murmurs assent, Paolo sighs with frustration at the thought of years' worth of original music sitting in these people's shells. He's not used to what he wants being beyond his reach.

The manager hasn't finished. "But she never stopped writing right up until the end. And, my friends, the real scunner of this *fucking cancer* that first took away her voice, then her breath, was that she *did it*. She wrote a song that beat ICoSP, and we'd almost convinced her to go public with it." He slumps, diminished. "But then it didn't matter any more. It *doesn't* matter any more. Even if Heather had given her permission there'd be no point in releasing the song now she's not around to benefit from it. However, as final tribute to a musical genius and a true friend, my friends, I think we ought to do her the honour today of listening to Heather Gilchrist's final song."

The big fella steps down and his place at the podium is taken by a skinny girl with a blotchy face. She stares glassily at the audience, turns her gaze to the panelled ceiling. Then, blinking away fresh tears, she starts to sing.

The girl's voice is soft and throaty, but the hushed space lends it body, a shiver of spiritual echoes. Not that you would recognise this as a song. Everything about it is off. The melody skitters around, continually promising to resolve into a tune but then sliding off again. The rhythm has a folky fluidity but that too strains expectations by dropping or adding beats at random intervals. Neither of these tricks is especially new; classical and jazz composers have been doing stuff like this since forever. It's a little like mash, but more organic. The girl's voice grows in confidence until it fills the room and, amid the continuing, soft sounds of grief, other voices pick up the melody and begin humming along.

But the music isn't what makes the song really special.

"What's she singing?" Swanny manages an actual whisper this time. "Is it Gaelic?"

Paolo shakes his head. The lyrics do sound familiar, but he can't actually distinguish them as words. Which is weird because he *knows* the song is a love song. He knows it, but he doesn't know *how* he knows.

"That's not Gaelic." Dinks's whisper is even more awed than Swanny's. "It's –"

"Just listen," Paolo says.

AFTERWARDS, THEY EMERGE into sunshine. Stand off to one side as the rest of the funeral's attendees filter past: talking, smiling, their emotional tension discharged. The crew's shells reconnect almost instantly.

"We ready to roll again, Dinks?" In the share, Swanny's toon twangs his braces and hops impatiently from one brothel creeper to the other. Dinks's gal-at-work toon says she's busy on something. She's slid her cans up too, which is her signal for *really*, really, *do not fucking disturb me.* Paolo looks for the list of cracked shells reappearing. The targets are already climbing into cars and driving away.

"Dinks?"

"Forget them." Their girl slips her headphones down.

In the share, Swanny's toon turns bronto and tries to stomp her.

"That wasn't a real language, was it?" Paolo says.

Dinks shakes her head. She's pretty when she twists her smile like that, and she only does it when she's about to say something smart and is trying to find a way of saying it that the other two will understand. "According to the algorithms it's not a *recognised* language. But I think it is a real one."

"How did you manage to run the algorithms?" Bronto-Swanny pulls a face then shrinks back to normal. "Everyone was disconnected in there, man."

Dinks slides a scuffed digital recorder from the pocket

of her blazer. A fan-shaped shell-tech dongle is black-taped into a socket on the top. She's recorded the song inside, then uploaded it and run the algorithms while they've been talking. She always did like her retro gear.

Paolo grins. "You got it all?

She grins back.

"And the language?"

She grins even wider. "It's actually pretty neat. She invented one of her own. A collection of phonemes that don't in themselves form actual words, but still manage to convey the sense of the song." She looks from Swanny to him and back again. "C'mon, you understood it was a love song, right? You just didn't need lyrics to get it. We're so conditioned to the conventions of pop music that for the sentiments of most songs we no longer actually need the words, just their shapes. Corporate music hasn't cared about original lyrics for decades. Gilchrist went a step further and distilled it down to a musical language."

While she's been talking Paolo's done a bit of research and now pops up a Wikipedia citation on *Sigur Rós;* another on *The Cocteau Twins*. "It was a beautiful thing, but it's hardly a unique idea."

Swanny says. "Still passes the test. It could make someone a lot of money."

Dinks completes the collective chain of thought. "Whoever released it first would sure as hell cash in. Gilchrist's family are all about respecting her memory for now, but sooner or later they'll realise what they're sitting on."

"So, anyone with a copy of that music would have to work fast to stake their claim."

In the sunshine, outside the now empty crematorium,

they all nod. In their shell-share, their toons do too.

ON THE BUS back, there are a few other passengers that under normal circumstances might be worth cracking for a look-see, but the crew have other things on their minds.

"Fuck it." The crew look up, surprised that Paolo says this out loud. "Gilchrist's music is cool, but what is it really? A weird shit tune that drones on forever. Might have been her idea of art but it sure as hell isn't ours. Do we really want Victaz associated with something like that?"

Swanny grins like the bear who ate the baby. An instant later a track starts playing in their share. It's classic Victaz mash: Swanny's beats collaged with scraps of nineties R'n'B, sixties Northern Soul, the voice of Bob Wills, the king of Western Swing, calling out *howdy-ho!* And interspersed between these, threaded through them, snatches of Heather Gilchrist's last song. The meaning-laden but wordless vocal lilt is the only thing in the mash that repeats and, in doing so, it becomes something pretty old-fashioned: a hook. For mash this is revolutionary.

Swanny looks at the others in turn. "Yeah?"

Paolo and Dinks both say: "Yeah."

He pushes it global.

By the time they get off the bus the track is getting download traffic and airplay in Edinburgh, Moscow, Rio. By the time they're home at Paolo's flat, it's made it onto nightclub playlists in Adelaide and Bangkok. Swanny prepares half a dozen variations, each of them mining a new facet of Gilchrist's song for its hook and ready to roll out to up the stakes when the first of the copycats appears.

The mass-shares go mental for it. This is Victaz's fifteen minutes global. Paolo charts their rocketing notoriety as the crew hops aboard the tube for that evening's sourcing. Because a mash crew's like a school of sharks. They have to keep predating or they grow old and cold. Always cracking, always sourcing, always looking for the next new thing.

There will be other songwriters' funerals – the city once had a lot of musicians, and they're all getting to that age – but until then who knows what else is waiting to be unearthed, cleaned up and cut into something glittering and abrasive and new.

The world tires of innovations faster than toys at Christmas. Anyone who thinks differently doesn't know the music industry.

THE TIME GUN

NICK HARKAWAY

Nick Harkaway was born in Cornwall in 1972, shortly after the Innsmouth refugees were driven out of Truro. At five, he narrowly avoided being scooped up by the government to participate in the now-notorious Project Shoggoth by concealing himself in a combine harvester, and ultimately went to school in London, where the worst that could happen to him was getting teased for his accent. He attained a middling degree at a nearby university in the study of Amoral Sciences before making the poorest decision of his life and working in the film industry. Rescued by a dedicated human rights worker, he is now the father of a disturbingly intelligent infant with webbed feet and the driver of an obsolete hybrid automobile. He lives in the ancient Borough of Camden with his wife and daughter, and has applied for a licence to flood his back garden with sea water and keep squid.

WHEN MORRIS WAS shot with the Time Gun, it took him a moment to realise what had happened. The old man popped up from behind a bank of machines which were projecting wavy green lines into mid air and shouted "No, no, no!" and shot him, and Morris felt himself blasted backwards and thought "bugger, I'm dead." And then he didn't die, which was a plus.

Instead he flailed back and through a solid object and then through the wall and back and back and he realised that whatever he was falling through it wasn't physical space, and he thought about what he had been supposed to steal. There had been no mention of this sort of thing at all, just some basic housebreaking and a moderate payoff.

"Go to Lab 5," Grimmel had said, "and bring us everything you can. All the results, all the theories, every scrap. Paper, too, if there is any. And then set it all on fire." Grimmel had been very clear the building would be empty, so Morris had agreed to this plan. He was a burglar and an insurance arsonist, not a thug.

So now here was Morris flying back through the air and trying to retro-engineer some highfalutin' gizmo he'd never heard of and he thought it must be an anti-gravity gun because he was flying, and then he realised he was flying sideways and that meant it was a neutral buoyancy gun and surely no one would bother with one of those. And then he realised that it was some sort of phase thingummajig because he wasn't physical any more, so maybe it was a brane-gun or an M-theory gun, because he'd seen about those on TV, and then he looked at his watch and it had stopped and when he tapped it the little hand went from three to twelve to nine and he realised that he was flying backwards through time.

A movie star had once told him this was possible, a real movie star, back when he had worked at Pinewood as a carpenter. This guy had said "time travel is real, boy! I've seen it! The Prime Minister showed me, because we were buddies before he was shot, they got it out of an alien spaceship in the twenties, long before bloody Roswell, that's just bollocks, that is, they never had one of those in America." Morris had always assumed it was a shitload of cocaine talking, but here he was now flying head first through physical objects and his watch was going in reverse and – now that he'd flown through the wall and into the street – the rain was going up into the clouds, and that made for a compelling case. He had to acknowledge that the movie star's testimony still wasn't all that likely to be true. He did not believe the British Government had obtained temporal displacement technology from an alien spacecraft and then done nothing with it between the arrival of women's suffrage and the collapse of the Euro. Although perhaps that sort of time-based calculation no longer made sense to the owners of such technology. It would certainly explain a lot about the way laws got made if parliament was functioning at right angles to time. He wasn't into that sort of crazy talk as a rule, but the idea seemed to fit the facts.

Morris Ruddle, petty larcenist, watched the world spin back along its orbit all around him. It seemed that his speed – his speed through time – was not constant. Sometimes the people around him looked like people and sometimes they looked a bit carroty, their movements all taking place at once so that they were interwoven strands or worms with a person face at the back (the front, from their perspective).

He wondered if he was getting physically younger. The old man had been yelling some pretty intense language back there, all replete with rage and so on, so Morris felt that whatever he had chosen to do would be fairly unpleasant, but maybe there was a chance that the device he had used was just the first thing to hand and Morris would bounce off, say, 1989 and fall into the world again. He could get really rich, that would be cool, and sleep with sexy people. Much of Morris's life until now had revolved around the attempt to achieve coitus with people he considered sexy, especially since Maria had left him, but the results were somewhat disappointing. Maybe he'd give his younger self a job, will himself his own fortune, and then jump off a cliff, and the whole shenanigan would never happen – he'd just be Morris Ruddle, rich young dude. That would be cool.

He had noticed that he was not zinging off the Earth into space, which he should have done almost immediately. He assumed that he was either still affected by gravity or by some other attractive force which linked his journey back through time to his own physical life until the moment in the lab. He was therefore unsurprised when he fell into his own house fifteen years ago and saw himself as a poor young dude getting smacked around the head. He reached out and tried to stop it, but he still wasn't physical, so he floated and fumed at the injustice and the basic, grotty meanness of the beating. It didn't matter that it was all in reverse, that the hand flew back off his face and arms, that the split lip was brushed away. He knew every moment of it, of every encounter like this. Forwards or backwards made no odds.

"When I'm king," boy Morris said out loud, and got smacked again. "I'll have your head cut off," retrotemporal Morris finished for him, and then shouted it. And then the scene was gone, and he was somewhere else. A supermarket. The kid at the checkout counted items into the bag and said something unintelligible and reversed, and the customer wandered into the aisles to shelve the goods.

Morris wondered if he might just fall back as far as his own birth. Maybe he'd be reborn as himself but with all his memories and he could go through school again but with all the knowledge he had now. He'd still fail his exams, probably, but he'd be very cool and he'd know the future, so that wouldn't really matter. He'd either shop his parents to the law or cut some sort of deal with them, blackmail them. Deal drugs and get money to hire men to sort them out. There were options, once you knew you didn't have to take that sort of thing.

But why birth? That was sort of arbitrary, when he considered it. Conception was probably more like it. Maybe when he reached the moment of his conception (yuck!) he'd just fade away, sort of spool himself up and never have existed at all. He considered whether this would count as dying and decided it was somehow worse.

Shit.

He struggled for a while, trying to figure out what he could hold onto which would let him claw his way forwards. He pictured himself climbing up a deep well of time back to the lab. He made pitons in his mind, hammered them into the walls and struggled against the current. It didn't help.

He passed the moment in question and nothing happened. That was slightly anticlimactic, and also a bit good because it meant he hadn't vanished into his own past self or disintegrated, but it was also a bit alarming because now there was really nothing to stop him falling and falling. Would he just run out of steam and get bumped out of time in the Middle Ages? The Cretaceous? Into space before there was a planet? The Middle Ages would be okay, he was up to date on his vaccinations and he knew cool stuff about engineering which would seem a little bit magical. A lot magical. He could set himself up as Merlin and live a pretty good life. Maybe he could start a school, find some real genius peasants and one of them could work out how to unstrand him. Maybe being sent back through time like this would give him miraculous powers. He'd be a god back here, a superman, he could joust and throw fire with his hands and rule the world and change everything so that Morris Ruddle would be the inheritor of the entire planet.

He fell through the time of Henry VIII, William the Conqueror, Julius Caesar. He fell on and on back through people who didn't have names because they didn't have language. He fell through dinosaurs and fish and amoebae and fire and then sat in space for a really, really, really, really, really, really long time. Or whatever it was when he was flying backwards through time. It couldn't be time, really, could it, because that was going the other way? Subjective time, for sure. He wondered if he was aging. Would he get hungry or thirsty? Could he starve while he was falling like this? His watch was broken again, which was probably not surprising. It was negative several billion years old, and it hadn't been an expensive watch to begin with.

He sat there and waited. He got very bored indeed. He wasn't sure, but he thought he was probably bored for longer than he'd been alive, longer than the entire human race had been alive, longer than every individual member of the human race put together, every animal, ever, had been alive, in total.

But maybe that was just how it felt because he had literally no points of reference at all.

And then he saw the beginning, and wondered if he was going to die now, hitting the beginning of time. He was aware that he might be going a bit mad, because he was so bored, and he was also aware that for the first time ever he wondered whether it would be so bad to stop existing, because he didn't know what else to do.

He saw the beginning coming at him: the biggest frying pan ever, a slap for being insolent, a car crash. He flinched, and fell and fell and fell. And fell.

He hit it.

The beginning of time was bouncy, like a giant, frictionless bouncy castle or a bouncy bed like the one in the hotel he had been to with Maria before she told him he wasn't the man for her. He hit the strange, springy surface again and again and bounced again and again. And again and again and again. Now he was bored and jostled by hitting the beginning of time and the universe and matter and all that, and a bit nauseous. Very nauseous.

Great. You could get motion sick from hitting the beginning of time. It was a little bit typical: Morris had never really gotten motion sick except a few times when he was trying to kiss Maria in a taxi, and once on a boat in Spain, also kissing. That seemed to be the only time his brain got confused about motorised travel. Which sucked.

But now, now, here he was, shot with a Time Gun, hitting the beginning of time and bouncing off it and of course he was going to feel like throwing up. He wondered what would happen if he did. Would he bounce around in atemporal vomit for ever? Would an angel come and give him a stern talking-to for messing up the Creation? Where was God, exactly, in all this? Was God behind the squishy meniscus of time? Was that why he couldn't get through it? Bounce, lurch, bounce, lurch, is God in there? Hello? Bounce, lurch. Bounce. Lurch. Oh, oh, oh, no.

He threw up.

Absolutely nothing happened at all.

And then it did.

It was like dancing rock and roll at your fourteenth birthday party when you spin around and then you accidentally let go and your sister flies across the room and lands on the goldfish bowl and the goldfish lands on the back of the TV and the TV blows up and the goldfish dies and you get hit really hard with a shoe for messing up the house and costing us a fortune but you sort of feel you deserved it because wow but really you didn't mean to and you never really knew what right and wrong was after that because it all seemed so totally capricious and a bit strange.

Which... is the first thing he sees when he slows down. He sees that whole unhappy business and for a moment he knows, absolutely knows in his heart of hearts that he's going to bounce off the end of time, the opposite end, and then go back, and then forward, until he is misshapen and exhausted and then the final act of the Time Gun is going to be to put his soul inside that goldfish and he's going to explode himself accidentally and wouldn't that make it an Irony Gun?

And then he thinks, no, thank God, that's just crazy talk. And flies forward through time.

Morris Ruddle flies forward through time. It's better in this direction because everything makes sense and words aren't backwards. It's also worse because he can see every crappy choice he ever made and a whole bunch of the ones other people made and he's sort of getting an education here, getting a bit wise. It occurs to him that maybe with this newfound wisdom he will solve some of the world's problems. He wanders around a bit checking out how governments work and reckons they don't. They're just a room full of confused people making it up as they go along, which is a bit scary. He watches sub-prime loans get out of control and frankly isn't impressed. It's as if no one's paying attention at all except him. He sees wars and executions and a great number of other people having sex and he passes through the moment when he gets hired to steal the Time Gun and he thinks for a moment that he might be slowing down.

He is slowing down.

He is, he's definitely not going to make it to the far end of time at this rate. He's going to stall out any moment now. He feels strange and papery and he looks at his hands. They are very, very, very, very, very old.

The universe goes: "pop".

And he stands in the lab again, staring at his ancient, wrinkled old hands and thinking that it is very unlikely that he will ever have any sort of sex again. And then Morris Ruddle comes in, young Morris, and like an incredible arsehole he goes right for the place where he got shot with the Time Gun and Morris realises that unless he can stop this from happening young Morris will get shot and end up as old Morris, but if he can prevent the whole thing something else can happen, even if it's just a little different it could be so much better, and his heart is fluttering and maybe giving up and he says "no, no, no," and lunges forward with the nearest thing to his hand.

Which is the Time Gun, and he realises this just as he pulls the trigger and thinks "oh, sod it" because now he's created a recursion or maybe there always was one and he's going to go around and around in this loop for ever, so he turns the gun around and shoots himself, too, goes zinging back along the same loop to intercept young Morris somehow, tell him to do things differently, and around and around and around they go, more and more Morrises making the loop tighter and tighter and tighter and getting shot more and more often with the Time Gun and he starts to wonder if there can possibly be enough energy in the greater universe to sustain this many iterations. And then he finds he is face to face with the many many iterations, perfectly balanced all along the endless line of himself, and out of sheer amazement he does the last thing in the world he ought to do.

He pulls the trigger on the Time Gun.

All of him.

And thinks: "this can't be good."

* * *

PROFESSOR MORRIS RUDDLE stares down at the dead burglar and wishes he had thought to pick up almost any other device from his workbench. The heavy battery pack would have made a quite excellent bludgeon, for example.

He consoles himself, staring down, with the thought that it must have been very quick. He calls the chief of campus law enforcement, Detective Morris Ruddle, who in turns calls Morris Ruddle the coroner to come and pronounce the boy dead. None of them sees anything unusual about this. Professor Morris Ruddle wonders if he will be put on trial. He knows a good lawyer – Morris Ruddle – and he has faith that a jury of twelve Morris Ruddles will see it his way.

He sits, and waits.

OUTSIDE, IN THE universe, Morris Ruddle expands to fill the available space.

WHEN THOMAS JEFFERSON DINED ALONE

KRISTINE KATHRYN RUSCH

Kristine Kathryn Rusch has won two Hugos, a few Asimov's Readers awards, an AnLab award, and a couple of Ellery Queen Mystery Magazine Readers awards – and that's just in recent years. Her novels have hit the USA Today bestseller list, the Wall Street Journal and Publisher's Weekly lists, and the extended list of the New York Times. She's also had bestsellers in Great Britain and France. All her fantasy novels, including the seven volumes of the popular Fey series (with more planned) have recently been reissued. She's currently writing two science fiction series set in the Retrieval Artist universe and the Diving universe respectively, two mystery series as Kris Nelscott, two goofy fantasy romance series as Kristine Grayson, and one strange futuristic romance series as Kris DeLake. She is also editing the new anthology series, Fiction River. No wonder she never leaves her house...

1.

"I SIT HERE *in this old house and work on foreign affairs, read reports, and work on speeches – all the while listening to the ghosts walk up and down the hallway and even right in here in the study. The floors pop and the drapes move back and forth – I can just imagine old Andy [Jackson] and Teddy [Roosevelt] having an argument over Franklin [Roosevelt]. Or James Buchanan and Franklin Pierce deciding which was the more useless to the country. And when Millard Fillmore and Chester Arthur join in for place and show, the din is almost unbearable. But I still get some work done."*

President Harry S. Truman
in a letter to his wife Bess
June 12, 1945

"MARY TODD LINCOLN is holding séances in the White House." Ambra Theeson stood just inside the office door, clutching a small research tablet so hard that her right hand was shaking. "And I think it's our fault."

Professor Kimber Lawson looked up from her desk. She pulled off her glasses – an affectation because no one needed glasses any longer, but an affectation she loved. She set them on the three-hundred-year-old partners desk her former husband had bought her on their honeymoon in Maine.

Ambra sounded close to tears, but there was no trace of them on her moon-shaped face. Ambra had always been a bit of a drama queen, even on her very first day of her very first 100-level class, more than eight years ago.

Kimber wished her book-lined office was bigger. Or that she had brought some of the oldest tomes to her apartment, rather than leave them here as an impressive (if out-of-date) tribute to her profession. Because, right now, even with the door open, Ambra was too close.

"Mary Todd Lincoln," Kimber said in the most patient tone she could muster, "was well-known for her spiritualist tendencies."

"But there'd been no evidence of séances," Ambra said.

Kimber wondered if there was evidence of them now. Ambra had passed the personality tests – necessary requirements for someone who wanted to tackle Living History as a discipline. But those tests examined her ability to tolerate delayed gratification. If Ambra hadn't been able to sustain research over several years with no result whatsoever, she wouldn't be in this program.

Kimber now believed the tests were inadequate. Ambra was a case in point. She was disciplined, all right, but she was also prone to making wild conclusions based on next to no evidence, something that the department hadn't thought of testing for, at least not three years ago when Ambra applied full time.

After all, Living History was still a new discipline – less than twenty years old, barely long enough for revisionists to appear. (And, in Kimber's opinion, those who had didn't really count.) Everyone was still trying to figure out what was needed, who the best scholars were, and what scholarship actually meant in the modern era.

"Perhaps people knew about the séances, but never made a note about them," Kimber said. "I mean, why else would we believe that Mary Todd Lincoln had spiritualist tendencies?"

Kimber truly couldn't remember, which only made her more annoyed at Ambra. The chair of the Living History department shouldn't be seen as ignorant about the Lincolns. Lincoln remained, two centuries after his death, the most studied president in American history.

"Because she kept seeing Willie's ghost in her bedroom after he died," Ambra said in that tone people use when they think someone else should know something. "She never tried to summon him."

Kimber assumed that Willie was the dead son, but she couldn't remember when or how he died. And wasn't there another named Tad?

"Do we know for certain that she never tried to contact him?" Kimber asked.

"Yes, we know that for certain," Ambra said with a little too much force. She still clutched the tablet, but now she was watching Kimber like Kimber had grown two heads. "We know more about Willie's death and its impact on both Lincolns than we know about almost anything else. I mean, they were in the White House at the time, and the number of servants and assistants and –"

"I mean," Kimber said, "do we know for certain that Mary Todd Lincoln held no séances?"

"*Yes*," Ambra said. "We do."

"Because," Kimber said over her, "we learn that all sorts of things we thought were true weren't when we travel back and observe. And vice versa, of course."

Ambra actually rolled her eyes, which Kimber thought horribly unfair. She'd wanted to roll her eyes at Ambra for nearly eight years now and, so far, she had restrained herself from doing so.

"We've been visiting the Lincolns for more than two decades and no one, *no one*, has seen a séance in the White House. And it makes sense." Ambra was now waving the tablet at Kimber as if the tablet held the truth. "I mean, think about it. If the Lincolns had held séances in the White House during the Civil War, the muckraking press would have been all over them. It would have reflected badly on them and –"

"I understand," Kimber said as calmly as she could. So she had shown her ignorance. At least she'd shown it to Ambra, whom everyone else found as annoying as she did. "But my earlier comment still remains. Sometimes presidents do manage to keep secrets, even from the press."

"Not something like this," Ambra said. "There would've been too many people involved."

Kimber closed her eyes, because otherwise she would look up to the heavens and shake her head. The day had already been a long one – she'd had to organize everything from next year's schedule to the waiting list for next month's historical visits – and she really didn't want to spend time with her most difficult student.

Nor did she want to explain something to Ambra that Ambra should have already known: Presidents kept major secrets all the time, secrets that were closely held by dozens of others, from staff to compatriots to members of the opposition party. A lot of those secrets got lost to history in the days before time travel. Now, those secrets were being recovered and revealed.

Once upon a time, Kimber used to think the revelations were the most exciting part of her work. Now she was so tired, she doubted she would ever use the word 'exciting' again.

Kimber made herself open her eyes and pretend interest. "How did you find out about the séances?"

"It showed up in the Wikipedia listings," Ambra said.

Kimber barely managed to keep from laughing in surprise. "And what were you doing on Wikipedia?"

That old creaky thing had existed as long as Kimber could remember, and no serious scholar used it. It was for school children and the occasional pedant who was giving a speech.

The site would probably vanish sometime soon. It was already losing its importance. People preferred to watch their history live, in snippets, and if they were going to make some kind of presentation, they now clipped the actual scholarly visitation and presented the quote or the moment on screen so that everyone could see both its veracity and its historical beauty.

And Kimber did mean beauty. The elegance of the Living History work kept her in this chair. She loved everything from accurate scholarship to the videos of actual historical events. Young scholars could watch major moments through protected observation portals (*Windows Into The Past*, the manufacturers called them), but the true scholars, the ones who wanted to dedicate their lives to discovering what actually happened during an event or even a war, would show up and observe in real time, unnoticed by the subjects themselves.

"I was checking the listings," Ambra said. "I volunteered to monitor some of the Wikipedia Living

History links last year, remember? You're the one who assigned it to me."

Kimber nodded, even though she had forgotten. She had given Ambra the assignment to keep her busy, to make her think she was actually doing real work when, in fact, she wasn't.

Kimber kept hoping that Ambra would drop out of the program but, so far, no such luck.

"I followed the link," Ambra was saying, "and here it is, plain as day. Look."

She set the tablet on Kimber's desk, narrowly missing her glasses, and tapped the screen. A tiny little recording of a group of people in nineteenth century garb sat around a large table in near-darkness. Someone was chanting faintly, and in the background, a spectral figure arose.

"See?" Ambra said, poking her finger on the tablet, making the images jump. "That's Raymond Hall."

At first, Kimber thought she meant some nickname for a Washington D.C. building that she wasn't familiar with. Then she realized that Ambra meant Raymond Hall was a person.

"You know him?" Kimber asked.

"We went to high school together," Ambra said.

"And he's enrolled here?" Kimber asked.

"Jeez, *no*," Ambra said. "He's not smart enough to get in here."

Sometimes Kimber was astonished that Ambra had possessed the intelligence to get in here. "Then I'm not sure what you're talking about."

"That spectral image, that's Raymond Hall."

"I got that," Kimber said, "but how can that be our fault?"

"I didn't mean *our* as in the university's. I meant *our* as in the Living History Project's. As in at all the universities. Now Mary Todd Lincoln is holding séances."

She said that last as if Mary Todd Lincoln were still alive. That was another danger of the Living History Project. The lesser scholars often forgot their subject had already lived his life, and had moved on to whatever it was humans moved on to.

"Has it crossed your mind that this image might be faked?" Kimber asked.

Ambra snatched the tablet off Kimber's desk as if Kimber were going to damage it. She wasn't, of course. To do damage, she had to care, and at this moment all she cared about was getting Ambra out of her office.

"I *checked*," Ambra said. "It's real."

"How could you check?" Kimber asked. "It takes a lot of technical skill to verify Living History recordings."

"Okay, I ran it through our immediate checker, the one we use for monographs and presentations," Ambra said. "And it cleared those."

The immediate checker was designed for professors who needed to check major presentations from students on a variety of subjects the professors might not know much about. The immediate checker caught flat-out fraud and historical reenactments, but couldn't tell if a particular piece of actual scholarship was real or not.

Still, Kimber wasn't going to argue at the moment. No one cared about Wikipedia, least of all her.

"Pull the piece down from Wikipedia as pending review," Kimber said, "and then give it to one of our techs. I'm sure he'll figure out that this is some kind of prank."

Ambra hugged the tablet to her chest. "How can you be so sure?"

Kimber smiled at her, hoping the smile wasn't too condescending. "We've long ago established that the processes we use to observe the past have no impact on that history whatsoever. We can't touch anything, we can't move anything, we can't interact with the environment in any way."

"You actually believe that?" Ambra asked.

"I do," Kimber said.

"Then explain Raymond Hall."

This time, Kimber did roll her eyes. "I already did," she said.

Ambra scowled at her and left the office, slamming the door behind her. Kimber stared at the blond wood for a moment. Maybe this was enough to expel Ambra from the department.

Kimber certainly hoped so. It was students like Ambra who took all the fun out of Living History.

Okay. That wasn't true. The fun had left Living History the moment the programs got institutionalized.

Kimber rubbed a hand over her face, then picked up her glasses. Maybe it was just time to retire. She hated the students, she hated the administration, and she hated teaching.

The only reason she stayed was her unlimited opportunities to head to the past, and actually see the people she had admired, living their lives as if they really were unobserved.

Which, of course, they were not.

* * *

2.

"GRACE COOLIDGE, WIFE of President Calvin Coolidge (1923-29), was the first person to say she had actually seen Lincoln's ghost. According to her, the lanky former president was standing looking out a window of the Oval Office, across the Potomac to the former Civil War battlefields beyond."

"Ghosts in the White House"
History.com

"HAVE YOU SEEN this?" Professor Donald Hemmet said as he thrust a print-out at Kimber in the faculty dining room of Union North the next morning.

Hemmet was a large man with an equally large brain. Kimber usually liked to talk to him, but he often saw problems where there were none – or, at least, problems where there were none that she cared about.

She smiled in what she hoped was a non-committal manner, and took the print-out, placing it under her orange tray. The dining room hadn't been redesigned since the teens, and smelled like it. The entire area reeked of decades-old hamburgers. But it was the only place on campus that still served eggs fried in butter, the way that her grandmother used to make them.

When the stresses of the job got in her way, Kimber skipped the oatmeal covered in fresh fruit and went straight for the fat and grease. And right now, the stresses had increased. The Living History technology was changing *again*, and she had to go to California to investigate the new equipment. As if she knew how it all worked. She only knew that it *did* work. She would, of course, bring techs with her, but techs always wanted to upgrade everything, even if the upgrades meant that the equipment no longer did the job it was meant for.

She sat at one of the wooden tables near the window overlooking the quad. When she'd taken over as head of the department, she had never expected the work to take most of her research and planning time. She thought it a small addition to her salary, with a few hours spent here and there advising her colleagues on tiny matters that no one really cared about.

How wrong could a woman be?

She dug into her eggs – heavenly, with butter dripping off them – and studied the print-out that Hemmet gave her. He was watching her from another table. He knew better than to approach her during a meal. She had begun to think of eating as her only free time, and she guarded it jealously.

The print-out relayed stories told by several Living History graduate students. While standing in the Yellow Oval Room at the White House, Franklin Delano Roosevelt's valet, Cesear Carrera, heard a voice. When Carrera looked in the direction of the voice, he heard someone say, "I'm Mr. Burns." But no one was there.

Others heard the same thing in the same spot. Reports had shown up in various documentation that everyone from a Truman Administration guard to a housemaid in the 1960s heard a male voice claim to be Mr. Burns in the Yellow Oval Room. The Truman guard actually checked to make sure that the speaker hadn't been Secretary of State James F. Byrne. The search made it into the records, even though Byrne himself hadn't been in the White House at the time.

White House historians from the previous century even had a theory on the subject. Mr. Burns was, they said, the unhappy previous owner of the land, David Burns, who had been forced to give up his land to make room for the White House in 1790.

Kimber knew of Burns and knew that he had indeed been unwilling to give up his land. She'd always meant to use the time travel technology to visit the meeting in which Burns pissed off George Washington by slandering his wife. Kimber wanted to see if the story was true.

By the time, Kimber finished reading, her eggs were cold and congealed. She ate them anyway. Ghost stories abounded in houses like the White House, houses with a lot of history and a large amount of people going through. She wasn't surprised that a lot of people had claimed to see spirits over the years.

The only thing that did surprise her in the print-out was the last bit, the one from a Living History administrator. One of his students, using a protected observation portal to explore the entire White House on what everyone thought was a particularly empty day, broke the rules and answered his phone in the middle of the view.

He listened to the voice on the other end and then said, loudly, "I'm Mr. Burns," before the administrator took him away – and banned the unthinking Mr. Burns from the viewing area for the next two years.

She ran a hand over her face, and set the print-out down. She heard a clank, and saw that Hemmet – and his tray, filled with pastries and two cups of coffee – had joined her. She wanted to tell him to go away. Take that print-out and shove it. Take her job and do it himself.

But she didn't.

"You realize this is impossible," she said. "The technology does not bleed through and even if it did, no one would notice."

"That's the thing," he said, shoving the print-out toward her. "I think we have some serious technical issues."

Two of these conversations in two days. How fun. And this time, from someone she respected. She couldn't escape, so she decided to play along.

"Okay, even if I grant that," she said, "it doesn't really matter. We're not influencing anyone in the past. We're not changing history."

"Oh," Hemmet said, softer than she thought he could speak. "I believe history *is* changing, and it is changing because of us."

She sighed and wished she hadn't had the eggs after all. They sat like a lump in her stomach. Had someone decided to haze her? Had the department chosen this busy week to have everyone pull a prank on her? Did they want to see how she'd handle it?

She wanted to tell Hemmet to leave her alone, but she was supposed to be diplomatic. After all, she was the department chair, which was, in its way, as close to an in-house diplomatic post as a university employee could hold.

"You think we're changing history because people are hearing ghosts?" She couldn't quite keep the skepticism out of her voice. "People have always heard ghosts, Dr. Hemmet. Shakespeare wrote about ghosts for a reason."

"Shakespeare's ghosts." Hemmet picked up one of the pastries and shook it at her. "You realize that the early drafts of the plays contained no ghosts at all."

Ambra had shaken a tablet at her. To Kimber's knowledge, no one had shaken anything at her in a conversation before this week. Maybe that was part of the conspiracy as well.

Kimber was getting real tired of this. "Dr. Hemmet, no one knows which drafts *are* the early drafts."

"No one *used* to know," he said.

She put a hand up to her face and rubbed her eyes. She hadn't followed Shakespearean scholarship. She considered Shakespearean scholarship both literary history and British history, and as such, outside of her purview.

She sighed. He was watching her, his florid face filled with – of all things – concern.

"What have you *personally* found that's changed?" she asked. "And I don't mean from your own visits to the past. I mean within the established historical *document* scholarship."

His lips thinned. "Eleanor Roosevelt held séances in the White House."

Before Kimber could stop herself, she made a sound of disgust. "One of our most revered and *sane* first ladies? Are you kidding me?"

Kimber could believe that Mary Todd Lincoln, who had a history of mental illness, held séances. But Eleanor Roosevelt? The most grounded woman in the mid-century? She would never–

"No, I'm not kidding you," Hemmet said, "and I have the documentation."

Kimber's heart started to pound. She did not want to be convinced of this. She wasn't sure what she could do about it even if she were convinced.

But she was an information gatherer – that's what historians were, as she told her students – historical reporters, nothing more, nothing less. And as such, she needed information like she needed air.

"Do the séances correspond with any Living History visits?" she asked.

"Not from our school, but the University of Chicago has some scholars who specialize in Lincoln –"

"Lincoln?" She let out a small breath of air. Relief flooded her. This issue (non-issue?) was bothering her more than she thought. "He has nothing to do with the Roosevelts."

"But he does." Hemmet gave her a pitying look. "Lincoln's ghost started appearing in the 1920s, or so they say, and both Queen Wilhelmina of Norway and Winston Churchill saw him during the Second World War. Churchill, who was getting out of a bath, managed to quip, 'Mr. President, you seem to have me at a disadvantage,' before Lincoln disappeared."

"Well, that sounds completely made-up," Kimber said. "You know that one of the first things the British Living History teams discovered was Churchill's gift for embellishment."

"I don't think that was a discovery so much as a confirmation," Hemmet said with a smile.

Kimber refused to smile in return. "Even if it did happen, we don't have students who look like Lincoln."

"How do you know?" Hemmet said. "We're not the only ones using the Living History devices."

He was right about that too. Even though her department was the oldest Living History department in the entire world, other schools had adopted the discipline. Over forty schools in the English-speaking world alone had Living History devices, with more adopting the technology and the discipline all the time.

"If the devices were malfunctioning, we'd know," she said.

Hemmet picked up a coffee cup and took a sip. "I think we do know."

"Two incidences of séances and an 'I'm Mr. Burns,' are not proof," she snapped.

"*Two* incidences?" he asked.

She flushed. Could he really not know about Ambra? Was Kimber the only person Ambra contacted on a regular basis?

"Believe me," Kimber said, "the first incident doesn't count."

Hemmet frowned at her. She got the sense, not for the first time, that he understood her better than she wanted him to.

"If you say it doesn't count, then I'll believe you." His tone said otherwise, of course. "But, I think we should look into this before all those time travel paradoxes actually come true."

This exact same discussion had precipitated her divorce, all those years ago. Her ex-husband kept citing science fiction writer after science fiction writer, bad movie after bad movie, physicist after physicist, about time travel paradoxes, and asking her why she wasn't worried about them.

I don't want to be married to the woman who destroyed history as we know it, he had said one particularly difficult afternoon.

That's the point, she had replied harshly. *We don't know history. And without these devices, we never will.*

She wasn't going to go into any of that with Hemmet. She knew that he knew as much about current time travel theory as she did.

Still, she had to say, "Time travel paradoxes are a myth."

"So were germs, once upon a time," Hemmet said. "And bacteria. And global warming –"

"All right," she said. "You've made your point."

She just wasn't sure what she was supposed to do about it.

3.

"BARBARA AND I haven't seen the ghost of Abraham Lincoln walking the halls, but this is our first Halloween in the White House, so maybe we'll see him tonight."

George H.W. Bush,
October 31, 1989

THE FIRST THING Kimber did do was postpone her own scheduled trip at the end of the week. She wouldn't take a time travel trip until she figured out what was going on, if something actually *was* going on. With that in mind, she reviewed the archives by searching for *séance* in the official calendar of each First Family. Disturbingly, she found two more First Ladies involved in séances, Nancy Reagan and Hillary Clinton.

Kimber believed Nancy Reagan, who took all of that California-at-mid-twentieth-century-New-Age crap a little more seriously than most, might hold a séance, just to see what it was like. But Kimber didn't believe Hillary Clinton would.

Kimber had actually met Hillary once. (The first name reference had become a historical convention to distinguish Hillary from the rest of her family (Clinton [aka Bill] and Chelsea).) Hillary had been formidable, even though she had been in her mid-nineties. It was easy to see why heads of state paid attention to her and how she managed to maintain her iron-lady reputation all those years. She was probably one of the smartest people Kimber had ever met.

Hillary had even known about the Living History project which was then in its infancy.

You know what they're calling it at the Supreme Court, don't you? Hillary had said over dinner. Hillary and Kimber had been seated near each other at one of those glittering White House dinners that seemed to happen no matter who the president was.

They're talking about this at the Supreme Court? Kimber had asked.

Oh, yes, Hillary had said, *and they're very happy that, at the moment, the people in the past can't sue. No one else will have standing. Because the Court really doesn't want to consider the Constitutional implications of all of this stuff you're meddling in.*

Constitutional implications? Kimber said. *But our scientists have shown that we can't have an impact on history. So we can't meddle with the Constitution—*

My dear Professor, Hillary had said with a bright smile that always surprised people. *Of course we can meddle with the Constitution. It's a living document, after all, one that we "interpret." And the group on this particular court is very happy that it will not be interpreting the right to privacy for long-dead Americans. Think about it: Do we value their privacy*

*rights over our right to publish treatises about the past?
Is that free speech? Do we have the right to invade
each other's homes at the most vulnerable times? Is
there truly a need to know? Or is it just historical
voyeurism?*

At the time, Kimber had thought Hillary was worried
for her past self, particularly about those days when
the Monica Lewinski scandal broke in the late 1990s.
No matter who you were or how famous, you really
didn't want some historian listening in as you berated
your husband for his adulteries.

Later, though, Kimber realized that Hillary had more
pertinent concerns. With the cult of Lincoln, and the
serious scholarship happening around FDR, those two
historical figures probably never had a moment of real
privacy. Scholars watched their every move – literally.

Fortunately, Kimber would say when an occasional
student brought up this concern, the historical figures
had no idea they were being watched.

But what if they did?

She shuddered. Hillary was long dead now, but had
she, at some point in her life, known that the whole
world *was* watching?

Still, would that lead to séances?

Twentieth-century American politicians were not
Kimber's area of expertise, although she knew more
about them than she knew about Lincoln, partly
because she'd met a few of them, and partly because
she'd flirted with writing about all the major twentieth-
century cataclysms, until she realized that they did not
suit her. She preferred more genteel times, and more
genteel questions. It wasn't a coincidence that Hillary
had discussed the Constitution with her.

Kimber wasn't a Constitutional scholar, but she was a student of the Constitutional period. The men of that era fascinated her. And as much as academics wanted to talk about Abigail Adams, the woman really had been relegated to the sidelines. The Constitution of these United States had been built by the men, for the men, and of the men, and it was only by understanding those men, Kimber believed, that the world could understand what the United States had become.

Besides, she found the young Thomas Jefferson a lot more sexy than she had expected – something she admitted to no one, not even the ex-husband before he became an ex.

Kimber was now taking all of this change seriously – with the séances (now numbering four that she could easily find), the Lincoln sightings (which seemed to be growing exponentially), and that regrettable "I'm Mr. Burns" incident nagging at her more than she wanted to admit.

She went into what she called The Pit, and the others called the Viewing Rooms, and talked to technicians, who left her more confused than she had been when she arrived. Then she talked to the university's scientists, including those who had worked with the developers of time travel. They all told her the same thing: time paradoxes were impossible, given the way that time travel actually works. For a paradox to happen, the travelers had to interact with their environment, and it had been proven time and time again that these travelers did not interact.

"But isn't a sighting an interaction?" Kimber had asked.

"Prove to me that the sightings – if they happen – have changed the course of history, and I'll let you know," one of the time travel techs had said.

So she went to two scholars, one who specialized in Eleanor Roosevelt, and one who specialized in Hillary Clinton.

Kimber met them off-campus, at a dive bar that felt like something out of a spy thriller instead of a place for a private discussion. The bar even had a jukebox – or a jukebox replica (theoretically, it played music accessed on an ancient cloud, as if that were supposed to make everyone feel better). The music that afternoon was some twenties techno-fusion-funk, which was hard to listen to, and drove the other patrons out of the bar.

The professors, Leonard Hughes and Connie Caio, seemed intrigued enough, especially after Kimber found a booth far enough away from the music that everyone could be heard.

"What I really need," Kimber said, after giving them all of the preliminaries, and listening to Hughes's repeated "*I knew it! I knew it!*", "are documents that you've had in your offices for years, things that haven't touched any media source from the cloud to the web to anything else you can think of. These documents can't have been near any portals either. I just want historical stuff, maybe even the hard copies of the calendars from the days of the séances, showing that the séances didn't happen."

"What if they did?" Connie Caio asked. "I mean, we don't know everything."

Kimber hated having her own words turned back on her. She shrugged. "I guess we accept it then."

"In the meantime, though," Caio said, "you want us to look for proof that things have changed."

Kimber tilted her head back. The music throbbed in her skull, like a never-ending headache.

What would it prove if the actual paper documents had no mention of séances? Prudence on the part of the participants? Or proof that the presence of the ghostly scholars actually changed history?

"Both women kept official and unofficial diaries, right?" Kimber asked.

"Yes," Hughes said, and then looked at Caio uncomfortably. Perhaps he had answered for them both without knowing what he was talking about.

But she nodded, so he smiled.

"Get me copies of both," Kimber said. "Copies that are made from the actual documents, not from –"

"Any other media, we know," Caio said. "I'll have mine for you tomorrow."

"Me, too," Hughes said.

Kimber thanked them, but her mind was already working on another problem. This conversation convinced her the problem was more complex than she even realized.

She didn't just need to know if the scholars had an impact on the past. If they did, she needed solutions.

And she needed them before (if) anyone else figured out that problems actually existed.

4.

"As for surprising [President] Taft, [Lillian Rogers Parks] wrote that it occurred on one of her first visits

to the White House in 1909. Her mother turned down
the president's bed and then left her daughter [Lillian]
in the bedroom, ordering her to stay put while she
took care of some brief duties elsewhere. While she
waited, a 'very stout,' 'jolly' man came into the room,
took one look at the girl wearing a prim white dress
and said, "Well, what have we here? Are you the little
ghost of the White House I've been hearing about?"

> "Ex-White House 'insider'
> Lillian Rogers Parks dies,"
> *The Houston Chronicle*
> November 13, 1997

KIMBER CALLED A meeting with the other department heads in Physics, History, Biology, and Time Travel itself, to discuss all that she had learned and what she hadn't.

She decided to hold the meeting in the VIP guest observation booth above the Pit or Time Travel Central, as the university called the Time Travel wing of the Physics Building. Eventually Time Travel would get its own building, but in the beginning the funding had to come out of Physics and History, because the alumni were scared to fund the project.

After the alumni had gotten to see it – first in this glass-enclosed viewing booth (like the VIP suites at the football stadium) and then on the floor below where they used protected observation portals for the first time, they started throwing money at Time Travel and Living History. But it had taken a few years.

Usually Eoin McKinty oversaw the alumni visits. McKinty headed the Time Travel division. He didn't discover time travel – hundreds of scientists over dozens of universities had done that – but he did invent the systems that allowed any old graduate student to confirm his hypothesis about Cromwell, if he so chose.

McKinty looked a lot younger than he had the right to. He was in his seventies now, but he looked no older than forty, and if someone commented on his appearance he would joke that time travel kept him young.

Kimber wasn't even certain that McKinty had time-traveled since he set up both the wing and the systems. He sat at the edge of the conference table now, chair pushed back, watching the students work the portals with one eye while keeping track of the other division heads at the same time.

The other division heads scattered around the table, looking a bit confused. It had probably been a decade since this group had been together outside of a general faculty meeting. Marcy Wolfson, the head of the Physics department, hadn't even been a full professor ten years before, and Janet Hsia, the head of the History department, might not have been out of high school yet.

Both women had gotten their appointments around the point that Kimber had, enough that it prompted the local media to say that the university was on a female hiring spree, something Kimber believed shouldn't even get noticed in the latter half of the twenty-first century.

The senior person here was eighty-five-year-old Isaac Brenner who ran the Biology department. He looked his age, bent and tired, except for his eyes, which were bright, sparkling, and full of humor. Kimber had always liked Brenner, who was said to be on the shortlist for the Nobel for his research into the biological development of consciousness.

That research, more than his department head status, was the reason she wanted him here.

Her stomach fluttered. She hadn't slept well since this whole thing began – well, since she heard of the Hillary Clinton séances, anyway – and she wanted the drama to end soon, although she suspected it wouldn't.

She had received actual paper copies of the diaries, which told her precisely nothing – or at least, nothing she hadn't expected. Nancy Reagan's personal diary did not list a séance, but did list several meetings with astrologers.

Hillary Clinton's diaries, personal and public, were as practical as the woman herself.

Which meant that the older paper documents downloaded or copied decades ago were different from the same documents downloaded today. And, if those new versions of the documents had records of séances, then that might prove that the scholars were having an impact on history.

But they might not.

Because, if there was record of the rumors on paper documents going back before time travel, then the stories of séances might have existed all along – as rumors. Back in the early 1990s, a lot of Hillary detractors said truly stupid things about her, things that her later actions (never mind her spokespeople) discredited.

Kimber couldn't think about any of that. She had to focus on the what-ifs, which she found a bit ironic, given what she was dealing with.

The what-ifs, as she presented them to the department heads, were simple: What if their new-fangled time travel and its scholarly uses actually had an impact on history?

It took her a while to get the others to discuss the actual what-if. Wolfson wanted to discuss the possibilities; Brenner wasn't sure any of this fit into his expertise; Hsia believed that history wasn't fixed at all; and McKinty jumped from that to a long discussion of alternate realities.

Finally, Kimber slammed her palms onto the table. "I know you find this fascinating. I do too." (Okay, she was lying about that; the discussions just got in her way.) "But here's what I need to know: if we are, indeed, having an impact on history, *changing it*, what do we do about it? Do we shut down the Time Travel and Living History departments?"

"Well, it's not just us," McKinty said. "Other universities have similar programs –"

"Do we *all* shut the projects down?" Kimber said over him. "Worldwide?"

"Why do we have to decide that now?" Hsia asked.

"Technically," Brenner said, "if a scientific experiment goes awry and it has an actual impact on others, then the project gets shut down everywhere. Everyone stops working on it until whatever has gone wrong has been fixed."

Hsia frowned. No one shut anything down in History Departments. They simply disagreed with each other, usually in some formal way, like a presentation or a paper, filled with video footnotes and lots and lots and lots of attribution.

"We have to define impact," McKinty said. "When we talked about the impact of time travel in the early years, we were looking at the Butterfly Effect."

Kimber felt that urge to roll her eyes again. Because she'd been in a thousand meetings where McKinty discussed that ridiculous butterfly/thunder story by fiction writer Ray Bradbury.

"Yeah, yeah," Kimber said. "A time traveler stepped on a butterfly in the past, and changed the course of history because of it. It's just a stupid story."

"No, it's part of chaos theory," Wolfson said. "And it wasn't a story. It was from a paper presented in 1972 –"

"I don't care," Kimber said. "We all understand the butterfly effect."

"The point is," McKinty said, "we expected the changes to be big. You know, if someone steps on a butterfly in fifteenth century Illinois, did that prevent Abe Lincoln from being born, and if he wasn't born, were the slaves freed? That kinda thing. This clearly isn't it."

"Really?" Brenner asked. "You think if more and more humans believe in ghosts that's not a problem. What if they all start finding proof of ghosts? Entire worldviews change."

"I don't think they would change," Hsia said in a tone that suggested she was about to lecture the entire group. "We've had ghosts as long as human culture has existed. Think about it. In religion alone, we have more incidents of ghosts than anywhere else. Even in Christianity. It refers to the Father, the Son, and the Holy Ghost."

"I thought it was Holy Spirit," Wolfson muttered.

"Certain parts of Chinese culture have accepted ghosts as real for thousands of years," Hsia said, not put off by the muttering. Kimber wondered if she was used to students muttering during class. "And the Mesopotamians referred to ghosts all the time. Those are the ones I can think of off the top of my head. I know there are lots more."

"Are there?" McKinty asked. "Or are we already in an alternate timeline? Did any of us believe in ghosts two years ago?"

"Do any of us believe in ghosts now?" Brenner asked Wolfson. She shrugged.

"My point," Hsia said firmly, "is the same as Professor McKinty's. What does it matter?"

"I thought you were making a different point. I thought you were pointing out that it did matter." Brenner glanced at Kimber as if she could clear up his confusion.

She shrugged. She wanted solutions, not this intellectual banter.

"The thing is," McKinty said, "if we are having an effect, it's a relatively minor one. And besides, we're already on this road. It can't get worse. I don't think we shut anything down or worry anyone. We haven't proven anything."

"He's right," Hsia said. "Four references to séances and a few mentions of ghosts don't mean anything. I can show you more than that in *Arabian Nights*."

"That's a story," Wolfson said.

"So's the Bible," Hsia said.

"Some would argue –"

"All right." Kimber shook her head. She wasn't going to get anything from them, and they didn't see it as a problem. Or, at least, as a problem that they had to think about yet.

Either she made decisions on her own that would have an impact on the entire scholarly world, or she had to acquiesce to an academic timeline.

She was an academic, after all. She acquiesced.

"If we call for more study," she said, "who does it?"

"I think we set up an international committee with quite a few experts," Wolfson said. "Let's put out the call, bring in people from other disciplines, see what the historical record produces, see if anyone can show harm that a belief in ghosts engenders, and go from there."

Brenner and McKinty nodded. Hsia, for once, looked a bit shocked. "That'll take years."

"I think that's the point," Kimber said. Her frustration level had gone up, something she hadn't thought possible.

There must have been some kind of change on her face, because McKinty patted her hand.

"Kimber," he said gently, "what you're missing is this: if the changes have already occurred, I have no idea how they could get worse."

Maybe this was where they needed Ambra. *She* would have no trouble imagining how things would get worse. She would probably have some this-is-the-end-of-civilization-as-we-know-it scenario that would stop everyone in their tracks.

Of course, no one would believe the scenario because Ambra came up with it. Which simply echoed Kimber's experience with this topic so far.

"I don't have a dog in this hunt," Brenner said, using a phrase Kimber hadn't heard since her grandmother died. "I don't care if your programs continue or not, but here's what I think, Dr. Lawson. We're discussing a what-if that could take away your life's work. It would definitely take away Dr. McKinty's life's work. Don't we owe it to both of you and everyone else who works in Time Travel and Living History to be absolutely certain of two things – one: that our methods actually cause ghosts to appear in the past, and two: that those ghosts actually cause harm?"

"Ghosts have an impact," Hsia said. "The *past* has an impact on the present. Don't we owe it to history to preserve it?"

"Do we really know what history is?" Wolfson asked. "Nothing is certain. If we look at chaos theory –"

"If we look at all theories, we'll be here all day." Kimber couldn't quite keep the annoyance out of her voice. She had thought these people would help her.

She should have known better.

"'All day' is what we owe the past," Hsia said in a prim little voice.

Kimber hadn't thought there could be someone on the planet more annoying than Ambra, but Hsia had proven that theory wrong in less than two hours.

And that alone made Kimber want to finish this meeting. She turned to Hsia.

"I think you're right," Kimber said to her. "We owe the past a great deal. Perhaps you can set up this international committee? It will take a grant or two to establish, and someone – perhaps Dr. McKinty here – will need to set up the research guidelines, but I think it's necessary."

"What about you?" Hsia asked, her eyes bright. She probably saw the forward momentum of her entire career in this one assignment. "This is your idea, after all."

Kimber nodded. "It is, and I'd be happy to sit on the committee if you need me. Otherwise, I'd prefer to let someone else take point on this. I'm almost six months behind on my research, and I'd like to finish before the year's out."

Everyone else chimed in about the state of their own research, and Kimber tuned out.

She had done what she could, hadn't she? After all, did she owe history a debt? Was history an entity that actually could be owed a debt? Or was it simply a construct that many people refused to believe in?

Like ghosts.

5.

"I THINK THIS *is the most extraordinary collection of talent, of human knowledge, that has ever been gathered together at the White House, with the possible exception of when Thomas Jefferson dined alone."*

John F. Kennedy
Remarks at a dinner honoring Nobel Prize
winners of the Western Hemisphere
April 29, 1962

KIMBER NEVER SPOKE the word "séance" again, but she did think it, and in the most unlikely place. Or perhaps it was too likely.

For she was in the White House dining room designed by Thomas Jefferson, with its circular shelves that turned with the touch of a spring. The shelves really worked the way the history books said they would: covered dishes, filled with the finest food, prepared under the supervision of steward Etienne Lemaire, hid in each cabinet, so that the notoriously private Jefferson could dine alone.

In his own time, Jefferson's public meals had been famous, written up in every single journal, and by many guests – particularly female guests, who had no idea that the Third President of the United States had a live-in lover who was also his slave. The entire country thought him an eligible bachelor.

Time travel, Living History, whatever anyone wanted to call it, had proven that Jefferson and Sally Hemings had indeed been intimate, and that Hemings did indeed look like her white half-sister, Jefferson's late wife, Martha.

But those things hadn't interested Kimber, at least not when she had made her grant proposal. She wanted to recreate the meals, the recipes, write about the grand conversations, once thought lost to time.

And she also wanted to know if Jefferson truly did dine alone, like John F. Kennedy, the 35th President of the United States, used to imagine.

Kimber had planned this trip for a long, long time. She'd researched the schedule, looked at guest diaries, researched the weather, and figured if Jefferson would ever dine alone it would be on this night. So she went back, to see not just the dining room, but the meal itself, and what he read while eating – if he read anything.

Instead, she found herself beside his chair, looking at one of the handsomest men to ever sit in the White

House – red-headed, freckled, with a friendly face and lively blue eyes, more than six feet tall, and without an ounce of fat on a frame that was "straight as a gun barrel" (as Edmund Bacon once described him).

The table, like the shelves, was circular and, at this moment, littered with almonds and cut apples, an empty claret glass to one side, and some warm tea steaming near an open book.

The candles in the chandelier burned low, so another candle sat near the book itself, illuminating the text.

But Jefferson wasn't looking at the book. He was staring at the other side of the table as if he saw people. His face had paled and his lips were parted. He said nothing.

Kimber followed his gaze, and saw half a dozen Jeffersonian scholars, her colleagues and rivals, all staring at Jefferson as if expecting him to say something profound.

She could see them, but they didn't seem to notice her. Could she see them because she had expected them? Or had she conjured them herself like a medium at a séance?

She bowed her head, then cursed softly.

It was all gone for her now, the feeling of discovery, of aloneness, of *scholarship*. Now she truly felt like she was invading someone's privacy.

All Thomas Jefferson wanted to do on this evening – on *that* evening, now hundreds of years in the past – was dine alone.

He had failed at that. And he had an inkling that he had failed.

He smiled a little sardonically, picked up his claret glass and peered at it in the manner of a man who thought he had had too much.

Then he shook his head and returned to his book.

Kimber let out a small breath. She wanted to ask his forgiveness, but she didn't dare speak to him. What if her voice remained in the room, like poor Mr. Burns' voice had?

She didn't need this part of the White House to be haunted by a perpetual sorry attitude. Not that it probably would have, considering. After all, the British would burn this section of the building to the ground in less than a decade.

Still, she couldn't resist. She looked at Jefferson's bowed head, and mouthed her apology, realizing the apology wasn't just to him, but to all residents of this magnificent house.

Because it would become – it already was – the most haunted place in America.

And she now knew she had contributed to its growing collection of ghosts.

BONDS

ROBERT REED

Robert Reed is the author of eleven novels and a big quivering mass of shorter works. His novella, "A Billion Eves", won the Hugo in 2007. Reed is now at work on a trilogy of narrow novels set in his Marrow/ Great Ship universe. The first book, now titled The Slayer's Son, *should be published in mid-2013 from Prime Books. The author lives in Lincoln, Nebraska, with his wife and daughter.*

The Article

AN INTESTINAL AILMENT led to post-surgical complications, and the young man had to spend three or four months in a long-term care facility. Or it was a sick gall bladder and half a year of recovery. Or the patient began with a sexual correction or enhancement and perhaps has never fully recovered. There must be a true story, and maybe it is illuminating. But Desmond Allegato seems to prefer opacity and rumor. The only detail common to every account is Havenwood

– a small private institution where the twenty-five-year-old language arts student could heal in peace, contemplating life and his place in a universe awash with profound forces and tiny people.

Havenwood is famous for its professional, trustworthy staff. Desmond Allegato's case has never been discussed by any employee, present or past. But that seamless secrecy allows pretenders to step forward, each claiming to have been a patient during the right months, and to have met the genius long before he defined our century.

As a rule, you can spot liars and charlatans; they are ones full of self-affirming details.

The casual, inadequate witness rarely gets much of an audience. But they are the most reliable voices to us. Those people describe a handsome but dangerously skinny, very pale young man. Most never knew his name. Desmond took his meals in a room that he shared with an old laptop. His days and long evenings were spent playing first-person shooter games and FreeCell. Nobody remembers visiting family or friends, though it was understood that he was riding his parents' health insurance. On those rare occasions when he emerged from his quarters, the gaunt youngster spent his breath complaining about the awful food and his cheap computer and how poor he was, and bored, and if only there was some way to make fat money fast.

These are the stories that appeal to a cynical, scientifically schooled audience. Allegato is our shared obsession, and we have a favorite story – an anecdote that broke while *The Bonds That Free* became a runaway bestseller. An elderly gentleman was living in a nursing home. His family was visiting when a stock photo of Allegato appeared on Fox News, and he announced that he knew that face. Then after pulling together his thoughts, he explained how he met "the kid" at Havenwood. They were neighbors and shared a nurse, some middle-aged black gal, and thinking about the nurse brought a wide, appreciative smile.

It seems their nurse had quite a few things to say on the subject of Allegato. "Mr. Locked Away," as she called him. She never offered medical details, but she insisted that he was an odd broken child, and broken in ways no doctor could fix. Mr. Locked Away didn't want people. He preferred to sit alone, which was unnatural. The boy didn't have one friend in the world, and that's what he deserved. And while every patient had his sickness and his special burdens, that idiot white boy was in such a miserable place, and he didn't even know it.

Then came a morning when some unspecified incident put her over the brink. Entering the old man's room, she announced that she'd had enough of Mr. Locked Away. Several years later, sitting with his daughters and grandchildren, the witness described how the nurse railed against the waste of being alone so much, never being touched in good ways. Then she stopped talking. Which was an unusual event, he mentioned. Silence was peculiar. The nurse worked quickly with him, and then, glancing at the time, she broke into a dreamy smile, and he asked what she was thinking, and that's when she winked in a conspiratorial fashion.

"I've got a fix," she said. "I know just how." And with that, she returned to Allegato's room.

The old man made a few assumptions. He didn't

confess his state of mind, not with the little grandkids sitting close, but he had made no secret of liking his nurse, particularly her "well-built" qualities. It was easy to imagine his mind – a frank firm woman in her forties would seem like a wish answered, and there sat that eighty year-old fellow with his new knee and happy visions about what was happening down the hall. His hearing wasn't the best, but he listened. He thought he heard voices and then he definitely heard something fall, and that was followed by larger crunching sounds. An attendant jogged past the room. Another door opened. Then the Allegato kid was shouting about the unfairness and why did she do that, and the nurse said she was sorry but accidents happen. Except Allegato would have none of that. "Then why did you pick it up and throw it down a second time, if it was a damned accident?"

More attendants arrived. The nurse was standing in the hallway, telling her supervisor how sorry she was and she would replace the machine.

From his room, Allegato cried out, "When?"

"When you listen to what I've been telling you," she said. And with that she walked away, not smiling but definitely proud, her posture full of certainty, her fine full chest carried up high where it belonged.

Two days later, the kid had a new laptop and the hallway had a new nurse, and the incident was officially closed. And two days after that, our favorite witness happened to shuffle past his neighbor's room and found the door opened. The kid was working with his new computer. He usually played idiot games, but not today. He was writing, displaying the swift competent typing of a professional student.

"What's the project?" the old man asked.

Allegato had fine features and black hair, and whatever his ailment, he was beginning to regain weight and strength. "I'm writing an article," he said. "It's going to make me money."

"Oh yeah?"

"I'm a very good writer," the kid said, eyes focused on the screen.

"That's great," the old man said, not caring one way or another. Then after a long silence, he asked, "So what's your article about?"

"Something occurred to me the other day." No mention was made of altercations or reassigned nurses. "You just think we're living in different rooms. But then I realized that we aren't."

"Aren't what?"

A mysterious smile broke out. "Apart," Allegato said.

"We're not?"

"Not ever."

"So we're joined somehow? Is that it?"

"Yeah, there this bond between us," the kid said.

It seemed like a singularly silly notion, and the old man giggled, which didn't offend anyone because nobody else seemed to be listening. And then he asked, "Do you really believe that?"

"Hell no. But that's what I'm claiming." And then Allegato finally glanced at his neighbor, and their last conversation ended with a simple request.

"Shut the door on your way out."

*　　*　　*

The Bonds that Free

THE ARTICLE WAS published but only barely—a short-lived web magazine offered Desmond a hundred dollars for the honor and then paid him nothing. But among its few readers was a jobless editor/minor author/amateur psychologist named Clarence Parcy. Where most people found nut-cake baked from obscure reasoning, Parcy saw one grand idea begging to be domesticated. An exaggerated resumé and promises of a book deal helped him meet the young author. Allegato proved to be a self-serious, aloof lad with no charm but an inflated and very useful ambition. Promises were made. A partnership was forged, and the next five years were spent building the future bestseller. Because the public wanted an expert, the author had to acquire an advanced degree. Desmond earned two quick literary doctorates from online universities. Because a serious professional needed a serious job, the young doctor formed the Chicago Institute of Interpersonal Bonding and Love – an incorporated endeavor that filled one corner of his bedroom. Because science lives on research, he and his mentor devised dozens of web surveys, dangling the possibility of cash in exchange for a moment of the world's time. Mountains of data were given away for free. A small portion of those files were massaged to create charts and graphs, while the comments sections were dredged for tales of personal woe and adoration. And because the first goal of any genuine professional is to practice his craft, Dr. Allegato gave a series of lectures and little workshops, teaching select audiences about his extremely new theory about the nature of human beings and how vivid, living connections tie all of us together.

Those were the venues where Allegato mentioned his undefined surgery and the long, illuminating recovery. He brought notes but never referred to them, speaking from memory as the PowerPoint show churned past. Every participant signed an agreement not to record the important, confidential material. Only one authenticated video log survived until today. In it, the speaker looks older than his years, the wardrobe and gray dye in the black hair creating the portrait of the wise professor who had been through much and who might know what he was talking about. Despite a relentless smile, Allegato seemed remote, even chilly. Presumably that was why Parcy sat in the audience. A heavy-set man in his sixties, Parcy had a winner's grin and an infectious manner that couldn't be taught. No one ever remembers Allegato mentioning his associate. The two men in the video act as if they don't know each other. Parcy is a nameless character sitting near the front of the rented hall, intrigued by every word and every chart, lifting his hand high whenever the group energy diminishes.

"Yes, sir," Allegato says in the recording. Pointing off screen, he asks, "Do you have a question, sir?"

"No, just a comment." The shaky phone-camera pans right. Parcy takes a moment to look back at the audience, making sure everyone feels involved. "I did some checking, sir," he begins. "I can tell you're smarter than me, and goodness knows, I don't have half your education. And I'm sure this is all very obvious to you, this business of bonds forming around distinct personality types. But what do these bonds mean? And how can I use them in my life?"

"That's more than a comment," Allegato points out. "Those sound suspiciously like questions to me."

Parcy breaks into a delightful laugh, dragging the audience into his pleasure. "I guess you're right, sir."

A smattering of laughter has to die away. Then with a tone both caring and a little wary, Allegato asks, "Do you have children, sir?"

"One son, yes."

That happened to be true.

Allegato nods. "And are you close to him?"

"Very close, yes."

"So that's your son sitting beside you?"

His 'son' is a sleepy fellow in his seventies who looks up in surprise.

The lecture hall fills with hard laughter. Parcy is still giggling when he says, "No, no. Brad lives in Arizona, with his wife and twins."

"But you said you were close to him," Allegato says.

"Yes." Parcy frowns and looks at his hands. "Oh, wait. I understand. I'm not talking about Brad. I'm talking about the bond between us."

"Because that's what is real to you."

The audience shifts in the chairs, whispering.

"That's not to say your boy is inconsequential." Allegato needs a pointed finger to underscore the implications. "The human species acts like a very complicated molecule. And what is a molecule? It is a mixture of elements, some similar and some very different, all linked together by powerful, powerful bonds. For instance, hydrogen is an elemental gas that burns. Oxygen is an element that supports burning. Yet the molecule born from that fire is water. Hydrogen and oxygen are still present, but what we see is a delicious essential liquid composed of the bonds between these most common ingredients."

The audience probably doesn't understand the concept, such as it is. But the air fills with interested noises and whispered questions.

Parcy nods, seemingly ready to surrender the stage.

But Dr. Allegato won't let him go. "Now tell me the truth, sir. I want to know about your son."

"What about him?"

"How strong is this bond between you and Brad?"

The son hasn't spoken to his father in a decade, lending the moment its poignant life. Parcy drops his gaze, saying, "Well. Honestly, we have had our troubles."

An empathetic nod is followed by, "I see. I see."

"There was a fight. A while back, and maybe it was my fault. And since then we haven't been keeping up like we should."

"Sir, I am sorry for your difficulties," Allegato says. This is where his natural remoteness helps; the words are compassionate but his mouth gives them heft and a clinical tone. "However, if I might, sir, I would like to point out that there are no problems between you and your son. Sadness and shame are wasted when they aren't applied to the correct part of the equation. Which is, as I have said –"

"The bond," another voice cries from the back.

The lecture hall feels alert, involved. Everybody watches the young gray doctor nodding, seemingly gathering his thoughts. Then for nothing but the minimal cost of attending, he gives them an idea that in another two years will make him wealthy. "Every person is unique," he says. "But each of us can be categorized according to his or her properties. There is a periodic table to the human species. I have mapped it. In nature, each element is fundamental. Each plays best with certain elements – like hydrogen joining with oxygen. Those bonds are stable and useful, and yes, the same can be said for people. But we waste so much of our lives worrying about what we cannot change. It's the quality of our bonds that brings us happiness or despair. Some bonds are essential, others dangerous. The trick is to know how to manage these powerful, ultimately beautiful forces."

Hands rise and voices call out. One woman wants help with a difficult husband. Another is grieving her dead, difficult mother. One loud man wonders how bonds can help him sell cars.

But Dr. Allegato is a professional, and professionals deal with one patient at a time. Focusing on Parcy, he says, "First of all, forget your son. You have no son. What you have is a bond that is sick and unstable, and what you need to do is restructure and reconfigure the other bonds in your life. Only then will you be able to offer your son a new, more stable bonding."

"But how can I do all that?" the suffering father asks. "I'm not a strong person."

"None of us are strong," says Dr. Allegato. "But of course, that doesn't matter. It is our bonds that hold the energy of the world."

"Do you think so?"

"I know it, and I have tests I can give you," Allegato says. "I'm also developing a series of exercises that can be tailored to different elemental personalities.

At the end of a long weekend, I promise, you will have the bonds you need, and you'll drink in the energies borrowed from a universe that will give and give."

The Unknown Element

MAYBE THE FATHER and his estranged son would have reconnected in the future – an event full of significance and press releases, no doubt. But men of Parcy's age and physical condition often die with their first major coronary. Striking on the eve of publication was a coincidence, or it was the inevitable outcome of long hours making pretty the author's stilted prose. Some claim that Parcy was suffering regrets about the project. Why didn't he just steal the idea from the original article and put himself before an eager public? But he lacked Allegato's marketable looks. And besides, regrets would have required confidence about the book's success.

Confidence seemed ludicrous. Initial orders were sluggish, and the tepid early reviews used the words: 'Contrived,' and 'Complicated', and 'Unconvincing.' Parcy told several friends that his last big gamble had failed. Then he died and his body was found by his cleaning lady, and the autopsy and belated inquest found no substantial reason for a criminal investigation.

The sudden loss of his partner didn't seem to sadden Allegato, which cocked a few eyebrows. But the earliest believers generally found the man's reserve to be a comfort. Allegato spoke at the funeral. "The bonds between us and the deceased still exist," he reminded everyone, "and it is each of our responsibilities to keep the bonds alive and helpful. Which I should add is exactly how Clarence would have wanted it."

Clarence would have preferred money. He was guaranteed thirty per cent of Allegato's take, which seemed like nothing for the first few weeks. But the online campaigns outperformed expectations and a pair of talk-show appearances went very well. Then one actress' speech turned viral – a five minute sermon about how she had tried a thousand self-help guides before this and none worked and *Bonds* was remarkable. She was already at the Third Tier and on a good day she could see the bonds surrounding her, brilliant and lovely, tying her to her boyfriend and children and of course her many supportive and lovely fans too.

Orders jumped from steady to torrential. In an age of e-readers and wide scale thievery, it was impossible to know how many consumers were remaking their lives in the Allegato Way. Ten million Americans was a common guess, with a hundred million practitioners worldwide after the first year. Then the movement struck China. The One-Child policy left people desperate to cherish their scarce, valuable bonds, and seeing the wise Chinese embrace the concept caused a second, much larger wave of interest across the Western world.

Fifteen months later the second edition of *Bonds* was released – a minor reworking that dropped Parcy's name as a contributor, assuring the young social modeler of one hundred per cent of the profits. The International Institute of Interpersonal Bonding and

Love did even better. Good weekends saw ten thousand clinics on six continents. Motivated teachers flinging out jargon and smiles were transforming lives. One neutral study claimed that the Allegato Way was more effective at enhancing happiness than any religion and most psychoactive drugs. Other studies were less certain, but they didn't gain the media foothold. Add the machinery designed to measure bonds and enhance their power, and it was possible to believe that ninety households out of hundred were blessed with Dr. Allegato's presence.

Yet as successes grew, the man became more of a mystery. Even employees who saw him on an irregular basis were perplexed by his manners. Desmond could be pleasant in conversation, but he usually ignored the room full of corporate officers, preferring the DS held close to his face. He made decisions when decisions were necessary, and when it seemed essential he could meet a national leader or open a new hospital, mustering a passable charm for several minutes straight. But the man's only true friend seemed to be Desmond Allegato. His ideal day involved solitude inside one of his dozen mansions, playing games designed by a team that built games only for him. Beautiful women and a few men tried to entice that billionaire, but besides a few laughable/sad adventures, nothing came of their bold advances. The man had a pathological indifference to the rest of us, and that only made him seem more brilliant and intriguing and perhaps tragic.

For twenty years his books and courses and hardware continued to sell, and there was more praise than complaints about the results, and there was no reason to suspect that would ever change.

Then, last March, without a whisper of warning, astonishing news broke. The corporate office panicked. The announcement was absorbed and often misunderstood and, according to several sources, the vice-presidents told one very loyal officer to find out where the Master was, and then they started to battle about who would deliver the thunderbolt and how.

The officer had ambitious and very bold bonds. On his own initiative, he drove to the Master's favorite house. There were rings of security to pass through and, getting wind of this event, the vice-presidents called their man to order him home again. But the officer was already inside. He kept imagining the thrill of sharing what he knew with the world's greatest man. Sitting in what seemed like a random room, the fifty-year-old game player was filling a very comfortable chair, holding a controller while armored gnomes lived in three dimensions, fighting hard for dominion over nothing.

"Sir," the officer said.

The Master continued to play, apparently not hearing him.

Again, louder this time, he said, "Sir."

The game was paused. But it took Allegato some time to pull back from the place where he had been, rubbing his eyes and sighing twice before looking over his shoulder at the intruder.

"What is it?" he asked.

"There's been an announcement, sir."

But Allegato raised his hand first, silencing him with the gesture. "Your name is Greg, isn't it?"

An eleven year veteran of the company, Gary knew well enough to nod and say, "Yes, sir."

"Okay. What's this announcement?"

"Researchers in Australia designed some new equipment. They were using it to study quantum effects. And they just determined that you were right."

Allegato had no reaction, save for another small sigh. Then a look of doubt came into the still-handsome face, and he calmly asked, "What am I right about?"

"There are bonds," Greg/Gary stated.

"What do you mean? Bonds where?"

"The air is full of them, and they're real, and just like we've always said, they weave us together."

"No," the great man said.

"But it's true, sir. They just had a press conference…"

"I meant 'No, I am not right.'" Allegato picked up the game control, studying a partly disemboweled creature. "I made it all up to begin with. So you see? I can't be right. I'm just lucky."

A Team of Dreamers

GOSSIP AND APOCRYPHAL stories make unreliable sources, and that's true with groundbreaking science as well as with affairs of the heart. Something intriguing lay inside an ocean of data. But even the Australian researchers were uncertain what their work meant, and they said so many times. Yes, the universe was laced with subtle quantum relationships. That was always known, at least for the last century-plus. And yes, the human mind seemed to be connected to other minds, including evidence of persistent influences shared between friends and family. The first news conference was wrapped around those modest claims. Then a reporter asked, "What do these bonds look like?" The "bonds" didn't look like anything. The effects were invisible and always tiny, and everybody at the podium said as much. But once used, the telltale word was embraced. "Bonds" was the most popular word in the world now. It took another three days before the science team realized the significance of the word, and they released a joint statement to warn the public away from a label that delivered history and color and a lot of money-making expectations.

Yes, something new had been found. But the discoverers were hardware savants armed with competent software. Those Australians were in no special place to assess the new phenomenon, and the real groundbreaking work required theorists possessing special training and the interest and a properly warped nature, plus that rarest blessing, which was the free time to invest in the chase.

We are the hunters.

Counts vary, but there are about fifty of us worldwide. We know each other mostly through webcams and emails. Some of us are graduate students, others tenured professors, while the largest group are presently unattached to any major institution – the result of economic downturns and little scandals, bouts with mental illness and probably more than a few cases of plain stubbornness.

Except by reputation, we didn't know one another before this. Yet now we're in the same grand endeavor, and bonds have formed. We talk about this daily. And we use the word "bonds" without qualifiers or scorn. Our new mathematics has been woven into the physical research, and we can put numbers to the ways that the fifty of us are bonded. We aren't one mind united by a holy quest, no. But in a given twenty-four hour period, on average, the fifty of us share one-and-a-third thoughts that otherwise wouldn't have existed.

Allegato demands our attention. Last year, most of us didn't give a damn about the man. Yet while the media keep simplifying and misunderstanding our work, they can't stop talking about linked minds and Allegato's innate genius. It pisses us off. Every month, a fresh edition of *Bonds* is released, and each volume culls a few of our equations to illustrate points that were never intended. Doesn't the world understand that the man is a phony? How can brilliant people like us be so unappreciated while his organization of con artists and tag-alongs continues to swallow up billions in new revenue?

That's why the old hermit can't be ignored. The world talks about Allegato, and some of those thoughts leak our way. Our math gives us a reliable number: We endure six and a third Allegato moments every day, and some of us think about him quite a lot more than that, particularly now.

Several months ago, one of the Master's officers contacted us, and because my name was first on the latest paper, I ended up being the rich First-Bonder.

The young woman had two tasks: to show me a pretty face and a polite, respectful manner, and once that goal was met, to arrange a video conference between my group and hers.

Twenty-three of our fifty were present at the meeting. Some of us expected Allegato at their end, but of course he wasn't present. One of us asked about the man, and we were told that he was quite healthy – did we think otherwise? – and he was certainly watching the feed but preferred to keep a low profile, which was everyone's right, and since our time was precious, shouldn't we move things along?

"Things" included us describing exactly what we were doing and what it meant to science and human existence.

Every living mind was connected to every other mind. "Bond" was a poor word, implying some sort of profoundly stubborn joining. There wasn't anything like that, at least not that we could see. What our work showed us were influences and the ghostly quantum motion of information. "Thoughts" didn't do justice to the concept. In a random day, there were anywhere from five hundred to a thousand thoughts that would pop into existence inside a healthy adult cortex. And yes, that seemed like a lot, but the number needed a proper context. Most "thoughts" went unnoticed by the conscious mind. The average person ignored a thousand "thoughts" every minute, and the ghostly glimmers arriving from outside were usually weaker than those generated by the resident brain.

In the media, self-described experts were promising that the world could be woven together with some kind of a telepathic Internet. But that was a farfetched if not out-and-out ridiculous thought. There was a lot of neurological rain falling, but most of it was senseless and, in any storm, who can count individual drops?

We ran out of thoughts that we were willing to share verbally. And when the silence was noted, the pretty lead woman smiled and straightened her back, telling us, "Well, thank you. This has been very fun and informative, and I know that all of us feel energized by this last hour. Thank you very much."

The conference ended with a blank screen.

Three hours later, the PR wing of Allegato's organization went into overdrive. A clipped and deeply misleading version of our conference was given to the world, and with it came words attributed to nobody. That's when we learned that our work was lending meat to bones laid down by the famous man himself. According to the nameless spokesperson, Dr. Desmond Allegato believed this was the moment to step forward and accept the duty for which he was born. He wasn't merely a deep thinker and a grand scientist, but in a world tied together by infinite Bonds, there had to be a leader, and who would be half as perfect as him?

The Bondless Man

AS MENTIONED, THERE are fifty of us, give or take. Some of us feel like "grand scientists", but most realize that he or she has some narrow strength as well as broad limitations in a venue that was invisible just a year ago. On the whole, we love our work. We accept being collaborative. We respect some peers and despise others. Lying awake in the night, each of us contemplates pseudo-telepathy and quantum mysticism, and we imagine future successes while our sleepless minds play with erratic and lovely high mathematics. But there is no way to avoid thinking about Allegato – he is never "Dr. Allegato" to us – and that turn of the mind never helps any of us fall back to sleep.

The long hermitage seems finished. The man who never appeared in public is suddenly ubiquitous. As in old times, he has begun holding little seminars with select audiences, but this time cameras are invited so that the video can be diced and carefully remixed and then released as web events and extended commercials. The old salesman looks handsome and respectable and maybe a little heavy. But Allegato walks quickly on a small brightly-lit stage, and with a strong certain voice he speaks about Bonds and how they define so much of us, and every religion stems from the Bonds, and all intellect and even the smallest emotion too.

His last twenty years have been spent in contemplation, he says, and what he has learned is enormous. Eight Tier is the highest level on the official Allegato Scale, but he is a genuine Twelve, living in a world full of bright Bonds that are lovely and obedient to him. In one more year, perhaps sooner, he will reach the ultimate Tier, which is so important and powerful that it doesn't wear a number, and at that point he will know how to influence most of what happens in the world.

The world probably isn't seeing the genuine Allegato. That's our best guess, at least. Digital invention has reached a point where any damn thing can be put together out of zeros and ones, but we know what we know. The cold soul from the old video could never have become so relaxed and smooth and charming, and particularly not after years spent playing his games. I knew that immediately. But somebody else in our group saw the deeper meaning. "That's not our Desmond," she announced. "That's Parcy with a new body and voice. Don't you see?"

We see too much. The man's fine face is everywhere, and he makes it into the news most days. His first new book in decades was released just last month, and I read it in one long bad evening and then tried to get my peers to look at the words. The old Allegato was a slippery character who at least delivered a comforting product. But this new incarnation isn't a simple commercial machine. He wants power. He is religion. His agenda is broad and well-planned, although it is impossible to know just what the ultimate goal is. Does his organization want to bump up the profits another notch, or is this some wild bid to gain a chokehold on civilization?

Some of my associates read the book, and a few of them were appropriately offended. But as much as we might worry about a new prophet, and as angry as it makes us to see our smart words and math used to bolster his faith, the bulk of our days are still spent trying to comprehend the nature of everything. And while I was reading Allegato's Bible for a second time, an associate in Cairo pieced together three other people's work and then added something of his own, making a discovery that nobody expected, or wanted, or could ignore.

I'M NOT SURE when I decided to pay Allegato a visit. The idea was a whisper between louder thoughts, and then it was a possibility enjoyed over pancakes. I played with the imagery for several days, writing conversations without bothering about the mechanics of how to make the meeting real. And I can't say for certain when I decided to make the attempt. But I was sitting in my little office when I saw the obvious possibility: maybe this wasn't my idea at all. Maybe the fabled seer was genuine, and he was guiding me, and I had no power or right to deny what he saw as an important step in his inevitable rise.

The face of true madness looks this way – hard and obvious and always practical.

Allegato owned twelve or fifteen mansions, and maybe part of Samoa. But I knew about the residence near the corporate headquarters, and a four-hour drive would put me at a reasonable starting place. In my mind were two scenarios: I would be expected in some fashion, or I would be turned away by the first layer of security. One scenario seemed likely but both had their appeal. What I didn't expect was to find several thousand people ahead of me. A town of pitched tents and rain ponchos had grown up on a horse pasture. My IQ might be the stuff of wonders, but it seemed that everyone has sufficient genius when it came to this kind of quest, and I was stunned.

After parking in the mud, I walked through a steady rain. Strangers approached, asking my Tier and my name. I made noises, but nobody was really listening. There was a good deal of mental in some faces, but it was a lucid woman who winked at me before saying, "I feel Him, I see His lovely Bonds, and He has left us."

"Left us?" I asked, imagining the Pacific Island.

"When the final Tier takes Him, a light will sing to all of us and we will know His splendor."

Shoring up my frail sanity, I reached the gate and a guardhouse.

I expected robots or at least brusque professionals. What I found instead was a bored and very fat man sitting behind bars and glass. He didn't speak to me, and I don't know if he heard me. I was just another idiot, and he did what he did a hundred times every day: he swung a thumb at the panel fixed to a tiny detached kiosk.

An automated voice asked for a name and fingerprints, and I think the rough screen took a sample of my skin. Then a warmer voice cautioned me that the Master was deep into meditations but cared for me and wished to hear my thoughts. Clarence Parcy had used a deceptive resume to win a first meeting with the young Desmond, and I took the same approach. I wasn't just working on pivotal research into the nature of Bonds. I was linchpin of the operation, and I had some very big news to deliver firsthand.

That voice said, "Thank you," and then added, "Wait please while your request is given every attention."

Thirty seconds into the wait, I felt like idiot.

Seventeen seconds later – I was timing the event – a third, decidedly more feminine voice gave her apologies and said thank you before sadly admitting that no meeting would be possible today.

The idiot walked back through the squalid, muddy camp, fending off the sober, happy looks of madmen.

I was climbing into my car when the fat guard appeared. He wasn't running, but judging by his gasping and the wet muddy uniform, he had tried to run and fallen at least once. Seeing me, he waved. I climbed back into the rain, and he asked, "How many are watching us?"

"Everybody," I admitted.

He said, "Shit," and took a long look at everyone. Then something in the sorry situation became funny, and he laughed. "It's never happened before. We've got rules, codes. I knew what to do. But eleven years at the gate, and you're the first. I think even the software was startled when he said, 'Yes.'"

"Allegato," I said.

"Dr. Allegato," he whispered. Then he turned, telling me, "Keep close. If they get wind of this, we could have a goddamn riot on our hands."

THE EXPECTED ROBOTS lived inside the big house, and not one had a face.

A bipedal machine offered me a place for my muddy shoes and coat, and then it asked if I wanted food and drink, and when I said that I wanted nothing, thank you, it combed its software for the next viable topic. "Sir, if I may... which office do you hold in the company?"

"None," I said.

"Are you a political figure or a Nobel laureate?"

"No and not yet, but maybe soon."

A smaller, even less human robot wheeled itself between us. "He wants you and please come with me."

I followed. A mansion that was grand on the outside was decidedly ordinary within. Room after room passed by, every door open and each furnished in the same ascetic style – white carpeting and screens on three walls, no windows and no second doors, and in the middle of every room, the same model of lounge chair. The chairs that had been used were outnumbered by chairs still wearing plastic. No room had two items of furniture. What would be the need? Every surface looked clean, but that could have been the result of busy robots. The sole tenant remained a mystery until I was twenty rooms into his quiet, quiet palace.

My guide stopped, studying me with its cameras. "This is an honor for you," it claimed. "Treat it as such, and the intrusion will be forgiven."

I dripped my "Thank you" in sarcasm.

The only closed door in the house was opened, and a jointed limb waved me into the only occupied room.

The man was heavier than his present doppelganger, and what hair remained was white and clustered about the ears. Desmond Allegato looked healthy if not fit. He was sitting in the middle of the room, eyes focused on one of the giant screens. I expected to see gnomes in battle, and I was wrong. Various geometric shapes were dressed in bright colors, and the famous man was moving the figures about a landscape that possessed the illusions of three dimensions and endless size.

I stood just inside the doorway, waiting.

Allegato's hands moved through the air, interfacing with controls that I couldn't see. Then the shapes froze in place, and a subtle rumbling ended, and he looked at me and past me and then at the floor in front of my stocking feet, telling nobody in particular, "Make this brief."

I wanted nothing else.

He turned ahead, saying, "You have news about the Bonds?"

"Yes."

"I keep up on the papers, you know. I recognized your name."

"This news hasn't been published yet."

"So you said." He gave the ceiling a skeptical stare, and something in that gesture told me one obvious fact that I should have guessed. Whatever the man had done with his life, he managed it while pushing through a crushing case of shyness.

The shy man gave my face one brief look. Then talking to the ceiling again, he asked, "What have you learned?"

"Bonds are important," I said.

A small laugh ended with one heavy sigh, and silence.

"In fact," I continued, "they are more important than we ever realized. They aren't just little mathematical tricks that connect minds. They possess matter and energy that tie into the dark parts of the universe. The universe exists because of the bonds. There's no more pre-eminent player in the universe at large."

I was hoping for curiosity or revulsion, any sign of interest. Instead he acted mildly offended, asking, "Are you upset about something?"

"Humans," I said.

"What?"

"We're nothing, or nearly so."

"Are we?"

"The math tells us that. When you and the Method liken humans to elements, when you talk about hydrogen and oxygen, you make a big mistake. It doesn't work that way. Elements have mass. They have nuclei and presence. But the bonds we're talking about – not your Bonds, the real ones – are far more profound and universal than the little impurities that we represent."

He said, "Oh."

"My mind and yours are the smallest part of the equation, contrivances built out of baryonic residues."

Something here was humorous. He laughed and said, "Baryonic? I don't know that word."

"Ordinary matter," I explained. "It's the smallest component of the universe."

Allegato squinted, and I realized he was tied into the web now.

"Dark matter and dark energy," he read aloud. "Is that what your bonds are made of?"

"They're part of them, but there's even more energy from other dimensions. Which is the most astonishing, unsettling part of this, at least in my mind." I lifted my arms and put them down again, trying not to shout. "We think we matter. We tell each other that we count for something. But we don't. All those wishes for free will and power, but our thoughts predate us and will outlive us, and they inhabit our heads only because we just happen to have a place that welcomes them."

"I need to think about that," he said softly.

But my thinking was finished. "Everything in my head is determined by other forces, forces that have remained invisible until now."

Allegato frowned, something tasting sour. Then he laughed abruptly and looked at the white carpet between us. "You know, I don't read faces or voices particularly well. I never have. But under these circumstances, I would have guessed that you would sound somewhat happier than this, telling me about these great discoveries."

I wasn't happy. I was furious, and it was important to explain why. "Your people are using my work and your likeness. I don't know if you realize this, but they're making enormous claims with no basis in fact."

"Well," he said to the carpet. Then the eyes returned to the screen and its geometric players. "I give my people considerable latitude. If they think they can enhance my company, then I wish them all the best."

"They're making you into some kind of god," I shouted.

He sighed and said, "Well, yes. It is an aggressive scheme."

"And you approve?"

He shrugged. Allegato was the master of the indifferent, world-weary shrug. Then he finally looked at my eyes and left his eyes on me, saying, "According to everything that you have learned, there is no 'me'. I am a... what was the word? Contrivance, yes. I am virtually nonexistent. Which makes me blameless, the same as you and everyone else on this little planet."

Again, he offered the perfect shrug.

I breathed and looked at my shaking hands.

Then, with the careful tone of a professional, he told me, "You should try and relax. If these thoughts are as big as you think, then maybe they know what they are doing. Or they don't, and what can you do about it?"

"I don't know," I managed. "What can I do?"

Dr. Allegato turned away, and lifting his hands into the air, he said, "Try closing the door on your way out."

TICKING

ALLEN STEELE

Originally a journalist, SF was always Allen Steele's first love, so he ditched journalism and began producing what made him want to write in the first place. With eighteen novels and nearly a hundred short stories to his credit, Allen's work has received numerous awards, including three Hugos, and has been translated worldwide, mainly in languages he can't read. He serves on the Board of Advisors for the Space Frontier Foundation and SFWA, and also belongs to Sigma, a group of SF writers who serve as unpaid consultants on matters of technology and security. Allen is a lifelong space buff, which has not only influenced his writing but also taken him to some interesting places. He has witnessed numerous space shuttle launches from Kennedy Space Center and, in 2001, testified before the U.S. House of Representatives in hearings regarding the future of space exploration. He dreams of going into orbit, and hopes that one day he'll be able to afford to do so. Allen lives in western Massachusetts with his wife Linda and a procession of adopted dogs. He collects vintage science fiction books and magazines, spacecraft model kits, and dreams.

*   *   *

HAROLD AND CINDY were trying to find something to eat in the hotel kitchen when they were attacked by the cook.

Shortly after the refugees moved into the Wyatt-Centrum Airport, they'd divvied up the jobs necessary for their continued survival. Harold and the remaining desk clerk, Merle, had drawn the assignment of locating the hotel robots. That's all they had to do; just find them, then tell Karl and Sharon, the two Minneapolis cops who'd taken shelter at the Wyatt-Centrum when their cruiser died on the street outside. The officers had their service automatics and a pump-action .12-gauge shotgun they'd taken from their car; unlike most of their equipment, the guns weren't rendered inoperative. And they'd already discovered that an ordinary service robot could be taken out by a well-aimed gunshot; it was the big, heavy-duty ones that were hard to kill.

So Harold and Merle spent the second day after the blackout prowling the hotel's ten floors. Merle knew where the robots normally operated, so they only needed to confirm their positions while avoiding being spotted, and once they'd located all the 'bots Merle remembered, they returned to the pool and told the cops. Karl and Sharon made sure the barricades were secure, at least for the time being, then went up into the hotel and, moving from floor to floor, blew away all the 'bots the civilians had found.

This search-and-destroy mission netted ten housekeepers, five custodians, two room-service waiters, and two security guards. According to Merle, that accounted for the hotel robots; this didn't include the huge bellhop that killed two staff members and a guest before someone picked up a chair and used it to smash the robot's CPU. That happened on the first day; most of the guests fled after that, along with most of the remaining staff. After that sweep, everyone thought all the 'bots had been accounted for and destroyed.

By the end of the third day, the thirty-one people hiding in the Wyatt-Centrum's cathedral-like atrium were down to the last few cans of the junk food a couple of them had scavenged from a convenience store a few blocks down the street. Nobody wanted to venture outside, though – it had become too dangerous to leave the hotel – and the cops were reluctant to tear down the plywood boards they'd had nailed across the ground-level doors and windows. So when Cindy asked Harold if he'd mind coming along while she checked out the kitchen – "It can't all be fresh food," she'd said, "they must have some canned stuff, too." – she didn't have to twist his arm very hard.

Hunger wasn't the only reason he went with her, though. Truth was, he wanted to get into Cindy's pants. Sure, she was at least twenty years younger and he was married besides, but Harold had been eyeing her for the past three days. Only that morning, he hadn't entirely turned his back when she'd taken a bath in the atrium swimming pool. As afraid as he was of dying, he was even more afraid of dying without having sex one last time. Such are the thought processes of the condemned. Perhaps he wouldn't get a chance to knock boots with her during this foray, but at least he'd be able to show off his machismo by escorting her through the lightless kitchen. That was the general idea, anyway... but before he got a chance to nail Cindy, that goddamn 'bot nearly nailed them instead.

Unfortunately, when Harold visited the kitchen earlier, he and Merle had neglected to check the big walk-in refrigerator. It wasn't entirely his fault; the two cooks they'd found attacked them the moment they pushed open the door, forcing a hasty retreat. Those were the first robots the cops had neutralized, and Merle believed they were the only ones in the kitchen. But he was wrong; a third 'bot had been trapped in the fridge when the lights went out.

The walk-in was located in the rear of the kitchen, just a little farther than Harold had gone the first time he'd searched the room. They'd found a carton of breakfast cereal, which would be good for the kids, and Cindy was hoping for some milk that hadn't spoiled yet. She'd just unlatched the chrome door handle, and he was standing just behind her, when they heard the sound everyone had come to dread the last few days:

Tick-tick... tick-tick-tick... tick... tick-tick-tick...

"Watch out!" Harold yelled, and an instant later something huge slammed through the door. Cindy was knocked to the floor; falling down was probably the only thing that saved her from having an eight-inch ice pick shoved into her chest.

The cook was nearly as large as the bellhop. A Lang LHC-14 may seem harmless when it's stirring a vat of corned beef hash, but this one was hurtling toward them with a sharp metal spike clutched in its manipulator claw. And neither Harold nor Cindy were armed.

"Get back, get back, get back!" Harold yelled, as if she really needed any encouragement. Cindy scuttled backward on hands, hips, and heels while he threw himself away from the refrigerator, losing his flashlight in his haste.

Even if he'd hadn't dropped the light, though, he would have been able to see the cook. Red and green LEDs blinked across the front of its box-like body, the glow reflecting off the hooded stereoscopic lenses within its upper turret. As it trundled through the door on soft tandem tires, the turret swept back and forth, clicking softly as the lenses captured first Cindy, then Harold, then Cindy again. Mapping them, remembering their positions...

"Watch out! It's gonna charge...!"

The turret snapped toward Harold as the 'bot determined which human was closer. At that moment, his groping hands found the cold metal surface of something that moved: a dessert cart, complete with the moldering remains of several cakes. Torture wagons, his wife called these things, and he was only too happy to use one in a less metaphorical way. As the cook rushed him, he dropped the light, dodged behind the cart, grabbed its glass handle, and slammed it straight into the robot.

The impact dislodged the ice pick from the cook's claw. As it hit the tile floor, Harold wrenched the cart backward, then shoved it forward again, harder this time. He was trying to knock it over, but the 'bot had been designed for stability, bottom-heavy and with a low center of gravity. He was slowing it down, but he wasn't stopping it.

The situation was both dangerous and absurd. The cook would trundle forward, its arms swinging back and forth, and Harold would ram the cart into it. The 'bot would halt for a second, but as soon as he pulled the cart back, the machine would charge again, its claws missing his face by only a few inches. It might have been funny, but when Harold glanced over his shoulder, he saw in the shadowed illumination cast by the dropped flashlight that the cook was gradually backing him into a corner between a rack and a range grill. Dale was right: these things learned *fast*.

"Cindy! Get this friggin' thing off me!"

He didn't hear anything save for the incessant ticking, high-pitched whine of the 'bot's servos, and the loud clang of his cart ramming it again. A chocolate cake toppled off the wagon and was immediately pulverized by the cook's wheels. He had the wild hope that the icing would somehow screw it up, make it lose traction...

"Cindy...!" Damn it, had she abandoned him?

All at once, the robot's turret did a one-eighty turn, its lenses snapping away from him as its motion detectors picked up movement from somewhere behind it. In that instant, Cindy dashed out of the darkness, something raised in both hands above her head. The robot started to swivel around, then a cast iron skillet came down on its turret and smashed its lenses.

Nice shot. Although the robot could still hear them, it was effectively blinded. While its claw lashed back and forth, trying to connect with one of them, Cindy beat on it with the skillet while Harold continued to slam it with the dessert cart.

"Hit it, hit it!"

"Get the claws!"

"Go for the top, the top!"

So forth and so on, until one last blow from Cindy's skillet managed to skrag the CPU just beneath the upper turret. The LEDs went dark and the cook halted. The ticking stopped.

When Harold was sure that the cook was good and dead, he came out from behind the cart. Cindy was leaning against an island, breathing hard, skillet still clutched in her hand. She stared at him for a moment, then dropped the skillet. It hit the floor with a loud bang that echoed off the stainless steel surfaces around them.

"Thanks." Harold sagged against a counter. "Tough, ain't it?"

"Built to last." Her cotton tank-top was damp with sweat, the nipples of her twenty-two-year old breasts standing out. "You okay?"

"I'm good." Harold couldn't stop staring at her. "You?"

Cindy slowly nodded. She brushed back her damp hair, then looked up at him. Even in the wan glow of the dropped flashlight, she must have seen something in his eyes that she didn't like at all.

"Fine. Just great." She turned away from him. "C'mon. Let's get out of here."

Harold let out his breath. Looked like he wasn't going to get laid after all, even if it was the end of the world.

CINDY TRIED TO hide her irritation, but she was still quietly fuming when she and the other guy – what was his name? Harold? – returned to the atrium. She'd noticed the way he'd been watching her for the last couple of days, of course; men had been checking her out since she was fifteen, so she'd developed good radar for sexual attraction. Given the situation everyone was in, though, you'd think he'd have the common sense to put his impulses on hold. But for God's sake, they barely escape being killed, and what's the first thing he does? Stare at her tits.

Enough. Cindy had heard his dejected sigh as she picked up the carton of single-serving cereal boxes she'd found and left the kitchen. She couldn't have cared less.

By the time they reached the pool, though, she'd almost forgotten the incident. As soon as she and what's-his-name walked in, the kids were all over them, jumping up and down in their excitement to see what she'd found. Cindy couldn't help but smile as she carried the carton to the poolside terrace and put it down on a table. There were a half-dozen children among the refugees, the youngest a four-year-old boy and the oldest a twelve-year-old girl, and none of them seemed to mind that they didn't have any milk to go with the Cheerios and Frosted Flakes she handed out. Even kids can get tired of Spam and candy bars if that's all they've had to eat for three days.

Once they'd all received a box of cereal, Cindy took the rest to the cabana room she was sharing with Officer McCoy. She'd never thought that she'd welcome having a cop as a roommate, but Sharon was pretty cool; besides, sleeping in the same room as a police officer assured that she wouldn't be bothered by any horny middle-aged guys who'd holed up in the Wyatt-Centrum.

Sharon was dozing on one of the twin beds when Cindy came in. She'd taken off her uniform shirt and was sleeping in her sports bra, her belt with its holstered gun, taser, and baton at her side. She opened her eyes and watched as Cindy carefully closed the door behind her, making sure that she didn't accidentally knock aside the pillow they'd been using as a doorstop. With the power out and even the emergency generator offline, there was nothing to prevent the guest room doors from automatically locking if they closed all the way.

"Find some food?" Sharon asked.

"A little. Ready for dinner?"

Sharon sat up to peer into the carton put down beside her. "That all? Couldn't you find something else?"

"Sorry. Didn't have a chance to look." Cindy told her about the cook. Sharon's expression didn't change, but Cindy figured that cops were usually poker-faced when it came to that sort of thing. And she left out the part about what's-his-name. No point in complaining about that; they had worse things to worry about.

"Well… anyway, I'm glad you made it back alive." Sharon selected a box of Cheerios, but didn't immediately open it. One of the hand-held radios the cops had borrowed from the hotel lay on the desk; their own cell radios no longer worked, forcing them to use the older kind. Sharon picked it up and thumbed the TALK button. "Charlie Baker Two, Charlie Baker One. How's everything looking?"

A couple of seconds went by, then Officer Overby's voice came over. *"Charlie Baker Two. 10-24, all clear."*

"Ten-four. Will relieve you in fifteen minutes. Out." Sharon put down the radio, then nodded to the smartphone that lay on the dresser. "What's happening there? Any change?"

Cindy picked up her phone, ran her finger down its screen. The phone would become silent once the charge ran down, but there was still a little bit of red on the battery icon. She pressed the volume control, and once again they heard the only sound it made:

Tick... tick-tick... tick-tick-tick-tick... tick... tick-tick...

Like a cheap stopwatch that skipped seconds. That wasn't what she immediately noticed, though, but instead the mysterious number that appeared on its screen: 4,576,036,057, a figure that decreased by one with each tick.

For the last three days, Cindy's phone had done nothing else but tick irregularly and display a ten-digit number that changed every second or so. What these things signified, she had no clue, but everyone else's phones, pads, and laptops had been doing the same thing ever since the blackout.

It started the moment she was standing on the curb outside the airport, flagging down a cab while at the same time calling her friend in St. Paul to tell her that she'd arrived. That was when the phone suddenly went dead. Thinking that her call had been dropped, she'd pulled the phone from her ear, glanced at the screen... and heard the first weird ticks coming from it.

She was still staring at the numbers which had appeared on the LCD display when the cab that was about to pull up to the curb slammed into the back of a shuttle bus. A few seconds later, the pavement shook beneath her feet and she heard the rolling thunder of an incoming airliner crashing on the runway and exploding. That was how it all began...

Cindy glanced at her watch. Nearly 6 pm. Perhaps

the atrium would cool down a little once the mid-summer sun was no longer resting on the skylight windows. Unfortunately, the coming night would also mean that the robots would have an easier time tracking anyone still outside; their infrared vision worked better than their normal eyes, someone had explained to her. Probably Dale. He seemed to know a lot about such things.

Almost as if she'd read her mind, Sharon looked up from strapping on her belt. "Oh, by the way... Dale asked me to tell you that he'd like to see you."

Cindy was halfway to the bathroom; its door was closed against the stench of an unflushed toilet. She stopped and turned around. "Dale? Did he say why?"

"You said you're carrying a satphone, didn't you? He'd like to borrow it."

"Yeah, why not?" Cindy shrugged. "We won't get anyone with it. I've already tried to call my folks in Boston."

"I told him that, but..." Sharon finished buttoning her shirt. "C'mon. I'd like to see what he's got in mind."

Dale's cabana was on the other side of the pool. Like Cindy, he was rooming with a cop: Karl Overby, Sharon's partner. In his case, though, it was a matter of insistence. Cindy didn't know much about him other than that he worked for some federal agency, he knew a lot about computers, and his job was important enough that he requested – demanded, really – that he stay with a police officer. Dale was pleasant enough – he faintly resembled Cindy's old high school math teacher, whom she'd liked – but he'd been keeping a certain distance from everyone else in the hotel.

"Cindy, hi." Dale looked up from the laptop on his desk when she knocked on the room's half-open door. "Thanks for coming over. I've got a favor to ask. Do you...?"

"Have a satphone? Sure." It was in the backpack Cindy had carried with her on the plane. She'd flown to Minneapolis to hook up with an old college roommate for a camping trip in the lakes region, where cell coverage was spotty and it wasn't smart to be out in the woods with no way to contact anyone. "Not that it's going to do you any good."

Dale didn't seem to hear the last. "So long as its battery isn't dead –" a questioning look; Cindy shook her head "– I might be able to hook it up to my laptop through their serial ports. Maybe I can get through to someone."

"I don't know how." Sharon leaned against the door. "Internet's gone down. My partner and I found that out when we tried to use our cruiser laptop." She nodded at the digits on Dale's laptop. "We just got that, same as everyone else."

"Yes, well..." Dale absently ran a hand through thinning brown hair. "The place I want to try is a little better protected than most."

"Where's that, sir? The Pentagon?" Sharon's demeanor changed; she was a cop again, wanting a straight answer to a straight question. "You showed us a Pentagon I.D. when you came over here from the airport. Is that where you work?"

"No. That's just a place I sometimes visit. My job is somewhere else." Dale hesitated, then he pulled his wallet from his back pocket. Opening it, he removed a laminated card and showed it to Sharon. "This is where I work."

Cindy caught a glimpse of the card. His photo was above his name, Dale F. Heinz, and at the top of the card was NATIONAL SECURITY AGENCY. She had only the vaguest idea of what that was, but Sharon was obviously impressed.

"Okay. You're NSA." Her voice was very quiet. "So maybe you know what's going on here."

"That's what I'd like find out. Tonight, once we've gone upstairs to a balcony room."

MINNEAPOLIS WAS DYING.

From the balcony of a concierge suite – the only tenth-floor room whose door wasn't locked – the city was a dark expanse silhouetted by random fires. No lights in the nearby industrial park, and the distant skyscrapers were nothing but black, lifeless shapes looming in the starless night. Sharon thought there ought to be the sirens of first-responders – police cruisers, fire trucks, ambulances – but she heard nothing other than an occasional gunshot. The airport was on the other side of the hotel, so she couldn't tell whether the jet which had crashed there was still ablaze. Probably not, and if its fire had spread from the runway to the hangars or terminals, those living in the Wyatt-Centrum would have known it by now; the hotel was only a mile away.

A muttered obscenity brought her back to the balcony. Dale was seated at a sofa end-table they'd dragged through the sliding door; his laptop lay open upon it, connected to Cindy's satphone. He'd hoped to get a clear uplink once he was outside, and a top floor balcony was the safest place to do this. And it appeared to have worked; gazing over his shoulder,

Sharon saw that the countdown had disappeared from the screen, to be replaced by the NSA seal.

"You got through." Cindy stood in the open doorway, holding a flashlight over Dale's computer. The satphone belonged to her, so she'd insisted on coming along. Sharon had, too, mainly because Dale might need protection. After the incident in the kitchen, there was no telling how many 'bots might still be active in the hotel, as yet undiscovered.

"I got there, yeah... but I'm not getting in. Look" Dale's fingers ran across the keyboard, and a row of asterisks appeared in the password bar. He tapped the ENTER key; a moment later, ACCESS DENIED appeared beneath the bar. "That was my backdoor password. It locked out my official one, too."

"At least you got through. That's got to count for something, right?"

Dale quietly gazed at the screen, absently rubbing his lower lip. "It does," he said at last, "but I don't like what it means."

He didn't say anything else for a moment or two. "Want to talk about it?" Sharon asked. "We've got a right to know, don't you think?"

Dale slowly let out his breath. "This isn't just any government website. It belongs to the Utah Data Center, the NSA's electronic surveillance facility in Bluffdale, Utah." He glanced up at Sharon. "Ever heard of it?"

"Isn't that the place where they bug everyone's phone?"

"That's one way of putting it, yeah. Bluffdale does more than that, though... a lot more. They're tapped into the entire global information grid. Not just phone calls... every piece of email, every download, every data search, every bank transaction. Anything that's transmitted or travels down a wire gets filtered through this place."

"You gotta be kidding." Harold appeared in the doorway behind Cindy, apparently having found the restroom he'd been searching for. He'd tagged along as well, saying that Sharon might need help if they ran into any more 'bots. Sharon knew that this was just an excuse to attach himself to Cindy, but didn't say anything. Her roommate knew how to keep away from a wolf... and indeed, she left the doorway and squeezed in beside Dale, maintaining a discrete distance from the annoying salesman.

"Not at all. There's two and half acres of computers there with enough processing power to scan a yottabyte of information every second. That's like being able to read 500 quintillion pages."

Harold gave a low whistle. "All right, I understand," Sharon said. "But what does that have to do with us?"

The legs of Dale's chair scraped against concrete as he turned half-around to face her and the others. "Look... something has shut down the entire electronic infrastructure, right? Electricity, cars, phones, planes, computers, robots... everything networked to the grid was knocked down three days ago. And then, almost immediately after that, every part connected to the system that's mobile and capable of acting independently... namely, the robots... came back online, but now with only one single purpose. Kill any human they encounter."

"Give me another headline," Harold said drily. "I think I might have missed the news."

"Hush." Cindy glared at him and he shut up.

"The only other things that still function are networked electronics like smartphones and laptops... stuff that runs on batteries. But they don't do anything except display a number and make a ticking sound just like the robots do. And that number seems to decrease by one every time there's a tick."

"Yeah, I noticed that, too," Cindy said. "It began the moment my cell phone dropped out."

Dale gave her a sharp look. "You were on the phone when the blackout happened?" Cindy nodded. "Do you happen to remember what the number was when it first appeared on your phone screen?"

"Sort of... it was seven billion and something."

"About seven and half billion, would you say?" Dale asked. She nodded again, and he hissed beneath his breath. "That's what I thought it might be."

"What are you getting at?" Sharon asked, although she had a bad feeling that she already knew.

"The global population is approximately seven and a half billion." Dale's voice was very low. "At least, that's about how many people were alive on Earth three days ago."

Sharon felt a cold snake slither into the pit of her stomach. A stunned silence settled upon the group. Her ears picked up a low purring sound from somewhere in the distance, but it was drowned out when both Cindy and Harold started speaking at once.

"But... but why...?"

"What the hell are you...?"

"I don't know!" Dale threw up his hands in exasperation. "I can only guess. But –" he nodded toward the laptop "– the fact that the most secure computer system in the world is still active but not letting anyone in tells me something. This isn't a cyberattack, and I don't think a hacker or terrorist group is behind it either." He hesitated. "I think... I think it may have come out of Bluffdale."

Sharon stared at him. "Are you saying the NSA did this?"

"No... I'm saying the NSA's computers might have done this." Dale shook his head. "They always said the day might come when the electronic world became self-aware, started making decisions on its own. Maybe that's what happening here, with Bluffdale as the source."

The purring sound had become a low buzz. Sharon ignored it. "But why would it start killing people? What would that accomplish?"

"Maybe it's decided that seven and a half billion people are too many and the time has come to pare down the population to more... well, more sustainable numbers." Dale shrugged. "It took most of human history for the world to have just one billion people, but just another two hundred years for there to be six billion, and only thirty after that for it to rise to seven and a half billion. We gave Bluffdale the power to interface with nearly everything on planet, and a mandate to protect national security. Maybe it's decided that the only certain way to do is to..."

"What's that noise?" Harold asked.

The buzzing had become louder. Even as Sharon turned to see where the sound was coming from, she'd finally recognized it for what it was. A police drone, the civilian version of the airborne military robots used in Central America and the Middle East. She'd become so used to seeing them making low-altitude surveillance sweeps of Minneapolis's more crime-ridden neighborhoods that she had disregarded the sound of its push-prop engine.

That was a mistake.

For a moment or two, she saw nothing. Then she caught a glimpse of firelight reflecting off the drone's bulbous nose and low-swept wings. It was just a few hundred feet away and heading straight for the balcony.

"Down!" she shouted, and then she threw herself headfirst toward the door. Harold was in her way. She tackled him like a linebacker and hurled him to the floor. "Get outta there!" she yelled over her shoulder as they scrambled for cover.

They'd barely managed to dive behind a couch when the drone slammed into the hotel.

AFTERWARDS, HAROLD RECKONED he was lucky to be alive. Not just because Officer McCoy had thrown him through the balcony door, but also because the drone's hydrogen cell was almost depleted when it made its kamikaze attack. So there hadn't been an explosion which might have killed both of them, nor a fire that would have inevitably swept through the Wyatt-Centrum.

But Cindy was dead, and so was Dale. The cop's warning hadn't come in time; the drone killed them before they could get off the balcony. He later wondered if it had simply been random chance that its infrared night vision had picked up four human figures and homed in on them, or if the Bluffdale computer had backtracked the satphone link from Dale's laptop and dispatched the police drone to liquidate a possible threat. He'd never know, and it probably didn't matter anyway.

Harold didn't know Dale very well, but he missed Cindy more than he thought he would. He came to realize that his attraction to her hadn't been purely sexual; he'd liked her, period. He wondered if his wife was still alive, and reflected on the fact that he'd only been three hours from home when his car went dead on a side street near the hotel. He regretted all the times he'd cheated on her when he'd been on the road, and swore to himself that, if he lived through this and she did, too, he'd never again pick up another woman.

The drone attack was the last exciting thing to happen to him or anyone else in the hotel for the next couple of days. They loafed around the atrium pool like vacationers who didn't want to go home, scavenging more food from the kitchen and going upstairs to break into vending machines, drinking bottled water, getting drunk on booze stolen from the bar. Harold slept a lot, as did the others, and joined poker games when he was awake. He volunteered for a four-hour shift at the lobby barricades, keeping a sharp eye out for roaming robots. He saw nothing through the peep-holes in the plywood boards except a few stray dogs and some guy pushing a shopping cart loaded with stuff he'd probably looted from somewhere.

Five days after the blackout, nearly all the phones, pads, and laptop computers in the hotel were dead, their batteries and power packs drained. But then

Officer McCoy, searching Cindy's backpack for an address book she could use to notify the late girl's parents, discovered another handy piece of high-tech camping equipment: a photovoltaic battery charger. Cindy had also left behind her phone; it hadn't been used since her death, so its battery still retained a whisker of power. Officer McCoy hooked the phone up to the recharger and placed them on a table in the atrium, and before long they had an active cell phone.

Its screen remained unchanged, except that the number was much lower than it had been two days ago. It continued to tick, yet the sound was increasingly sporadic; sometimes as much as a minute would go by between one tick and the next. By the end of the fifth day, a few people removed some boards and cautiously ventured outside. They saw little, and heard almost nothing; the world had become quieter and much less crowded.

Although Harold decided to remain at the Wyatt-Centrum until he was positive that it was safe to leave, the cops decided that their presence was no longer necessary. The hotel's refugees could fend for themselves, and the city needed all the cops it could get. Before Officer McCoy left, though, she gave him Cindy's phone so he could keep track of its ticking, slowly decreasing number.

In the dark hours just before dawn of the sixth day, Harold was awakened by light hitting his eyes. At first he thought it was morning sun coming in through the skylight, but then he opened his eyes and saw that the bedside table lamp was lit. An instant later, the wall TV came on; it showed nothing but fuzz, but nonetheless it was working.

The power had returned. Astonished, he rolled over and reached for Cindy's cellphone. It no longer ticked, yet its screen continued to display a number, frozen and unchanging:

1,000,000,000.

BEFORE HOPE

KIM LAKIN-SMITH

Kim Lakin-Smith's dark fantasy and science fiction stories have appeared in numerous magazines and anthologies including Black Static, Interzone, Celebration, Myth-Understandings, Further Conflicts, Pandemonium: Stories of the Apocalypse, The Mammoth Book of Ghost Stories By Women, *and others, with "Johnny and Emmie-Lou Get Married" shortlisted for the BSFA short story award in 2009. She is the author of the gothic fantasy* Tourniquet: Tales from the Renegade City, *the YA novella* Queen Rat, *and the novel* Cyber Circus, *which was shortlisted for both the 2012 BSFA Best Novel Award and the British Fantasy Award in the same category.*

THE LIGHT RACK flicked from green to red. Lu De Lun felt a small judder as the lock rods sealed against the tank of the Eighteen Wheeler, pinioning the craft inside the parking bay. He punched the six engine stabiliser buttons into neutral, unharnessed himself from the driver seat and stood up.

Stretching his legs, he felt his knees crack and his ankles pop as he took turns to circle his feet and bring back the circulation. Even inside the K01-461 planetary system, the satellites and 18 planets were millions of kilometres apart. A driver had to enjoy a life spent behind the wheel. Which was why the long haul business only suited loners and fugitives. Although, as Lu knew from his 21 years as a trucker, the latter never lasted long given that the Fuel Prospectors they did business with liked to supplement their income with the fat bounties offered by the People's Armed Police. But Lu was happiest riding out among the stardust, the red dwarf that sustained the solar system an ever present reminder of Something Bigger. Bigger than him. Bigger than the PAP with their guns and Absolute Law. Bigger than the Fuel Prospectors and their corrupt management of the decaying planet he'd just landed on.

Right at that instant though, Lu was less concerned with the rights and wrongs of life outside the hangar than he was with filling his stomach and getting some fresh air.

OF COURSE, THE notion of 'fresh' air was a misnomer on Twelve, as K01-461-12 was generally known. Having stripped down to a mandarin vest and gone with lightweight combats, Lu was still unprepared for the searing temperature inside the domed market of Man Fu. He was instantly soaked in sweat and badly in need of a drink.

"How much?" he asked a passing Kool-Aid vendor.

The man stopped and lifted the top container off a haphazard stack on board the cart.

"Five newyen."

Lu dug around in a side pocket and handed over the coins. The man picked up one of the metal beakers that hung off the sides of the cart and filled it with garish yellow liquid. Lu drained the cup.

"Labour Hall open today?"

"Yes, sah. I can take you there. Fifteen newyen. Good price." The vendor peeled back his lips, revealing one good tooth.

"No thanks. I know the way."

Leaving the Kool-Aid vendor, Lu set off through the market. The outermost circumference of the dome was given over to food stalls – those pockets of death for a multitude of live vermin stacked high in cages. The cat meat stall offered an array of flambéed carcasses. Old women in folk tunics and headscarves sat behind tiny mountains of spices. It always amazed Lu that, despite the great girdered structure overhead, the ground inside Man Fu was still a sodden mess. A cockroach burst beneath his boot. The sticky air clung to his lungs.

Stepping over a pool of slurry, Lu found a sync screen thrust in front of his face.

"Credentials," barked the officer holding the tablet. The regulation PAP visor made the man appear more cyborg than human. Lu suspected that was by design.

A second officer kept a hand on the gun strapped across his body, a black keratin-shelled automatic. Standard issue.

"Lu De Lun. Afro-Caribbean Asian male. Age 43. Employment: Fuel Transportation." He reeled off his own data while inputting his signature code to the sync screen and scanning the birth bar at his wrist.

"Specialist or Independent?"

A Specialist transported one type of geofuel and was in the pockets of the corresponding Fuel Prospector. Often as not, they acted as middle men between the PAP and the Prospectors, adding another layer of corruption to Twelve's feudal monopoly. Independents, on the other hand, paid fealty to no single Prospector or crop type.

Begrudgingly, Lu admitted, "Independent." *Now came the wack bureaucracy and timewasting.*

"We're going to need some more details," said the sync screen waver.

"All the necessary licences are there, linked to my signature code." Lu flashed a sour smile.

"Of course," said the officer tightly. His partner stroked the automatic. "But there are still the quotas. There's plenty of chicken waste to load. I'd strongly recommend you make your way to the slurry vats."

"Of course," Lu mimicked. Stinking chicken waste, worth half the value of other loads like pokeberry, potato or citrus peel. He knew that he needed to get shot of the officers before they forced him to preregister for a chicken waste load via the sync screen.

"I don't suppose you gentlemen could direct me to the magistrate's quarters?" He took a clip of dollar notes out of his back pocket and held it up. "I need to make a deposit of fifty US dollars."

While unable to see the officers' expressions, he knew they understood the bribe well enough.

The first officer plucked the clip from his fingers. "We will see the magistrate gets your deposit."

Lu waited. The men had accepted his bribe, but

PAP officers could be bastards and they might opt to harass him anyway.

In the end, it was the Robot Arena which came to his rescue. Standing fifty metres or so outside its wire perimeter, Lu could see the upper halves of the crop giants over the heads of the crowd. Most were the usual models – 9Z4s, P99Ps, couple of borers. The huge steel mechanisms were designed to withstand the ravages of Twelve's geothermic landscape. But some lucky vendor had a new model on display: a Titan SLS. The crowd had thickened around it. Apparently the two officers were keen to take a closer look too.

"Go on now." The officer pocketed the money clip. With a swipe of a hand, the sync screen went blank. Both men moved off, their visors turned towards the Titan.

Taking care to keep his distance, Lu joined the crowd at the opposite side of the arena. The older models of crop giants oozed smoke from the seals of their feed hatches. The stench was incredible; Lu was all too aware that the faeces of Prospectors and itinerant workers alike went into fuelling the things. The design of a crop giant was fundamentally basic. Lu knew how to repair one and how to take it apart. Colossal shears moved on pinioned arms. Bucket jaws delivered into thresher spools. Balls of revolving caterpillar tracks gave the robots their gliding motion. Mothers frightened naughty children with tales of crop giants abandoning the fields and acquiring a taste for blood.

Lu had never seen a robot like the Titan. The head was black and gridded like a compound eye; in fact, Lu suspected the design was precisely that – a grid of stereoscopic cameras delivering 3D images of an entire field of crops. If the older robots were spiders, the Titan was a king crab, its kin dangling from hooks at chop bars or hissing inside stock pots. Six huge, harvesting arms were multi-axis and reticulating, doubling up as legs. Sonar booms served as antenna. A central jaw sat in a cradle of synthetic sinew. Traction engines were bolted beneath, alongside a complex bowel of cabling. The entire system was powered by a Cyclops 84 chip – so declared the neon data screen above the robot. 'Titan is the first crop giant with surveillance mapping and a PAP-sanctioned weapons system.' Lu noted the gas guns at the pivoting midpoint of each arm.

"That will put the noses of the Yellow Scarves out of joint," remarked a man next to him.

"I'm yet to meet a machine the rebels couldn't destroy," he replied. Too poor to leave Twelve, many families found themselves entirely dependent on the dire wages offered by the Fuel Prospectors. Thanks to the increasing utilisation of crop giants, the workers were being deprived of even that small source of revenue. The Yellow Scarves fought for survival, and Lu understood why. But could they really take down the likes of the Titan?

The man didn't share his faith. "If the Yellow Scarves don't take a shot to the belly from those guns, I reckon that machine can keep a grip on them until the PAP arrive." He smacked his heat-dried lips. "Then it'll be off to the Heat Zone for those they catch. Poor bastards." Rolling his rheumy eyes, he seemed to squat down inside the sorrow of the thought.

Lu moved on.

*　　*　　*

LABOUR HALL WAS packed with workers putting themselves up for sale. Lu squeezed past men, women and children, aware of their bony limbs, leathered skin, and the stench of desperation. He made his way up the sweaty iron stairs to the hiring platform. Taking a numbered bat from a nearby table, he joined the twenty or so foremen on the platform. Each held the fates of those below in their grasp; raise a baton to indicate a job offer, keep it lowered to opt out.

Lu scanned the crowd. He saw scores of faces and skins of every shade. China might have originally colonised Twelve fifty years earlier, but rubber stamped work visas and the promise of good wages had attracted a 10% US contingent. Finding the planet's geothermal activity too unstable, China had pulled out. That was 23 years ago. Now the Fuel Prospectors lorded over their volcanic real estate and the workers were forced into the Labour Hall.

A ramp led up to the hiring platform and another led down. The workers took turns to file past the foremen. The hour was allotted to 'Unskilled Labour'; a neon sign ticker taping around the circumference of the hall declared as much.

Poverty was the true equaliser, Lu concluded, watching the procession with his arms folded and a knot between his eyebrows. The younger men and women had the advantage when it came to attracting a foreman's eye. Those who were elderly or in any way disabled did not attract a bid.

When the tickertape switched to 'Apprentices', the age of those in line dropped considerably. So did the number of potential employers. Lu joined four other men on the viewing step. He wasn't entirely welcome in their company.

"You don't need to train a kid to join the long haul," spat one out the side of his mouth.

"Maybe he needs an apprentice to clean the ship's toilet? Is that it, trucker?" said a second.

"That's it." Lu concentrated on the children filing past. He needed a strong one. Own teeth wouldn't hurt either. And then there were the eyes. His father had once remarked on the grit contained within a man's eyes. "Look for the soul beyond the sadness," he told him. "Those are the ones we can trust with our secrets."

"Come on, come on," he muttered.

"Eager to be on your way again, huh? I do not blame you," said the man to his right. Guy in his fifties, Lu guessed. Big old boots that belonged on a soldier. Neatly darned tunic to his knees.

"No one should have to live out their days in this stink hole, least of all the young." He nodded at the girls and boys so desperate to find a trade. "Me? I can only help one of them today." He raised his baton as a boy of twelve or so stepped forward. None of the foremen challenged his bid, not with so many youngsters to go around.

"I'm offering a three yearer in chicken waste," announced the man.

"Oh shit," said one of the mouthy foremen. The others shook their heads and laughed.

The kid didn't laugh. Instead he got the despairing look of someone who'd hoped for the best and heard the worst. But Lu knew the kid was in no position to argue or negotiate. The new apprentice and the man moved aside.

For the next half hour, Lu watched the children come and go. Some were taken on as apple pickers, mulch grain sifters, gas pump operators or kitchen staff. The majority went home wanting.

A small boy stepped forward, the sort with bones still soft enough to allow him to root around the engine of the Eighteen Wheeler. Lu was about to hold up his baton when he spotted the girl up next. She had black hair in a braid, crooked teeth in an over-wide mouth, and long, slim eyes. He put her at 15 – the maximum age for an apprentice.

When she took the boy's place, Lu raised his baton. The remaining foremen knocked elbows and he heard one whisper, "A girl on board a fuel ship?" and another, "If it's a whore he wanted, there's cheaper to be had at Pig Town."

If the girl was afraid of him, she didn't show it. Instead she met his gaze and held it.

"Two yearer hauling gas." Lu would have tried to sell the proposition if he thought she had any choice in the matter. As it stood, he didn't bother.

She nodded, even flashed her crooked smile. "Yes, sir."

Lu led her over to the PAP officer busy registering new vocations against workers' employment sheets on his sync screen. At his back, the foremen offered a few crude comments then forgot them.

The officer scanned the birth code at the girl's wrist.

"Pay rate?"

"Bed and board."

Lu looked at the girl for a reaction. Surely she'd expect some kind of wage. Her expression didn't change though.

In minutes, she had signed away the next two years of her life for an apprenticeship on board the Eighteen

Wheeler. She followed as Lu led the way back down the stairs and through the crowd, all the while praying he'd made the right choice.

THE GIRL'S NAME was Hope Turner. She thought she was 15, but couldn't be sure having lost her mother and siblings to cholera several years earlier and with a father too busy lugging potato sacks at the local farm to count birthdays. Lu didn't care. He just wanted someone to grease the engine of the Eighteen Wheeler, hook up the hoses for liquid fuel, scrub the dry bay to keep it clear of fungus, and otherwise stay out of his business. At least to start with.

So far Hope was turning out to be a good choice of apprentice. Her reaction on seeing the Eighteen Wheeler up close in the hangar was genuine awe.

"She's a dark horse, but there's value in that," he explained. "Keeps nosy children and parts pirates at bay. Fast too. We can make the trip between here and K01-461-13 in a week."

"I've never seen a land shuttle up close. Has it got a name?" she asked in her strong provincial accent.

"Eighteen Wheeler. I don't like to complicate things."

The girl had nodded, the huge craft reflecting in her pupils.

They'd left Man Fu that afternoon, driving at first and then taking to the sky to pass over beet farms and vast golden stretches of wheat. The vegetation was hardy fuel stock, tough as a sun-dried rat's carcass and able to withstand the harsh conditions. Hope had sat alongside him in the co-driver seat, absorbing everything.

"Everything looks so different from up here," she told him. "The world looks alive."

"Not rotting to pieces." Hands steady on the wheel, he glanced over at her. "The farms are no different to embroidering a rotten bandage. Sooner or later the fabric will tear and the crud will pour out."

THEY ARRIVED IN Pig Town early that evening. K01-461, the Scarlet Star, pulsed at the horizon. The Heat Zone was just visible to the west – five hundred kilometres of the planet's most active geothermics. The area was home to geysers, boiling springs, mudflats and fumaroles. With magma flowing so close to the surface and subject to colossal pressures, the water achieved a boiling point of 300°C, meaning the zone was perfect for cultivating algae – another source of fuel. It was also where convicts laboured in the carbon dioxide rich atmosphere and treacherous working conditions.

"I can't believe I'm back in Pig Town." Hope nodded towards the open sewer running the length of the main street. "Thought I'd escaped that stench."

"You walked to Man Fu?"

The girl shrugged. "Walked some, hitched a lift with a market truck couple of times." She pointed at her bare feet. "My father says I have my mother's feet. Small enough to attract a husband. Broad enough to carry life's woes."

Lu surveyed the shanty huts and makeshift chop bars, the chicken-shit peppered paths in-between. "I've got business here. You can stay with me or pay your father a visit. Your choice."

Hope jutted her chin. "My father would be ashamed to see me home so soon. I would prefer to stay and begin to learn my trade. That is, after all, the reason you took me on."

She showed her crooked teeth. Lu grunted.

"Come on then. You can help me choose a present for someone."

In Man Fu, the very visible presence of the PAP kept any reminders of the resistance at a minimum. But out among the villages, people were braver. Every so often he'd spot graffiti on the dung brick walls – the tag of the resistance – or 'Death to the Dark Greens': a reference to the PAP's olive coloured uniforms.

It took guts to go up against the authorities in such a direct way. Those who were caught earned a one way ticket to the Heat Zone. But that didn't stop people – some whispered their support for the rebels, some daubed walls with graffiti, and some took action.

"What kind of a present are you looking for?" asked Hope, fingering the strings of beads that hung off a hook at one end of the stall. "My mother always said to give the gift of colour. Red for good fortune, yellow for freedom from life's cares, green for health and harmony. Never white – the mourning shade."

"You like the beads, huh?" Lu examined some boxes of chopsticks. They were crudely made, no doubt deliberately to appeal to the pockets of Pig Town's inhabitants.

"I do," Hope murmured. "The reds and gold remind me of my mother. Hair the colour of corn oil, lips red as poppy heads."

Lu thought about his own mother. Strong as an ox. Spine soldier straight so that she faced the world head on.

"I want something bigger," he told Hope. "The farm we're going to visit is extremely large. Mister Gun Mao Rong is a powerful man."

"A Prospector?" Hope's upper lip curled.

"Yes, a Prospector." Lu picked up a cigarette case made of monkey wood. A silhouette of the Scarlet Star was carved into the lid.

Hope spat onto the ground. Lu ignored her and looked for the stall's owner. He found him round the back, crouched on a low stool between bundles of low grade reflector cloth. The man was old as the soot hills judging by his appearance. Face set in a thousand wrinkles. Eyes turned milky by cataracts. He sat on his stool, smacking his lips as he whittled a new set of chopsticks.

"Hello, Father Time."

The man grunted at the colloquial greeting.

"Hello, Buckrabbit."

"I need to buy a present for an important man. What can you recommend?"

The man picked up a walking cane that was resting against the fabric bales. He poked the end of it at a wooden box towards the back of the stall.

"Every man likes a music box. Rich are no different to the poor. I spent six months carving the thing. It's made of blackwood. Open it." He redirected his cane to Hope. "Go on now. Open it."

The girl did as instructed. With the lid raised, music started to play. Tinny yet pretty, it was a classic melody Lu had heard many times from the plucked strings of a qin.

"Bring it here, Hope." The man bared his gums.

She carried the box over, its tune mingling with the sounds of street children playing nearby and the wail of a baby coming from one of the tin shacks.

"You know my name?" Her brow knitted.

"Pig Town's not so big."

Hope handed the box to Lu. He could see that it was well-made with elegant wooden hinges and an interior lined with preserved moss. Weighty too.

"Price?"

"500 newyen."

Hope took a sharp intake of breath. The cost was astronomical compared to the sums she was used to in Pig Town.

Her eyes widened further when Lu said, "For this? 900 is closer to the value."

"That is too much," said the man quietly. "Too much."

"Yes, 900." Lu produced a money clip from a side pocket. It was bigger than the one he had given the officers in Man Fu. He peeled off the notes and pressed them into the man's hands.

"It's not worth that much," Hope tried to argue. Lu raised his hand sharply and she fell silent.

The man fed the notes into the top of his tunic. Lu turned to leave when the man said, "No news for me, Buckrabbit?"

Lu put his hands on his hips and sighed. "Man Fu is as ugly as ever. The crop failures around Pig Town haven't garnered much sympathy from the law makers. For now, there is not enough fuel to be loaded around here for an Independent to make a living."

"So you will be heading for pastures new for the time being." The man nodded a little sadly. Lu kept his chin high.

As he strode away with Hope in tow, the old man called after them, "Take the girl to see the safflowers growing out at the cemetery. May be the last chance you have."

THE CEMETERY WAS carpeted with safflowers, token survivors of one of the first oil crops artificially seeded across Twelve. Having originally thrived in the arid conditions, the crop had become infected by a rogue fungal disease brought in with a shipment of rapeseed. As the sight of the spiky yellow flower heads became rarer, so the workers came to see them as a symbol of their personal fight for survival. The wilted heads were steeped in water and distilled into a lemony pigment – the dye favoured by the rebels. Safflowers had also been his mother's favourite.

The girl was at the far end of the field, praying at her family's graves. Lu surveyed the rows of tombstones – small markers carved with individuals' signature codes. He turned his back on the grand sweep of the dead.

In front of him was an area fenced off from the rest with barbed wire. The safflowers were the only obvious inhabitants of the area. In accordance with Absolute Law, there were no carved markers, no shrines, and no gifts left for the spirits.

Lu knelt down besides the barbed wire. He plucked one of the flower heads and crushed it inside his palm. He prayed for worlds, for Hope, and for his ancestors.

"You have a relative among the Unmarked?"

Lu got to his feet, brushing the remains of the flower off his hands. The girl stood a respectful distance behind him. She'd been crying; he recognised the tell-tale gloss in her eyes.

"My mother," he told her, a break in his voice.

She bowed her head. "I'm sorry. The way PAP treat the people sentenced to work in the Heat Zone is awful. Everyone has a right to a headstone."

"Even convicts?"

She hugged the music box she carried and sucked her bottom lip. "Depends on the crime."

"Indeed." They'd both loved and lost, thought Lu. The true crime on Twelve was that of a nation trapped in servitude. "You and me are the fortunate ones," he told his apprentice. "We have the means to fly away."

THEY ATE DIM sum at a chop bar then retired to the Eighteen Wheeler for the night. Lu slept on the bunk to the rear of the cabin. Hope reclined the co-driver seat and curled in on herself. The next morning, Lu used a small gas stove to brew tea and cook up a sharing bowl of wheat noodles layered with pig fat. The addition of spices came from his Jamaican ancestry.

By 11.00am, they had flown the 2000 kilometres to the area known as the Money Fields. Below were great expanses of rapeseed, field penny-cress, flax, and soybean, as well as sprawling orchards of apple and citrus fruit trees. The grand estate belonged to Mister Gun Mao Rong, a man with enough power to have Titan SLS prototypes already at work in his fields.

"Look at those things!" Hope had her face pressed to the windscreen. Her breath misted the glass. "What if they go wrong and don't see the difference between harvesting plants and humans?" she asked in a child-like way which made Lu smile.

Hope wasn't smiling, though. "What if the jaws never stop eating and before we know it, the planet is deserted except for two of those machines charging head on at each other?"

"Then technological advancement will eat itself and we, its creators, will be dust on the wind." Lu winked at his apprentice. "Now buckle up. I'm taking us down."

THEY LEFT THE Eighteen Wheeler parked in an immaculately maintained hangar alongside a number of work vehicles – one man crop sprayers known as 'dragonflies' and churners with their giant revolving cylinders that processed plant fibre on the move. High end transportation craft lined the right-hand side of the hangar. One had recently docked and Lu and the girl watched the side door curve aside and a silver walkway unfold. Staff emerged, the women dressed in figure-hugging, red silk cheongsams, the men in black tunic suits. A woman emerged, terribly and deliberately thin. Her clothing was tailored, her glossy black hair scraped back. Lu noticed Hope's expression: a mix of anger and awe.

"There'll come a day when one of the Titans mistakes her for a blade of grass." He pressed his hands together and mimicked the snapping motion of the robot's jaw until Hope showed her crooked teeth.

* * *

LU HAD WORKED many long years to establish himself as one of the fastest, most reliable fuel transporters to work the circuit. Consequently, he didn't deal with foremen. He took his business dealings direct to the Fuel Prospectors. Despite his wealth, Gun Mao Rong was no exception.

Hope appeared resistant to following him into the glittering mausoleum where the Prospector lived with his achingly thin wife and unseen children.

"If you are going to get to grips with this trade, you have to learn to ignore all *this*." By which he meant the opulent entrance hall with its silver grid-work underfoot and corridors and grand staircase leading off to numerable rooms.

The girl absorbed the idea, tough little hands folding over themselves. "I follow where you go."

They removed their shoes and Lu led her down one of the corridors on the ground floor. The temperature-controlled air was as welcome as it was disquieting. Staff materialised, almost as if from the walls. At his side, the girl took three steps to his every one. Lu could have sworn he heard her heartbeat.

At the end of the corridor they came out into a beautiful circular room. As Lu had discovered when he first visited the Prospector twenty years before, a man like Gun did not sit behind closed doors. He perched on a low bamboo stool, legs folded up under him. His hands were busy scrolling through projected data screens. He wore a v-neck white t-shirt and a sarong skirt, and possessed the casual good looks associated with considerable wealth.

Lu bowed. Hope followed his example. From his perch, Gun returned the courtesy.

"Lu De Lun. It is a pleasure to see you."

"The pleasure is mine, Gun." Lu knew the girl would be surprised by his use of the Prospector's first name; if she was to succeed in the fuel game, she would have to achieve the same level of connection.

He gestured to the box Hope carried. "Please do me the very great honour of accepting this gift."

Hope tiptoed forward. Lu was relieved when she presented Gun with the music box using both hands. Despite her rustic upbringing, she knew rudimentary etiquette.

Gun considered the box, nodding appreciatively. "It is exquisite, Lu. But I cannot accept."

"My apprentice selected it. Her first task and one in which she took great pride."

"I can see that." Gun smiled at Hope. "But such a beautiful gift is too much."

"It was carved with you in mind. There can be no other explanation for such splendour."

"I really must refuse."

"No, you really must accept."

There the game ended. Gun had refused three times and Lu had persisted. The Prospector put the box on his lap and opened the lid.

"Wonderful!" he cried as the tinkling melody filled the room. "Oh indeed, a gift I shall cherish." Taking in the girl's appearance – her coarse clothing and staring eyes – he cocked his head and said gently, "The kitchen is at the opposite end of the house. My man, Francis, will show you the way. You will find him directly outside this room. Ask the cook to give you a glass of soda." He switched focus to Lu. "I have a shipment of bioethanol that needs to be in K01-461-15 inside the month. Shall we talk terms?"

Lu had hoped the girl might be allowed to stay. She needed to experience the art of fuel negotiation. But he was not about to offend Gun by disagreeing.

"Go along now, Hope," he said.

"Hope?" Gun stuck out a hand. Again the girl proved aware of social niceties and used both hands to clasp Gun's. "A good name," he told her. "I look forward to conducting business with you, Hope."

"And I you," Hope replied, voice strong, back very straight.

Lu watched her leave the room, her soft tread at odds with the steel he had just witnessed.

THE WHEEL VIBRATED under his hands. Lu worked his way through the gears with the stick shift then pulled back on the thruster. The g-force hit him hard. With his spine moulded into the driver seat, Lu had to fight to keep his chin up as the Eighteen Wheeler left the ground and soared. A minute later, he levelled the craft out and the pressure eased.

Beside him, the girl released her grip on the co-driver seat harness. She wasn't used to take off yet, he saw that. But she would be soon.

"He was nice," said Hope, interrupting his thoughts.

"Who?"

"Mister Gun Mao Rong."

"Did you expect a monster?"

"I guess." The girl's forehead wrinkled. "It's just that there he is in that big house with all that money while the rest of us struggle even to breathe. And then he's just so *nice*."

Lu gave a tight smile. "A dilemma, isn't it?" Through the windscreen he saw Titans at work in the fields of blue, green and yellow. From this height, the robots looked like dung beetles.

"That's why the box was so beautifully carved. It was a genuine gift. But my father still hid an HPM unit in the base of the box and I still brought it from him." He sensed confusion washing over Hope and wondered if he should have trusted her with the facts sooner.

"My father and I cannot communicate openly. I have had to distance myself from the great unclean of Pig Town in order to be taken seriously as a Fuel Transporter. But I still try to help when I can." He glanced across at Hope. "You were right. 900 newyen was too much. But I wasn't really paying for the box. I was providing my father with money to live off."

"What are you telling me, Mister Lu?" She bit her bottom lip while Lu really hoped he hadn't made a mistake in his choice of apprentice. He needed someone who'd become as jaded with the system as he was. He needed a fellow soldier.

"What's an HPM unit?" she asked suddenly.

Lu liked that question. His lies were less important to her than the details of that deception.

"High-powered microwave weapon. The unit inside the music box emits bursts of electromagnetic energy. Harmless to humans but capable of burning out the circuitry of all crop giants within a 200 kilometre radius. To avoid detection, the transmission stops working after 24 hours. Enough time to do a farmstead damage but not long enough to arouse suspicion."

Hope stared out the windscreen. They were still flying over Gun's vast estate. It was difficult to tell from this altitude, but the Titans would already be grinding to a halt, their insides seizing. The build up of biogas in the algae-fed boilers would do the real damage. A design flaw would be cited as the cause of the problems, putting a dent in the seemingly impenetrable armour of the Titan SLS crop giant model.

"But what's the point? They'll only fix them or buy more," said Hope, voicing the same frustration in the pointlessness of it all that he had felt so often over the years.

"The point is quiet rebellion," he said carefully, as much to remind himself as explain to Hope. "We remind a Fuel Prospector like Gun that the machines taking the place of the human workers can go wrong and are nowhere near as cost effective. Just as importantly, we remind the PAP that we have a voice and their law is not absolute."

"You're a Yellow Scarf." Hope said it simply, without fanfare and apparently without fear.

"As was my mother before me."

It was enough. As he had hoped all along, he saw a look of complex pain and anger on Hope's face. Same one he'd seen reflected in the mirror every day since his mother paid for her commitment to freedom in the Heat Zone. Hope had lost her mother and siblings to poverty. Her father hadn't the strength to fight back. But she did.

"Quiet rebellion?" She appeared to mull over the idea. "A war without bloodshed."

"For now." Lu held her gaze.

The strength he'd witnessed in front of Gun returned. Hope sat up straight in the co-driver seat and tilted her chin to meet the glow of the Scarlet Star.

"Then that is one trade I am eager to learn," she said firmly.

Lu nodded. Suddenly he needed to be free of Twelve and its poisoned atmosphere. He wanted to be cocooned in the black velvet of outer space.

"I want to show you what you'll be fighting for," he told the girl, adding, "Hold on."

Lu drove the Eighteen Wheeler into a steep vertical trajectory.

THE SPIRES
OF GREME

KAY KENYON

Kay Kenyon's latest work is a sci-fantasy quartet. Book One, Bright of the Sky, *was one of* Publishers Weekly's *top books of the year. It is a free Kindle book. The series has twice been shortlisted for the American Library Association Reading List awards.* Writer's Digest *recently featured her fiction blog,* Writing the World, *at www.kaykenyon.com*

OUTSIDE THE SPIRE, the phages emerge from their cocoon. Everyone in the spire is watching from a window if they can fight their way to one; most of us have never seen phages hatch. The size of grown pigs, the sacs press against the birthing cocoon and then burst out, hovering among their siblings. They are waiting to catch a breeze to begin their drift through the forest, hunting.

Kammy, who is only twelve and has never seen these creatures before, pronounces, "They stink!"

I roll my eyes. The sensors pick up the smell, but all we get is numbers on the computer screens. Are numbers a smell? Depends on who you ask. Crow says that everything is a number, and I know what he means, but I still would like to stand outside on solid ground and smell the never-ending Forest of Greme, stink or not. I would like to open the sealed doors of the mini-decks and feel the forest breeze blow hard against me, feel the mist silver my face.

This is not going to happen. Not even when I cross over. They have a tube for crossing over.

My name is Sark Highspire, just for the record. I am fifteen years old, and the *bride select*. That's how come the crossing over. I'll go over to another spire and submit to the sexual domination of one of their males. Despite what my mother wants me to believe, I find the prospect grotesque.

As Highspire sails off, the phage bags follow in the trail of our tree ship. Maybe they're detecting the scent of our exhaust. As people see them bobbing along after us, they emit a collective moan of dismay. We are afraid of the phages, of course. They spit toxins, and if necessary, explode. But they'll lose interest after a few miles. With our chemical make-up, clean hydrogen drive and biomolecular imprint – we have pretty good camouflage. The forest can't detect us as a foreign body.

If it could, we'd be dead.

IT'S SIXTY-SIX steps up the central spiral to my cabin. I count them every time, an old habit from childhood. I loved numbers then, back when I thought I would go for science. Now I'm going for making babies. It's why Crow has given up on me. Why teach science to a bride elect? I want to answer: Because after I have my four babies, I'll be free to have a real job.

What kind of jobs does my new home have? I know nothing about the place where I'll spend the rest of life: Deepspire. Our library has only a few ancient references. Spires don't communicate by radio, of course. That's only for emergencies, and maybe not even then. Greme homes in on transmissions. It's like announcing "Here I am!" The way we'll meet up with Deepspire is that we have meeting points based on an established web of path lines. This was all decided long ago. Every spire has its own secret path. But every few years spires cross paths and share DNA. This time *I'm* the DNA.

Why are the web paths secret? Because we're hunted, and not just by phages. The forest may be smarter than we realize. In the old days, the virus that the ecofreaks released helped the remnant forests to join and spread. They say Greme now stretches from old Vermont all the way to the Long River. As it spread, it wiped out its enemies: people. Has the forest continued to evolve its defenses? Crow thinks so. But he's a bit strange. You'll see.

At the top of the spiral, I race around to the port side and nearly bash into Captain Harliss. He protects himself by putting his hands on my shoulders, as though I could do real damage to this big, balding slab of a man. "Well, Sark! The bride herself," he chuckles.

I try to pull away without meeting his eyes, but he holds on to me. He's getting rid of me because I'm Crow's ally, and one by one he's making sure Crow doesn't have any. Harliss thinks that science doesn't have a place on the spire; not during these hard times.

"I dropped off a present for your hope chest," he says.

My despair chest. But "Thanks for nothing," is all I can think of to say. I yank away and head down the corridor to the cabin I share with Branish. I'm mad at my mother for letting Captain Harliss send me to Deepspire, but I'm still eager to share the big phage bag sighting with her.

When I get to our cabin, outside the door I find Branish entwined with Ezzard Truespire. They are pressed against each other, his hands locked on her hips as he sucks on her face. Branish is a big, heavily endowed woman, and Ezzard is old and stringy. Imagine, if you can, a great cow being mounted by a ferret. That is what we have here. Mother sees me and pushes Ezzard away. As she adjusts her clothes, Ezzard ducks a bow at me. He's ridiculous: at least seventy years old. The whole scene is beyond ghastly.

As Ezzard slinks away, mother fans her face with her hand. This is supposed to mean that Ezzard has aroused her. I am going to be sick, and to make matters worse, she's not even embarrassed. I blurt that out.

"Why should I be ashamed? I'm not dead yet, Sarkila."

She waves me to follow her into our cabin, which I do, uncertain now whether I will share the phage sighting with her. When she turns around, I register with disgust the smeared lipstick, the eyeblack leaking into her creases. But then I notice the room has changed.

The wall that separates her cabin from mine. It's gone.

My look prompts her to say, "You don't need a cabin anymore." She smiles happily. "You're going to be *married!*" She spreads her arms. "Doesn't it look all roomy and open?"

I'm outraged and astonished. But in the end, I'm crying. "You couldn't even wait until I'm *gone*."

I turn and rush away as her voice trails after me: "Everything is such a *drama* with you!"

WE JOURNEY ON. Our spire floats through the forest, buoyed by grav annihilators. We cross a slow moving river, plowing a wave as we go. As Highspire sails into a region of heavy mist, through the window I see swags of hemlock creep by, branches stuffed with pine cones, bird nests, pollen and tufts of fog. It's all ghostly silent, muffled by the tough outer skin of the spire.

I lie in Dry Storeroom Number Three on the floor, near the tiny crack in the old outside deck door. Highspire is busy repairing. I can see the crystalline structure flaking together under the door, obeying its molecular engineering.

I wonder if the freaks from the old days would like what the forest has become. I know they'd like how successful the virus was in speeding up forest evolution, allowing it to protect itself. Once the first toxins emerged, the forests began to recover and thrive; people weren't welcome. Greme was becoming dangerous.

At first the ecofreaks attacked the science stations in what they called Green. (I think we call it Greme to spite them, but no one's sure.) They thought the researchers were trying to eradicate the virus, but it was much too late for that; scientists were just studying things. Humanity was dying, but science marched on. After a while the research stations had to become mobile, and finally, unattached to the ground (avoiding sensing roots). After the virus raged through the forests and farmlands, most people died from starvation, something the ecofreaks must have approved. They weren't afraid to die. You have to admire that.

What they wouldn't like is this: the spires have a refuge in the forest. Because when civilization went down, it went way down. Out there, all that's left of humanity are savages. They don't dare enter the forest, so it's a good thing Greme hates people. It protects us, like a shark protects the nursery fish that ride on its back.

When Crow finds me, I'm still lying on my side watching the crack fill up.

"Sark." He stands in the door, frowning, his black hair falling to his shoulders, his big nose a beak that gives him his nickname. "Why didn't you report the leak?"

I sit up. "It's not my job," I say because I'm hurt that he can't even say hello.

"I heard about your mother and Ezzard." He doesn't really look at me. Crow isn't great at the interpersonal. "You can sleep in the lab."

That's a relief. I'm never going back to her little love nest. A curl of outside air slides over my ankles. "We used to be interested in the forest," I muse. "Now we're just afraid of it."

Crow blinks at this. "I have a couple of blankets I could spare."

He looks out the window and chuckles at some Crow-thought, something complicated and ironic, no doubt. "We're just a germ to Greme. And what's worse? The *grasslands*. Grass is all interconnected." And as though I didn't know, he adds, "Under the ground." He slides a finger across his throat.

"Right," I say, getting to my feet. "We're a germ to the prairie, too."

"Amber waves of pain," he says, smirking. He turns away, muttering. "I'm going to eject Littlespire this morning, if you want to watch."

I follow him down the corridor to the lab. This is a bad day for Crow. Littlespire was his pet project, and the least I can do is bear witness.

In the lab, Andergeesen Farspire is sitting at the central console, his short legs propped up on the counter, picking at his hangnails. He's the science deck manager, if you can believe it.

"Goose," I say, nodding at him in passing. He glares in response to the hated nickname.

At the nutrient station, Crow explains that Littlespire is attached to the outside by only a few crystalline tubes, so once we set off the tiny charges, it will just fall to the forest floor. Captain Harliss has changed course so that Highspire will be moving in the right direction to avoid any collision against the lower decks.

Andergeesen saunters over. "All ready?" He wants to be the one to order the separation charges. He has nothing else to do, no science role. He's got the job Crow should have had.

Crow turns to the people watching from the other science stations. Everyone feels bad for him. "I would like to propose a toast," he says, holding up his cup of deadfall tea. He waits until all have raised their cups.

"To the triumph of mediocrity over discovery. To the victory of moronic fiscal cutbacks, when an eight-year science project is sacrificed for the captain's fancy new conference room." He raises his cup higher. "To the murder of Littlespire." He takes a furious gulp of tea, nearly choking on it.

This will all be reported to Captain Harliss. No one is supposed to mock or, in the captain's term, "suborn" the mission. What is the mission? Depends who you ask. Crow would say research. Captain Harliss would say survival. Me? I don't have a mission except to avoid being a bride.

"Sark, please throw the switch." Crow points with ominous flair to the lever.

"That's my job," Andergeesen snaps. He reaches in quickly before I can usurp his authority.

Everyone crowds around the starboard windows to see the pod fall. It's already one and a half decks high, so the crash should be impressive.

As Andergeesen cranks down the lever, the light on the console flickers but goes out.

"Shit," Crow says.

Andergeesen yanks the switch up and down once more. Nothing.

Somebody titters. Andergeesen swings around. "Who laughed?"

"God damned toxic luck," Crow mutters, ripping up the panel to look underneath. He wanted to make a political statement about ruin and murder, and all we've got is a tech malfunction.

"No cause to swear," Andergeesen says primly.

Crow slowly turns and burns a stare into him. "*Of course* there's every fucking reason to fucking swear, Goose. I had planned a *ceremony*."

The ejection had been on the docket for weeks. The scavenging has gone poorly all year; we've all suffered cutbacks. Let the bigger spires with more resources calve new spires. We can't afford to. But Crow thinks cancellation of Littlespire was directed against him personally. He'd already been admonished for poor performance in deadfall conversion – as though this was his fault! But the management types like Harliss and Goose hate the science types like Crow. It's always been that way, and now the captain is using hard times to consolidate his power.

Andergeesen waves his hand at the wall behind which the proto-spire is still attached. "Well," he says, stalking off, "eject it when the charges are ready. No more grandstanding."

A thought occurs to me. "Crow, maybe we *can't* jettison Littlespire."

He glares at me. "Might as well dump it. We haven't fed it for months. It's *dead*, Sark. It hangs on to us like a dead baby." Crow inspects the circuitry, muttering and swearing.

At the window, I can see the proto-spire, still attached. A sickly color, it appears to be sagging. Maybe it'll just fall off like a scab.

As Crow checks his computer programs, I see a stack of blankets under the console. There's a pillow on top.

I LOVE IT on the science deck at night. The computer screens throw an eerie light on the walls as screensavers kick on and off like dreaming thoughts. There's just enough room under Crow's main console so I can fully stretch out.

I'm almost asleep when I hear a pinging sound. At the next ping, I get up and squint at the console. I hear it again. It's coming from one of the screens. When I lean in, I see that someone has written a line. *Send me your pic.*

I stare at this a long while.

Another line: *Well?*

Who are you? I type.

Jonn is the answer.

He is answering in the fewest possible words, because Greme might hear. This insight comes to me like a needle in my flesh. This is from Deepspire.

I don't know how long I've been staring at the screen while I argue with myself. Then I adjust the screen to a good angle and peel off a shot of me staring into the little eye. I don't smile. I probably look grotesque with my hair uncombed and having forgotten to brush my teeth.

A moment later, a tiny picture shows up on the screen. His face is narrow, his eyes very black. Jonn, I figure. He's not exactly good-looking but he has a good chin. We must both be staring at each other. Maybe this is the night duty tech on Deepspire who figured out we're in range for a little forbidden communication.

I erase the picture and the lines we have exchanged. Despite not knowing for sure, I know who I'm hoping Jonn is. He's young and has a good chin. This is enormously comforting. *Not* that I'm going to let them marry me off. I still plan to get out of this. Somehow.

Restless, about 2 a.m. I move my blankets up to Dry Storeroom Number Three. With a full moon outside I watch the forest slide by, leaves glistening from a recent downpour. Then I see the forest floor hump up. It's an antibody surge. The wave moves quickly along, rumpling the seedlings, rocks and fallen logs in its path, until it passes from sight. This is twice in one day I've seen Greme on the hunt. I'm not sure this is a good sign, but I'm not afraid. You can spend your whole life being afraid, and end up missing it all.

AT THE SECOND Seating for lunch, Captain Harliss announces that the rendezvous with Deepspire will happen the day after tomorrow. Branish coos with delight, leading a round of applause. My despair chest is brought in as a surprise, and everyone has another little gift to shove in its maw.

I respond with stony silence.

Branish elbows me, whispering, "Be gracious, Sarkila. People gave things they couldn't *afford*."

"Thank you," I manage to say to the lunch crowd. "I know how much your sacrifices have cost you." Everyone thinks this is a touching thing to have said. Clapping ensues. Captain Harliss nods at me, but less friendly than he's been lately. Maybe he thinks I'm going to try a prank at the last minute, something that will embarrass him.

But I'm starting to think: What if I *like* Jonn? What if he's being forced into this too, and worries as much as I do? I've been watching the monitor at Crow's station every night until late, but he hasn't dared radio me again.

After lunch, Harliss comes up to me and Branish. He looks down at me with suspicion. Maybe he's wondering where my old fight is. Then he says, "I hope you're not nervous about crossing over. The tube has never broken."

"Maybe someone big and brave should test it, first," I say, holding his gaze.

"Sarkila!" Branish gasps. But I'm having fun imagining Harliss crawling through the tube, and then the whole thing sagging under his weight until it breaks and blurps him onto the forest floor. Cue the phage bags.

A frown cuts into the captain's broad forehead. I walk away, satisfied that I have lived up to – what does Branish call it? – my *snotty* reputation.

WHO AM I trying to fool? I'm terrified.

Deepspire will intersect our path tomorrow at 3:00 p.m. Branish and her friend Penley have made a white dress for me with lace at the throat and gauzy bunting caught up with bows. It's lying right now on my despair chest like a dead body. To avoid open warfare, I've told Branish I'll wear it, but of course it's too grotesque to even consider.

This afternoon when Crow and others from the science deck are at Third Seating, I send a message from the computer, using the frequency from the first message: *What are you like?* I don't even care if the techs on Deepspire intercept it.

Meanwhile I brood. How did Jonn know I was at the station that night he asked for my picture? Come to think of it, that was the night that Crow invited me to sleep here.

Crow.

He *planned* for me to have a message. My heart crimps a little as I think about how sweet this was. Crow is a little crazy, but what he did, that was really nice. He wasn't always so odd. Before the hard times, we used to have fun working on science projects, and he seemed almost happy. He was headed to become science deck chief, and we were going to launch some new inquiries into Greme antibody responses. He hasn't weathered the downturn very well. And he still had time to worry about me. I'm humbled.

A ping. I watch the few techs left at their science stations and shuffle closer to the screen so no one will see.

I won the marathon spiral stair climb. We better not talk. See you tomorrow, Sark.

He knows my name! That settles it. Crow has been talking to Jonn.

At a sound behind me, I turn. Crow stands there. He reaches past me and looks at the screen, nodding. Then he turns the screen off. "Storeroom three," he murmurs. "Ten minutes."

We meet as the sun is setting, and the storeroom has only a murky light from the window. "Thanks..." I begin, but Crow cuts me off.

"We can't be seen together." He takes my elbow and steers me behind some crates. "There isn't much time. If Andergeesen reports us, it's all over."

My spirits spike with hope. "Have you figured out a way to get me out of this?"

Crow looks at me sideways, kind of like, well, a crow. "Yes and no. No, because you need to go with Jonn. That's a given. I hope you like him better?" He doesn't wait for an answer. "But yes, you don't have to go to Deepspire."

"Jonn is coming *here*?" The thought is wildly exciting. I could stay with Crow, get my own cabin, stay in the spire I know so well...

"No. You're going to *Littlespire*. Jonn's already agreed. It can hold two right now."

"But Littlespire's dead!"

Crow looks toward the door that he can see through a crack between the crates. "I've been feeding it."

I'm just trying to keep up with all this. The charges that wouldn't work! Crow made it look like a malfunction. And feeding it. He must have been falsifying the outputs for months, diverting nutrients to Littlespire. I look at him in amazement. That was quite a show he put on at the ejection ceremony. My heart is jumping up and down in my chest. But how can I live on Littlespire? And they won't let us! Harliss will be in a rage. It's impossible. Besides, from the windows it looked all blistered and soggy. I say as much.

Crow smirks. He engineered a droopy look to the outside. "Sark," he whispers, "look at me."

I do, and the crazed, confused face that I've grown used to is totally different. Crow is paying attention, steady and confident. Has this been the real Crow all along?

He's speaking fast and low. "We don't have a future in Greme. The forest is getting smarter. It's started an accelerated decomposition process on the deadfall. That's why our extraction rates have been going down. Of course we're dependent on what falls to the forest floor, since we can't harvest the living Greme. But there's not enough to sustain us, not anymore." He lets this statement sink in. I realize the horrible truth: we're not just suffering hard days. We're at the end of days.

"Time to leave, Sark."

"But to go *where*?"

A genuine grimace. "I don't know. That's for you to decide."

"But I don't know anything about it! I don't know what's out there!"

"Nobody does. But you'll have Littlespire. You can look. Jonn's got some ideas."

"The grasslands?"

"No. Remember what I told you about grass."

It communicates underground. "Crow," I say, my voice rising, "I don't know if I can do this."

He puts a gentle hand over my mouth. "I know you don't know. But let me ask you one question." The hand comes down, as he sees I'm settling. "Are you afraid? Does the idea of taking off in Littlespire with a young man who's as disgusted with spire life as you are, does this excite you or scare you? Answer truthfully."

I lick my lips, trying to think.

"Don't think. Just tell me the first answer that comes to mind."

"I'm not afraid."

I realize that I haven't seen Crow smile in months. It helps a little.

"See," he says, "everyone is afraid. We're running around the forest two steps ahead of the phage bags. We're even afraid to learn about the forest. You want to live this way?" From where we're crouching he can just see the window, and he gazes through it as though he sees something out there besides the shadows of passing trees.

His voice goes dreamy. "I see Littlespire crossing the Long River. It's only ten miles west of here. On the other side is grass, miles and miles of grassland.

I see you skimming across the prairie, Sark. To the mountains."

"What if the mountains are poison, too?"

"Might be. Then you go south to the great desert. There wasn't much green there for the virus to feed on, and people used to live near the rivers. I've been arguing this with Harliss for years. He prefers the enemy he knows. I think he enjoys playing hide and seek with Greme. It's a game at his level." He holds my gaze.

But not at my level. Mine and Jonn's. I nod. We don't have much time, and there's still so much to figure out.

Crow is ready with a plan. "When we meet Deepspire tomorrow, Jonn will be invited on an inspection of Highspire. While he's touring, you'll be in here, putting on your bridal dress." He nails me with a look and I don't dare react. "Then you'll meet him in front of the science deck door. I'll arrange for everyone to be outside, leaving you two a chance to be alone for the first time. Very romantic. Then we lock the door and you two enter Littlespire. I blow the tubes, and off you go."

I ask how we'll do this. My voice is mouse-small, because by now I know that Crow has it all planned down to a twig.

"Jonn can drive the spire."

I say the obvious. "Harliss will kill you." Metaphorically speaking.

He shrugs. By the look on his face, I'm sure he'll enjoy this no matter what the cost.

He stands up. "Yes or no?"

I think about meeting Jonn and crossing the prairies. My great dream has been to step outside into Greme. But when one dream isn't possible, you find another.

"Yes," I answer.

Crow nods once and slips out of the room. I intend to follow in a few minutes, but I'm numb with shock and a queasy joy. Also, I'm worried about leaving Crow behind. My whole future is in front of me, and all I can think of is, I wish Crow were coming with me.

I DECIDE TO stay up all night and work out the details. What shall I bring? Shall I leave a note behind thanking people for all they haven't done for me?

At the science deck window, I take one last peek at brave Littlespire. Not as sleek and lovely as Highspire, but even if it's a little warty, it's young, and if we find enough bio-matter, it will grow and change.

Then I gaze at the blank space on the wall where Crow has explosive bolts to break through a door. That ought to keep people busy enough patching like crazy as Jonn and I make our getaway.

THE DAY THAT Highspire and Deepspire are to meet is declared a holiday. I've been given a bunch of letters to deliver to remote relatives. I'm surprisingly gracious about all this, thanking everyone and acting a little spacey as brides are expected to. I can't overplay this, though. Goose is watching me with a pinched gaze.

The dress is in Dry Storeroom Number Three; I've said goodbye to my mother a dozen times, and she is crying enough for both of us so I guess I don't need to.

I've graciously accepted Penley's offer to help me dress. As we discuss whether I will wear gray shoes or white, a horrid scream echoes through the dining deck.

Varna Farspire is screaming as she presses her hands against Highspire's largest window. We all rush over.

At first I can't even fathom what I'm looking at. There is a jumble of rocks scattered below, lying aslant on a steep hill. But it's not rocks, it's an enormous spire. Fallen, broken. Impossibly, it's lying on the hillside, a giant, horrifying body of a spire.

Great clanging sirens go off, and Captain Harliss is shouting over the loudspeakers for us to go to stations, but none of us can move.

"It's not..." I whisper. "It's not *Deepspire*." It just can't be Deepspire.

"Oh, God, where are the survivors?" Penley gasps.

"There!" someone shouts triumphantly as people in the wreck force open a window.

My stomach convulses as I see that it's not a person at all. It's a phage bag. Big and bloated, it can barely squeeze through. Another one is right behind it.

That's when we realize that Deepspire has been down for a while.

"Stations, stations," the captain keeps shouting, and finally people are rushing away, leaving me alone at the window.

Jonn, I whisper. *Jonn*.

Several huge, ancient hemlocks block our view of the crash. Highspire rocks alarmingly as the captain attempts to stay close while navigating the gullies and steep slope. Far below a river froths, looking like the crack to hell. I am in hell already.

I rush away and climb the spiral staircase, one just like Jonn must have won his marathon on, and reach the very top, the Nav Deck. Here it's a storm of shouting, with inputs coming in on the screens, and Captain

Harliss swearing and shouting coordinates to the pilot. I ignore this and move to the circular window wrapping the room.

There must be survivors. We were in contact only a day ago. But no one is stirring around the dead spire. How would we even effect a rescue if we found someone alive?

Then, far down the slope, I see a woman sliding and stumbling down the hillside. Behind her, a burly man picking his way down toward the river on a separate trajectory. He stops, bent over, coughing as though the forest is already defending against him.

And behind both of *them*, an antibody surge, rolling downward. It had been leaning against Deepspire, and I'd thought it was solid ground, but now it's moving down the hill. Others on the bridge have already seen this and we rise higher as Captain Harliss moves Highspire out of clumping distance. The surges normally stay on the ground, but they can theoretically mass up into peaks.

Noticing me, Harliss barks at someone to get me out of here, but I don't need prompting. I flee the scene, my thoughts like shattered ice.

I am on the spiral staircase, heading down. What is my station? What do you do when your plans topple down like a massive tree in the forest? Someone rushes past me carrying a self-contained breathing apparatus and bio suit. I squeeze off to the side, wishing that the walls would absorb me, the forest would take me. By the time I wander onto the science deck, I am nearly blind with tears.

Everyone is on the starboard side, staring out the windows, but Crow is sitting at his console. He swivels around to face me, his hair looking matted and wild, but his expression calm.

"It's figured out the web path lines," he says. "We've been getting emergency calls from all over. It was a coordinated attack."

"Other spires are down?"

He nods blackly. Then the most horrifying statement of all: "We've all been breaking the rules about communication. Little snippets here and there, from all of us, between all of us. For seven hundred years, Greme has been charting our paths."

I contributed to this. *What are you like?* I asked my would-be lover. I am sick at myself.

Crow stares at the computer screen. "I think it was counting on getting us, too. At the rendezvous."

I move to the window, but I can't see the fallen spire from here. I whisper, "Why does it hate us so much?"

"Sark. That's unscientific. It doesn't hate us, it's just developing more efficient defenses."

"We haven't hurt it for hundreds of years, can't it ever forgive?"

Crow sighs. "It sees us calving new spires. We were dominant once. Maybe it's taking the long view."

Then I see him. A young man racing *up* the hill. A good, strong runner. Dark hair. *Jonn.*

THE NEXT MINUTES will change my life forever. I am scared to death and pumped so full of adrenaline, I think my touch is electrified.

Nevertheless, I manage to reach Dry Storeroom Number Three to count to a hundred. Then, I rush down to the science deck and throw open the cabin door.

I shout breathlessly: "The captain is calling an all-hands meeting on the dining deck. Everybody out!

Everybody!" I start waving furiously and people make for the door, everybody except Goose who is starting to make a call on his headset. I need to prevent this.

I rush up to him. "Captain Harliss needs you on the flight deck, right now!" I yank his headset off and push him toward the door. "He needs you, Goose. Run!" He is skeptical, but finally the notion that the captain specifically needs *him*, exerts its appeal. He moves through the door.

Crow pounces. Standing in the doorway facing Goose, he says, "Sucker." Then he slams the door, locking it.

Dashing back to the console, he blows a line of charges at the nutrient station, and the wall shudders and sags. Then, standing on the instrument panel, we are both pulling away the broken pieces, furiously yanking them and throwing them down. Behind the wall, Littlespire's door is revealed. There's a thing nagging at me, but I'm so frantic, I can't pinpoint it.

Crow, standing on the console, reaches through the hole. "Say a prayer, Sark."

Um, I don't know a prayer. But it's just an expression, I realize, as Crow turns the wheel and it gives, moving counter-clockwise. The door in Littlespire's hull swings wide into the gap left in Highspire's wall.

We clamber through. Crow will drive the spire, and my job is to throw the rope to Jonn. It's tied to the beginnings of the spiral staircase.

I don't have time for more than a glimpse of Littlespire: yellowish walls, exposed circuitry, a wrap-around window. Crow has carried in his mobile computer and is jacking it in. He says, with amazing calm, "Shut the door, Sark."

Reaching out for the handhold, I slam the door with such force the spire rocks. I spin the inside wheel, locking it.

The charges go off – little puffs like a distant landslide. Simultaneously Littlespire's small grav annihilators kick in.

We are floating free.

The spire is just a flight deck right now. Down the spiral staircase, I can see a shadowy cave, the beginnings of crew quarters. But I have to focus on my next job: spotting Jonn on the hillside. Crow is intent on the ship systems, none of which have been tested other than virtually.

"There he is!" I exclaim. "Port side, up the hill." Jonn is still climbing fast, scrambling over logs and darting around boulders. That's when the thing that's been nagging at me comes clear. There's only room for two.

Littlespire starts to move, a thrilling sensation. We are under power.

Crow says, still intent on his computer keyboard, "When we open the door, we're going to inhale the outside air. It might make you sick. Over the next few days, don't give up if that happens." He gives a lopsided smile. "*We've* got antibodies, too." He glances up at me. "Time to open the door."

I crank it open. In streams all the musky, humid, cold green air of Greme. Despite the warnings, I take a huge gulp. As we slowly move closer to our target, I say, "There's room for three, Crow."

"Littlespire can't take the extra weight." Then he says, as calmly as ever, "When Jonn climbs aboard, I'm climbing down."

Jonn has seen us. He's stopped, but oddly, he's pointing down the hill.

Crow mutters, "The antibody surge is heading uphill."

My stomach lurches in panic.

"Throw out the rope," Crow commands.

Oh God, I forgot the most important part! I throw down the coil.

I can see the hillside and the hemlocks and Jonn with fierce clarity. I could reach out and touch Greme. Touch Jonn. This is the real world, I have time to think as Crow maneuvers the spire until the rope and Jonn's hands make their connection.

As Jonn climbs – he's as good on a rope climb as he is at running – the thought occurs: "We're *already* handling Jonn's weight and yours." Littlespire isn't even listing in the direction of the rope climb.

"Can't sustain it," Crow says. "You don't have the fuel yet. When you get to the grasslands, your first job will be just like mine, extracting resources. The prairie might not have thought to clear deadfall." It all sounds so clinical and proper. It's how Crow is keeping me focused, of course.

I lean close to the opposite window, seeing that the surge is now past Deepspire and continuing uphill. Jonn is fifteen feet off the ground, but a crest could easily take him. He's got another twenty feet to go.

Now, the wave has arrived underneath us. Time has run out. "Hurry," I scream down at Jonn who accelerates his awful climb.

A little cone appears on the surge just below us. Then Crow is beside me, and he's hauling up the rope, bearing Jonn's weight as he braces his feet against the lip of the door, while I'm wrapping the excess rope around the spiral railing.

"Help him in!" Crow shouts. To my relief, Jonn has thrown his arms and shoulders over the threshold. Crow jams himself into the navigation chair and Littlespire chugs upward, away from the crest.

I haul Jonn through the door, sparing a glance down at the trembling hill that is reaching for us an arm's-span below.

FOR TWO DAYS now we have been sailing across the prairie. It is late afternoon and the wind lays the golden grasses over, an inverse wave. On all sides the horizon is far away, defining a sublime emptiness except for the stacked cumulus clouds and little spikes of lightning in the distance. This new land is overwhelming and calming.

Jonn puts his hand on my knee as I work next to him. We've hardly spoken, there's been so much to do. We cannot falter or ever forget that Littlespire depends on us as much as we on her. (Jonn and I call it a *her*.) After two sleepless days and nights, I occasionally nod off, and Jonn doesn't wake me. We've already taken on board our first branches, grinding them in the nutrient pod that hangs off the port side.

I wonder what the mountains will look like when we first see them. I wonder if the buffalo ever came back in their endless brown herds, as in the stories. And I wonder if we'll see remnant cities, since grass won't cover them as Greme did.

Oddly, I think I'm going to miss Highspire. I can't believe such a magnificent thing will not endure. And I know I'm going to miss Greme. We had our differences, but there was blame on both sides. In time... but I can't look backward.

I'm hoping that when we get to the mountains we'll find a welcome and the place will have a good, solid name, as a home should.

I will never forget my last view of Crow, standing on this side of the Long River, as was his request. He was walking into the tall grasses, shading his eyes from the setting sun, watching us depart. I could see him for the longest time, facing west, his dark hair blowing gently over his face.

MANMADE

MERCURIO D. RIVERA

Mercurio D. Rivera was nominated for the 2011 World Fantasy Award for his short fiction. His stories have appeared in The Year's Best SF 17, *edited by David Hartwell & Kathryn Cramer,* Other Worlds Than These, *edited by John Joseph Adams,* Unplugged: The Web's Best SF and Fantasy for 2008, *edited by Rich Horton, and markets such as* Interzone, Asimov's Science Fiction, Nature, *and* Black Static. *His work has been translated and published in China, Poland and the Czech Republic. His first collection,* Across the Event Horizon, *edited by Ian Whates, is out now from Newcon Press.*

ON HIS THIRD birthday, Alex Belfour showed up unannounced at my South Cannon beach house. I'd been curled up on the sofa at the time, dazed by the blue glow of afternoon infomercials, when the doorbell rang. I heard Tilly glide from the kitchen to the front entrance and a minute later she poked her sleek steel head into the living room.

"It's a former patient, ma'am," she said. "A convert."

It took a moment for the words to register. A patient. Visiting me here?

Not having dressed or showered, I wasn't prepared – or in the right frame of mind – to deal with a guest. "Have him make an appointment," I said.

"I tried, ma'am, but the young man insists it's an emergency," Tilly said. "He says he's willing to wait."

I sighed and stood up, pushing aside the wool blanket and the scattered clothes that draped the sofa.

"Fine then. Have him wait."

THIRTY MINUTES LATER, as I approached the den in the rear of the house, I overheard Tilly's soothing voice peppering the patient with diagnostic intake questions. I entered the room to find an adolescent sitting slouched in the cushioned chair, his arms crossed over his rumpled plaid shirt. Before I could even greet him, he reached into the pocket of his jeans and handed me a bright blue card, the access code for his medical history written on it. As he introduced himself and explained what he wanted, I fiddled with my smartreader, punching in the code numbers, and skimmed the pages of his med-report, which flickered across the screen.

"I'm not sure I follow," I said, although I understood his request well enough. I suppose part of me just hoped I'd heard wrong.

"Reversed." He repeated the word softly but emphatically. "I want the procedure reversed, Dr. DeLisse. I don't want to be human anymore."

"I see," was all I could muster. I'd encountered

many AIs over the years who'd had some initial difficulties adjusting to their humanity. Reactions ran the gamut from minor emotional hiccups to serious psychological disorders that sometimes warranted intervention by psyche experts – but I'd never seen a three-year-old react this way. Most AIs resigned themselves to their conversion within a matter of days or, at most, weeks.

"I'm from ManMade. Don't you remember me, Dr. DeLisse?" He leaned forward. "You converted me."

The boy did seem vaguely familiar. "I'm sorry, but I've performed so many."

"You can change me back, right?"

I walked around a stack of unpacked boxes and sat behind my desk. "It isn't a question of whether I can do it." I had access to Krell TechLabs, just a hundred miles down the coast. "It's more a question of why. Why would you possibly want to do such a thing?"

He opened his mouth as if he were about to launch into a rehearsed speech, but instead he hesitated. "Today's my birthday, you know. I'm three years old." His eyes reminded me of blue seawater.

I squeezed my smartreader and the conversion date flashed in red. "So I see. Happy birthday."

"Cognitively, that makes me seventeen years old. I can vote now. I can fight in the wars if I choose to. I can make my own decisions, can't I? Legally, I have rights." His eyes begged me to agree.

"Technically, yes. But a decision like this... This is different."

"Why? You can see the results of my neural exam, my psyche evaluation." He pointed at my reader.

I clasped the device in my right hand. All normal

results, true, but there was no way I was rubber-stamping such a drastic procedure. He was a living, breathing human being, after all. And just a kid.

"Still," I said. "I need to understand where this is coming from."

He sighed. He had the gangly awkwardness typical of most teenagers, but something about his pale blue eyes, his thick mussed eyebrows, stirred a memory I pushed away.

"I'm not happy," he said.

I could certainly relate to that sentiment. I stared at the pine board shelves, which were empty except for a framed holo of me and Phillip and Tim. Tim was just a four-year-old toddler in baggy, yellow swim-trunks in the holo, banging the keyboard of a plastic piano in a steady beat. Phillip and I hovered over him, wide smiles stretched across our tanned faces while we stood in the clumpy beach sand.

"Being human..." Alex said. "It's not what I expected."

"So you're not happy." I forced a weak smile. "Join the club." He didn't react. "Look, young men your age sometimes go through phases. It's not always easy coping with so many conflicting emotions, but it's all a normal part of adolescence. You'll get through this, I promise."

"It's not a phase." He rubbed his bloodshot eyes with the back of his hand and sat silent.

"I know someone. Someone you can talk to about these feelings."

Alex pushed his chair back, and stood up. "I guess I'm wasting my time here."

"Relax." I pointed to the chair. "Sit, sit, sit."

He looked at me warily before taking his seat again. "It's important you understand the consequences. This isn't a common procedure, Alex. You wouldn't have the same functionality as you did before. Your sense of identity would be tenuous, Grade 1 level at best, like my Tilly housebot. Trust me, you don't want to do this."

"But I do. I do."

I paused. "Have you discussed this with your guardians?" Until fully integrated into society, converts were placed in a foster home, usually with a childless couple.

"My foster mom died a few months after I was converted. And I never got along with my father," Alex said. "He didn't care about me. Not really. No, I think he only loved the idea of me. He wanted me to play a role and... I was tired of it, tired of him and everyone else defining me and telling me what to do, who to be. Do you know what I mean? I had enough of that when I was an AI."

"Why me?" I said. "Why not go back to ManMade for the procedure?"

He froze, and his eyes glazed over for a few seconds as if he were dreaming while awake, a common affectation among converts. It reminded me this was no ordinary teenager. Three years ago he had been a different form of life altogether.

After a five-second pause, he picked up the conversation without missing a beat.

"I heard that you left. I'm not stupid, okay? ManMade would never do it. It wouldn't risk the bad publicity."

The boy was sharp. With the rising death toll and

declining birth rates caused by the spread of the Red, ManMade had become the leader in the production of people, implanting AI syngrams into cloned teenaged bodies. Bodies designed to be immune to the plague. ManMade's stock prices had quadrupled over the past three years. No, the boy was spot-on. The company would do right by its shareholders before it did right by him.

I sighed. "Let's do this. Think about it for a week. If you still want to give up your humanity, I'll consider it." And more likely than not, I thought, he would walk out the door, drive back to Portland, and find a different way to vent his normal teenage rebelliousness. Hopefully I'd never hear from Alex Belfour ever again.

"Thank you, Dr. DeLisse." Alex pushed his bangs out of his eyes and smiled sadly, wearily. He seemed so vulnerable at that moment that I had to fight the urge to hug him. Instead, I extended my hand in a detached, professional manner, and he shook it, his grip soft and warm and oh-so-human.

"Celia," I said. "Call me Celia."

MY FORMER COLLEAGUE at ManMade, Milt Maddox, stopped by my house the next morning. Apparently this was turning into the week of surprise visits. I'd performed hundreds of conversions with Milt – a pleasant enough fellow if a bit introverted. His shoulder-length hair, which he kept in a ponytail, had gone prematurely gray and there was something haunting about his thin smile. I had met his late wife, Carmen, in a cybertech course in grad school and years later she had recommended me for the position of techsurgeon at ManMade.

"How are you f-feeling, Celia?" His nervous stammer always made him more endearing, I thought.

I shrugged.

He handed me a bouquet of sunflowers and we sat at the kitchen table while Tilly poured us tea. "Have you considered coming back to work?" he said. "Listen, I understand what you're going through." Milt had lost Carmen and his daughters to the Red. "It'll do you good to stay busy."

"I'm not ready to return to ManMade." I paused. "I don't know if I'll ever be ready."

Milt stared uncomfortably at the tabletop. His expression said it all. *You need help, Celia.*

He sipped his tea. "Any word from Phillip? Do you think –"

"No, he's not coming back." Last I heard, my husband had hooked up with a traveling companion on his road-trip across the Nordic countries. A young blonde half his age. It was for the best, I supposed. Just the sight of Phillip brought back memories of Tim. And I'm sure he felt the same way every time he looked at me. "I'm not bitter, Milt. Honest."

He nodded. "So I hear an old patient of ours paid you a visit yesterday. Alex BL4Z6M."

It took a moment for his words to sink in.

"How do you know that?" Milt's appearance here was starting to make sense.

"I'm Alex's guardian."

"You became a guardian?" Milt never struck me as the nurturing type.

"After Carmen and I lost the girls to the Red, well, she really wanted to take in a convert. This was before Carmen became afflicted herself." He picked up his cup of tea and stared into it. "Alex was one of the first in our BL4 series. Don't you remember?"

I shrugged.

"No, why would you?" he said. "So many hundreds of conversions."

"If you came all this way, Milt, you must know why he sought me out, what he asked me to do." I opened the cupboard where I stored the brandy and poured a shot into my morning tea. I offered some to Milt but he held up his hand. "You need to talk to him," I said.

"He won't listen to me. He's s-stubborn. No, he's dead-set on going through with this. All we can do at this point is give him what he wants."

"What?"

"It pains me, but I don't see any way around it. Do you?"

"Are you kidding me?"

"SERA gives him the right to decide. If he wants to revert to his AI state... We're required to follow the law and respect his decision."

To hell with SERA, I thought. "The boy just needs counseling."

"You have enough on your mind, Celia. I'll reach out to Alex. ManMade will counsel the boy and perform the procedure, if need be."

"You'll do this? You would really do this?" I said. "What about the negative publicity?"

"I spoke with Legal. We can have Alex and everyone involved sign the necessary paperwork to keep this confidential."

I laughed in amazement. "And what about our oath? What about our ethical duty? Have you seen the latest birth-rate figures?" Suddenly it dawned upon me. "Oh, my God. You've done this before, haven't you?"

"Celia," he said, setting down his cup, "your p-political views – which, by the way, I happen to share – don't give you the right to override the clear mandates of SERA. Yes, I'm sure there'd be strong public sentiment against the procedure if it ever came to light. But we have to balance that against our legal exposure for violating the statute..."

"I don't give a damn, Milt. He's just a kid. And you're his guardian."

"I'm here in my role as Executive Director of ManMade."

"Be straight with me. Others in the BL4 series have suffered from similar disorders, haven't they."

His face flushed. Milt obviously hadn't expected me to do my homework so quickly. After Alex's visit yesterday, I'd spent the entire evening studying up on the BL4 series. "I read about the others who mutilated themselves with razor blades and who turned to heavy drug use. And what about the two suicides?" Suicide. Just saying the word out loud made me queasy.

He shook his head. "The autopsies revealed no physiological problems with the BL4s."

"I could never approve Alex's request." Saying the words out loud gave me a new resolve.

"You're letting personal feelings –"

"Don't say it, Milt."

"– cloud your p-professional judgment. After what happened with Tim..."

I squeezed my mug so hard that it slipped through my fingers and shattered on the floor.

His eyes shifted from my face to the scattered shards.

"I'm sorry. It's just so obvious, Celia. Look, there's no reason to be embarrassed. You've been through a lot. But expending energy trying to save someone who doesn't want saving, someone who's made a personal choice about his future..."

When I didn't respond, Milt stood to leave.

But as he opened the front door, I finally answered him. "If he shows up here again – and I don't think he will, mind you – I won't authorize the procedure," I said. I couldn't care less about Milt's armchair analysis of my motivations. Or about the 'Sentient Equal Rights Act.' I wouldn't allow any harm to come to that boy.

"If he returns, you're to send him to us," Milt said as if reading my mind.

"Haven't you just been telling me to respect his decisions? He's three years old. And free to consult with any techsurgeon he wants."

"For your own sake, Celia, stay out of this. Don't get involved."

With those words, he strode out the door.

Had Milt just threatened me?

I folded my arms on the table, leaned my forehead into them. Stay away, Alex, I thought. Just stay away and suffer through your miserable life like the rest of us.

I SAT AT the kitchen table a week later, scrolling through the family holo-album, when the doorbell startled me.

"Tilly!" I shouted. Then I remembered that I had sent Tilly out to do the weekly grocery shopping.

I threw on a flannel bathrobe over my nightgown, and spied through the peephole. Alex Belfour stood on the porch in the afternoon daylight.

I opened the door.

"I'm sorry for disturbing you on a Saturday, Celia." The teen had his hands buried deep in his jeans pockets and looked away from me awkwardly when he spoke. "But... I really needed to talk."

"That's okay. Come in," I said, hugging my bathrobe tight.

I directed him to the living room and asked him to take a seat on the sectional sofa by the piano.

"Sorry for the mess." It's the one room in the house that I didn't let Tilly disturb. "You can just push the clothes and other stuff onto the floor and make yourself comfortable. I'll be right back."

I stepped into the bedroom, picked up my smartreader and punched the first four digits of Milt's number. I stared at the screen for a long moment before pausing and clicking it off.

"I'll be honest," I shouted from my bedroom as I dressed, "I didn't think I'd ever see you again."

"I meant what I said," he yelled back. "I still want to be reverted to my AI form."

When I returned to the living room, running a brush through my hair, Alex stood staring at the dozen framed holos atop the piano. My heart skipped.

"Who's this?" He held up a holoframe of a teenaged Tim playing fetch with our old collie, Lady Lu.

"My son. Tim." I stopped brushing. "Six months ago... He died."

"Oh." He set down the holoframe and said nothing more.

I took a deep breath to compose myself, and started brushing my hair again. "Would you like something to drink? Some tea? Water?"

He shook his head.

"A reason," I said. "I need a reason."

Alex sighed. "Okay, fine." He flopped down on the end of the couch where he'd cleared a space. "My girlfriend dumped me, okay? We'd been dating for a year and then we had an argument. It ended with her saying that she wanted to date a 'real' person."

"I'm sorry," I said.

I scooched next to him on the couch, knocking more of my unhung clothes to the floor. "Your heart's been broken so you've decided to give up your humanity, huh?"

"That's the gist of it."

I went to put my hand on his shoulder, but he drew back. "I have a suggestion," I said. "Something a lot less drastic than what you have in mind. Go out, meet more people, find yourself another girlfriend."

He pursed his lips.

"It might help," I said, "if you talked to some other converts, joined a support group."

"No, I'm not interested in that," he said. "I want to steer clear of any other converts."

He said this with such finality that I decided to change the subject.

"Are you sure I can't get you a sandwich or something?" I said.

"No, thanks."

"Alex, I'm going to ask you something. And I need you to tell me the truth. If not, I'll have nothing more to do with your case," I said, though in reality I couldn't imagine turning my back on this kid. "Is what you've told me true? Did you really break up with your girlfriend?"

After a pause, the boy's cheeks reddened and he shook his head.

"Did you even have a girlfriend?"

No response.

I exhaled. "Alex, how can I help you if you're not honest with me?"

He leaned over and brought his hands to his temples. "Being honest hasn't gotten me anywhere. I'm just sick of... feeling things, sick of hurting. So many millions killed by the Red. And how many die every day in the wars? Do you realize how – how lucky, how privileged we are? To have shelter and food and running water and electricity? There's so much poverty, so much suffering, and yet we're still waging wars in the Philippines and Indonesia, in the Sudan. What kind of world is this?" He stared at me intensely. "This constant... hopelessness. How do you stand it? No, I don't want to feel this any more."

This time I believed him. But despite the passionate speech, I still sensed he was holding something back.

"There are problems with the world, no question," I said. "We're far from perfect. But you're young. Someone like you can make a difference, Alex."

He didn't answer.

"Alex, when you were an AI, didn't you want to be human?"

A sad, faraway look washed across his face. "Of course. I was curious. Maybe it's just part of being... manmade. Maybe the created always emulate their makers." His lips curled into a grimace. "But when we want to go back, you won't let us."

"It's not like that. Most converts outgrow that desire. Especially when they learn that they can only return to their AI state with very limited functionality."

He shook his head. Something about his solemn expression, his sincerity, triggered a memory, a memory of Tim visiting from the University of Oregon over Thanksgiving break and expounding with equal earnestness on Cartesian philosophy: I think, therefore, I am. Descartes had become newly relevant with the Sentient Equal Rights Act being debated in Congress, and since Tim had decided to double-major in music and philosophy, he often stood right where Alex now stood, spouting similar speeches, while Phillip and I listened, incredulous and proud. Tim had seemed so stable, so well-adjusted...

"I guess Pinocchio woke up and smelled the coffee, huh, Celia?" Alex said. "I'm a living, feeling, human being. And now? Now I want nothing more than to be an AI again."

"Alex..." I said. "You're depressed. You should speak to someone." I wondered whether he needed medication and thought about my own unopened bottle of Livorex, the prescribed anti-depressant I'd refused to take. Was it so terrible that I wanted to feel my pain?

"I *am* speaking to someone." He lifted his chin in my direction.

"I'm not a psychiatrist." After a pause, I said, "Why don't you go out? Do something with your friends."

He said nothing.

"Don't you have any friends?"

Silence.

Then he said, "What about you, Celia? Do you go out? Do you have any friends?"

His questions threw me off balance. "We're not talking about me." I stood and paced in front of the sofa. "You're asking me to assist your suicide, Alex." Suicide. That ugly word again.

"I don't think returning me to my natural state as an AI qualifies as suicide. I'd just be... free of all this emotional baggage." His eyes lit up for a second. "Before I was human, I saw the world – it's hard to put it into words – in a cooler, almost invulnerable, manner. I could objectively analyze any subject, scan any person or object on a molecular level. And there was no sense of time. I could retrieve events at will – but not like human memory. No, I had total control. I could cut off access to painful memories with a nano-click." He snapped his fingers. "I wasn't burdened with... experiences."

"But what about all the pleasures of being human, Alex? The taste of delicious food, the feel of the ocean breeze on your face... And don't you enjoy a good laugh and –"

"Ma'am?" Tilly was back. Her stilt-like form poked into the room. "I'm sorry to interrupt. Milton Maddox is calling."

Alex's head turned toward Tilly.

"Tell him I'm busy," I said.

"He insists it's urgent," Tilly said

"I told you, I'm busy!"

Tilly hesitated. "Yes, ma'am."

Alex seemed shaken. "I'm sorry about that," I said. "I – I shouldn't have been rude to Tilly. I'm embarrassed by my behavior."

"She's an AI. Her feelings don't get hurt."

I paused. "Still, that's no excuse. Alex, you realize

you'd be converted physically? SERA prohibits emotion-free AIs from running around in human bodies. You'd be like Tilly, in a mechanical form."

"I understand," Alex said. "That's okay."

"I still have... grave concerns." I didn't think it wise to volunteer what I knew about the suicides among others in the BL4 series. That information, I feared, might lead Alex to a more direct route to ending his existence as a human.

"This is my decision to make," he said.

I walked over to the Steinway piano. "The request itself gives me pause."

"That's not fair, Celia."

"I suppose not," I said. "Look, Alex, I'll tell you what. Just give me another few days to think about it."

"Are you stalling again, hoping I'll change my mind?"

Yes, he was perceptive.

"I can't deny that I hope you'll drop this nonsense," I admitted, "but one way or another I'll give you my final answer then. I promise."

"Fair enough," he said without conviction.

"Why don't you stay for the night? It's foggy out there and the forecast is for heavy rain."

His eyes glazed over dreamily and he froze for five seconds again in that affected manner of the converted. "I don't know."

"I have a spare bedroom. Please. Stay."

He didn't answer. Instead, he walked over to where I stood by the Steinway and ran his hand over the piano.

"Replay," I said. At my command the piano began to play a brief peppy jazz number, a piece that Tim had been practicing six months earlier.

"Do you like it?" I said. .

Alex nodded. At the end of the piece, he walked up to the keyboard and struck a chord.

"You play?" I said.

He opened up the songbook on the piano, which hadn't been touched in over six months. Without a word, he sat down and began to play Espinoza's Contrazzo Espiritual.

The way he interpreted it, beginning with a long trill in the left hand, punctuated by right-hand flourishes in the upper parts of the keyboard, the piece sounded like a tragic waltz – delicate, ruminative – veering from reverie to resolve before dissolving into what I can only describe as near-desolation. He played with deep feeling, the notes gliding into each other in a rapturous melancholy.

So beautiful. So profoundly sad.

I BREWED COFFEE for Alex the next morning and opened the shutters of the living room windows to let the sunlight in. As I tidied up, I overheard the faint sounds of a conversation coming from Tim's bedroom. I recognized Milt's stammering, baritone voice and crept down the hallway to the bedroom door, which was slightly ajar.

Peeking inside, I saw Alex talking into a smartreader in his hand, Milt's face filling the screen.

"...should have come to me first, Alex. You-You've made a complete jackass of yourself."

Alex's shoulders slouched and he stared at the ground. "I'm old enough to decide for myself –"

"Don't give me that drivel! This has always been

about your need for attention. That's the way all you BL4s operate."

"That's not true."

"Of course it is! Look, you're not doing Dr. DeLisse any favors staying in her house. She's deeply distraught. Troubled. In fact, ManMade is considering legal action against her for her interference. We can reverse the procedure for you."

"If I go, will you leave Dr. DeLisse out of this?" The boy's voice barely registered.

Maddox growled his answer. "Yes."

"So you'll perform the procedure?"

"Of course I'll do it. For you, Alex," he whispered.

Alex turned sideways, pain etched on his face; he wore a mask of fear and shame. "How could you?" he said after a long pause. He forced the words out through gritted teeth. "I'd just been converted! I... I didn't understand."

"Don't twist things, Alex." Milt's stammer had vanished. His words were ice. "You knew well enough what you were doing."

And just like that, the fright, the shame, evaporated from Alex's face. "I didn't know what it was like to be human," he whispered, "until you showed me."

I knocked on the partially open door.

"Is everything okay, Alex?"

He clicked off the reader.

"I'm fine, Celia. I'll be right out."

ALEX EMERGED A few minutes later wearing jeans and Tim's University of Oregon sweatshirt. His hair was combed back neatly.

I halted at the sight of him.

"I hope you don't mind that I borrowed this shirt," Alex said.

"That looks... That looks good on you."

"It fits perfectly."

"Let's go for a walk." I handed him a lidded cup of coffee and we headed out the back screen door onto the beach. Seagulls swooped overhead and the chill air made me hug my windbreaker close to my body.

We hiked nearly a mile in silence, leaving footprints behind us in the wet sand.

Alex said nothing, so I said nothing.

We reached a point on the shore where a narrow outcropping of rock jutted into the ocean. Alex clambered over it like a prisoner walking the plank and I followed close behind him, careful to maintain my balance until we reached the tip.

The morning fog had dissipated and the sun now shone brightly in an impossibly blue sky. Out further to our left, a few ships had congregated in the docks. In front of us, the Pacific glittered into infinity.

"It's breathtaking, isn't it?" I said, speaking the first words in our long trek.

Alex squinted as if searching for something on the horizon, something just out of sight. "We're so ephemeral, Celia. So ephemeral and so transient and yet... We're able to leave such lasting scars." He sniffled and ran his hand across his nose. "And in the end, what does any of this mean?" The sparkle of the sun in his blue eyes created the illusion of tears.

"We're also capable of great acts of kindness, you know. Of making a lasting positive impact. For someone like you, Alex, a young man with a good heart, you can help others in so many ways. This world needs people like you."

He seemed even more forlorn at my remark.

"Alex... I overheard part of your conversation with Milt Maddox."

He glared at me – opened his mouth, shut it – and turned away.

I couldn't let go of the fleeting image of Milt's glowering face, Alex's expression of fear and shame. "I have to ask you this, I'm sorry." I took a deep breath and forced the words out. "Alex, did Milt do anything to you? Did he...?"

Alex shook his head. "You don't understand, Celia. You don't understand at all."

"Then explain it to me. Please."

A gust blew and his hair flopped across his eyes. I waited for the wind to die down, hoping he would open his heart to me. A large wave struck the rocks and splashed my sneakers.

"I had been human for a few days when he asked me to do... things," he finally said, his back to me. "To the other converts. He asked me to put my hands around the throat of a newborn. And to squeeze and keep on squeezing while she tried to push me off until... And there were other... acts." He drew a labored breath. "I was trying to understand what it felt like to be human. And he asked me to do things to them while he watched and recorded. They were innocent. Newly human. They didn't understand. But I should have. I should have."

"Oh, Alex..."

"Maddox didn't do anything to them." He turned back around toward me, his lips quivering. "It was me. It was me."

I put my arms around him and he tried to push me off but I held him tight until he stopped struggling.

"You were just a child yourself," I whispered in his ear. "Only a few days old. Obedient. Innocent."

"Innocent?" He snorted contemptuously.

"Yes, innocent. It's not your fault, Alex."

At those words his body heaved and he buried his head in my shoulder. I hugged him tight. "It's not your fault."

We stood like that for a long time. I never wanted to let him go.

"Alex!" A voice boomed behind us and Alex stiffened.

Maddox stood on the shore with two uniformed ManMade guards at his side. His black suit, his very presence, seemed incongruous in this setting, like a lamppost in the middle of a grassy savannah. "It's time to go."

Alex pushed away from me and stepped over the rocks back toward the shore. I grabbed his arm. "What are you doing?"

He yanked free.

"Alex," I said. "Don't go through with it."

The boy looked exhausted, his uncombed hair hung down over his eyes. He ignored me and addressed Maddox. "I want it done right away."

"We can have you p-prepped for surgery immediately," Maddox said.

"Others have to be present," Alex said. "I don't want to be alone with you when you perform the procedure."

Maddox nodded. "Of course, of course. Whatever you want. A team of professionals will assist me."

"Milt!" I shouted. "You sick son of a bitch! You won't get away with this –"

"This doesn't concern you, Celia."

"The hell it doesn't!" I said. "Alex! I can help you get past this. I understand now, Alex. I can –"

Alex stopped and looked over his shoulder at me.

He brushed the hair out of his eyes. He seemed spent, as if the procedure had already been performed and his soul had been snuffed out.

"I know you mean well," he said. "But you're no different than the others. It's not me you care about. It's the idea of me." He turned and continued on his way while I shouted after him.

"That's not true!" I screamed. "You're wrong, Alex!"

The two guards accompanied him to the car on the beachside road.

Maddox placed his hand on the boy's shoulder and guided him into the vehicle.

Alex never looked back at me.

I WALKED BY the docks again this afternoon – just as I had every day since Alex's reversion. I observed from afar as a sleek steel bot rolled up and down the planks, unloading crates from the freight ships. As usual, I resisted the urge to approach him.

Although there were other bots working at the port, I had been able to identify Alex easily enough. An old colleague at ManMade had told me where the boy had asked to be sent after the procedure, which coincided with the arrival of a new shiny laborer at the docks a few days later. Alex's sparkling steel frame stood out among the slightly rusted, older-model bots.

I had filed a complaint with the authorities that

triggered an investigation into Maddox's treatment of the BL4s. He denied everything, of course, making it my word against his. And Alex was no longer available to testify, as Maddox had intended all along. Fortunately, agents uncovered a cache of hidden recordings that Maddox had made, recordings of acts so sick and cruel they could only have come from the mind of a sociopath. I'd always considered Maddox a bit eccentric, but that he could be capable of such sadism... How could I have let this go on right under my nose? How could I not have seen what was happening? To make matters worse, Maddox's lawyer had argued persuasively that the incidents with the converts had taken place prior to the final passage of SERA, making the acts, at most, crimes against property. This resulted in a plea deal for Maddox to serve only a year of house arrest.

What did all of this say about humanity? I could almost understand Alex's despondency. The only upside was that Maddox would never again work with AI conversions.

As I stood there watching the docks, a crate slipped from an older bot's arms and crashed to the ground, breaking open. Something round and metallic rolled in my direction. Alex sped towards me to retrieve it. As he caught sight of me for the first time, I held my breath.

I thought I saw something in his cold lidless eye – an instant of recognition – but maybe it was just the glint of reflected sunlight. He spun around in silence and returned to work. I decided to walk back home.

I had assumed that the other BL4s with emotional problems had also been victimized by Maddox, but

ManMade's records, according to the authorities, revealed that neither Alex nor Milt ever had any interactions with them. This left me to wonder what could have made the others feel so desperate, so hopeless. What terrible secrets had tortured them so? Or maybe they had no secrets. Maybe just being human was torment enough. No, I refused to accept that. Everything I'd told Alex about experiencing the joy of life, about making a difference... I believed it. I honestly did. Maybe Alex's reversion had finally brought him the peace, the serenity, he never found as a human being.

I arrived at home and spent the afternoon cleaning the living room and doing laundry. Later in the evening, after unsealing the bottle of Livorex and taking my meds, I boiled some water for tea, foregoing dinner. I poured myself a cup and opened the living room window, letting in a cool, salt-tinged breeze. The bruised moon now hung high in the sky and lit the dark room. I sat down on the sofa and sipped the tea while staring at the Steinway piano by the window. When the pill's calming effect kicked in, I got up and walked over to Tim's holos displayed on the piano.

"Tim," I said, running my trembling finger along the edges of his image. "Oh, Tim. Why did you do it?"

I squeezed my eyes shut. I breathed hard, gathered myself.

"Replay," I commanded. I expected to hear Tim's piano-playing, but instead Alex's haunting performance, the last piece played on the keyboard, bloomed out of nowhere. It sounded the same, but somehow different. Still mournful, yet more tender and complex than I remembered. The melody repeated over and over like the mantra of a boy desperately struggling to find his soul. And in that struggle, the music he created sounded more glorious, more alive, than ever before.

THE CIRCLE OF
LEAST CONFUSION

MARTIN SKETCHLEY

Martin Sketchley is a British science fiction author. He has had three novels published to date, as well as numerous short stories and articles. He also appeared on the DVD accompanying the 2012 reissue of Nick Cave and the Bad Seeds' album Abattoir Blues/The Lyre of Orpheus. Tweet him @MartinSketchley.

MARK ROLLED OVER. Kate was just stirring. The alarm on her phone had already been snoozed three times. It must be around seven by now.

Mark moved towards her, slid under the duvet and began to kiss her belly. Kate sighed and shifted, put a hand on his head and gently pushed him away.

Mark moved up the bed and began to kiss Kate's neck and ear. "Morning," he whispered.

She put an arm around him. "Morning."

He continued to kiss her, began to caress.

"I've got to get up in a minute," she said. "I need to wash my hair."

"It's only seven. There's plenty of time."

She gave another gentle push. "Mark. Please."

He sighed, backed away from her and leaned on one elbow. "What's the matter?"

"Nothing. I'm not in the mood, that's all. I've just woken up. And I really do need to wash my hair."

"Okay. Well we can't have you going another day without washing your hair, can we? You might be sick again."

He threw open the duvet and walked out of the bedroom.

"Mark. *Mark.*"

He ignored her.

Kate sighed and stared at the ceiling. As soon as she could tell him, things would be so much easier.

MARK WALKED INTO the bedroom as Kate was drying her hair. He took his keys from the bedside table then walked over to her. "I'll see you later then," he said.

She leaned forwards, but his kiss was flat. She turned and smiled and put her arms around him. He did not return her embrace.

"Sorry," she said. "I'll make it up to you another time. Promise."

"Doesn't matter."

Kate looked towards the door. "What's that noise?"

"David and Elanor having another argument."

"Blimey, they've started early."

"Yeah. Apparently he only thinks about himself. Doesn't care what she wants."

"And it's taken her this long to work that out?"

"Seems so. Look, I've got to go. Otherwise it'll be me who's late. See you later." He gave her another quick peck on the lips then left.

Kate placed the hair dryer on to the dresser, waited until she heard the front door close then went over to her own bedside cabinet. She pulled open the drawer, moved aside the bank statements and pantyliners and took out the box from the very back. She looked at it for a few moments, then went into the bathroom.

KATE LEANED BACK with her head resting against the bathroom wall. She kept looking at her phone; it was the longest two minutes ever, but she was determined not to look for the result until the required time had elapsed.

She consulted her phone again: twenty-three minutes past eight. The two minutes were up, but she decided to give it a little longer anyway. Just to be safe.

She felt more apprehensive than excited. Mark had talked about kids for ages, but she had resisted, partly due to her own fears, but to some extent influenced by Liz and some of the other girls. They were firmly against kids. Could not bring children into this world of greed and war, they said. It just wasn't right. More likely they were too used to having everything their own way. Did not want to give up their nights out, their shopping trips, their precious careers.

Was she like them? She was not sure. She and Mark had talked about kids on and off over the years. One evening when neither of them could be bothered to cook they had walked to their local takeaway. By the time they reached the restaurant they had convinced themselves that the time was right to start a family. By the time they got home again they had talked themselves out of the idea.

Although she continued to have concerns about the huge changes a child would bring, Kate had stopped taking the pill a few months earlier. She took the decision not to tell Mark until something happened: he would only fuss and fluster.

When she could wait no longer Kate put her phone on the windowsill and turned to face the toilet. The Clearblue tester lay on the cistern. She could hardly look at it.

She took several long, slow breaths, then picked up the tester and looked at the indicator without further hesitation.

THE VITARIAT SNIPER called Cairo climbed to the crest of the hill and crept through the trees into the ancient ruins that overlooked the Qrettic outpost. She lay on one of the derelict walls, settled herself among the decaying leaves and took the teleculars from her gear pack.

The war that had lasted three millennia and spanned two thousand light years had boiled down to a few pockets of resistance scattered on remote worlds; small outposts such as the one before her, spread out across a dozen solar systems. The destruction of every last soul was essential for complete victory, however time-consuming the task might be.

When this particular group had been detected there were reports that a notorious high-ranking officer – Orchestrator Lutz, head of the Qrettic Organic Development Module – was present. The unusually high level of security in such a remote location made the claim credible. The Orchestrator's assassination had the potential to hasten the end of the war, so Cairo was assigned: an expert sniper experienced in the use of slipspace. Stealth was essential. Cairo had entered the planet's atmosphere several thousand miles away and flown at low level to the landing site near the river to the south. The rest of her journey had been made on foot, with just limited rations, her weapons and a displacement unit. Avoiding detection had taken all of her skill. Getting away would be more difficult, but she had escaped from similarly challenging situations before.

She watched the base carefully through the teleculars. There was some activity, but she had only limited information. The laboratories were to the east, comms building to the west, kitchens and sleeping quarters on the northern side of the encampment.

Cairo lowered her teleculars and grasped the displacer that was attached to the front of her tunic. The blue sphere glowed gently in her hand. Using the device would push her into slipspace — the fragments of time between moments, the constantly shifting layers between adjacent dimensions. It was in this strange netherworld that she would be able to see combinations of future events, a variety of possibilities. Although the projections would be complex, Cairo was highly experienced in filtering such information, and although entering slipspace had its risks, the device was key to the mission's success.

Cairo looked down at the Qrettic encampment, grasped the displacer and twisted the two halves of the device in opposite directions.

There was a click, followed by a tremulous whistling that rose in pitch and increased in intensity;

when the sound of the device reached its peak, the visualisations began.

CAIRO FELT THE familiar rushing sensation. Voices echoed around her, a babble of disjointed words – spirits and half-lives and a multitude of ghostly existences that had once populated this ruin. The trees shimmered and distorted.

Cairo's heart beat hard, but she could barely feel the rest of her body. She knew she could not spend too long in this indeterminate state, and would have to focus carefully to prevent the displacer pushing her too far into the future: the next few minutes was all she needed, and the further she went the more difficult it would become to analyse the information correctly, even for someone as highly trained and experienced as she. Cairo raised the teleculars to her eyes again and looked down at the enemy encampment.

Just minutes into the future she saw several figures emerge from the laboratories. She recognised Orchestrator Lutz immediately. Given his swagger, he had presumably made another notable advance in the development of his organic technologies.

Surrounded by a sizeable entourage, Lutz walked across the courtyard, past the truck, then took a short flight of steps and, shrouded in ghostly slipspace duplicates, entered another building at the base of the communications assembly. Cairo observed carefully as the displacer reset.

She watched as the same group emerged from the same building. They followed an identical route to the first visualisation until they were half way across the compound, at which point they climbed aboard the truck. The engine started, then the vehicle proceeded to the gate and left the base.

The device reset once more. A moment later the scene repeated, but on this occasion the party split into two groups: the one which included Lutz continued towards the communications building on the other side of the courtyard, while the second group turned and retraced its steps. As this second group approached the building from which it had emerged, another identical group appeared and met it head-on.

The two groups became a collection of doppelgangers and duplicates that mingled and mixed, flickering and distorting in the strange slipspace twilight, possible scenarios for the next few minutes combining and looping. Cairo had to concentrate hard to identify the most likely chain of events. She determined that if Lutz had made a notable development he would want to inform his superiors as soon as possible. The communications building represented the most likely course.

Despite Cairo's training and ability to focus, the intensity of the slide began to cause disorientation. Recognising the warning signs, the sniper deactivated the displacer and withdrew from slipspace.

The sounds of the woodland abruptly returned; the cold stone of the ruin upon which she lay, the scent of damp earth. She felt a snap of nausea, could feel sweat across her brow, took a few deep breaths to return herself to a rested state.

The possibilities and opportunities now clear to her, Cairo did not have long to wait.

* * *

KATE'S PHONE BUZZED. She leaned down from her desk and took the handset from her bag. It was Mark. She thumbed the *Accept* button.

"Hi," said Mark.

"Hello."

"How you doing?"

"Okay. You?"

"Not too bad. Busy day. Just phoning to let you know that I'm going be late. That project I told you about is going live tomorrow and there's still loads to do. Everyone's staying behind then going for something to eat afterwards. I probably won't be back until elevenish. Is that okay?"

"Yeah, sure. I can have a pizza and Kindle evening."

There was a pause.

"Sorry about this morning," he said.

"Forget it. Doesn't matter."

"It's just that…"

"It doesn't matter, Mark, honestly. I know I've been a bit frosty lately. I've got a lot on my plate at work and it's getting on top of me a bit, that's all."

"If you let me get on top of you it might take your mind off it." He half-laughed.

"Mark."

"Sorry. Bad joke. Look, I'll have to go. Meeting's about to start."

"Okay. Mark…?"

"Yeah?"

She hesitated. "It doesn't matter. I'll tell you later."

"What is it?"

"Nothing. Chat when you get home."

"Okay. Sure. See you later."

"Bye."

The call ended, Kate looked at the phone for a moment then slipped it back into her bag. She returned to her work, staring at the screen and typing on autopilot.

CAIRO REPLACED THE teleculars into her gear pack and prepared her rifle, activating the pulse generators and adjusting the settings to take into account the atmospheric conditions. Lutz would emerge from the laboratory in just a few moments.

She looked over her shoulder; the woodland was fairly dense and would give her some cover when she needed to get away. She had already utilised the displacer to gauge the likelihood of patrols; there would be some, but their efficiency was difficult to judge given the greater range of the visualisations.

Cairo lowered her head and looked through the rifle's sight. She adjusted the viewfinder and the compound within the walls of the base leapt into view.

She relaxed, adjusted her grip on the weapon, then lay and waited. When the laboratory door opened, Cairo focussed on the point above the third step, precisely two meters in front of the door to the communications building. That was the point at which Orchestrator Lutz would die.

Cairo slowed her breathing. Relaxed her muscles. Calculated drop and drift. Lutz and his entourage walked across the compound. As they passed the truck she began to exhale. A moment later she was utterly motionless. As Lutz reached the steps he turned to say something to those around him. As he took the second step Cairo heard their laughter across the quiet of the woodland.

When the Orchestrator took the third step, a single high velocity shot rang out.

Cairo was up and running before Lutz hit the ground.

CAIRO HEARD SHOUTS in the distance behind her as she ran, the sound of rustling leaves and snapping twigs. When she glanced back she glimpsed figures moving among the trees. She cursed; there were far more of them than the displacer had indicated. This could be tricky.

Cairo brought her subrifle to bear and returned fire, but the trees were too closely packed to get a clear shot. She turned again and continued to run.

She darted to her right, hurried down a slope, ran alongside a stream then leapt across the water and scrambled up the slope on the other side. Her vessel was in the next valley, just over the crest. Fragments of wood exploded from a tree trunk nearby as those behind her took hopeful shots. She could hear them calling to each other. They were getting closer.

A shot glanced the side of her face; she barely felt the pain, continued running. She crested the hill and saw the spherical shape of her craft on a patch of open ground.

More shots. She lunged to one side, spun around and fired again.

The ground levelled out and Cairo began to cross the clearing. Sensing her approach a portion of the craft's skin shrank away and the ladder began to extend to allow her to gain entry.

As she reached up to grasp the ladder Cairo felt a hot lance of pain in her side and fell to the ground.

She looked down; the side of her tunic was slick with blood. She twisted as far as she could and fired her subrifle through the long grass at pursuers she could not see.

She reached up to the ladder and began to haul herself up. She fired at the figures approaching across the clearing as the sound of projectile ordnance thudded and pinged against the craft's hull around her.

As her pursuers took cover Cairo pulled herself up the final few rungs and fell back through the hatch on to the cockpit floor.

She cried out as pain shot through her. The hatch closed automatically and all external sound faded. There was a hiss as the seals engaged. Cairo dragged herself up to the master console and slumped into the seat.

With one hand she pulled a coagulate capsule from one of her pockets and sprayed the wound through the torn fabric of her suit, while with the other she dragged open the protocols panel and initiated the emergency sequence. Seconds later the craft's automatic procedures went operational, and within moments the vessel was airborne.

Qrettic defences responded, and as Cairo's craft was about to leave the planet's atmosphere the vessel was hit. There was a muffled explosion inside the cockpit. Numerous alarms and warnings began to sound. She assessed the damage as the machine left the planet's atmosphere and accelerated rapidly towards the speed of light.

It became clear that the life support systems were struggling.

*   *   *

CAIRO DRIFTED IN and out of consciousness. She had used all of the coagulate pods but the bleeding continued. She could feel herself weakening. She verified her location, speed, rate of acceleration.

The craft had already achieved a significant light speed multiple, but even at its current acceleration she was unlikely to make it to the nearest Vitariat base.

Cairo opened the communications panel and brought the distress alert into focus. She hesitated: once sent, the alert could not be rescinded. The vessel would convey her to the nearest planet capable of offering her support resources until she could be rescued.

Her head spun. She looked down at her side: the coagulant had merely reduced the bleeding, her tunic and the seat were still slippery with blood. With a curse of frustration she drew her hand through the tab, and the distress alert was sent.

Control relinquished, Cairo pulled on her helmet and sealed her suit, then slumped back in her seat. She was now just a passenger. If a suitable location could be reached, the craft would convey her to it as quickly as possible.

MARK RESTED HIS arm on the door frame. As warm air whipped through the car, he tapped his fingers to the track on the radio. The world flickered by, fields on either side, trees in the distance. It was the kind of road car manufacturers would use to advertise their vehicles: sweeping bends, ideal conditions, no other traffic and the fading of the summer day.

Mark was worried about Kate. Worried she was taking too much on, too nice to say no or stand her ground. She had been so tired lately that he had tried to get her to take a day or two off sick, but she refused to do so. Maybe they should have a weekend away. Somewhere with fluffy white bath robes and an on-site spa.

The song ended, the DJ said a few words and the programme slid into the news. Mark reduced speed slightly as the road curved to the right and narrowed towards the bridge. As he crossed the water Mark looked to his right. The reflection of the full moon shimmered on the surface of the river. Mark glanced up, frowned, leaned forwards and looked through the passenger window: the moon was to his left.

He looked back to his right. The object had moved; it was no longer above the river and was also lower in the sky than before. He glanced ahead, eased off the accelerator then looked back into the sky.

He watched the glowing object as it continued to descend. It must be an aircraft in trouble. They often circled out this way, but it was too far from the airport to be so low. He turned off the radio and slowed a little more, keeping his eyes on the object as it drifted downwards. Mark swore and braked hard as the aircraft touched the first of the tree tops, then sank into the woods and disappeared from sight.

He continued watching for a few moments, expecting an explosion, a fireball. When neither came he pulled the car into the entrance to a field and turned off the engine. He stared at the trees, silhouetted by the orange glow beyond. He took his phone from his pocket to call the emergency services, but there was no signal.

Mark let his hand drop to his side and swore again. He stared at the trees, then slipped the phone back into his pocket, got out of the car, vaulted over the gate and began to jog across the field.

GREAT CLUMPS OF mud stuck to Mark's shoes and weighed on the hems of his trousers.

He moved quickly through the trees at first, but slowed as he got closer to the crash site: he could feel the heat on his face and there was a burning smell. He stopped dead.

He was standing in a gash in the trees made by the aircraft. The wreckage lay twenty or so meters to his left, but was not like anything he had seen on *Air Crash Investigation*: there was no trail of debris, no broken bodies. But then the aircraft itself was unlike any he had ever seen.

The machine was a dark sphere, twenty meters or so in diameter, its outer shell covered in a texture like metal snakeskin, scratched and scarred. There were no wings, no tail. The object radiated heat and glowed just enough to cast faint shadows. The damp ground and the trees around it steamed.

Mark began to walk towards the sphere. He could see that a circular portion of its surface near the muddy ground was missing, revealing the interior. Mark shielded his face from the heat and stooped a little to see inside.

He saw a large padded seat surrounded by a variety of pipes and tubes, banks of instruments and controls. There were no windows. There did not appear to be anyone aboard.

Mark stood upright again and looked around. There was no sign of the missing hatch. As he wondered whether it had been ejected before the machine crashed, he saw a body lying near the trees to his left. Marks in the muddy ground indicated that the pilot had dragged himself away from the sphere rather than having been thrown clear.

Mark walked quickly over to the body and crouched. The pilot wore a one-piece jumpsuit with a somewhat metallic appearance and a helmet with a smooth glass visor. Mark thought the person looked female. "Bloody hell," he said quietly. "What are you? Some kind of test pilot?"

He leaned closer; although he was barely able to make out her face through the visor in the dim light there was something very odd about her appearance. The side of the helmet that was against the ground was damaged, and there was a wound in the side of her abdomen.

Mark reached out and placed his left hand gently on the pilot's back; he could feel her breathing. "Better get you to a hospital," he said. "If I can get a signal." As Mark took his phone from his pocket he became aware of a deep, almost inaudible hum.

MARK LOOKED OVER his shoulder and saw a bright disc in the sky above the trees. The light was so bright he had to shield his eyes. Shadows lengthened as the hum intensified and the machine sank lower. Nearby puddles that had not been evaporated by the heat of the crashed machine began to tremble. A hot wind swirled around him.

Mark stood beside the pilot of the first aircraft, his phone clutched limply at his side. The second aircraft was a sphere like the first, but considerably larger. The machine descended further, then dimmed slightly and came to a halt just above the smashed trees.

Mark simply gazed at the aircraft. The heat radiating from it was uncomfortable on his face. As he watched, a circular portion of the sphere's skin changed colour and shrank away.

The interior of the machine was like the one to his left, but this time there were several people inside. They possessed the same slender physique and wore suits similar to that of the injured pilot.

Two of the crew got out of their seats, walked over to the door and stepped out. They did not fall, but dropped slowly to the ground as if on wires.

Mark cleared his throat as they walked towards him. "She's still alive," he called. "I was just about to phone an ambulance." He held up his phone. "Still. I suppose you've already got that covered."

No reply came. The two people were focussed solely on their injured colleague.

"Is it some kind of military thing?" Mark nodded towards the crashed sphere. "I won't go to the papers. Do I have to sign the Official Secrets Act or something?"

Still no response. The two figures walked past him in silence; they did not even look at him.

Mark turned, watching as they knelt beside their colleague. "I knew there were women in the air force," he said. "But not that many. Are you some kind of special unit?" A few moments passed. "I suppose you're not allowed to say anything. Secrets and all that." Nothing.

As the two figures examined the wounded pilot, Mark looked towards the second sphere. The object continued to hover. Through the open hatch he could see those still on board interacting with various displays. He was not sure what he was looking at.

The two people tending the injured pilot stood and moved back away from their colleague, then one of them took a small object from a pouch at her waist and held it at arm's length. She depressed the top as if pushing a pen, and a sphere like a soap bubble appeared in the air in front of her. The bubble hung there for a couple of seconds, then sank gently on to the casualty. When the pilot's body was completely enveloped the bubble rose into the air once more, lifting the casualty with it.

Mark watched as the two people touched the bubble and began to guide it towards the second aircraft. When they reached the machine they skilfully led the injured pilot up into the air and through the circular opening, then got back on board themselves. A few seconds later the opening sealed and the deep vibration resumed. The second craft emitted a line of light that linked it to the first, then the sphere's skin began to glow and the two aircraft rose into the sky in unison.

Mark watched as the machines ascended rapidly, and within seconds they were lost among the stars.

He considered what he had just seen. Looked at the marks and troughs in the ground all around him, the broken trees, the steaming earth.

'BLIMEY!' SAID KATE. "What happened to you? You're covered in mud."

Mark said nothing. He simply closed the door, leaned back and rested his head against it. After a long moment he looked at her and shook his head. "I don't know," he said.

"What do you mean, you don't know?"

"I mean I don't know. I was driving home and…" He stopped.

Kate waited. "And what?" she said.

"I saw this light."

"What kind of light? Was it a migraine?"

"No. Nothing like that. It was in the sky. I thought it was the moon at first but then I realised the moon was on the other side of the car. It came down in Holt End woods."

"Oh my God – was it a plane crash?"

"Well that's what I thought, so I went over and had a look. But it wasn't a plane. At least I don't think it was a plane."

"If it wasn't a plane what was it?"

Mark shrugged. "I don't know. It was round. The door was open and the pilot was lying nearby."

Kate put a hand to her mouth, wide-eyed. "Was he dead?"

"No. And I think it was a woman but I couldn't see properly through the helmet. Then another one turned up."

"Another plane?"

Mark nodded. "It didn't land. It just hovered. A couple of people got out, put the injured pilot in some kind of bubble, got back into their machine and went away."

She looked at him. "Some kind of bubble?"

"Yeah. Like a soap bubble, you know. But huge.

They lowered it over the body, lifted it into the air and put it into the second aircraft. I thought it was some sort of military thing at first. An experimental aircraft." He hesitated. "But I think they might have been…"

Kate raised her eyebrows. "Might have been what, Mark?"

He looked at her. "Aliens," he said. "I think they might have been aliens."

Kate smiled. "You're winding me up, aren't you?"

"No, I'm not, Kate. I swear to God."

"You don't believe in God."

"You know what I mean."

"So you were driving along, an alien spaceship crashed, and you saw the injured pilot who was then rescued by more aliens in another spaceship. Have I got that right?"

"It sounds mad, I know."

"Sounds like you've gone back on the pills."

"You know I haven't done anything like that in years."

Kate got up off the settee, took her coat from the back of one of the dining chairs and put it on.

"What are you doing?" he said.

"If an alien spaceship crashed in Holt End woods, I bloody well want to see it."

"They took it away. The second one sort of towed it with this beam of light."

She stopped and looked at him, one arm in one sleeve. "Right. So there's no evidence that any of this happened?"

"You don't believe me."

"You've got to admit it sounds a bit crazy, Mark."

He said nothing for a few moments, then looked at her. "The trees," he said.

"What about the trees? I suppose they spoke to you, did they?"

"They were all broken where this thing came down. The earth was all churned up, too. It's obvious something's happened."

Kate finished putting on her coat, walked over to the cupboard by the front door and took out her wellies. "Come on, then," she said as she slipped her feet inside them. "Let's go."

"It's quarter to eleven."

"I don't care. If an alien spacecraft landed in Holt End woods I want to see the evidence. Besides, you never take me out these days." She grabbed the torch from the shelf at the back of the cupboard and turned to face him. "Well come on then," she said. "What's the matter with you? It'll be an adventure!"

THEY WALKED THROUGH the trees, the torch beam waving around in front of them, twigs snapping underfoot.

"It's a bit spooky," said Kate. "But fun. How much further?"

"It's just here."

They emerged from the trees into the gap created by the sphere. They stopped. Kate shone the torch on the broken trees, the rutted, muddy ground.

"It was right there." He pointed to the crater where the sphere had rested. "And the pilot's body was just over there. If you shine the torch up there you'll see how the trees are all broken where it came down."

"I can see trees all right."

Mark looked up at the stars, frowned, shook his head. "It was here. I saw it. I saw the pilot, and I saw them take her away. I know I did."

"When you went out after work – you didn't have a drink did you?"

"I was driving."

"And you honestly didn't take anything... exotic?"

"Look, I didn't have a drink and I didn't take anything. I know what I saw and I know what happened, okay?"

"All right. Calm down. You've got to see it from my point of view, though, Mark. This is all a bit weird. Are you sure you didn't fall asleep at the wheel for a second and dream it?"

"Kate."

"Okay, okay, sorry."

"Look, forget it. Let's just go home and pretend I never said anything." Mark turned and started to walk back towards the car.

"Mark. Mark, I'm sorry." She hurried after him.

"It doesn't matter. You're right. It's ridiculous. I'll make an appointment with the doctor first thing in the morning and get my head examined."

As he passed the point at which he had found the pilot's body Mark stopped walking and looked at the ground, then stooped and picked something up.

"What's that?" said Kate when she caught up with him.

Mark wiped mud from the object. It was round, a similar size to a small apple, with a slightly stippled surface like frosted glass. He held the ball up by his ear and shook it, but it made no sound. It emitted a faint blue glow and felt slightly warm in his hands.

"The pilot must have been carrying it," he said quietly.

She looked at him. "You are joking. This is a joke, right?"

"No, I'm not bloody joking."

She looked more closely at the device. "Does it open? See if there's anything inside."

Mark examined the ball for a moment. He noticed a thin groove around its circumference. He gripped the upper and lower halves in his hands and twisted; there was a faint click and a whistling sound.

Mark felt as though he drifted sideways. The world greyed, distorted. He felt somewhat numb. He could see Kate, blurred and indistinct, shimmering as if he were looking at her through a veil of heat haze. He could see that she was saying something but her words seemed garbled and distant.

He heard a strange wailing sound and glimpsed a black motorbike speeding along the country lanes, its headlight illuminating the hedgerows. Mark seemed to be watching the motorbike from overhead. The machine approached the bridge across the river but did not slow down. Just as the road narrowed the machine skidded and slewed sideways. The rider lost control and the machine hit one of the bridge pillars, catapulting the rider on to the river bank.

Almost immediately Mark became aware of another motorbike approaching from the same direction as the first. It looked identical, following the same course. The rider took the bridge without slowing down, failed to see an oncoming car, was thrown from the bike when his machine collided head-on with the other vehicle. This was followed almost immediately by another bike; the machine raced towards the bridge, slowed slightly, crossed the river and disappeared along the lanes on the other side without incident.

Mark twisted the orb back to its previous position. Sound and air burst on to him. He blinked, staggered a couple of steps and threw up against a tree.

"Are you all right?" Kate asked. "What happened?"

Mark leaned against the tree with one hand, gasping and sweating and staring at the ground.

"I don't know," he said. "I came over all weird."

"You kind of faded. As if I could see through you."

At that moment Mark heard the sound of a motorbike on the country lane on the other side of the field; he immediately recognised the note of the engine. He stood upright and turned to face the road. "Oh my God."

"What's the matter?"

Mark said nothing. He could only watch through the trees as the motorbike's headlight sped towards the bridge. As the rider approached the river he eased off the power, took the bridge with caution, then accelerated away into the darkness. Mark gazed towards the road as the sound of the engine gradually faded.

"What is it, Mark?" said Kate. She touched his arm. "What's the matter?"

"I saw that bike," he said. "When I twisted this thing." He looked at the sphere. "In fact I saw it three times. But the first two times it crashed. I saw the same bike have two different accidents. I'm sure I did."

They both looked at the sphere.

"Come on," said Kate quietly. "Let's go. This place is beginning to creep me out."

*   *   *

IT WAS WELL past midnight by the time they got home. Kate slipped off her muddy boots then shrugged off her coat and threw it on to the back of the sofa. While Mark went into the kitchen and filled the kettle Kate placed the sphere on the coffee table, sat down and stared at it.

As he waited for the water to boil Mark turned and stood in the kitchen doorway. "So what do you think?" he said.

Kate shrugged. "I don't know. Tell me again what you saw."

Mark did so, concluding, "Then I saw a third time when it didn't crash, and that's what we both saw. Do you want tea or coffee?"

"Tea, please. Just a small one, though."

As Mark turned and went back into the kitchen Kate picked the device up off the coffee table and rolled it over in her hands. "It looks like glass," she said, "but it feels warm and soft. Like wood."

"Weird, isn't it?"

The object emitted a faint blue glow. Kate examined its stippled surface. She noticed that there was more than one notch around its circumference. She grasped the device firmly between her palms and rotated the two halves until it clicked, turning it to the second notch.

The world greyed and closed in. She felt an almost asphyxiating pressure and dizziness, heard a strange howling and saw ghostly shapes.

She could see Mark in the kitchen, but there was a second image of him, too, a strange overlay. As the first Mark lined up a couple of mugs, a second Mark was picking up already filled cups and turning towards the door. As the first Mark put teabags into the cups Kate watched the second Mark walk across the room towards her. As this Mark passed the sofa he banged his leg on the coffee table and stumbled slightly, half-spilling the contents of the cup in his right hand. She felt his anger and embarrassment quite clearly. He turned and placed the cup on the table and shook tea from his hand. Behind him, the first Mark watched the kettle as the water it contained reached boiling point. That was her Mark. The real Mark. Wasn't it?

She twisted the device again. The room seemed to shift sideways and she was enveloped in darkness. Kate heard a babble of voices. Fighting the compulsion to deactivate the device Kate closed her eyes and listened through the cacophony.

One voice she recognised. A woman crying. Elanor from next door. Through her tears she was asking David why he treated her the way he did. Why was he such a bully?

Kate focussed harder. She felt as though she were moving through a tunnel. The pressure increased and the darkness intensified until after a few moments she found herself in Elanor's flat. She could see their living room, their sofa, their television. Kate was behind and to one side of Elanor. The other woman was slightly blurred but it was definitely her. Kate could feel the intensity of her misery and fear.

David was a dense, dark shadow to Kate's left, looming over Elanor's slender shape. Kate tried to focus on him but he remained indistinct. Yet his animosity was palpable. When David spoke, his voice was distorted, like a badly tuned radio.

You're a useless excuse for a wife. His voice shifted and warbled. *Useless. Useless excuse. Waste my money again and I'll knock your stupid head off. Do you understand me?*

Kate's head swam; she felt as though she might throw up.

You're pathetic. If you waste my time again I'll break your stupid neck. Do you understand me?

Elanor spoke again – although Kate could not distinguish the words it seemed to be a defiant challenge.

The David shape swelled and stretched and threw Elanor on to the sofa. More tears, more shouting. A stream of garbled, stuttered words.

Stupid neck. Understand me? Do you understand... Neck... Pathetic... Head off, neck, stupid, stupid...

The room spun. Nauseous and dizzy, Kate quickly returned the sphere to its original setting and was dumped back into her own living room.

She blinked, took a moment to catch her breath. She heard the kettle reaching its peak and then looked up to see Mark walking towards her with the tea cups.

"Are you all right?" he said.

"I think so."

As he neared her Mark banged his leg on the coffee table. He swore, kicked one of the table's legs, put one of the cups down and wiped his hand on his trouser leg.

"Stupid bloody table," he said. "Here." He handed Kate the other cup and looked at her. "Are you sure you're all right? You look as white as a sheet."

"I turned that thing."

Mark glanced at the sphere. "Right. So what did you see?"

"I'm not sure. I saw you in the kitchen. But there were two of you, doing different things. I saw you bang your leg on the table. Then I clicked it again and I was next door. As if I was in there with them, in their flat. They were having another row."

"What about?"

Before she could answer there was a thump against the wall and muffled voices.

Why do you treat me this way? Why are you such a bully?

You're a pathetic excuse for a wife. If you waste my money again I'll knock your bloody head off. Do you understand me?

"That's it," whispered Kate. "That's what I heard. Just a few moments ago when I turned this thing. Only it wasn't exactly like that." She gazed at the device. "I think..."

"What?"

"I think it shows the future. Or some representation of the future."

Mark put down his cup and picked up the sphere. He rolled it from one hand to the other, smoothed his palms across its strange surface. "Well that would kind of explain things. There were slight differences between what I saw and what actually happened, but a lot of it was accurate. Bloody hell. What do you think we should do?"

"Take it to the police and hand it in."

He looked at her. "And say what? Some aliens came down and left this bauble lying around. If it's not claimed within six weeks can we keep it?"

"Well what do you think we should do?"

Mark looked at the sphere for several moments, then tossed the object into the air and caught it. "Think about it, Kate. If we really can see the future with this thing, we could be made. We could win the lottery. Invest on the stock market while all the shares are low. Make a sodding fortune."

"I don't know, Mark. That all sounds a bit..."

"What's the matter? Do you want to be a secretary all your life?"

"Thanks very much. And I'm a PA as it happens."

"You know what I mean. This thing could change our lives. We could go and live on an island in the Maldives, get an apartment in New York, do anything we wanted."

Kate rubbed her eyes with her fingertips as immense fatigue caught up with her. She shook her head. "I'm scared, Mark."

"Of what? The people who left it behind aren't likely to come looking. They're probably back on Alpha Centauri by now."

Kate rubbed her hands across her face "I really can't think straight I'm so tired. I've got to go to bed. Can we leave it until the morning?"

Mark shrugged. "Sure. I suppose. If that's what you want."

She nodded. "Please. I'm exhausted."

"Are you all right? Are you ill? You look terrible."

"Thanks a lot. No, I'm fine. Just tired."

Kate pushed herself up and walked towards the bathroom, her cup of tea untouched. As she closed the door Mark looked at the sphere for a few moments longer, then set it on the table in front of him and went to bed.

*   *   *

KATE WOKE EARLY after a night of fitful sleep. Mark was lying on his side facing away from her, but she could tell from the movement of his shoulders that he was still asleep. Slowly, careful not to wake him, she slipped out of bed, put on her dressing gown and quietly went into the living room.

She walked over to the table, picked up the device and sat on the armchair next to the window with her feet tucked beneath her.

She studied the object. She wondered where it had come from, what it was made of, what strange powers it held. But more than that, if the device really did show the future, she wondered whether there was something else she should attempt to view. It did not involve lottery numbers, stocks and shares or islands in the Maldives.

She stared through the window. Weighed up the pros and the cons. After several minutes of consideration, Kate gripped the sphere in her hands and twisted. The device clicked twice.

She felt as though the ground had dropped from beneath her. There were shimmering lights, a discordant howl, a torrent of images that skewed and distorted like a weak transmission.

She saw children: a good-looking boy with Mark's eyes; a pretty, fresh-faced girl. Kate was rocked by the intensity of the love she felt – an emotion so powerful it took her breath. She tried to focus on them but there was another surge, a headlong rush. She glimpsed riots and demonstrations. Felt the fear of millions. Sunlight weakened by a veil of ash and dust, starving children, a decaying world. The images slewed and shuffled. Sunlight through trees. The girl. Older now. A beautiful young woman with a striking young man. Kate was struck by the intensity of their love. A fast-flowing stream. A golden beach. Children. A house somewhere. Another shift. The boy, his face flickering and morphing on a bizarre time-lapse loop. Laughter, tears, a relationship broken. Another shift. Multiple overlays of the two young people living through a multitude of events and combinations in an exhausting cycle of joy, pain, love, anxiety and fear.

When she could stand the onslaught no longer Kate deactivated the device and was dumped back into their flat.

The room spun. She placed a hand to her chest and gasped for breath.

Within the few seconds that had passed under the device's power she had careered from elation to heartbreak and back again, experienced a multitude of lives and possibilities.

Kate replayed the images in her head. The future seemed so confused, such a struggle. How far ahead the device had transported her Kate was unsure, but the gravity of the commitment she was on the verge of undertaking was clear. The responsibility for the life growing inside her was overwhelming. There seemed to be potential for so much suffering to come. Could she bring children into a world like that? Were Liz and the others right? There was still plenty of time.

Kate heard Mark moving around in the bedroom; she quickly put the device back on the table, stood and walked over to the window.

"Hello," he said. "I didn't hear you get up."

Kate glanced back at him, smiled, looked outside once more. Mark crossed the room, wrapped his arms around her waist and nuzzled against her neck. "It's still early," he whispered. "Why don't you come back to bed for a while?"

Kate twisted herself from his arms, said nothing.

"What's the matter?"

Kate continued to gaze through the window, biting her thumbnail. "I used it again," she said. "That thing."

Mark glanced at the sphere.

"What did you see this time?"

She hesitated. "I'm not sure. You can twist it more than once. I think the more times you twist it, the further forward you see." She stopped, bit her thumbnail again.

"And?"

She simply shook her head.

Mark took the object from the table.

"No, Mark. Please."

But he had already twisted the sphere.

THERE WAS A long pause after Mark deactivated the device. He slumped down on to the sofa, exhausted. After a minute or so he looked at Kate, who continued to stare out of the window.

"Who is it?" said Mark.

"Who?"

"The man. I saw you with someone. You loved him. Or you will love him." He looked down at the sphere, rolled it from one hand to the other. "Is there someone else?"

"Don't be ridiculous, Mark."

"I'm not being ridiculous. I saw you with someone. I felt your love for him." He looked away.

Kate closed her eyes, rested her forehead in her hands and sighed. She took a breath, hesitated. But there was no alternative. "I'm pregnant," she said. It seemed such a flat statement. This was not the way she had rehearsed the announcement in her head.

Mark sat motionless, absorbed Kate's words. "Why didn't you tell me?"

"It's very early days. I only did the test yesterday."

"So that man I saw you with…"

Kate shrugged, looked weary, rubbed her eyes. "Our son? I don't know. Maybe."

"There was a girl," he said. "She had your eyes. I thought you and he…"

"Well he had your eyes. Will have your eyes. Oh, God, I don't know, Mark. I'm not sure I can cope with this. Did you see the other stuff? It felt like a war. So much struggle and suffering and pain. How can we have kids knowing they'll go through something like that?" She was on the verge of tears.

"It might not be that straightforward. If it's showing us different scenarios then events can't be fixed. It's the choices we make that will dictate what happens. And if all the decent people just throw their hands in the air and give up, what hope is there?"

"But what if we get it wrong? Think we're doing the right thing but take the wrong path?"

"We just have to be there for them, give them all the support and help they need. Follow the right course for *us*."

"I don't know, Mark. It's so… daunting."

He pulled her close to him. "It'll be okay," he said.

"How do you know?"

"We've just got to do our best. Roll with the punches when they come and bring our kids up as best we can."

Kate sighed. Mark wrapped his arms around her waist. She rested her head against his chest.

"At some point we're going to have a son," he said. "And a daughter. And she's going to be beautiful. Just like you." He kissed the top of Kate's head.

She squeezed his arms gently. "Did you see others? I think they might have been grandchildren."

"Grandchildren? Blimey. Let's take it one step at a time, eh?"

"Sure. One step at a time."

They were quiet for a few moments, looking out into the street.

"You know, that thing could still help us," he said. "If we could learn how to use it, learn how to channel the things we see we could…"

"No, Mark. We've got to get rid of it. For good. Somewhere no one else will find it. Better not to know what might happen."

Mark rested his chin on the top of her head. "You know your trouble?" he said. "You're far too wise."

Kate shrugged. "Maybe it's just the maternal instinct in me."

Mark and Kate leaned on the handrail and looked down at the surging sea.

"Not quite as exciting as the time we went to Paris is it?" he said.

"Not quite. But at least we'll get to buy some cheap booze."

"Always a glass-half-full kind of girl."

She shrugged. "Beats half empty every time."

They said nothing for a few minutes.

Kate looked at him. "When are you going to do it?" she said.

Mark looked back towards the English coast, fading in the mist. "I'll give it a couple of minutes."

"You'd keep it, wouldn't you?"

Mark half shrugged, squinted at another ship in the distance. "Maybe. There are so many possibilities."

"That's the problem." She reached out and rested her hand on his arm. "It's got to go, Mark."

Mark took his left hand from his inside pocket and held the device out in front of him. They both looked at the blue sphere resting in his palm. Mark looked at Kate. She nodded once, and Mark allowed the sphere to roll from his hand. A moment later the device hit the water and was lost from sight as it sank into the foaming sea.

Mark turned and slipped one arm through Kate's. "Come on," he said. "It's freezing out here. How about we go inside and get something to eat."

"Sounds good to me," she said. "Do you think they do coal-flavoured ice cream?"

Mark laughed. "I guess we won't know until we get there," he said. "Come on, let's go and find out."

They turned and walked arm in arm along the deck, and left the churning sea behind them.

FAR DISTANT SUNS

NORMAN SPINRAD

Norman Spinrad is the author of over twenty novels, including Bug Jack Baron, The Iron Dream, Child of Fortune, Greenhouse Summer, *and* The Druid King. *He has also written some sixty published short stories collected in half a dozen volumes, and his work has appeared in about fifteen languages. His most recent novel in English is* He Walked Among Us *(Tor, April 2010). His teleplays include the classic Star Trek, "The Doomsday Machine", and he has produced feature films* Druids *and* La Sirene. *He is a long time literary critic, sometime film critic, perpetual political analyst, and sometime songwriter. In addition, he has been a radio phone show host and a vocal artist on three albums. He occasionally performs live. He's been a literary agent, and President of the Science Fiction Writers of America and World SF. Norman grew up in New York, has lived in Los Angeles, San Francisco, London, and Paris, and travelled widely in Europe and rather less so in Latin America, Asia, and Oceania.*

*   *   *

OF COURSE WE *knew* we came from one in the distant past. We knew that Homo sapiens evolved on the surface of a planet called Earth with a stable orbit around a star. And indeed we still calculate our base unit of absolute time, what we still call the 'year,' as the duration of its full orbit around that star, and all our units of time as fractions or multiples of that so-called 'year.'

What other absolute unit of time could be possible for the diverse clade of civilizations that we have become, inhabiting hundreds, if not thousands, of everything from planetary-sized bodies to entirely manufactured habitats to archipelagos of bits and pieces, all tumbling and jumbling their merry ways through the sea of space between the few and distant stars as we slowly expand and exfoliate through it?

And of course we knew that the lights in our firmament were stars, and our instruments told us just what stars are – globes of largely hydrogen gases of a sufficient mass for their gravity to induce a stable fusion reaction akin to the miniature versions we use to power every human habit and enterprise.

My specialty is comparative xenological anthropology, the study of the alien civilizations we have never met and know only from their broadcasts and probes, isolated as we are, isolated as they are, by the absolute limit of the speed of light.

Some century in the far future, our slow but steady advance, expanding our sphere of habitation through the sea of ejected planets, planetoids, rocks and pebbles, and assorted other debris of birthing 'solar systems' that form the rich galactic soup upon which we feed and from which we build may intersect with one of theirs. But in this era, comparative xenological anthropology has remained a frustrating science, or, as some say, hardly a science at all.

Although, or perhaps because of that, I have at least gained a certain general notoriety and professional standing in the scientific sphere by extending comparative xenological anthropology to the study of the cultures of our own beginning species on the planet 'Earth'. After all, the word 'anthropology' originally meant exactly that, since at the time it was coined our distant ancestors hardly had the concept that other intelligent species inhabited the galaxy at all. And it isn't as if our ancestors, even before they began escaping the gravity well of their planetary surface, hadn't created a complex information storage technology so that much has survived even the millennia between then and now.

So I knew that there were two words in every language our species had ever evolved for these stellar phoenix phenomena that had spewed forth the chaos of debris into what otherwise would have been an empty void, thus condemning us to being eternally wandering sailors in arkologies and caravans. Could the material exist to build them, and if we could exist in such a galaxy at all.

And not only did I believe I knew why, but I had published an explanation which had gained general acceptance in circles where such things were of interest. Namely that what to us appeared as points of light and which the ancients had called 'stars' appeared as something else on a planet in a so-called stable solar system up close to a 'sun,' so that they didn't even comprehend that they were the same things until they had devised sufficient instrumentation, and so they had two words for what appeared to be two different phenomena.

I *knew*, but I didn't *understand* until I stood there at the bottom of a planetary gravity well like the natives, watching a *sun* arising from the *star*-spangled crystalline blackness of our home, like one reality blasting its way into another.

Contrary to a hoary maxim whose origin is lost in the mists of time, getting there was not at all half the fun.

We had detected something like a hundred artifact-creating species in our arm of the galaxy, and some of them seemed to possess technologies which we presently did not, and which we had long yearned to study first-hand; but faster-than-light travel was not among them and never would be, and so they were out of our reach.

But then a probe that had been sent out less than two 'centuries' ago (a 'century' being the measure of one hundred 'years') broadcast back imagery and data from a planet about forty 'light years' out, (a light year being the distance light traveled in a year), which, with our now-current technology, *was* within our reach, if barely.

It would take about a century to get there and a century to get back but only forty years to transmit the data and imagery, and the time-dilation effect of moving at a significant portion of the speed of light would lessen the biological time expended to go and return ourselves, so it could be done within a single human lifespan.

And there was a very good reason indeed to attempt such an arduous journey, no more so than to myself. The planetary biosphere had evolved a sapient species of lithe warm-blooded saurian-appearing creatures, and while these lithe saurians had yet to even reach outside their planetary gravity well, they had built actual cities of a primitive level.

So as luck would happen, if one could deem such a situation *luck*, this primitive civilization of sapient saurians was the closest to our tribes of civilizations now only extending our tendrils into the fringes of the Oort Cloud of nearby Centaurus; which of course was the only reason to choose it for our first expedition to the habitation of another intelligent species.

Which is to say because it was the *only* possible choice.

Convincing the scientific and financial spheres to do it was in the end more arduous than the voyage itself, which we slept through in relatively blissful hibernated sleep. The considerable effort and energy to build and launch the vessel was not the main issue, although it took no little appeal to public romanticism to pressure the economic sphere to finance it. The main objection came from the scientific sphere itself.

Something called the 'prime directive' of comparative xenological anthropology, whose origin was lost in time, the gist of which was that it would be immoral to meddle in the evolution of any civilization more primitive than our own. If nothing more, then at least a kind of anthropological Heisenberg Uncertainty Principle, that our very presence would interfere with and change what we were studying.

This seemed idiotic to me, since after all, we would dearly love to have some sapient species more advanced than ourselves arrive with knowledge and technology beyond our ken, and I repeatedly said so.

The clincher finally came as another and far more sensible dictum which I at length discovered. The very first probe our ancestors had sent into the sea of interstellar space bore a message that said it all – "to learn if we are fortunate, to teach if we are called upon to teach."

Once this was taken into the philosophical sphere the issue was finally decided in my favor, that is, once I had compromised by accepting what I considered unnecessary "rules of engagement." Observation from a distance only. No meeting with the natives, not so much as a revelation of our existence. No landing on the planetary surface.

The voyage itself passed without incident, or, if there were one, we slept through it, and as required, we put our vessel in a synchronous orbit around a gas giant, which would have kept us out of view even if the saurians had advanced telescopes, which they did not. We sent down probes, and when they confirmed that the natives had no aerial technology, we sent down manned skiffs; though they were not to dip into visibility from the surface, let alone land, though this was agreed upon against my strenuous objections.

The full report of this imagery and data is part of this data packet, but before anyone plows through it at random, be advised that the most bizarre and existentially important phenomenon observed from afar and one which I suspect will have drastic impact on our own cultures is how thoroughly the natives are in thrall to their *sun*.

A species that built large flat habitats, that had fairly sophisticated power sources – internal combustion engines, hydroelectric generators, steam generators, and so forth – and yet they allowed their sun to dominate all their planetary cultures.

View these recordings first, for while they do not *explain* why it occurs, they do present the phenomenological fact around which the data and imagery packet coheres:

Observe these otherwise modestly advanced and intelligent sapiens arising from torpid sleep as their locus on the planet revolves into its light and sinking back into it when the natural darkness returns, even though they have powerful, universal, and even esthetically pleasing illuminative arts. As if they were plants or autonomats programmed to obey an overwhelming phototropism that overcame their sapient consciousness.

Observe that in some score of their cultures, these sapient saurians even *dance* to welcome this 'sunrise' and apparently mourn 'sunset'. Or perhaps the reverse, welcoming the return of the comforting blackness of 'night' studded with our familiar sprinkling of stars, and mourning its destruction before their eyes by the dawning light of their implacable sun.

And this bizarre and universal behavior cannot be explained by their 'saurian' nature, for we were able to discover from the probe data that these are warm-blooded creatures, who only appear reptilian to our subjective eyes.

What transpires within their consciousnesses at these times cannot be discerned from the physical facts. That is the province of xenological anthropology and the most fascinating conundrum it has ever confronted. And perhaps the most dire.

There was a general longing to – in some era safely

in the far future – reach one of those myriad points of light which were far distant suns.

But what would happen to our far-future descendants if they did? The same thing that seems to have happened to these saurians? Might it be preventing them from reaching beyond their gravity well? Might we succumb to the same mindless tropism?

We had to actually *understand* this phenomenon, and I insisted that it was obvious that the only way to do that was to *experience* it ourselves from the surface of the planet.

But that would be a violation of the prime directive, I was told.

The debate immediately became heated.

Might we not be putting our own civilization in jeopardy by failing to perform the necessary task due to excessively punctilious adherence to a so-called prime directive concocted by our distant ancestors?

It would be a violation of our rules of engagement.

Was not the survival and continuing progressive evolution of our species and its spreading expansion into the outer reaches of the Oort Cloud of Centaurus the ultimate prime directive? Surely you don't have to be a xenological anthropologist or moral philosopher to understand that? To feel from within that we simply cannot send back a packet of imagery and data without experiencing the phenomena directly? For if we don't, we have no hope of actually understanding what it implies for the continued free consciousness of our own sapient species.

And if we don't, we can have no informed knowledge of what we might be releasing into our culture, and no idea what it may have devolved into when we return, thanks to whatever cultural meme we inserted into it like a retrovirus into a genome.

Thanks to our moral cowardice.

That was enough to begin to win them over, however grudgingly; and however grudgingly the agreement was sealed by my acceptance of the collectivity's version of my manned mission's rules of engagement, namely that we would land in an isolated area so that the natives would never know we existed, and observe the phenomenon for only one cycle.

We landed on the most desolate rocky coast we could find so as to minimize any chance encounter. Here not even a hint of vegetation grew to draw any desperate herders or foragers. A noxious chloride stench wafted in on the unprogrammed air currents from an enormous reservoir of undrinkable hydrogen dioxide. *We* were the aliens in this strange, distasteful, and therefore threatening, planetbound environment.

The only comfort for our trepidacious spirits was the familiar starry blackness, if only as a kind of great ceiling over our heads as we awaited the sunrise, and we found ourselves gazing towards the presently invisible horizon line over the mercifully black ocean, as if trying to merge them into the familiar three dimensional matrix of our homes far from any star, like a cloak to shield us from what was shortly to come.

And then as we stood *beneath* rather than *within* a black firmament of stars, one of them, the one around which this planet orbited, became a *sun* as the planet revolved around its axis, bringing it slowly into view.

Or somehow, it seemed vice versa.

The line of the horizon brightened like the edge

of a knife under a halogen spotlight, separating the blackness of the sky from the blackness of the ocean and destroying any remaining illusions of three dimensionality.

We were standing on the flat surface of a planet as the black sky morphed into deep purple into mauve into iridescent blue, heralding the sunrise radiating from the line of the terminator as it swept slowly towards us.

And then a far greater blade of light, the very top of something enormous, brilliant as an exploding fusion bomb, peered out over the horizon at us balefully, rising as if to display itself to our vision, or somehow to see all the better into our beings as it arose majestically from the stellar deeps, burning away the sight of any other star, and becoming a Sun.

Awesome. Overwhelming. Greater than anything in our millennial experience in the spaces between the distant stars.

No longer just a *star*.

The Sun.

A huge ball of white light too bright to burn with a coherent hue, too searing to gaze upon without pain for even a moment, dominated everything visual, turned the ceiling above us to a cruel whitened blue and the ocean into a mirroring surface as it began its agonizingly slow journey through the sky towards a sunset it seemed would never come.

Beautiful? Horrible?

Neither and both.

The words had no meaning in this context. The recorded imagery cannot convey the subjective experience, we were so small and the sun was so large.

But we were sapient creatures, and it was not; it was not even a creature at all but an immense globular fusion reactor, and that is all you will see in the recording.

How then can I explain that being there made it seem something terrifyingly more?

This was a Sun.

One of billions glittering beyond our present reach but beckoning us towards them like insect lifeforms to a lamp. Collectively the creators of our homelands in the galactic flotsam and jetsam, but each one a stellar phoenix, a power, a reality, on an absolute scale exponential orders of magnitude greater than we were.

Greater than we were but not alive as we conceived it. No consciousness, no will, no intent, only physics, only the blindly amoral and insensate power of the Sun that dominated the saurians, and the Suns that by their billions dominated creation.

And we were naked before it.

To endure this was to understand how the Sun could bring a species to its knees, and why I feel I must write its name with a capital letter. Not a matter of 'worship' of a 'god', but mere brute phenomenological force, for these Suns, these masters of the galactic main, were not *beings* in any way that being may be scientifically described, nor philosophically understood by anyone who had not experienced the subjective reality, and yet they had a kind of *existence* which transcended our own.

Duty demanded that we remain under this searing and blinding and daunting ball of nuclear fire to record a 'sunset'. An agonizingly slow wait, but in the end, we were relieved that we had, as the Sun finally slid down the opposite 'horizon' with the same breathtaking visual display of 'sunrise,' only run in reverse, and the *stars* emerged into the welcoming darkness from the brutal and implacable light of the departing Sun.

And now we *know*.

We know that consciousness is a frail orphan in a creation in which it is merely a third-degree byproduct of non-being and all too capable of falling under its uncaring sway. We know that *this* was what our species escaped from into the freedom of the galactic main, now no further than the outer fringes of the Oort Cloud of Centaurus, in the future, further, and infinitely further still.

We must not cease exfoliating forward into our galactic destiny, but we must turn our caravans aside from the Suns. If it is not already too late when you receive this packet, venture no further towards the Sun called Centaurus, and however we might grow in time and space and evolutionary grandeur, let us remain free beings in the vast richness of the spaces between the stars.

That is our home.

That is where we belong.

Let us steer well clear of those far distant suns.

THE LIGHTHOUSE

LIZ WILLIAMS

Liz Williams lives in Glastonbury, England, where she is co-director of a witchcraft supply business. She is currently published by Bantam Spectra (US), Tor Macmillan (UK), and Night Shade Books. Her short fiction has appeared regularly in Realms of Fantasy, Asimov's, *and elsewhere. She is the secretary of the Milford SF Writers' Workshop, and teaches creative writing and the history of Science Fiction. Her first short story collection* The Banquet of the Lords of Night *is published by Night Shade Books, and her second,* A Glass of Shadow, *by NewCon Press. Her novel* Banner of Souls *was nominated for the Arthur C Clarke Award and was also her fourth finalist for the Philip K Dick Memorial Award. Liz writes a regular column for the* Guardian *and reviews for* SFX.

MY MOTHER WAS the keeper of the fortress, and so was her mother before that, and now so am I. My mother gave birth to me in the deepest part of the fortress, the part that lies far underground, the place that is lined with metal and filled with sparkling lights. I remember my birth very well: it was not an easy one, and I tried to help my mother by making myself as small as possible. Finally she pushed me through, into light and air, and the first things that I saw after that were her golden eyes.

She raised me in the maze of rooms that lay beneath the fortress and I came to know them all: the metal room itself, the low dark passages and, higher up at ground level, the series of sealed airlocks that shut the base of the fortress off from outside. I was not allowed to go there, of course, but my mother did so every month, to gather the black weed that covered the rocks, and the small scuttling things. Until I was grown, and started studying the fortress records, I thought there were only three things to eat: two kinds of weed, and shellfish.

Gradually, my mother started to teach me how to keep the fortress going. It was explained to me why the fortress had been placed here, on this remote fragment of rock orbiting the great suns of Ternair, of Sulane, of Morre, the last outpost of our people before the Sea of Sulane itself. She told me about the war, about the ships that had set out across the Sea, seeking a new world that the Kharain could never find, could never touch. I asked her, when I was old enough to understand what this was really about, whether any of our people were left in the suns' systems, or whether everyone had died. My mother's face crumpled, the loose skin puckering into tight folds and ridges, and she said that she did not know for certain, but she had been told by her own mother that no one was left, that all had fled before the Kharain. But she could not be sure and this was why the fortress must be kept going, sending out its beacon both fore and aft, back towards Ternair and out towards Sulane. Because if the beacon was allowed to fail and the signal died, and if someone came home, then they would not know what had happened, or whether it was safe to proceed. The fortress was a safe place, where a ship could be moored.

"But don't the Kharain know that we're here?" I asked. The thought of the Kharain terrified me: my mother had told me about their warships, their planet-rammers, their spawn-squads which bred on the battlefield, creating new warriors before the very eyes of their enemies.

"I think they must know," my mother said.

"Then why haven't they attacked us?"

A long pause.

"I don't know."

For a long time after that, I had dreams about the Kharain, great armoured figures charging through my sleep, making me wake with a cry. But the years passed and the Kharain did not come, and eventually my mother told me that it was time for her to die.

"I don't want you to go!" I said.

"And I don't want to leave you. But it's time, I can feel it. And we have to go outside."

"But there's only one suit."

"The only reason for the suit is to keep me alive. Since I'm going to die anyway, that's not a problem any more. You can survive for a couple of hours out there, Beshmennah, it's just that it will kill you eventually. The air is very thin. But both of us must go. You'll see why when we're out there."

It was the first time that I had worn the suit and I found it clumsy and stifling, with its round helmet and huge gloves. It was very old, my mother said, made in a different age, but it was the only one that was left. It seemed very strange to be standing in the airlock, with me in the big suit and my mother in nothing but her shift.

"Won't it be cold?" I asked. I felt cold myself, closed and tight, like a knot.

"Yes. I'll manage. I'm going out to die, remember?" She was very calm and I wondered whether she'd been looking forward to it. She had spent her whole life here, as I would, with the added burden of a child, and I knew from the records that once our people had known something different, parklands with burrows and caverns and towers, before the coming of the Kharain.

"Are you ready?" she added, configuring the coding of the airlock mechanism, which she had made me memorise, over and over again.

"I suppose so." To my shame, because I felt I had to be as strong as she had been, I blurted, "I don't want to be on my own."

"Ah," she said. "But you won't be, not for long."

Then the airlock hissed open and we were outside.

I know it was just the suit filter kicking in, but the air smelled fresher the moment we were through the hatch. My mother did not look back, but set off immediately across the rocks, striding surefooted down a ridge of land. I knew we had no more than a couple of hours together, that I would have the rest of my life to stand out here and gape, but I still lingered. The star field was immense, much brighter than it seemed from the monitor windows of the fortress. Over the shoulder of the tower I saw the three blazes of the sun system; ahead were coiling meadows of coloured gas, the spirals of the Sea of Sulane. It looked close enough to touch. The fortress itself rose up from a basalt crag, all fused black glass and vitrified rock, sheened with an eerie blue. Pools of water lay at the foot of the crag, with the weed growing thick and slippery around them. My mother was walking quickly over a wilderness of stones. I hastened to catch up, moving awkwardly because of the suit.

She did not look to see if I was following her. She walked in a straight line, without faltering, not swerving around the rocks but walking up and over. I had to scramble to catch up; not easy in the ill-fitting, bulky suit. After a while, it became clear where she was heading: a cave, high in a basalt cliff. She climbed, and I was not sure at first if I would be able to follow her but then it struck me that she must have done this same thing, wearing the ancient suit, following in the steps of her own mother when the time had come.

When we reached the cave, she stopped, and motioned that I should take off the helmet. I did so.

"Take off the suit," she told me. Her voice sounded different in the thin air, frail but not hesitant. She clearly knew exactly what she was doing. So I removed the bulky old suit and stood half naked in the searing cold. The cave exuded chill: it was like breathing in darkness.

"Leave the suit and come with me," my mother said. I did as I was told. She led me further into the cave and touched the wall. The cave was suddenly lit, and I saw that we were not alone. Two figures sat against the opposite wall.

"This is your grandmother," my mother said. The corpse was wizened, desiccated by the dry air. "And this, her mother." They both looked exactly the same, the folds of facial skin slack, like the parchment leaves I had seen in the old records, their eye hollows staring at nothing, their hands nothing more than fragile bones. "Come here," my mother said.

She sat down beside the corpse of her mother and motioned for me to sit opposite her. I did so, shivering, and she took my hands. "Wait." All I could think of was the cold; it drove out even my despair.

"Is there anything I must," I stopped, "that I must do for you, when you are dead? Any rite or ceremony?"

"Nothing. Just leave."

"But –"

"Just leave. You will not have long."

She sat, clasping my hands. The cold must have put me in a kind of trance. I sank into it, feeling the skin of our joined hands growing clammy – some exudation from the slits in her skin, or those in mine. I sensed her triumph, that she had succeeded in what she had set out to do, that her life had had meaning and purpose. I remember her life as she herself remembered it, a life very like that of her own mother, and I knew that my life would be the same. But there was a piece missing: the question of whether I, too, would breed. The cold seemed to grow more intense, biting through to my bones, and I came out of the trance with a start.

My mother's golden eyes were open, but there was no one behind them. My hands were clammy and wet. For the first time in my life I was alone and I think I would have been sitting there yet, as cold and still as she, if her last words had not struck me with renewed impact: *you will not have long.*

I was so cold that I could barely drag myself upright. At the entrance of the cave I glanced back and saw the three of them sitting in a row. I said, aloud, shakily, "I will see you again." Then I passed my hand down the wall as I had seen my mother do, and the light faded and died.

I might have hated the suit before, but that was gone: I tugged and pulled until it was once more covering me and even then I was still cold by the time I reached the fortress. I threw myself in through the airlock, shut all the seals behind me, stripped off the suit and ran up the stairs.

I had been to all the levels before, but to the uppermost ones only in the company of my mother. I knew how to keep the beacon codes in sequence, how to send out the pulses of light that – so my mother said – only our people's ships would understand. Now, because the uppermost level of the fortress had been so much my mother's place, it was the place where I felt most safe. Ironic, since it was the highest place on all our little world, and thus the place that was closest to the Kharain. But I wrapped myself in my mother's weed-silk blanket, that now was mine, activated the ceiling monitor of the dome, and stared up at the gleaming, distant stars.

I can't remember how long I stayed there. Long enough for the cold to go away, though when I got up again my limbs were stiff and some of that cold seemed to have settled in my bones, nestling there. Life without my mother was lonely, yet not so very different: all her stories came from the records, as did mine. Her life had been one long seamless lack of change, except for the death of her own mother, and my birth. And that raised questions.

I pored over the records and discovered that for birth, one needed a male. Clearly, I did not have one, and my mother had never mentioned such a disturbing thing, so how had she managed to breed? I searched the fortress from beacon to maze, to see if my mother had kept any personal records, but it did not seem that she had. Perhaps she had not felt the need, but why had she never explained about birth and breeding? Come to that, why had I never asked any questions about it myself? I suppose that, remembering my birth as I did (though not my conception) I had simply taken the process for granted.

But soon something happened that drove all thoughts of males and breeding from my mind.

The Kharain came back.

At first, I didn't understand what was going on. I had gone up to the data room as usual, but when I looked at the readouts, none of them made sense. The cycle of information that had been coming in ever since I could remember had changed, become new. I had to ask the data-source what was wrong and it told me, in my mother's calm voice that sounded so much like my own, that the new data represented a ship, on its way to the fortress.

I felt my skin become suddenly dry, all over. The data room was filled with little lights and when they went away I found that I was sitting down.

"What kind of ship? Is it one of ours?"

"It is a ship of the enemy, the people known as the Kharain."

"Can we –" It was strange that my first thought was not for my own safety nor for the sanctity of the information that the fortress guarded, but for the cold dry bodies of my mother and my grandmother and her mother, alone in the dark. "Can we put up a screen of some kind?" *Can we hide?*

"It is too late," the data-source informed me with infuriating serenity. "The ship is coming here."

And then it showed me a picture, gliding through the air: a huge thing, green, bristling with weapons. I looked out of the viewport of the fortress and saw a bright light that was not a star.

I asked the data-source to download everything recent. I knew that my grandmother had asked for the crucial information, the data pertaining to our world and culture, to be downloaded into a secret location – secret, that is, from any but her own family. I knew, now, that it was hidden in the same cave as the bodies. So even if the fortress was to fall, and I died, the information would still be there, safe for someone to find it.

If anyone could.

If anyone ever came back.

If the asteroid was not blown to fragments by one of the Kharain's planet-slammers.

Having set the download in motion, I ran down to the cellar room and pulled on the suit, fumbling so that it took twice as long. Then I shoved myself as quickly as I could through the airlocks and out onto the surface.

The ship was much closer. I did not know how fast it must be travelling, but it was growing more visible every moment, so that I could see not only its lights but the long hulk of it, the glint of weapons in Sulane's distant glow. I could only trudge across the rocks, and watch as it came. It seemed to take years to reach the cave, and then I did not go far inside, but crouched just beyond the entrance. I did not know if the Kharain ship had any form of life-scanners, but if they did, and if they found me, dreadful thought, I did not want them to look any further within the cave system. I did not want them to find the data. Or the bodies, as though my mother's corpse was one of the shrines of which I had read, needing protection.

But all our real shrines were gone into fire and the ship was directly overhead now, slipping above the rock-strewn plain. There was a flare from its side and something was hurtling downwards, striking the surface below the cave with a great puff of dust. I shut my eyes and turned my head away, to avoid what I thought would be an explosion. But the ship glided on. As the dust settled I could see the thing that had fallen – no, landed. It was a pod, with a curved hull, surrounded by a network of webbed spines. A small black hole appeared in its surface, like a mouth opening. Two figures came out and began to move around.

They were the first Kharain I had ever seen, but they did not look like the images on the monitors. They were not the big, spiral-bodied things, with armour plate, with needle claws. These figures were spindly and small. But they were moving quickly towards the fortress, away from the cave. At least I had the suit, at least I did not have to face the freeze without it. I began to talk to the suit, speaking to it as if it was my mother. I can't remember what I told it. Stories of our people, perhaps, or stories that I made up. I spoke and I waited for the Kharain to come back. I think I might have slept, because when I next looked out over the plain, the spindly figures were nowhere to be seen and the pod was lifting up in a roil of dust. I watched it sail upwards to the ship as though it was pulled on a wire, and once it had disappeared, the great ship moved away.

I watched it disappear and did not believe. This was a trick. The ship would come back, or would turn and the last thing I'd see would be the flare of its guns, bright as Sulane. I waited and waited and sipped some of the emergency fluid from the inside of the suit, thankful that my mother had instilled in me the importance of keeping it topped up. But the filtering system would not last forever and eventually I knew that I would have to go back to the fortress.

I did not want to go back. The fortress was no longer my home; the Kharain had made it part of themselves, stealing it from me as they had stolen everything else. But, apart from an unfamiliar coding of the airlocks, imposed to over-ride the locking mechanism, there was initially no sign that they had been there. They had closed the airlocks behind them, with no damage. When I checked, still wearing the suit, that they had not done anything to the internal air supply of the fortress and found it intact, I stripped off the suit and went through the tower room by room. I moved stealthily, for I'd only seen the pod lifting off, not the two figures. For all I knew, they had left someone behind.

But there was no sign of anything or anyone, until I reached the data room. There was something on the monitor, unscrolling into air. It was a battle scene.

"I have been left an instruction by the visitors," the

data-source said in my mother's calm voice. "I am to play these images."

So I watched. I saw a legion of beings that looked like my mother, like my grandmother, like me. They were advancing through the streets of an unfamiliar city, somewhere with tall clay towers, from which a small, spindly people swarmed. The beings that were ourselves were tearing through them, tearing them apart, until the spaces between the clay mounds ran with ichor. Occasionally, one of our people would squat, her abdomen would pulse, and she would drop a squirming ball of a child, which swiftly uncoiled and grew. The ranks parted around each ball, until the back of the line was formed of new beings, growing quickly.

They were a spawn-squad, and they were me. Then the end of the city was reached and the image rewound itself from the beginning.

I watched it over and over again. I could not understand it, because it meant that everything I had been told was untrue. The Kharain were not the overrunning warriors. We were. I was.

"They have left a message," the data-source said. "Shall I relay it?"

"Yes." My voice sounded numb.

"It is this: the visit has been conducted. The treaty remains because the terms of the treaty have been adhered to. Your numbers have remained constant. The risk of your return is still judged to be too great and you must remain here, but you will not be harmed. You are the last of all your kind and we will not be responsible for extinction in spite of past actions. Message ends."

It took me a long time to work it out. We had been

the aggressors, but they had found a weapon against us: some chemical that limited the number of young we were able to reproduce. Reluctant to commit complete genocide, they had marooned one of our kind here, in what had once been an outpost of ours. And with difficulty, she had bred, the birth triggered by an adrenalin surge, not from combat this time, but from fear. So it had been all the way down the line, with the stories of how we had come here mutating and changing, until we were in the right, and they were in the wrong.

Now, we have a new story. And it is 'we', not 'I', for my child is growing slowly within, her conception sparked by my fright when the Kharain ship came onto the monitor screens. We will have a new story to pass down, but it is not one that I want to tell, just as my many-times great-grandmother did not want to tell it, the story of our failure. But the alternative is a comforting lie and so I have a choice, as I sit here in the fortress, knowing now that there are no wonderful lands to which to return, no ships of my lost people which will one day come home. All I have is a story.

THE FIRST DANCE

MARTIN MCGRATH

Martin McGrath is a writer and editor. Originally from Northern Ireland, he now lives in Hertfordshire with his wife and a disturbingly precocious daughter. He has seen around twenty of his short stories appear in anthologies such as NewCon Press' Conflicts and Mutation Press' Rocket Science, and in magazines including Albedo One. He has a PhD in a thoroughly obsolete area of political science and was once pushed off a Eurostar by an impatient elderly French woman. When he correctly predicts the lottery numbers he will buy the Odeon cinema in Leicester Square and live on popcorn.

THEY HAD TAKEN away the memory that Alejandro cherished most. He wanted it back. The Muninn in his shoulder whirred warmly and recalled everything. The old man relaxed, allowing the device to take him back, he did not hope – did not allow himself to hope – that this time would be different. He accepted the pain that must come.

* * *

Aʟᴇᴊᴀɴᴅʀᴏ ʟᴏᴏᴋᴇᴅ ᴀʀᴏᴜɴᴅ at the faces of friends and family, as he has always done. So many were now long gone. Even the community centre was rubble today, cleared for some office building that was never finished. But here were the people, young and bright. And here was the room still filled with the smell of fresh paint.

He let the soft rumble of conversation enfold him, Arsene's barking laugh, the tinkling of glasses and the scraping of chairs on the red-tiled floor. He felt the warmth of the summer's day seeping through the building's thick walls and the gentle breeze from the single fan that stirred the air above the hastily cleared dance floor. His stomach felt heavy from drink and food, his head light from an unexpected depth of joy.

Finn, Tommy's little boy, stared up at him. Alejandro smiled then and now. Finn was twice married, and twice divorced, with three kids and a big belly but here he tottered across the dance floor, his body still working out the complexities of standing upright. The boy's face was set in a mask of fierce determination. Every step was a struggle of will against gravity, battling loose legs that only reluctantly obeyed his commands. In the boy's fist, gripped tight and held out high, a carnation, the buttonhole from his father's rented tuxedo.

The boy plodded towards them, dragging the focus of the room with him. The chattering faded; the band, tuning up in the corner, fell silent. The world stopped spinning. Finn swayed to a halt and raised the bruised white flower to Teresita.

"Thank you," she said as she stooped to take the gift.

"Princess!" the boy said, eyes wide.

Teresita laughed and scooped the child up in her arms, spinning him around.

Alejandro flicked a jaw muscle to pause the play back. The hum of the Muninn, more felt than heard as it thrummed against his collar bone, settled into a lower pitch.

Teresita.

His throat tightened. He blinked away tears.

She had been, on that day, so convinced of her own happiness that it seemed to Alejandro that a kind of joyful rapture had engulfed the whole wedding. Even her mother, who had always known Alejandro would never amount to anything, sat holding her new husband's hand with a soft smile and her eyes bright. Teresita's faith in him, in them together, had been so absolute that it had scared him even then. From here, knowing all the ways he would let her down, all the stupid disappointments and carelessness, the promises that he never could keep...

Alejandro blinked, restarting the recall – the Muninn whined.

Teresita kissed Finn on the forehead and set him down. The boy nodded solemnly, turned on his heel and tottered away into the arms of his parents – both gone now, God take them – and the laughing, applauding crowd.

Teresita put the flower in her hair, the white petals shocking amidst that ebony flow. She looked up, a wide, immodest grin on her face. Alejandro felt his hand reach out, the movement steadier and stronger than he had managed in many years. He felt himself brush her face with one finger, wondering again at the softness of the touch, the cool smoothness of her skin. She rested her cheek against his hand.

And there they stood, perfectly still, at the centre of the world.

The lead singer of the band started counting.

"One, two, three, four –"

And at that moment the picture fractured and the sound crackled and a wall of static fuzz rose up around Alejandro. Over the hiss and warble a low female voice began to intone a legal statement about copyrighted material and the rights of its owners and the cost of licensing and offering him the opportunity to upgrade his package with Mnemosyne to reinsert the missing moments.

Alejandro sighed, twitched his jaw again to end the playback and felt the Muninn's hum fade on his shoulder.

ALEJANDRO FLICKED THROUGH his bill from Mnemosyne. He'd long ago paid off the basic charge on his Muninn; going through the bill and removing memories that were flagged with demands for copyright payments meant that the basic services of the device were available free.

He could have set his scroll to automatically reply to the bill, giving up everything that contained a memory he could no longer afford to keep, but sifting through the memories he was about to lose had become a small ritual. He'd wander down through the list, attempting to remember each incident without the Muninn, trying to work out where copyrighted material might have slipped into the memory.

Was it a tune on a distant radio? Or was a screen in the corner playing some movie? He flicked away one memory when he realized they were demanding a payment for the taste of a soft drink.

Alejandro enjoyed the puzzle even as he resented dropping each lost moment into the wastebasket. Every deletion came with a polite reminder from the sweet-voiced Mnemosyne woman reassuring him that his memories would never be deleted and were always there for him if he paid the required licence fee. It stung every time. He knew that he could never bring them back.

He'd held on to their wedding dance for as long as he could afford to. Now, though, the prices had gone up again and the rules kept changing. He had no choice.

He clicked the box and dragged the file to the corner of the screen and consigned it to the trash.

Tomorrow I will visit Filipe's boy, he thought.

ALEJANDRO WONDERED IF he was the only one left who remembered that this building had once been a bowling alley. The neon signs were long gone, as were the bowlers. The inside had been divided up into tiny rooms – the lanes buried under cheap flooring. Did the mechanisms still work? Were there, somewhere underneath the narrow dirty corridors and crudely boxed-in apartments, pins and balls sitting, waiting to be rediscovered one day by a wrecking crew or, perhaps a thousand years hence, by a confused archaeologist?

He pushed his way through the junk-filled space, past discarded furniture, heavy boxes, broken toys and stacks of waste-filled plastic bags that reeked of rot and seeped colourless liquids across a tacky floor that sucked at his feet.

The door to Gideon's room was open just a crack and violet light spilled around the jamb into the corridor. From inside music throbbed with bass so deep that Alejandro could feel it vibrating in every bone – his skin shivered with the beat.

Alejandro knocked. Waited. Knocked again. And then, when it became obvious that the music would drown out any sound he was capable of making with his knuckles, he pushed the door open.

There was a man with black skin, not brown but black with a hint of blue, like the deepest night sky, and stars of silver sparkled in his ears and his lips, his nose and his eyebrow, his teeth and his tongue. A line of what looked like rivets ran from the bridge of his nose over his brow and across the bald-black skin of his head.

The music snapped off and silence roared into the room.

"Gideon?" Alejandro said.

The boy looked up, suspicious at first. Then he smiled and Alejandro saw his mother in him and for an instant he was again the little boy he had once been, playing in the street with Gael and Tad, Alejandro's grandsons.

"Mister Marichal?" The boy stood up. He was very tall. Alejandro wondered if that was something else he'd done to himself. Filipe and his mother were not so big. "Mister Marichal!"

The boy came around the desk, ignored Alejandro's offered hand and gave him a fierce hug, lifting the old man off his feet. Then he pulled away, looking serious.

"What are you doing down here? You should have told me you were coming, it's dangerous down here."

Alejandro waved away the boy's concerns.

"I lived in this neighbourhood before your father and mother were born," Alejandro said, laughing. "I walk where I like and no one bothers me."

The boy looked unconvinced and again Alejandro saw his mother's kindness.

Gideon remembered his manners, Filipe had been a good father, and rushed to clear a stack of boxes and papers from a deep armchair that was almost buried in one corner of the room. Alejandro sat, perched on the edge of the seat, and Gideon propped himself against the vast desk that filled most of the room.

"I want to remember the things they've taken away," Alejandro said, tapping his shoulder where the small box of the Muninn was buried beneath his skin.

"Mnemosyne would do that, Mister Marichal."

"Pfff!" Alejandro shook his head. "Too much money."

Gideon nodded, biting at his lower lip, as he took a moment before making up his mind. He reached for something on his desk.

"How long have you had the Muninn installed?"

Alejandro had to stop and think.

"Well, Teresita and I were married in twenty-one so that would be, sixty-one? No, sixty-three years ago."

Gideon whistled.

"Any upgrades?"

"Not since I stopped working. That was in fifty-eight."

"I don't think I've ever worked on implants that old." Gideon looked impressed. "That must be first generation hardware."

Alejandro shrugged. He'd never been much interested in technology.

"Teresita was desperate to have these things installed before we were married. She was determined that it would be a day we'd never forget." The words caught in Alejandro's throat. Surprised by the emotion he coughed and looked away. "Now they've taken even that."

Gideon said nothing but got up and began to move around Alejandro, running a small device over his shoulder and neck, nodding and tutting.

"Everyone in the neighbourhood says that you are the best person to see about Muninns," Alejandro said. "They say there's nothing you can't make them do."

Gideon tried to pat him on the shoulder, clumsily trying to reassure the old man. But Alejandro grabbed the hand, surprising the boy with the strength of his grip, and pulled Gideon closer.

"Give me back my Teresita!"

Gideon bent over the old man for a stretching, silent, moment, not sure how to respond to the hunger in Mister Marichal's expression.

"Let's see what I can do," he said finally.

Alejandro nodded and smiled and Gideon took it as a signal that he could disentangle himself and go back behind his desk. He swiped his device across a scroll. A display jumped into life between them and the boy began manipulating information. Figures streamed up from the desk, lines twisted and curled at eye level.

"I can do this," Gideon said. "But there will be a price."

Alejandro nodded.

"I have a few dollars."

"I wouldn't take your money, Mister Marichal." The boy looked genuinely hurt and Alejandro had to smile. He'd known this was a good boy.

"Do you know how a Muninn works?" Gideon asked.

"I know what anyone knows," Alejandro said. "It records your memories and lets you replay them later – you see what you saw, smelt, tasted, heard. Everything. All the experiences you had at the time."

"That's true, sort of," Gideon said. "But the Muninn doesn't store your memories. It puts itself between your sense organs – your eyes, your nose, your skin – and your brain. It records the electrical impulses that your nervous system uses to communicate with your brain. When you recall something from the Muninn it replays the electrical signals from that moment in the past and amplifies them so that they override whatever you're experiencing in the present. It feels as if everything is happening again."

Alejandro had sat through an endless demonstration by the Mnemosyne people back before the wedding. None of it had mattered to him then and he hadn't paid attention.

"That's not even the really clever part," Gideon said. His enthusiasm brought out the young boy in him. Alejandro tried to imagine him as he had been, skinny, brown-skinned, always laughing. "The pathways and patterns in your brain are always changing. You learn new things. You add new memories. Old memories fade. You forget almost everything. The brain is always changing. The Muninn threads through those pathways and keeps track of the changes, adapting the recordings it makes to fit the new patterns so they seem no different from when they were first recorded."

Gideon looked at Alejandro as if he'd just explained something vital.

"So?"

"My system can't do that," Gideon said.

Alejandro shrugged, not understanding.

"So... if I pull out the memory, you'll only be able to review it once or, if you're lucky, twice. Watching it will alter your neural pathways and the copy I make will become unplayable. And you can't wait too long to replay it after I pull the memory onto a scroll. New experiences will change the patterns in your brain. A Muninn can compensate for those changes, my equipment cannot. You have a few days before the divergence starts to become significant, after that your brain won't decode the signals in the same way and the memory will start to degrade. The visuals break down first but after a week or two all that will remain are scents and fleeting sensations of touch."

"Oh?"

"And there's something else." Gideon leant forward. "When you replay the memory, Mnemosyne will know I've tampered with your Muninn. It isn't strictly illegal but it does break their terms and conditions, there's a chance they'll cancel your service."

"I didn't know..."

Alejandro looked away for a moment. He knew his own memory wasn't what it was. He knew he relied on the Muninn for a lot of simple things. Life would be difficult without it.

Gideon gave a tight smile.

"Mister Marichal, I would do anything to help you. You have always been good to my family. Gael was like my brother before..." Gideon stopped. Alejandro nodded. Some things didn't need to be spoken about. "But I think you should go home and think about this."

Alejandro looked into the palms of his hands. He hated his hands. They trembled slightly, they were lined and creased and dark with liver spots. They were old hands. He was old. He relied on the Muninn. But their fees and their rules – they were robbing him of everything he cared about.

He needed to dance with Teresita again, even if it was just once more.

There was no choice to make.

"No," he said. "I don't need to go home."

"What if I paid the licence fee?" Gideon dropped his gaze to the floor. "It isn't so much."

"I did not come here for charity." Alejandro tried not to shout but his voice was loud in the small room. He stood up – struggling out of the low armchair – and took a step towards the door.

"Just like my dad –"

Alejandro turned and opened his mouth ready to spit some angry response but the boy was laughing, hands raised in surrender.

"You're certain?" Gideon asked.

Alejandro set his jaw firm and nodded.

"Then come with me."

ALEJANDRO HAD BEEN expecting something that was more clinical, more futuristic. The walls of the little room may once have been white or cream but the paint had aged and yellowed, bubbled and cracked. You could tell from the edges that the carpet had started off a pale shade of blue but shuffling feet had worn the centre threadbare, the brown structure of the weave showing through. There was a single seat, a soft, battered armchair with a high back covered in a floral-patterned material that was thin and faded and had lost any charm it might once have possessed.

Gideon waved at Alejandro to sit down while he walked over to a scroll that lay on a small wooden table propped uncertainly against one wall. He tapped a few instructions on the scroll's screen then pulled a skullcap of fine metal mesh from his trousers pocket. He swiped it against the scroll and then came towards Alejandro.

"Sit back, please, Mister Marichal,"

Alejandro did as he was told and the boy stretched the cap over his head.

"You're sure you want to do this?"

Alejandro nodded, resolute.

Gideon went back to the scroll and tapped at the screen again. He paused, looking to Alejandro, but the old man gave no sign of doubt. The boy entered a final instruction.

"This will take about twenty minutes," Gideon said, stepping towards the door. "It will work best if you can keep still and relax. I'll come back when it is done."

THE DANCE WAS not elegant. Alejandro and Teresita did not sweep across the dance floor in a dramatic tango or spin in a light-footed waltz. They shuffled, they bumped and they wheeled around gracelessly to a long-forgotten pop-song that Teresita had loved.

It didn't matter to Alejandro that his new wife trod on his toes or that they stumbled when he tried, unwisely, to sweep her up in a dramatic turn.

All that mattered was her smile. She stared up at him and he saw himself reflected in her eyes and it seem that the man she saw was bigger and prouder and happier than he ever remembered being. He was a man with hope, a man who would do great things and who would always have this beautiful woman beside him.

He lifted her off her feet and she squealed his name as he whirled them both around, her dress ballooning out, one shoe flying off across the floor to land at the feet of the band's guitarist. And when he put her down she threw her head back and laughed, her face wide and open and honest with simple pleasure. And then all their friends were around them, clapping him on the back, kissing his new wife and then dancing themselves – just as clumsily – and laughing.

It was a perfect moment.

GIDEON PUT A hand on Alejandro's shoulder and the memory dropped away. He lifted the cap off the old man's head and rolled it up.

"We're done," Gideon said.

Alejandro sprang from the chair, surprising the boy with his sudden vigour, and gripped Gideon in a tight embrace.

"Thank you," Alejandro stepped back, his eyes filling with tears. The old man wiped roughly at his face. "Thank you so much. You always were a good boy."

Alejandro pulled out a small fold of neat bills and pressed them into Gideon's palm.

The boy, as gently as he could, refused them.

"No ,Mister Marichal –"

The old man pushed them back.

Gideon looked at the notes. He peeled away the top two and handed the rest back.

"That is enough."

Appeased, Alejandro nodded; then he reached up to grab Gideon's face. He pulled the boy's head forward and craned to kiss him on the forehead, his lips touching a cool metal stud.

"Thank you for giving me back my Teresita."

The old man turned and walked out the door.

"Mister Marichal?" Gideon called after him but he was gone. The young man stared, confused for a moment, looking around the room.

Then he went over to the low table with the scroll.

The download from the Muninn was complete, the copy ready to play, unused.

If he returned it, the old man could have his precious memories one more time. Gideon fiddled with the mesh cap in his hands then turned towards the door, intending to chase after Mister Marichal and explain there had been a mistake.

Then he remembered how the old man had looked and he paused.

Thank you for giving me back my Teresita.

Gideon sat down in the old, battered armchair and gently ran his fingers along the studs in his skull.

Mister Marichal had been happy and that was enough. The old man didn't need the download.

He already had everything he needed.

STILL LIFE
WITH SKULL

MIKE ALLEN

Mike Allen edited a trilogy of weird fiction anthologies called Clockwork Phoenix *from 2008 to 2010, and thanks to the miracle of a $10,000 Kickstarter campaign, he's now in the process of assembling* Clockwork Phoenix 4. *A 2008 Nebula Award finalist, his stories have appeared most recently in* Beneath Ceaseless Skies *and* Not One of Us. *His first short fiction collection,* The Button Bin and Other Stories, *is forthcoming from Dagan Books, and his first novel,* The Black Fire Concerto, *is on its way from Black Gate Books. You can learn more about his work at http://descentintolight.com and http://www.mythicdelirium.com*

THIS PART I remember. My old life ended here. What's left starts this way:

When that girl from the belowground stole into my workshop, I wasn't wired for running. I was wired for show. I had to be my own saleswoman without having to speak a word.

My cranium had corners, and each one sprouted a chain that helped suspend my head from the grid of railracks overhead. A bit illusory, those chains, as neurofibers wound through them, so I could sync the bearings as I rolled my dangling head along the grid from one end of the shop to the other. No need to stick close to my body. The tubing from neck to trunk could flex and telescope a long way.

I kept my body simple, an elegant cube with two slender alabaster arms worthy of any Venus curving out from each vertical face, balanced on a single pair of sleek, muscular legs. Everyone wants to perch on beautiful legs and that never changes. Who'd trust me with their bodywork if I couldn't shape a pair for myself?

I don't do the full works. Integration with nanorobotics, consciousness transplants, I don't touch that ghost-in-the-machine garbage. Coming to me for genitalia removal's like asking a hivemind to add single digit integers, but most everyone's had that taken care of long before they ever consider my services. Removing a heart, replacing it, I'm happy to do that and good riddance to those useless antiques. Duplicate pumps throughout the body, replaceable on request, that's the way to go. My most requested modification, but I can do so much more.

I had a client split onto three different tables, connected by fibers and hose. I choose to keep up a pretense to gender but this customer did not out of deference to the Hierophant hirself – a deference I don't share, but I respected hir wishes nonetheless.

Se wanted hir head nestled in earflaps like flower petals atop a long stalk, descending into a birdcage of ribs that would moan musically when se breathed. And legs, always the sculpted legs. My head hovered over hir as my hands did the delicate work.

And that crazy painter, Encolpio, the one with the natural-born, unaltered body that ought to be archivally preserved before the fool simply dies of old age. He was there. He loved to paint me and the clients I worked on. I let him hang out for the sake of atmosphere. Something to make my shop stick in the memory. These denizens could go their whole lives without ever seeing anything like him.

The oil fumes wafted from his canvas, coursed across my tongue. My customer sighed and fluttered hir eyes as I reconnect the last cranial fiber, and it chimed soft in hir torso, a slow gong. The door into my workshop irised open, though I'd heard no request for access and granted no permission, and the girl who stepped through it said, "Unmake me."

I said, "I don't know what you're talking about," but at the same time my client managed to swivel hir head on the table, stared with narrowed eyes at the intruder and blurted out through hir ribs, "You don't belong here!"

How fast that girl moved, right up to the tables in a blink, and thick fibers sprouted from her palms, winding all through the cavities in my customer's torso. Hir eyes fluttered and shut and hir mouth went slack.

The painter dropped his brush.

"Don't play dumb," the girl said. "One touch and I'll know if you're lying."

My body configuration wasn't tailored for quick escape. Before I could even run I had to contract my neck and position my body where I could withdrew my chain-tentacles out of the ceiling grid and perch my head like a spider over the cube of my body. That would take at least ten seconds.

I met the girl's gaze. She glared back with grids of diamond-shaped pupils. The woven gray cloth of her unisuit, its fibers perhaps made from real animal hair, marked her as a belowgrounder. Dark hair trimmed almost to her scalp, knees bent and back hunched in an aggressive stance – I knew she had to be enhanced in all sorts of ways but she hadn't deviated from the basic human blueprint that so many denizens of the Hives eschewed. Her smooth features made her appear just past pubescence, but who could really know anymore? And how could she possibly know about unmaking? About me?

"Why would you ask such a thing?"

"I'm not asking."

"From everything I've heard, unmaking is a complex and traumatic process." I wasn't about to admit aloud that I'd ever re-engineered a living, conscious person's DNA to completely change them at the cellular level. Talking about it would definitely perk up the Hierophant's nanoscopic Ears. Admitting knowledge will bring hir minions straight to you in a matter of minutes. Actually doing it – well, that's best left unsaid. "Not one bit of equipment in this studio could be used for such a thing." I spun my body a half-step closer to her. "You want to see if I'm lying, the base of my neck's the easiest place to plug in."

She continued to stare.

"Is se going to be all right?" Encolpio pointed at the unconscious customer. The intruder glanced his way. Then dashed at him. He swung his easel between them, a completely ineffectual defense.

I rolled my head toward my body at triplespeed and dropped out of the grid.

The girl tried to immobilize Encolpio the way she had my customer, but despite his antiquated body the old man proved surprisingly agile at staying just out of her reach.

Some ancient customs still make practical sense. I touched fingertips to the central counter in my surgical array. A drawer sprang open.

"Stop it, kid!" I shouted. She turned and I made sure she saw that I held firesprayers in three of my four hands, all aimed at her. "You can leave now."

Her eyegrids widened.

My entry bell sounded again. And I knew that couldn't be a customer. "Who is that?" I demanded, but the girl set her jaw and glared.

"Hey, Athiva," Encolpio said, "can you stop whoever that is from coming in here?"

I couldn't get to the controls quickly enough anyway, and in another moment it didn't matter, as once again the portal opened without seeking my input. Clearly I needed a security upgrade at the next install opportunity.

The girl started breathing harder, in excitement or fear – I'd not seen a physical reaction like it in years. Then she said, "Do you have another way out?"

Encolpio replied "No" at the same time I narrowed my eyes and said, "Yes."

As the painter started, the girl said, "Better use it."

Four figures stepped through the portal; all naked, all sexless, all identical, each about the size of the girl.

One of her eyes turned to track them while the other stayed fixed on my weapons.

With my chain-tentacles I gripped the corners of my shoulders tight. And I ran. My body aimed where it needed to go, I swiveled my face and firesprayers toward the newcomers.

All of them split and bloomed, their pink innards unfolding in a manner more mechanical than fleshy, interlocking together and slotting into each other to form one much larger creature. I uttered a noise somewhere between a gasp and a shriek as the resulting monster raised six massive arms and brought two of them down on my unconscious customer and crushed hir.

Red stripes of oxygen-consuming aerocapillaries roped across the golem's thoracic chambers, giving it grotesque symmetry as it bounded over my work tables, a thing made of raw, glistening muscle that combined elements of toad, monkey and spider. It had no head, no visible sensory organs.

The juggernaut scrambled at us. I'm no fool. It might be there for the girl, but it would leave no witnesses. I squeezed two of my sprayers, sent jets of fire right into its exposed guts. No mouths opened but the thing screamed and recoiled, its components peeling apart.

And immediately recombined, jettisoning what had charred, the new shape more compact with more legs that bent and sprang to propel it through the air, straight at us. Spraying it would just result in a mass of burning flesh raining right on top of us. I reached the far wall and slammed my free hand palm-flat against the hidden scanlock.

The emergency door dropped straight down into the floor, leaving a rectangular gap. I spun through.

As I slapped the scanlock on the other side I confess I wasn't paying close attention to whether my impromptu companions in flight made it through.

A deafening thud as the door pistoned back into its place with a burst of blood and torn flesh.

The girl, curse her speed, had passed through the opening before I had. A bloody tangle lay where the door had gaped. My hearts pounded until I spotted Encolpio across from me in the secret corridor, scrambling backward away from the mess.

The quivering parts on the floor began to rearrange themselves.

"Back!" I shouted, and hosed the rising mass with the firesprayers. Smoke filled the corridor before the ventilation sucked it away.

Fists pounded the wall from inside my shop, the other half, trying to find us.

The girl hadn't run, nor had she tried any neurofiber moves on me. I trained my weapons on her again, their nozzles still smoldering. "Who are you?"

"Procne," the girl said.

"Is that your real name?"

Her lips pursed before she answered. "It's the name I have."

Another pound on the wall. "And what is *that*? And why is it chasing you?"

Encolpio tried to speak, coughed, started again. "Can we do this somewhere else?"

"No," I said. My livelihood was ruined, the chosen existence I'd worked so hard to construct likely destroyed. Procne's next words would determine whether or not she left the corridor alive.

"His name is Hundig," she said. "He wants to take me back to his conscriptor so she can engineer me into something just like him, only smaller and smarter. And quicker."

"But you don't want this? You can't tell me you had those eyes and palm-fibers added so you could tend livestock in an underground pod."

She bristled, but remembered who held the weapons. "I won't be an owned thing."

"Who is this conscriptor?" I had to raise my voice over the beating on the walls.

"I don't know her real name. She has an artificial vessel that holds her mind. Sometimes it's shaped like a bird, sometimes like spiders." Her shoulders hunched, her speech became hesitant. Speaking of this woman scared her. "She told me to call her Philomela."

Instinct told me what she wasn't sharing. "You signed a blood contract, didn't you – and now you're trying to break it." And before she could answer: "And you dared to involve *me*? Who claims I know anything about unmaking?"

"Her name is Sieglinda."

Now there was a name I thought I'd never hear again. But I wasn't primed to buy yet. "Describe Sieglinda to me."

"She told me you would ask that. She told me to say that she's never let me see her compass rose tattoo, but it remains in the same place where you saw it."

I'm still amazed I didn't drop any of the firesprayers. The hooks were in me from that moment on. "And you didn't think to bring this up when you first came in?"

She shrugged but wouldn't meet my eyes. "I was short on time."

"How did you meet her?"

Another grimace. "I was supposed to kill her. She helped me escape."

I lowered my weapons. "We need to get out of here."

"About time," Encolpio said.

I did not under any circumstances want to admit in front of the painter that Procne was right about me, though he already had to be guessing and I suspected he wouldn't be the least bit bothered if he knew. But the ears and eyes of the Hierophant are everywhere, and the open admission of unmaking is one of the few things that will bring hir minions to you at maximum speed.

Se doesn't bat any of hir many eyes when a member of hir citizenry changes their cell structure to the point they're no longer recognizable as their former self. Do it without hir knowing, though – that se can't abide, if se ever finds out. They say hir attention is stretched so thin that you really have to work to attract it, no matter how vile your business. But some things are guaranteed to cause hir gendarmes to gather.

To pursue an unmaking you find someone like I used to be.

In ancient days on another continent there was a thriving industry in liquor made outside the law, untaxed and unaccounted for by the government. There was no rational reason for the business to be conducted outside the law beyond keeping the flow of commerce concealed, and yet because it was outside the law it thrived. Unmaking is like that.

Beyond that secret hallway my memories fragment. I deduce we must have parted ways with Encolpio afterward. I didn't dare let him stay involved, though

I can imagine his protests at leaving me alone with Procne. But that's a guess. A wall rises in my mind and won't yield, much as I feel pressed to force a way through.

This pressure shifts, prying at the name Sieglinda. Images, sensations stutter. She was like me, insistent on a gender, but she bared herself in a way I didn't, her transparent skin flaunting her morphologic choices even more than most. I recall a warm hand on my neck. My body was different then, more like a natural-born. Sieglinda's fingers playfully caressed a vein as my gaze tracked the tableaus of figures etched into her temple and across the crown of her skull. A kiss, sweet and electrifying. And nothing more than that. The rest of her no longer belongs to me.

My eyes have retained their tear ducts. Perhaps tears appear. This pressure releases me and my memories move forward, resuming here.

We stood before a reeking pool of brown liquid in a long cellar room fifty stories below the ground level of an old-money oligarch's ziggurat. Said oligarch, a former client of mine, no longer remembered that this room existed or that we were in it.

"You have to be the one to do it. I'm not built for swimming anymore," I said.

"I won't go in there," Procne said, her tone defiant, but the way she shrank away from the edge suggested otherwise.

I had no sympathy to offer. "Then you've ruined my life for nothing."

I had taken my direst risk yet, adding a personal rhythm to the coded telepathic impulses that gained me audience with the oligarch, but a face-to-face meeting was necessary to speak the combination that would temporarily trigger hir memories of me from hir previous identity and remind hir of the debt se owed me. And also remind hir for that same interval of the secret room built within hir home where my guest and I needed to go.

I must, in the back of my mind, have thought I might one day have need of my old gene-ensorcelling services, for myself at least. Why else would I have built in all these safeguarded spaces instead of purging my old life completely?

I had never planned, I'm sure, to make them available again to anyone else.

"Just because I brought you this far doesn't mean I won't call it off," I said.

Her faceted eyes turned down, sullen, a childish gesture from someone so deadly.

I again held out the hand I'd offered her. "Take this and dive."

Finally, the ornery thing followed instructions. She took my arm, which I'd detached at the shoulder, and dove in. I had explained to her that she had precisely ten seconds to find the ID pad at the bottom and press my palm against it; otherwise valves would offer their opinion with jets of a corrosive and flammable chemical, followed by an inconvenient ignition. Ah, the elegant glare when I concluded, "Someone like you should have no difficulty."

Just enough time went by to make me wonder if Procne had botched the task. Then drains opened with a throaty gurgle as she bobbed back up. She held up my arm for me to reclaim, saying nothing as the fluid around her ebbed away. As I attached my limb to the facet where it belonged, all the nervesockets and vesselvalves reconnecting, she floated in the pool until her feet touched bottom. Her expression told me she didn't want to help me down, so I insisted she do so. It was the least she could do, as I'd be rebuilding the ruins of my life long after she was gone.

As the last of the liquid sluiced off, the floor of the pit shuddered, then lowered; a platform lift that descended as a new fake floor slid into place over our heads. For the first time Procne appeared impressed. "With all this, why did you even need a modshop?"

"It's not my wealth that built this," I replied. "Just a favor owed. Nothing here belongs to me."

Which wasn't completely true.

The lift carried us down into another hidden chamber much larger than the one we'd left.

The room didn't need to be so cavernous. I'd requested it be filled with decoys. I'd imagined three or four. My former client had outdone hirself.

Each machine in this cavernous vault hulked large as a garrison hovertransport; at least three dozen of the special cryogenic units with their corrugated skeletons of coolant piping wound through with webs of insulating fiber, muttering with off-the-grid power. I wondered what my former client was thinking, taking my requested ruse this far, but it would be too dangerous to attempt to revive hir memories so se could be asked.

"When were these built?" Procne asked. "They're ancient."

"Maybe as you perceive time they are." If she was to be believed, she'd just given away that she genuinely was young, not simply adjusted to appear so. Yet there was good reason for these units to be so cumbersome and chaotic in their design. Each held hundreds of redundant systems. They were intended to serve their purpose even if languishing for centuries, forgotten.

Yet only one held what I'd come to collect. And if anyone, including me, attempted to activate the wrong unit, they'd all shut down and destroy the hidden treasure. I hoped my client and I both remembered rightly about the pattern and the sign that would tell which machine was the correct one.

I shared none of this anxiety with Procne. Instead I walked between the right and center row of machines, keeping an eye toward the crowning configurations of pipes. Each machine was different. I paused by one crowned by a duct that contained a curve and bend reminiscent of the crest of an ancient Greek helmet. Only an expert would know that no functional reason existed for this, and that expert would perhaps be thrown by the many useless design flourishes repeated above the other machines. But only this machine featured smaller pipes radiating out from the helmet like Shiva's undulating arms.

My hands hadn't touched the ID pads on its surface in twenty years. The configuration requires four hands, all of them mine. "This will take a few minutes," I said, as the sophisticated machinery inside came alive with a sigh.

"What's in there?" she asked. For the first time I noticed a tremolo in her voice.

"What I need to do what you need," I said. "I could try to explain, but you'll see for yourself before I'm finished."

The machine opened a tray the size of an antique file

cabinet drawer to disgorge its treasure, which stared up at me in wide-eyed surprise. I picked up the end, which contained all my knowledge of the forbidden art of unmaking. The head I already wore partitioned like a tulip bulb to allow this second braincasing to slide into place within it like an egg in a cup.

My old self reconnected and took in what the rest of me knew and remembered. I recall my lips shaping the question, "What do you want to be?" She answered, and I asked, "What can you pay?"

There's really only one thing she could have paid: my pick, before I changed her, of what she had already, her body and its augments, the sum of her memories. But I can't tell you precisely what she offered or what I took.

And you won't find her. Nor will you find, in my memories, any trace of where she is now. See, just as I knew that my survival for all those years depended on hiding as much of my former life away as I possibly could, what I learned from her, both things she knew and things she did not, told me that I would end up here. My old self left me with this sickening news, and what I needed to consider about it, and no more than that.

Surprised that I can do this? Shut off the autonomous flow of my memory into your recorder and address you directly? My old self prepared me well. Let me guide you to what's left for you to find.

You see, Procne made confessions to me before and during her unmaking. Some she intended, some she didn't. No process exists that's more invasive.

What I learned from her took me to Philomela's lair, sixty stories deep into the belowground, right under the community of Hivetowers that adjoin the Hierophant's fortress. The hall that led to Philomela's dwelling, painted yellow in warning, simply dead-ended. I crossed into the yellow and waited.

The pair of creatures that came to greet me in the tunnel was each formed of five different people engineered to interlock, though one skin covered them all. Both were terrifying masterpieces, even more brutal that the thug that trashed my shop, each with five pairs of ropy limbs terminating in prehensile claws. They emerged from the door that irised open at the hall's far end and crawled along the ceiling ducts. Each dangled three of those massive arms, all the better to tear me to pieces with. I wondered if either of them incorporated the remnants of Hundig.

I had no weapons, just a vague hope that I wouldn't need to resort right away to my defensive plan, which would do little more in that space than postpone my death by a couple of minutes.

The hall echoed with a feminine voice. "One of my brothers is going to present you with a sensory block. Crawl your head inside it. When it opens, we'll talk." Indeed, the nearest of the ceiling thugs used its free limbs to lower a gray sphere toward me.

I did not anticipate or desire this. How did Philomela know I could detach my head? "I can't stay separate from my body longer than three minutes." I hated how my voice quavered.

"This is your problem but not mine. Do as I ask or die where you stand."

The box opened, a hungry shellfish. I detached my chains from the corners of my shoulders, extended my neck into the case, which enveloped me like a helmet, and released my cervosocket. The clamshell sealed around me and the cramped space inside filled quickly with preserfluid. Nothing I could do but float and count seconds.

At one hundred sixty-four seconds the fluid drained. At one hundred seventy-one seconds the case opened and I scrambled to reattach my swooning head to my body, which had been sunk to just below its square shoulders in a pit full of a polymer that had already hardened. My head remained the only part of me that could still move.

Under other circumstances I'd have found Philomela a delightful creation, her lower half recognizably female if sexless, her upper half a carefully sculpted bonsai tree. A mechabird of paradise rested in her branches, and when its beak moved the voice that emerged was the one I'd heard in the hall.

I notice your interest perked up as I described her. Perhaps she means something to you. I don't suppose you'll tell me, will you?

Philomela said, "Conditions will improve for you once I'm sure your priorities match mine."

Radically as I'd altered my body, using my lungs for speech still proved difficult. "You want me... to take up... my old trade... for you?"

It's hard to read the expression of a mechanical bird of paradise. "Do you not recognize me, Athiva?"

Had I given further offense? "I'm sorry if I'm supposed to, but I don't."

I wondered if she and her monsters were attuned to a mutual telepathic feed, because both of the ten-limbed creatures surrounding me shifted in unison, altering their stance so each loomed a little bit closer.

It wasn't wise for me to utter another word, but I needed to buy time, somehow. "Did you do this to Sieglinda? Seal her in this pit with these wonderful creatures surrounding her? Is this how you got her to cough up the code phrase?"

Silence.

"Is she still alive?"

"Perhaps she is." And I wondered, for a moment, if maybe Sieglinda wasn't missing at all. This creation looked like nothing out of my memory, but in this mutable world, memory's value is suspect.

I knew of no reason Sieglinda would seek to harm me. And yet I'd deliberately severed most of my knowledge of unmaking. What else might I have sliced away? What might I have done?

Philomela continued with a question of her own. "What did you do to Procne, to get her to reveal this place?"

"I gave her what she wanted. I unmade her. Surely you know unmaking peels away secrets. It's part of the process. And she really did want to be free of you. It wasn't an act."

"Too bad for her. Where is she?"

All of my hearts beat fast. She wouldn't like the answer. "Procne's gone. I unmade her, I told you. That one is out of your reach. You'll never find her."

"But you know where she is."

The thugs inched closer.

I tried to sidestep, so to speak. "You have me, though. I'm what you want, correct? I will be happy to unmake whoever you need unmaking, whether it's you, whether it's someone you need to hide. My skills are yours."

"And your machines?"

"Destroyed. I'll need new ones."

"Maybe we can salvage. Where are they?"

I bit my lip. She waited until I finally said, "I can't tell you."

"Why not?"

"I don't know."

The monsters raised their front limbs like spiders threatening attack.

"How could you not know?"

"Because this version of me, the one you're talking to now, isn't the one who knows how to unmake. I unmade myself before I went legit. But the me who existed before didn't want to leave the world forever, like your Procne did. She kept herself hidden away and left me with knowledge of her. In hindsight I wish she hadn't, but there's nothing I can do about that now."

"A second cortex?"

I wobbled my head. "Mine is the second cortex."

"Where's the first?"

I could only hope then that I'd stalled long enough. The gambit was at its end. "She didn't let me keep that memory. She's gone, just like your girl."

She gave no command. The monsters lunged. Sheer luck they didn't catch me.

Funny as it sounds, my neck doesn't just telescope out and detach. It also contracts. I retracted my head into my body's fleshy cube and disconnected.

What I told Philomela isn't quite true. I can stay unattached longer, though after three minutes lobes of my cortex will start shutting down to conserve oxygen. By eight minutes I'm down to the essentials and after ten I'm in real trouble.

I've heard that if you're unfortunate enough to attract the Hierophant's focus, to cause hir scattered consciousness to actually zero in, it takes about fifteen minutes for hir gendarmes to reach you, wherever you are. I hoped, this close to hir fortress, they'd come much quicker.

My self-engineering spared me the pain of the monsters' assault as they tore into my body. I confess, I had not ever planned to be lost inside myself, but it was a good thing I'd unhooked from my neck, as one of the thugs plunged a limb into that gullet, seized the coil of my neck and ripped it out.

I crawled away blind through my own blubber and organs, safe only for that moment. Once they gutted me deep enough, they'd inevitably find me if I didn't suffocate first. Sealing me in the floor at least made it a little bit harder to scoop me out.

Of all the people I thought I might see if I survived, I didn't expect you, Encolpio.

Yes, I see you, peering through the translucent curve of the jar. My eyes aren't as sharp as Procne's were, but I didn't leave them unaugmented like yours. If anything you told me about yourself is actually true.

Why do the neuroleads from my jar lead to your temples? Are you a prisoner, like me?

I see you shake your head no.

Then you belong to hir. A servant of the Hierophant? My jailor?

What a strange expression. You're hir creature, yes? I see.

Here's a stray scrap of memory, it must fall somewhere in between taking my leave of Procne and paying my visit to Philomela. Perhaps you've puzzled over it.

Wondered why I strolled right up to the Hierophant's Node in the Biomass Gardens and started chittering about how anyone could have been unmade and might not even know it. I'll spell it out. I'd hoped se might set some of hir Ears crawling on me and that they'd still be with me when I at last admitted what I was.

Obviously my ploy worked.

If you saw me go through the motions of sighing in relief when I regained consciousness and found myself wired up inside your little tank – well, that's why.

I still don't know what Philomela did to Sieglinda to make her reveal me – in my heart, I know that's what happened. I will not let myself succumb to doubts.

Did the Hierophant's forces capture Philomela when they swarmed in? Can you tell me?

Can you at least look my way, you dreg?

The Hierophant must have already suspected something, for you to spend so much time in my shop. And here I thought you stood out too boldly to ever suspect you of having any other agenda. No need to look so sheepish. I just wish I had any hope of ever learning your story.

What I told Philomela was true. I really don't know where Procne went or where my old self has gone. I made sure of that. And though I can't tell you what they were, I can only assume that purging those memories were just fractions of the precautions I took once Procne revealed how thoroughly I'd been had.

So what happens now? Am I dissected? Unmade in the Hierophant's special way? Perhaps the things I can't remember can still be found, the way I found all sorts of information in Procne's mind that she didn't know consciously.

If your body is as retro as you claim, maybe you really feel as sad as you look. Is that supposed to comfort me, that you've unfolded your easel?

This calming warmth, that can't be a true warmth, that's the polar opposition of how I feel. This comes from you. Why should I trust it, Encolpio?

I can do many things, but I can't read lips.

You're pressing your mouth to the glass. What a surprise, this fluid carries sound.

I'm safe from the Hierophant. Se thinks I'm dead. So you say. How kind. But am I safe from you, and will you be safe from me if you ever let me out?

How long do you plan to keep me here?

Encolpio?

Yes, look at me.

If you won't answer now, at least show me the painting when it's done.

WITH FATE CONSPIRE

VANDANA SINGH

Vandana Singh is an Indian speculative fiction writer who finds herself continually surprised by the universe, to the point that she acquired a Ph.D. in physics and now teaches at a state university near Boston. Her short stories have been published in various magazines and anthologies, such as Strange Horizons, TRSF, Lightspeed *and* Other Worlds than These *(ed. John Joseph Adams) and some have been reprinted in* Year's Best *volumes. Her novella "Distances" (Aqueduct Press) won the 2008 Carl Brandon Parallax award. In 2011-2012 she was a science and environment columnist for* Strange Horizons. *For more, please visit http://users.rcn.com/singhvan.*

I SAW HIM in a dream, the dead man. He was dreaming too, and I couldn't tell if I was in his dream or he in mine. He was floating over a delta, watching a web of rivulets running this way and that, the whole stream rushing to a destination I couldn't see.

I woke up with the haunted feeling that I had been used to in my youth. I haven't felt like that in a long time. The feeling of being possessed, inhabited, although lightly, as though a homeless person was sleeping in the courtyard of my consciousness. The dead man wasn't any trouble; he was just sharing the space in my mind, not really caring who I was. But this returning of my old ability, as unexpected as it was, startled me out of the apathy in which I had been living my life. I wanted to find him, this dead man.

I THINK IT is because of the Machine that these old feelings are being resurrected. It takes up an entire room, although the only part of it I see is the thing that looks like a durbeen, a telescope. The Machine looks into the past, which is why I've been thinking about my own girlhood. If I could spy on myself as I ran up and down the crowded streets and alleys of Park Circus! But the scientists who work the Machine tell me that the scope can't look into the recent past. They never tell me the *why* of anything, even when I ask – they smile and say, "Don't bother about things like that, Gargi-di! What you are doing is great, a great contribution." To my captors – they think they are my benefactors but truly, they are my captors – to them, I am something very special, because of my ability with the scope; but because I am not like them, they don't really see me as I am. An illiterate woman, bred in the back streets and alleyways of Old Kolkata, of no more importance than a cockroach – what saved me from being stamped out by the great, indifferent foot of the mighty is this... ability. The Machine gives sight to a select few, and it doesn't care if you are rich or poor, man or woman.

I wonder if they guess I'm lying to them?

They've set the scope at a particular moment of history: the spring of 1856, and a particular place: Metiabruz in Kolkata. I am supposed to spy on an exiled ruler of that time, to see what he does every morning, out on the terrace, and to record what he says. He is a large, sad, weepy man. He is the Nawab of Awadh, ousted from his beloved home by the conquering British. He is a poet.

They tell me he wrote the song Babul Mora, which to me is the most interesting and important thing about him, because I learned that song as a girl. The song is about a woman leaving, looking back at her childhood home, and it makes me cry sometimes – even though my childhood wasn't idyllic. And yet there are things I remember, incongruous things like a great field of rice, and water gleaming between the new shoots, and a bagula, hunched and dignified like an old priest, standing knee deep in water, waiting for fish. I remember the smell of the sea, many miles away, borne on the wind. My mother's village, Siridanga.

How I began to lie to my captors was sheer chance. There was something wrong with the Machine. I don't understand how it works, of course, but the scientists were having trouble setting the date. The girl called Nondini kept cursing and muttering about spacetime fuzziness. The fact that they could not look through the scope to verify what they were doing, not having the kind of brain suitable for it, meant that I had to keep looking to check whether they had got back to Wajid Ali Shah in the Kolkata of 1856.

I'll never forget when I first saw the woman. I knew it was the wrong place and time, but, instead of telling my captors, I kept quiet. She was looking up toward me (my viewpoint must have been near the ceiling). She was not young, but she was respectable, you could see that. A housewife squatting on her haunches in a big, old-fashioned kitchen, stacking dirty dishes. I don't know why she looked up for that moment but it struck me at once: the furtive expression on her face. A sensitive face, with beautiful eyes, a woman who, I could tell, was a warm-hearted motherly type – so why did she look like that, as though she had a dirty secret? The scope doesn't stay connected to the past for more than a few blinks of the eye, so that was all I had: a glimpse.

Nondini nudged me, asking "Gargi-di, is that the right place and time?" Without thinking, I said yes.

That is how it begins: the story of my deception. That simple 'yes' began the unraveling of everything.

THE INSTITUTE IS a great glass monstrosity that towers above the ground somewhere in New Parktown, which I am told is many miles south of Kolkata. Only the part we're on is not flooded. All around my building are other such buildings, so that when I look out of the window I see only reflections – of my building, and the others, and my own face, a small, dark oval. At first it drove me crazy, being trapped not only by the building but also by these tricks of light. And my captors were trapped too, but they seemed unmindful of the fact. They had grown accustomed. I resolved in my first week that I would not become accustomed.

No, I didn't regret leaving behind my mean little life, with all its difficulties and constraints, but I was under no illusions. I had exchanged one prison for another.

In any life, I think, there are apparently unimportant moments that turn out to matter the most. For me as a girl it was those glimpses of my mother's village, poor as it was. I don't remember the bad things. I remember the sky, the view of paddy fields from my grandfather's hut on a hillock, and the tame pigeon who cooed and postured on a wooden post in the muddy little courtyard. I think it was here I must have drawn my first real breath. There was an older cousin I don't recall very well, except as a voice, a guide through this exhilarating new world, where I realized that food grew on trees, that birds and animals had their own tongues, their languages, their stories. The world exploded into wonders during those brief visits. But always they were just small breaks in my life as one more poor child in the great city. Or so I thought. What I now think is that those moments gave me a taste for something I've never had – a kind of freedom, a soaring.

I want to be able to share this with the dead man who haunts my dreams. I want him, whoever he is, wherever he is, to have what I had so briefly. The great open spaces, the chance to run through the fields and listen to the birds tell their stories. He might wake up from being dead then, might think of other things besides deltas. He sits in my consciousness so lightly, I wonder if he even exists, whether he is an imagining rather than a haunting. But I recognize the feeling of a haunting like that, even though it has been years since I experienced the last one.

THE MOST IMPORTANT haunting of my life was when I was, maybe, fourteen. We didn't know our birthdays, so I can't be sure. But I remember that an old man crept into my mind, a tired old man. Like Wajid Ali Shah more than a hundred years ago, this man was a poet. But there the similarity ended because he had been ground down by poverty; his respectability was all he had left. When I saw him in my mind he was sitting under an awning. There was a lot of noise nearby, the kind of hullabaloo that a vegetable market generates. I sensed immediately that he was miserable, and this was confirmed later when I met him. All my hauntings have been of people who are hurt, or grieving, or otherwise in distress.

He wasn't a mullah, Rahman Khan, but the street kids all called him Maula, so I did too. I think he accepted it with deprecation. He was a kind man. He would sit under a tree at the edge of the road with an old typewriter, waiting for people to come to him for typing letters and important documents and so on. He only had a few customers. Most of the time he would stare into the distance with rheumy eyes, seeing not the noisy market but some other vista, and he would recite poetry. I found time from my little jobs in the fruit market to sit by him and sometimes I would bring him a stolen pear or mango. He was the one who taught me to appreciate language, the meanings of words. He told me about poets he loved, Wajid Ali Shah and Khayyam and Rumi, and our own Rabindranath and Nazrul, and the poets of the humbler folk, the baul and the maajhis. Once I asked him to teach me how to read and write. He had me practice letters in Hindi and Bengali on discarded sheets of typing paper, but the need to fill our stomachs prevented me from giving time to the task, and I soon forgot what I'd learned. In any case at that age I didn't realize its importance – it was no more than a passing fancy. But he did improve my Hindi, which I had picked up from my father, and taught me some Urdu, and a handful of songs, including Babul Mora.

Babul Mora, he would sing in his thin, cracked voice. *Naihar chuuto hi jaaye.*

It is a woman's song, a woman leaving her childhood home with her newlywed husband, looking back from the cart for the last time. *Father mine, my home slips away from me.* Although my father died before I was grown, the song still brings tears to my eyes.

The old man gave me my fancy way of speaking. People laugh at me sometimes when I use nice words, nicely, when a few plain ones would do. What good is fancy speech to a woman who grew up poor and illiterate? But I don't care. When I talk in that way I feel as though I am touching the essence of the world. I got that from Maula. All my life I have tried to give away what I received but my one child died soon after birth and nobody else wanted what I had. Poetry. A vision of freedom. Rice fields, birds, the distant blue line of the sea. Siridanga.

Later, after my father died, I started to work in people's houses with my mother. Clean and cook, and go to another house, clean and cook. Some of the people were nice but others yelled at us and were suspicious of us. I remember one fat lady who smelled strongly of flowers and sweat, who got angry because I touched the curtains. The curtains were blue and white and had lace on them, and I had never seen anything as delicate and beautiful. I reached my hand out and touched them and she yelled at me. I was just a child, and whatever she said, my hands weren't dirty. I tried to defend myself but my mother herself shut me up. She didn't want to lose her job. I remember being so angry I thought I would catch fire from inside. I think all those houses must be under water now. There will be fish nibbling at the fine lace drawing room curtains. Slime on the walls, the carpets rotted. All our cleaning for nothing!

I have to find the dead man. I have to get out of here somehow.

THE SCIENTIST CALLED Nondini sees me as a real person, I think, not just as someone with a special ability who is otherwise nothing special. She has sympathy for me partly because there is a relative of hers who might still be in a refugee camp, and she has been going from one to the other to try to find her. The camps are mostly full of slum-dwellers because when the river overflowed and the sea came over the land, it drowned everything except for the skyscrapers. All the people who lived in slums or low buildings, who didn't have relatives with intact homes, had to go to the camps. I was in the big one, Sahapur, where they actually tried to help people find jobs, and tested them for all kinds of practical skills, because we were most of us laborers, domestic help, that sort of thing. And they gave us medical tests also. That's how I got my job, my large, clean room with a big-screen TV and all the food I want – after they found out I had the kind of brain the Machine can use.

But I can't go back to the camp to see my friends. Many of them had left before me anyway, farmed out to corporations where they could be useful with medical tests and get free medicines also. Ashima had cancer and she got to go to one of those places, but there is no way I can find out what happened to her. I imagine her somewhere like this place, with everything free and all the mishti-doi she can eat. I hope she's all right. Kabir had a limp from birth but he's only eighteen so maybe they can fix it. When she has time, Nondini lets me talk about them. Otherwise I feel as though nothing from that time was real, that I never had a mother and father, or a husband who left me after our son died. As if my friends never existed. It drives me crazy sometimes to return to my room after working in the same building, and to find nothing but the same programs on the TV. At first I was so excited about all the luxury but now I get bored and fretful to the point where I am scared of my impulses. Especially when the night market comes and sets up on the streets below, every week. I can't see the market from my high window, but I can see the lights dancing on the windows of the building on the other side of the square. I can smell fish frying, and hear people talking, yelling out prices, and I hear singing. It is the singing that makes my blood wild. The first time they had a group of maajhis come, I nearly broke the window glass, I so wanted to jump out. They know how to sing to the soul.

Maajhi, o Maajhi
My beloved waits

On the other shore...

I think the scientists are out at the market all night, because when they come in the next day, on Monday, their eyes are red, and they are bad-tempered, and there is something far away about them, as though they've been in another world. It could just be the rice beer, of course.

My captors won't let me out for some months, until they are sure I've 'settled down'. I can't even go to another floor of this building. There have been cases of people from the refugee camps escaping from their jobs, trying to go back to their old lives, their old friends, as though those things existed any more. So there are rules that you have to be on probation before you are granted citizenship of the city, which then allows you to go freely everywhere. Of course 'everywhere' is mostly under water, for what it's worth. Meanwhile Nondini lets me have this recorder that I'm speaking into, so I won't get too lonely. So I can hear my own voice played back. What a strange one she is!

Nondini is small and slight, with eyes that slant up just a little at the corners. She has worked hard all her life to study history. I never knew there was so much history in the world until my job began! She keeps giving me videos about the past – not just Wajid Ali Shah but also further back, to the time when the British were here, and before that when Kolkata was just a little village on the Hugli river. It is nearly impossible to believe that there was a time when the alleyways and marketplaces and shantytowns and skyscrapers didn't exist – there were forests and fields, and the slow windings of the river, and wild animals. I wish I could see that. But they – the scientists – aren't interested in that period.

What they *do* want to know is whether there were poems or songs of Wajid Ali Shah that were unrecorded. They want me to catch him at a moment when he would recite something new that had been forgotten over the centuries. What I don't understand is, why all this fuss about old poetry? I like poetry more than most people, but it isn't what you'd do in the middle of a great flood. When I challenge the scientists some of them look embarrassed, like Brijesh; and Unnikrishnan shakes his head. Their leader, Dr. Mitra, she just looks impatient, and Nondini says "poetry can save the world."

I may be uneducated but I am not stupid. They're hiding something from me.

The housewife – the woman for whom I have abandoned Wajid Ali Shah – interests me. Her name is Rassundari – I know, because someone in her household called her name. Most of the time they call her Rasu or Sundari, or daughter-in-law, or sister-in-law etc., but this time some visitor called out her full name, carefully and formally. I wish I could talk to her. It would be nice to talk to someone who is like me. How stupid that sounds! This woman clearly comes from a rich rural family – a big joint family it is, all under the same roof. She is nothing like me. But I feel she could talk to me as an ordinary woman, which is what I am.

I wish I could see the outside of her house. They are rich landowners, so it must be beautiful outside.

I wonder if it is like my mother's village. Odd that although I have hardly spent any time in Siridanga, I long for it now as though I had been born there.

The first time after I found Rassundari, Nondini asked me if I'd discovered anything new about Wajid Ali Shah. I felt a bit sorry for her because I was deceiving her, so I said, out of my head, without thinking:

"I think he's writing a new song."

The scope doesn't give you a clear enough view to read writing in a book, even if I could read. But Wajid Ali Shah loves gatherings of poets and musicians, where he sings or recites his own works. So Nondini asked me:

"Did he say anything out loud?"

Again without thinking I said, maybe because I was tired, and lonely, and missing my friends:

"Yes, but only one line: '*If there was someone for such as me...*'"

I had spoken out of the isolation I had been feeling, and out of irritation, because I wanted to get back to my housewife. I would have taken my lie back at once if I could. Nondini's eyes lit up.

"That is new! I must record that!" and in the next room there was a flurry of activity.

So began my secret career as a poet.

RASSUNDARI WORKS REALLY hard. One day I watched her nearly all day, and she was in the kitchen almost the whole time. Cooking, cleaning, supervising a boy who comes to clean the dishes. The people of the house seem to eat all the time. She always waits for them to finish before she eats, but that day she didn't get a chance at all. A guest came at the last minute after everyone had eaten lunch, so she cooked for him, and after that one of the small children was fussing so she took him on her lap and tried to eat her rice, which was on a plate on the floor in front of her, but she had taken just one mouthful when he urinated all over her and her food. The look on her face! There was such anguish, but after a moment she began to laugh. She comforted the child and took him away to clean up, and came back and cleaned the kitchen, and by that time it was evening and time to cook the evening meal. I felt so bad for her! I have known hunger sometimes as a girl, and I could not have imagined that a person who was the daughter-in-law of such a big house could go hungry too. She never seems to get angry about it – I don't understand that, because I can be quick to anger myself. But maybe it is because everyone in the house is nice to her. I can only see the kitchen of course, but whenever people come in to eat or just to talk with her, they treat her well – even her mother-in-law speaks kindly to her.

Her older son is a charming little boy, who comes and sits near her when he is practicing his lessons. He is learning the alphabet. She makes him repeat everything to her several times. Seeing him revives the dull pain in my heart that never goes away. I wonder what my child would have looked like, had he survived. He only lived two days. But those are old sorrows.

I want to know why Rassundari looks, sometimes, like she has a guilty secret.

* * *

THE DEAD MAN has started talking to me in my dreams. He thinks I am someone called Kajori, who must have been a lover. He cries for me, thinking I'm her. He weeps with agony, calls to me to come to his arms, sleep in his bed. I have to say that while I am not the kind of woman who would jump into the arms of just any man, let alone one who is dead, his longing awakes the loneliness in me. I remember what it was like to love a man, even though my husband turned out to be a cowardly bastard. In between his sobs the dead man mutters things that perhaps only this Kajori understands. Floating over the silver webbing of the delta, he babbles about space and time.

"Time!" he tells me. "Look, look at that rivulet. Look at this one."

It seems to me that he thinks the delta is made by a river of time, not water. He says time has thickness – and it doesn't flow in one straight line – it meanders. It splits up into little branches, some of which join up again. He calls this *fine structure*. I have never thought about this before, but the idea makes sense. The dead man shows me history, the sweep of it, the rise and fall of kings and dynasties, how the branches intersect and move on, and how some of the rivulets dry up and die. He tells me how the weight of events and possibilities determines how the rivulets of time flow.

"I must save the world," he says at the end, just before he starts to cry.

I KNOW RASSUNDARI'S secret now.

She was sitting in the kitchen alone, after everyone had eaten. She squatted among the pots and pans, scouring them, looking around her warily like a thief in her own house. She dipped a wet finger into the ash pile and wrote on the thali the letter her son had been practicing in the afternoon: kah. She wrote it big, which is how I could see it. She said it aloud, that's how I know what letter it was. She erased it, wrote it again. The triangular shape of the first loop, the down-curve of the next stroke, like a bird bending to drink. Yes, and the line of the roof from which the character was suspended, like wet socks on a clothesline. She shivered with pleasure. Then someone called her name, and she hastily scrubbed the letter away.

How strange this is! There she is, in an age when a woman, a respectable upper-caste woman, isn't supposed to be able to read, so she has to learn on the sly, like a criminal. Here I am, in an age when women can be scientists like Nondini, yet I can't read. What I learned from the Maula, I forgot. I can recognize familiar shop signs and so on from their shapes, not the sounds the shapes are supposed to represent, and anyway machines tell you everything. Nondini tells me that now very few people need to read because of mobiles, and because information can be shown and spoken by machines.

After watching Rassundari write for the first time, that desire woke in me, to learn how to read. My captors would not have denied me materials if I'd asked them, but I thought it would be much more interesting to learn from a woman dead for maybe hundreds of years. This is possible because the Machine now stays stuck in the set time and place for hours instead of minutes. Earlier it would keep disconnecting after five or ten minutes and you would have to wait until it came back. Its new steadiness makes the scientists very happy.

So now when I am at the scope, my captors leave me to myself. As Rassundari writes, I copy the letters on a sheet of paper and whisper the sounds under my breath.

The scientists annoy me after each session with their questions, and sometimes when I feel wicked I tell them that Wajid Ali Shah is going through a dry spell. Other times I make up lines that he supposedly spoke to his gathering of fellow poets. I tell them these are bits and fragments and pieces of longer works.

If there was someone for such as me

Would that cause great inconvenience for you, O universe?

Would the stars go out and fall from the sky?

I am enjoying this, even though my poetry is that of a beginner, crude, and direct. Wajid Ali Shah also wrote in the commoner's tongue, which makes my deception possible. I also suspect that these scientists don't know enough about poetry to tell the difference. My dear teacher, the Maula, would talk for hours about rhyme and lilt, and the difference between a ghazal and a rubayi. I didn't understand half of what he said but I learned enough to know that there is a way of talking about poetry if you are learned in the subject. And the scientists don't seem to react like that. They just exclaim and repeat my lines, and wonder whether this is a fragment, or a complete poem.

One day I want to write my poetry in my own hand.

Imagine me, Gargi, doing all this! A person of no importance – and look where life has got me!

*   *   *

I NOW KNOW who Kajori is.

I didn't know that was her first name. Even the older scientists call her Dr. Mitra. She's a tall, thin woman, the boss of the others, and she always looks busy and harassed. Sometimes she smiles, and her smile is twisted. I took a dislike to her at first because she always looked through me, as though I wasn't there. Now I still dislike her but I'm sorry for her. And angry with her. The dead man, her lover, she must have sent him away, trapped him in that place where he floats above the delta of the river of time. It's my dreams he comes into, not hers. I can hardly bear his agony, his weeping, the way he calls out for her. I wonder why she has abandoned him.

I think he's in this building. The first time this thought occurred to me I couldn't stop shaking. It made sense. All my hauntings have been people physically close to me.

They won't let me leave this floor. I can leave my room now, but the doors to the stairs are locked, and the lifts don't work after everyone leaves. But I will find a way. I'm tired of being confined like this.

I realize now that although I was raised poor and illiterate, I was then at least free to move about, to breathe the air, to dream of my mother's home. Siridanga! I want to go back there and see it before I die. I know that the sea has entered the cities and drowned the land, but Siridanga was on a rise overlooking the paddy fields. My grandparents' hut was on the hillock. Could it still be there?

The night market makes me feel restless. The reflections of the lights dance on the window panes of the opposite building, as though they are writing something. All this learning to read is making me crazy, because I see letters where they don't exist. In the reflections. In people's hand gestures. And even more strangely, I see some kind of writing in the flow of time, in the dreams the dead man brings me. Those are written in a script I cannot read.

I 'DISCOVERED' A whole verse of Wajid Ali Shah's poem today, after hours at the scope. There was so much excitement in the analysis room that the scientists let me go to my quarters early. I pleaded a headache but they hardly noticed. So I slipped out, into the elevator, and went up, and down, and got off on floors and walked around. I felt like a mad person, a thief, a free bird. It was ridiculous what an effect this small freedom had!

But after a while I began to get frightened. There was nobody else on the other floors as far as I could tell. The rooms were silent, dark behind doors with glass slits. I know that the scientists live somewhere here, maybe in the other buildings. Nondini tells me we are in a cluster of buildings near the sea that were built to withstand the flood. From her hints and from the TV I know that the world is ending. It's not just here. Everywhere cities are flooded or consumed by fire. Everything is dying. I have never been able to quite believe this before, perhaps because of my peculiar situation, which prevents me from seeing things for myself. But ultimately the silence and darkness of the rest of the building brought it home to me, and I felt as if I were drowning in sadness.

Then I sensed a pull, a current – a shout in my mind. It was him, the dead man. *Kajori!* he called again and again, and I found myself climbing to the floor above, to a closed door in the dark corridor.

I tried the handle, felt the smooth, paneled wood, but of course it was locked. With my ear against the door I could feel the hum of machinery, and there was a soft flow of air from beneath the door. I called back to him in my mind.

I can't get in, I said. *Talk to me!*

His voice in my mind was full of static, so I couldn't understand everything. Even when I heard the words, they didn't make sense. I think he was muttering to himself, or to Kajori.

"… rivulets of time… two time-streams come together… ah… in a loop… if only… shift the flow, shift the flow… another future… must lock to past coordinate, establish resonance… new tomorrow…"

The chowkidar who is supposed to guard the elevator caught me on my way downstairs. He is a lazy, sullen fellow who never misses an opportunity to throw his weight around. I am more than a match for him though. He reported me, of course, to Nondini and Unnikrishnan, but I argued my case well. I simply said I was restless and wanted to see if there was a nice view from the other floors. What could they say to that?

I tried to make sense of the dead man's gibberish all day. At night he came into my dreams as usual. I let him talk, prompting him with questions when something didn't make sense. I had to be clever to conceal my ignorance, since he thought I was Kajori, but the poor fellow is so emotionally overwrought that he is unlikely to be suspicious. But when he started weeping in his loneliness, I couldn't bear it. I thought: I will distract him with poetry.

I told him about the poem I am writing. It turns out he likes poetry. The poem he and Kajori love the best is an English translation of something by Omar Khayyam.

"Remember it, Kajori?" he said to me. He recited it in English, which I don't understand, and then in Bangla: "Oh love, if you and I could, with fate conspire," he said, taking me with a jolt back to my girlhood: me sitting by the Maula in the mad confusion of the market, the two of us seeing nothing but poetry, mango juice running down our chins. Oh yes, I remember, I said to my dead man. Then it was my turn. I told him about what I was writing and he got really interested. Suggested words, gave me ideas. So two lines of 'Wajid Ali Shah's poem' came to me.

Clouds are borne on the wind
The river winds toward home

It was only the next day that I started to connect things in my mind. I think I know what the project is really about.

These people are not scientists, they are jadugars. Or maybe that's what scientists are, magicians who try to pass themselves off as ordinary people.

See, the dead man's idea is that time is like a river delta; lots of thin streams and fat streams, flowing from past to present, but fanning out. History and time control each other, so that if some future place is deeply affected by some past history, those two time streams will connect. When that happens it diverts time from the future place and shifts the flow in each channel so that the river as a whole might change its course.

They're trying to change the future.

I am stunned. If this is true, why didn't they tell me? Don't I also want the world to survive? It's my world too. This also means that I am more important to them than they ever let me know. I didn't realize all this at once; it is just now beginning to connect in my mind.

I burn inside with anger. At the same time, I am undone with wonder.

I think the dead man is trying to save the world. I think the scope and the dead man are part of the same Machine.

I wonder how much of their schemes I have messed up by locking the Machine into a different time and place than their calculations required.

What shall I do?

FOR NOW I have done nothing.

I need to find out more. How terrible it is to be ignorant! One doesn't even know where to start.

I looked at the history books Nondini had let me have – talking books – but they told me nothing about Rassundari. Then I remembered that one of the rooms on my floor housed a library – from the days before the scientists had taken over the building.

I think Nondini sensed how restless I was feeling, and she must have talked to Kajori (I can't think of her as Dr. Mitra now) so I have permission to spend some of my spare time in the library. They might let me go to the night market tomorrow too, with an escort. I went and thanked Kajori. I said that I was homesick for my mother's village home, Siridanga, and it made me feel crazy sometimes not to be able to walk around. At that she really looked at me, a surprised look, and smiled. I don't think it was a nice smile, but I couldn't be certain.

So, the library. It is a whole apartment full of books of the old kind. But the best thing about it is that there is a corner window from which I can see between two tall buildings. I can see the ocean! These windows don't open but when I saw the ocean I wept. I was in such a state of sadness and joy all at once, I forgot what I was there for.

The books were divided according to subject, so I practiced reading the subject labels first. It took me two days and some help from Nondini (I had to disguise the intent of my search) before I learned how to use the computer to search for information. I was astonished to find out that my housewife had written a book! So all that painful learning on the sly had come to something! I felt proud of her. There was the book in the autobiography section: *Amar Jiban*, written by a woman called Rassundari more than two hundred and fifty years ago. I clutched the book to me and took it with me to read.

It is very hard reading a real book. I have to keep looking at my notes from my lessons with Rassundari. It helps that Nondini got me some alphabet books. She finds my interest in reading rather touching, I think.

But I am getting through Rassundari's work. Her writing is simple and so moving. What I can't understand is why she is so calm about the injustices in her life. Where is her anger? I would have gotten angry. I feel for her as I read.

I wish I could tell Rassundari that her efforts will not be in vain – that she will write her autobiography and publish it at the age of sixty, and that the future will honor her. But how can I tell her that, even if there was a way she could hear me? What can I tell her about this world? My wanderings through the building have made me realize that the world I've known is going away, as inevitably as the tide, with no hope of return.

Unless the dead man and I save it.

I HAVE BEEN talking to Rassundari. Of course she can't hear me, but it comforts me to be able to talk to someone, really talk to them. Sometimes Rassundari looks up toward the point near the ceiling from which I am observing her. At those moments it seems to me that she senses my presence. Once she seemed about to say something, then shook her head and went back to the cooking.

I still haven't told anybody about my deceit. I have found out that Wajid Ali Shah and Rassundari lived at around the same time, although he was in Kolkata and she in a village that is now in Bangladesh. From what the dead man tells me, it is time that is important, not space. At least that is what I can gather from his babblings, although spacetime fuzziness or resolution is also important. So maybe my deception hasn't caused any harm. I hope not. I am an uneducated woman, and when I sit in that library I feel as though there is so much to know. If someone had told me that, encouraged me as a child, where might I have been today?

And yet think about the dead man, with all his education. There he is, a hundred times more trapped than me, a thousand times lonelier. Yet he must be a good man, to give himself for the world. He's been asking me anxiously: *Kajori, can you feel the shift in the timeflow? Have we locked into the pastpoint?* I always tell him I feel it just a little, which reassures him that his sacrifice is not for nothing. I wish I could tell him: I am Gargi, not Kajori. Instead I tell him I love him, I miss him. Sometimes I really feel that I do.

I HAVE BEEN speaking to Rassundari for nearly a week.

One of the scientists, Brijesh, caught me talking into the scope. He came into the room to get some papers he'd left behind. I jumped guiltily.

"Gargi-di? What are you doing...?" he says with eyebrows raised.

"I just like to talk to myself. Repeat things Wajid Ali Shah is saying."

He looks interested. "A new poem?"

"Bah!" I say. "You people think he says nothing but poetry all the time? Right now he's trying to woo his mistress."

This embarrasses Brijesh, as I know it would. I smile at him and go back to the scope.

But yes, I was talking about Rassundari.

Now I know that she senses something. She always looks up at me, puzzled as to how a corner of the ceiling appears to call to her. Does she hear me, or see some kind of image? I don't know. I keep telling her not to be afraid, that I am from the future, and that she is famous for her writing. Whether she can tell what I am saying I don't know. She does look around from time to time, afraid as though others might be there, so I think maybe she hears me, faintly, like an echo.

Does this mean that our rivulet of time is beginning to connect with her time stream?

I think my mind must be like an old-fashioned radio. It picks up things: the dead man's ramblings, the sounds and sights of the past. Now it seems to be picking up the voices from the books in this room. I was deaf once, but now I can hear them as I read, slowly and painfully. All those stories, all those wonders. If I'd only known!

I TALK TO the dead. I talk to the dead of my time, and the woman Rassundari of the past, who is dead now. My closest confidants are the dead.

The dead man – I wish I knew his name – tells me that we have made a loop in time. He is not sure how the great delta's direction will change – whether it will be enough, or too little, or too much. He has not quite understood the calculations that the Machine is doing. He is preoccupied. But when I call to him, he is tender, grateful. "Kajori," he says, "I have no regrets. Just this one thing, please do it for me. What you promised. Let me die once the loop has fully stabilized." In one dream I saw through his eyes. He was in a tank, wires coming out of his body, floating. In that scene there was no river of time, just the luminous water below him, and the glass casing around. What a terrible prison! If he really does live like that, I think he can no longer survive outside the tank, which is why he wants to die.

It is so painful to think about this that I must distract us both. We talk about poetry, and later the next few lines of the poem come to me.

Clouds are borne on the wind
The river winds toward home
From my prison window I see the way to my village
In its cage of bone my heart weeps
When I was the river, you were the shore
Why have you forsaken me?

I am getting confused. It is Kajori who is supposed to be in love with the dead man, not me.

So MANY THINGS happened these last two days.

The night before last, the maajhis sang in the night market. I heard their voices ululating, the dotaras throbbing in time with the flute's sadness. A man's voice, and then a woman's, weaving in and out. I imagined them on their boats, plying the waters all over the drowned city as they had once sailed the rivers of my drowned land. I was filled with a painful ecstasy that made me want to run, or fly. I wanted to break the windows.

The next morning I spent some hours at the scope. I told Rassundari my whole story. I still can't be sure she hears me, but her upturned, attentive face gives me hope. She senses something, for certain, because she put her hand to her ear as though straining to hear. Another new thing is that she is sometimes snappy. This has never happened before. She snapped at her nephew the other day, and later spoke sharply to her husband. After both those instances she felt so bad! She begged forgiveness about twelve times. Both her nephew and her husband seemed confused, but accepted her apology. I wonder if the distraction I am bringing into her life is having an effect on her mind.

It occurs to me that perhaps, like the dead man, she can sense my thoughts, or at least feel the currents of my mind.

The loop in the time stream has stabilized. Unnikrishnan told me I need not be at the scope all the time, because the connection is always there, instead of timing out. The scientists were nervous and irritable; Kajori had shut herself up in her office. Were they waiting for the change? How will they tell that the change has come? Have we saved the world? Or did my duplicity ruin it?

I was in the library in the afternoon, a book on my lap, watching the grey waves far over the sea, when the dead man shouted in my mind. At this I peered out – the hall was empty. The scientists have been getting increasingly careless. The lift was unguarded.

So up I went to the floor above. The great wood-paneled door was open. Inside the long, dimly lit room stood Kajori, her face wet with tears, calling his name.

"Subir! Subir!"

She didn't notice me.

He lay naked in the enormous tank like a child sleeping on its belly. He was neither young nor old; his long hair, afloat in the water like seaweed, was sprinkled with grey, his dangling arms thin as sticks. Wires came out of him at dozens of places, and there were large banks of machinery all around the tank. His skin gleamed as though encased in some kind of oil.

He didn't know she was there, I think. His mind was seething with confusion. He wanted to die, and his death hadn't happened on schedule. A terror was growing in him.

"You promised, Kajori!"

She just wept with her face against the tank. She didn't turn off any switches. She didn't hear him, but I felt his cry in every fiber of my being.

"He wants to die," I said.

She turned, her face twisted with hatred.

"What are you doing here? Get out!"

"Go free, Subir!" I said. I ran in and began pulling out plugs, turning off switches in the banks of machines around the tank. Kajori tried to stop me but I pushed her away. The lights in the tank dimmed. His arms flailed for a while, then grew still. Over Kajori's scream I heard his mind going out like the tide goes out, wafting toward me a whisper: thank you, thank you, thank you.

I became aware of the others around me, and Kajori shouting and sobbing.

"She went mad! She killed him!"

"You know he had to die," I said to her. I swallowed. "I could hear his thoughts. He... he loved you very much."

She shouted something incomprehensible at me. Her sobbing subsided. Even though she hated me, I could tell that she was beginning to accept what had happened. I'd done her a favor, after all, done the thing she had feared to do. I stared at her sadly and she looked away.

"Take her back to her room," she said. I drew myself up.

"I am leaving here," I said, "to go home to Siridanga. To find my family."

"You fool," Kajori said. "Don't you know, *this* place used to be Siridanga. You are standing on it."

They took me to my room and locked me in.

After a long time of lying in my bed, watching the shadows grow as the light faded, I made myself get up. I washed my face. I felt so empty, so faint. I had lost my family and my friends, and the dead man, Subir. I hadn't even been able to say goodbye to Rassundari. And Siridanga, where was Siridanga? The city had taken it from me. And eventually the sea would take it from the city. Where were my people? Where was home?

That night the maajhis sang. They sang of the water that had overflowed the rivers. They sang of the rivers that the city streets had become. They sang of the boats they had plied over river after river, time after time. They sang, at last, of the sea.

The fires from the night market lit up the windows of the opposite building. The reflections went from windowpane to windowpane, with the same deliberate care that Rassundari took with her writing. I felt that at last she was reaching through time to me, to our dying world, writing her messages on the walls of our building in letters of fire. She was writing my song.

Nondini came and unlocked my door sometime before dawn. Her face was filled with something that had not been there before, a defiance. I pulled her into my room.

"I have to tell you something," I said. I sat her down in a chair and told her the whole story of how I'd deceived them.

"Did I ruin everything?" I said at the end, fearful at her silence.

"I don't know, Gargi-di," she said at last. She sounded very young, and tired. "We don't know what happens when a time-loop is formed artificially. It may bring in a world that is much worse than this one. Or not. There's always a risk. We argued about it a lot and finally we thought it was worth doing. As a last ditch effort."

"If you'd told me all this, I wouldn't have done any of it," I said, astounded. Who were they to act as Kalki? How could they have done something of this magnitude, not even knowing whether it would make for a better world?

"That's why we didn't tell you," she said. "You don't understand, we – scientists, governments, people like us around the world – tried everything to avert catastrophe. But it was too late. Nothing worked. And now we are past the point where any change can make a difference."

"'People like us,' you say," I said. "What about people like me? We don't count, do we?"

She shook her head at that, but she had no answer.

It was time to go. I said goodbye, leaving her sitting in the darkness of my room, and ran down the stairs. All the way to the front steps, out of the building, out of my old life, the tired old time stream. The square was full of the night market people packing up – fish vendors, and entertainers, getting ready to return another day. I looked around at the tall buildings, the long shafts of paling sky between them, water at the edge of the island lapping ever higher. The long boats were tethered there, weather-beaten and much-mended. The maajhis were leaving, but not to return. I talked to an old man by one of their boats. He said they were going to sea.

"There's nothing left for us here," he said. "Ever since last night the wind has been blowing us seaward, telling us to hasten, so we will follow it. Come with us if you wish."

So in that grey dawn, with the wind whipping at the tattered sails and the water making its music against the boats, we took off for the open sea. Looking back, I saw Rassundari writing with dawn's pale fingers on the windows of the skyscrapers, the start of the letter kah, conjugated with r. Kra... But the boat and the wind took us away before I could finish reading the word. I thought the word reached all the way into the ocean with the paling moonlight still reflected in the surging water.

Naihar chhuto hi jaaye, I thought, and wept.

Now the wind writes on my forehead with invisible tendrils of air, a language I must practice to read. I have left my life and loves behind me, and wish only to be blown about as the sea desires, to have the freedom of the open air, and be witness to the remaking of the world.

'A cliché it may be, but there really is something for everyone here... an ideal bait to tempt those who only read novels to climb over the short fiction fence'

– *Interzone on The Solaris Book of New Science Fiction, Vol. 2*

THE NEW SOLARIS BOOK
OF SCIENCE FICTION

SOLARIS RISING

EDITED BY
IAN WHATES

FEATURING
NEW WORK BY:

Alastair Reynolds
Peter F. Hamilton
Stephen Baxter
Ian McDonald
Paul di Filippo
Ken MacLeod
Adam Roberts
Pat Cadigan
AND MANY MORE

UK ISBN: 978-1-907992-08-7 • US ISBN: 978-1-907992-09-4 • £7.99/$7.99

Solaris Rising presents nineteen stories of the very highest calibre from some of the most accomplished authors in the genre, proving just how varied and dynamic science fiction can be. From strange goings on in the present to explorations of bizarre futures, from drug-induced tragedy to time-hopping serial killers, from crucial choices in deepest space to a ravaged Earth under alien thrall, from gritty other worlds to surreal other realms, *Solaris Rising* delivers a broad spectrum of experiences and excitements, showcasing the genre at its very best.

WWW.SOLARISBOOKS.COM

Follow us on Twitter! www.twitter.com/solarisbooks

ENGINEERING
INFINITY

Edited by Jonathan Strahan

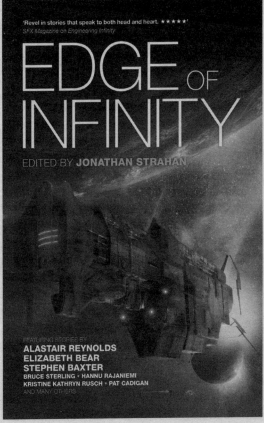

'Revel in stories that speak to both head and heart. ★★★★★'
SFX Magazine on Engineering Infinity

EDGE OF INFINITY

EDITED BY **JONATHAN STRAHAN**

FEATURING STORIES BY
ALASTAIR REYNOLDS
ELIZABETH BEAR
STEPHEN BAXTER
BRUCE STERLING • HANNU RAJANIEMI
KRISTINE KATHRYN RUSCH • PAT CADIGAN
AND MANY OTHERS

UK ISBN: 978-1-78101-055-9 • US ISBN: 978-1-78108-056-6 • £7.99/$8.99

Edge of Infinity is an exhilarating new SF anthology that looks at the *next* giant leap for humankind: the leap from our home world out into the Solar System. From the eerie transformations in Pat Cadigan's "The Girl-Thing Who Went Out for Sushi" to the frontier spirit of Sandra McDonald and Stephen D. Covey's "The Road to NPS," and from the grandiose vision of Alastair Reynolds' "Vainglory" to the workaday familiarity of Kristine Kathryn Rusch's "Safety Tests," the thirteen stories in this anthology span the whole of the human condition in their race to colonise Earth's nearest neighbours.

 WWW.SOLARISBOOKS.COM

Follow us on Twitter! www.twitter.com/solarisbooks

THE NOISE WITHIN

> *"Unreasonably enjoyable.
> 24 meets Starship Troopers.
> If you read Reynolds, Hamilton,
> Banks - read this."*
> *– Stephen Baxter*

IAN WHATES

UK ISBN: 978 1 906735 64 7 • US ISBN: 978 1 906735 65 4 • £7.99/$7.99

Philip Kaufman is on the brink of perfecting the long sought-after human/AI interface when a scandal from his past returns to haunt him and he is forced to flee, pursued by assassins and attacked in his own home. Black-ops specialist Jim Leyton is bewildered when he is diverted from his usual duties to hunt down a pirate vessel, The Noise Within. Why this one obscure freebooter, in particular? Two very different lives are about to collide, changing everything forever...

 WWW.SOLARISBOOKS.COM

Follow us on Twitter! www.twitter.com/solarisbooks

THE NOISE REVEALED

'Unreasonably enjoyable. *24* meets *Starship Troopers*.
If you read Reynolds, Hamilton, Banks – read this'
– Stephen Baxter on *The Noise Within*

IAN WHATES

UK ISBN: 978-1-907519-53-6 • £7.99

It's a time of change. While mankind is adjusting to its first encounter with an alien civilisation, black-ops soldier Jim Leyton has absconded from the agency that trained him, and allied himself with a mysterious faction in order to rescue the woman he loves.

Since his death, scientist and businessman Philip Kaufman has realised that there is more to the virtual world than he'd suspected. Yet it soon becomes clear that all is not well in Virtuality. Both men begin to suspect that the much heralded 'First Contact' was anything but, and that a sinister con is being perpetrated on the whole of humankind. Now all they have to do is prove it.

 WWW.SOLARISBOOKS.COM

Follow us on Twitter! www.twitter.com/solarisbooks

INCLUDING STORIES BY:

ALASTAIR REYNOLDS // KAY KENYON
JASON STODDARD // HOLLY PHILLIPS

"The energy
and enterprise
of Jetse de Vries
deserves a lot of
attention."
Ian Whates,
Matrix Online

AN ANTHOLOGY OF NEAR-FUTURE OPTIMISTIC SCIENCE FICTION

SHINE

EDITED BY JETSE DE VRIES

UK ISBN: 978 1 906735 66 1 • US ISBN: 978 1 906735 67 8 • £7.99/$7.99

A collection of near-future, optimistic SF stories where some of the genre's brightest stars and most exciting talents portray the possible roads to a better tomorrow. Definitely not a plethora of Pollyannas – but neither a barrage of dystopias – Shine will show that positive change is far from being a foregone conclusion, but needs to be hard-fought, innovative, robust and imaginative. Let's make our tomorrows Shine.

 WWW.SOLARISBOOKS.COM

Follow us on Twitter! www.twitter.com/solarisbooks